# The Suspension Bridge

# Praise for *The Suspension Bridge*

"Anna Dowdall delivers the shivers. Oh, and if you hear a corpulent sound, that will be Alfred Hitchcock stirring in his grave because he live long enough to film this quality novel. Yes, it's that good."
—ALAN BRADLEY, NYT bestselling author

"At once dark and moody and irreverently cheeky, The Suspension Bridge joins together literary mystery with municipal intrigue and a you nun's tell-all as she faces her own internal conflicts. Dowdall infuses ric atmosphere with captivating uncertainty and characters undeniably Canadi yet redolent of some other time and place."
—ANTHONY BIDULKA, author of *Going to Beautiful*, Crime Writers of Canada 2023 Best Crime Novel, and the Merry Bell trilogy (including 2024's *From Sweetgrass Bridge*)

"Please welcome a new and entertaining clerical sleuth: Sister Harriet is intelligent, determined, funny, and not a little perplexed as she investigates some very odd doings in a very odd town determined to be the very model of the very modern year of 1962—until it all goes pear-shaped. Filled with many twists and turns, *The Suspension Bridge* is a charming and deliciously convoluted tale served with both dark humour and a lighthearted air."
—C.C. BENISON, author of the *Father Christmas* mysteries

"Intriguing characters ... the reader senses the historic tensions of the real world of 1962 just beyond the page, kept back by a levee that might not hold."
—JANICE MACDONALD, creator of the *Randy Craig* and *Imogene Durant Mysteries*

Anna Dowdall's wry sense of humour gleams in this cautionary tale of bureaucratic speculation, cloistered subterfuge and secular mischief. As a nearly-completed bridge provides the link to a possible multiple-murder, Dowdall's Sister Harriet challenges her vocation and ventures beyond her cloistered walls to untangle the complex of clues.
—WINONA KENT, author of *Ticket to Ride* Book 4 in the Jason Davey Mysteries)

Copyright @ 2024 Anna Dowdall

All rights reserved. No part of this publication may be reproduced, stored in a retrieval system or transmitted, in any form or by any means without the prior written permission of the publisher or by licensed agreement with Access: The Canadian Copyright Licensing Agency (contact accesscopyright.ca).

Editor: Susan Musgrave
Cover art and design: Tania Wolk
Book design: Tania Wolk, Third Wolf Studio
Printed and bound in Canada at Friesens, Altona, MB

The publisher gratefully acknowledges the support of Creative Saskatchewan, the Canada Council for the Arts and SK Arts.

 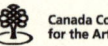 

Library and Archives Canada Cataloguing in Publication

Title: The suspension bridge / Anna Dowdall.
Names: Dowdall, Anna, author.
Description: Series statement: A Sister Harriet mystery ; 1
Identifiers: Canadiana (print) 20240432460
Canadiana (ebook) 20240432487
ISBN 9781998926121 (softcover) | ISBN 9781998926138 (EPUB)
Subjects: LCGFT: Detective and mystery fiction. | LCGFT: Novels.
Classification: LCC PS8607.O98738 S87 2024 | DDC C813/.6—dc23

radiant press

Box 33128 Cathedral PO
Regina, SK S4T 7X2
info@radiantpress.ca
www.radiantpress.ca

For Mary, and all the other Saint Reginald's girls

# Prologue

THE CROWDS STRETCHED *for miles on either side of the river. The dignitaries were assembled on the stratospheric crown of the Bothonville International Bridge. It was less dramatic than they had hoped, for television cameras obstructed the view at every hand's turn. This was necessary, so that all the yokels below could see them and hear their speeches on the giant screens lining the river, not to mention the other yokels watching on their television sets at home. Still, when the jets did their pass in a roar of noise, leaving the skies to the news helicopters, a palpable excitement filled the well-dressed crowd on the bridge. Somewhere else, the technical people had their fingers over the button that would trigger the rapid release of the coffer dams upriver. They'd get a cramp waiting for all the speeches to conclude, but that was the way of these things. Whole chapters of contrivance and delay were required, or how else could a climax be a climax?*

*At least the sky had cleared. It now blazed forth blue, mirrored with a wine-dark intensity below. Len Silverman became lost in admiration and got a crick in his neck gazing up at the gigantic lines of the bridge. It felt like being in an airplane.*

*Without a fear of heights, Dean Carter peered over the rampart. The water flowed far beneath him, its corrugated surface giving the faintest sense of what must be substantial waves, and this even before the dam water rushed down.*

*The freighters in the shipping lane beyond the velvet hump of Salamander Island looked like their old Tinker toys, men from the Retail Council said to men from the bridge consortium. Far in the* distance, you could just make out Bothonville on one shore, and even Sparta downstream on the other, their tallest buildings reduced to matchstick stubs.

It was a world between heaven and earth, and they were the chosen ones to occupy it. So said Mayor Martel in a lyrical aside to Police Chief Flynn, although he had to shout, up there in the middle of the air, for the wind was a howling beast.

The speeches took up the next hour. Perhaps the crowds below heard them better than the assembled elite on the bridge. No one heard a thing up there, what with the wind and the various noises made by the innovative combination of flexing cantilevers and quivering suspension cables. Not everyone on the river bank heard very well either. This was the time to get out the picnic, anchor the plastic tablecloth with rocks, and distribute the sandwiches, hard boiled eggs, cakes, amid shrill demands and competitive invective. Anyone who'd brought a sweater or jacket was happier than anyone who hadn't. Small children began to snivel and were ordered to shut up or they'd be removed.

"And then you won't see it when it happens," their mothers threatened, while a receding vista of giant mouths moved unheeded on giant screens now less interesting than the Vachon Flakies.

By the time the speeches wound down, many on the bridge's crown thought they imagined a subliminal bounce in the platform under their feet.

This special feature of the bridge dealt with stress, the Vivamus College chancellor immediately pointed out. A bridge of this size and design required it. For instance, take today's wind, which was certainly getting stronger. How else could a bridge like this withstand a wind, except by bending? It was the difference between the oak and the reed. The reed bent, the oak broke. Although, to be sure, the bridge was in many respects like an oak, half a million oaks, and it had to be, for what would the terrible force of the water rushing below do to a mere reed? After a general's wife lost her hat to a broadside gust, a few people moved away from the edge.

The bridge began to hum quietly to itself.

# 1: Arrival

HARRIET WOKE ABRUPTLY. She'd been dreaming she was hurrying across a frozen field under a darkening sky. She was being chased by something unseen and dangerous. A portentous dream voiceover told her she wouldn't like what lay ahead any better.

Patricia, sitting kitty corner to her in the facing seat, where they had spread themselves large for the trip from the regional motherhouse, didn't seem to have noticed anything. Anyway, her square impassive face gave nothing away.

Sister Harriet smoothed her habit, feeling unsettled. She blamed her summer bug, with its fitful fever. She'd have a few days, thank God, to get over it. But did she thank God? That was the problem, beside which her secret weakness in mathematics paled. Although not entirely, since she would be teaching upper year science at Saint Reginald's. She darted another furtive look at Sister Pat.

The train, on this muggy day in the late summer of 1962, was approaching their destination, a midsize river city where Harriet had lived twice before. And here she sat, going to Bothonville for the third time, to embark on her teaching vocation at swanky Saint Reginald's. How the city of her birth had changed, with all this prosperity you kept reading about, was one question she had. How she had changed was less a question than a fact.

"Bothonville," she said, feeling the need to engage the other nun. "I've always wondered, Sister, how it got its name." For a non-teaching sister in a drab brown habit, its unflattering short sleeves revealing arms you associated with convent chores, Patricia had a curiously subtle face.

Patricia wiped her forehead with a handkerchief, giving Harriet the time to feel guilty. Goodness knows, her own origins had been humble enough, and her post-secondary credentials hard won. However, someone always had to mash the potatoes.

"It was settled in the seventeenth century by the notorious Sieur de Bothon, after they kicked him out of New France. He made his way to this upriver wilderness with his retainers. Sounds to me like they didn't want him back in the old country. Who knows, though, there used to be a big button factory around here. Bothonville, Buttonville."

Harriet digested this unexpected reply. "A button factory? I don't remember that."

"Oh, before your time, Sister, it's been shut for decades. It was *big*." Patricia placed a strange emphasis on the word. She leaned forward, pointed. "Look, you can see the ruin on the horizon."

The countryside had become wilder. The train was taking a curve along the flank of a hill and Harriet could see the locomotive and cars, with a vista of rugged valleys beyond. Far away and strange that you could see it at all, sprawling against the misty horizon and endless storeys high, loomed improbably the Ontario Button Manufacturing Company.

"There's always this gap where it appears, although it's got to be a good ten miles away." Patricia's non-explanation struck Harriet as smug.

Harriet looked again. Perhaps due to the tricky haze of declining summer, the ruin seemed to swell, and how she could see its hundreds of windows and age-stained brickwork at such a distance was bizarre. She blinked and refocused. They were now around the curve and shaggy woodland hid the mill. Sister Pat looked as stolid as ever, but Harriet was left with a sense of hallucination.

More than unreal, it had verged on the sinister. Those endless windows had been like tiny eyes. Nerves apart, she really wasn't feeling too well. She schooled her face into sisterly blandness. She wanted to start her new life at Saint Reginald's on the right footing, exuding a calm confidence where academics were concerned, and an off-putting reserve in matters of faith.

She coughed into her handkerchief, aware that Patricia was studying her.

PATRICIA PICTURED the germs floating her way. Was she coming down with something herself, she wondered. Like the summer fever this sister evidently had. Unless it was heat stroke. Patricia moved a shoulder, itchy and hot. She didn't care for her humble habit, but at least she got to wear a white blouse under it, practical in terylene. Let the scholars swan around Saint Reginald's pseudo-hoary halls in hot and flowing black.

She took a thoughtful gander at the nun in front of her. Just turned twenty-nine, Patricia had taken the trouble to find out. The face before her was taut and finely modelled, the eyes well-spaced and large. A lovely young woman, all told, although she mistrusted the gleam of what she interpreted as charismatic piety in Harriet's hazel eyes. Slender and black-robed, a little antsy: the whole suggested fanaticism. You never knew, with these young sisters the Church attracted nowadays. Degreed up to the eyebrows, because Saint Reginald's was all about that, but sometimes lacking in common sense, not to mention humility.

It would be interesting to see what happened. Reverend Mother Perpetua was foisting oversight of the school bridge building competition on her, that is, co-oversight along with the melting Mr. Montserrat. Not that she, Patricia, was inclined to melt, she didn't give a rat's patootie for Marin Montserrat and his guitar-playing ways.

No, that interested her no more than Harriet's pity-inducing teaching load. The rather special diocesan role did intrigue Patricia. What with Perpetua and the bishop's furtive confabs, something about the city, the new Bothonville international bridge and the higher interests of the Church, blah blah blah, there was more to it than met the eye. Amanuensis to the bishop, anyhow, for the work of some important civic committee. She, no more than anyone else, was supposed to know even this much. Patricia didn't just mash the potatoes. She also listened at doors.

AND NOW THEY HAD left the countryside behind and were looking down on Bothonville. Harriet rubbed the warped window glass in vain. The Bothonville of her late childhood had shrunk to a memory of a boring narrow street where she'd lived with her married half-sister, and the trivial mishmash of a child still keen on bicycles, library books and candy stores. The view from the high trestle they were on presented a mishmash too, but to her feverish mind, unfamiliar and unexpected.

Harriet saw, or believed she saw, a vibrant downtown combining imposing buildings with the latest in snappy neon signage, tempered by basilica spires piercing the shimmering air; elegant neighbourhoods embowered in stately trees and shoulder by what their residents no doubt called exclusive suburbs; and beyond all this, far in the distance, the line of the old canal and the gleam of the magnificent river that had become here—she remembered this much—extremely wide in its headlong course.

The more she looked, the more she saw: piled up on the horizon a sort of factory city reminiscent in its uncanny threat of the button mill, the sprawl of mean workers' houses in its vast unwholesome shadow, whose squalor didn't lessen the shock of the far worse adjoining shanty towns; the whole enveloped in factory smoke which hung like a veil over all of Bothonville and which accounted for the shimmer.

"You'll see the bridge they're building in a minute," Patricia said, beginning to sort her things.

In the way of trains, the view from the trestle all at once disappeared, and they must have taken another of those sudden curves that radically alter the perspective. For now Harriet was looking over an impenetrable jungle of sumac that would swallow you whole for fun, directly to the river where, soaring above its blind white reaches, the colossal black skeleton of the half-built bridge clawed its way into the sky. Like the button mill, it loomed unnaturally close. Harriet suddenly realized she was burning up.

Perhaps this was why the bridge conveyed so much more: a ludic violence and attractiveness that beckoned like an evil friend. It was one sight too many for her. She felt a swooping wave of vertigo and nausea.

The rest of the trip to the Bothonville train station was a blank. She retained a fragmentary memory of being met by the school station wagon. When she came to, Patricia was saying something to Sister Rachel at the wheel, about this one needing to see the nursing nun stat.

HARRIET SAT IN the hard armchair, surveying her room in the overflow wing. She liked it more than the curtained area that was all the privacy she'd had at the motherhouse. The good-sized desk and bookshelves gratified her: she was, after all, a secondary school teacher of advanced academic stream subjects.

Her first glimpse of Saint Reginald's Academy, a reassuring grey stone sprawl, had been an antidote to her fainting spell. Whatever that had been about. Anyway, she felt better now.

Supper in the refectory had been tolerable. They didn't eat with the boarders, although she heard something about dining hall duty. No one had expected her to be chatty. Reverend Mother Perpetua had been a gracious presiding presence and the talk had been soothingly bland.

She'd caught glimpses of girls, making noise and shushing each other, giving the new nun the once over. They were bursting with life, attractive in their blue uniforms that reminded Harriet of her own boarding school uniform, which had been similar but green. The colour of renewal and hope, she'd told herself during those sad years.

Harriet lethargically fingered her brand new Saint Reginald's agenda. The view of the twilit grounds through the tall window distracted her. She didn't feel very productive. The lure of memory lane, this evening, was strong.

That bird's eye view of Bothonville from the train had clashed with memory, but now memory flooded in. She saw her twelve-year-old self, cycling around town with a pocket of gobstoppers, skating in winter, swimming in summer, blasting through homework like none of it mattered, and back then it didn't. Coddled carelessly by her half-sister Rhonda, with whom she was eager to live when her mother's health took a bad turn.

Of course sending her away from Lafrenière, a nowhere town on the far side of Montreal where she and her mother had come to rest, was the adults' decision. But she'd wanted to leave, eager for some attention and for a change of subject from doctors. She didn't seize on the severity of her mother's illness. Bothonville, phase two—Bothonville, phase one, featured an unremembered and soon vanished father—was a fool's paradise of a life, good, just not durable.

She'd wondered why she couldn't just stay on in Bothonville, finding out later that Rhonda had received money during those two years for her keep. The money must have dried up, along with Rhonda's casual indulgence. And yet, there was money around somewhere, presumably amid her mother's now barely remembered family in Lafrenière, for how else could she have boarded at exclusive Iona Preparatory on the provincial border?

Now another picture played vividly before her of motherless little Ruth, as she had then been called, in a too big uniform, standing before Iona Prep's gates all those years ago. An uncomfortable memory and she banished it. Ruth Savary, the name at least, was history.

It had been a pleasure to respond to the name of Harriet all day. Imagine starting her career at Saint Reginald's as Henrietta of Baumgarten. She'd dodged a bullet there. She tried not to feel self-congratulatory, but she always did.

In the determination of her saint's name, Mother Superior Alexandra at the La Tombe motherhouse had settled on Henrietta of Baumgarten for Harriet. Novices could pick from a list of three names—but the superior had the final say. Harriet had been helping out in the office, and had been horribly surprised by Alexandra's bizarre choice. Students would turn Baumgarten into Bumgarten, and why not Bumfarten? It had been ridiculously easy to switch the number one and two names on the paperwork. When Alexandra formally assigned Harriet her name, she had looked - confused over her bifocals. But she'd said nothing. Harriet's calculation that her octogenarian superior would seek to cover an embarrassing lapse of memory had been astute. Too bad, so sad, too late, shut the gate, she had gloated. Thus her name in religion became Harriet of Bingham.

Not only had she disregarded her oath of obedience, she had been guilty of deceit and vanity. If her flaws were many, in return she would work hard to be a good teacher. It was 1962, and the world belonged to girls and women. And science held the key. This, of course, had an unavoidably secular ring. History, her other subject, had value too. However, she sometimes felt uncomfortable with all these cautionary tales of perfidy exploding into the clueless present— for wasn't that what history was, a pulsing mass of errors coming back to bite you?

It may be that these thoughts were still with her during her dreams that night, for Harriet had her first bridge dream, in which she was trying to cross an immense arch and could neither see nor get to the other side.

## 2: Distractions

THE NEXT DAYS for Harriet, as the school filled with boarders, were a blur of gearing up for the school term, with little time left over for anything else.

She had been able to walk the extensive grounds once. Contained by low walls—there was no sense of a prison—the school and environs were as attractive as a movie set. As well as grass and clustered old growth trees, there were flower beds, a grotto to Saint Reginald and, at the end of a cinder drive out back, a former farmhouse with gingerbread trim, and an old barn in good repair. Rachel, the Home Economics nun, gave her a tour of the farmhouse turned home ec pavilion—cooking and classroom work downstairs, sewing under the eaves. Harriet had a peek inside the barn as well. Rachel told her they held special events here, conjuring a hope that even she would have fun mingled with all the work.

She would be exceptionally busy. The class registration numbers were in and hers were all courses she'd be teaching for the first time. Saint Reginald's was relatively new, despite the vintage academy look, and the school felt under pressure to prove itself. Their congregation, the Order of Saint Thomas Aquinas, and Perpetua personally had set their sights on shoving the rival schools of the Sisters of Divine Forgiveness to the curb. At the first academic staff meeting this became abundantly clear. They were in a postwar period of competition among convent schools, and Saint Reginald's wanted to snag high-flying girls from the best families. They also wanted other girls, fee-paying girls in plenty. Filler girls, Harriet thought. Better educated nuns were the bait.

Despite her tribulations, Harriet felt buoyed up at the staff meeting. It was her first chance to set eyes on the three lay teachers. Elsie Edison had been around for years, and struck all the expected notes, from tight greying curls to twinset. She was reputed to be a math whizz. Harriet studied her with mingled awe and envy. The other two lay teachers were young men. When a girls' school hires male teachers, one of them will invariably be the handsome one, and one of them won't. Mr. Ronald Hughes, teacher of Latin and a range of junior subjects, filled the latter role. He wasn't so much unhandsome as humdrum: dull hair, ordinary face, thickish neck. And his clothes, which included a rumpled yellow shirt, didn't help. Mr. Montserrat, on the other hand, knew how to dress. He exuded a *dégagé* tweediness, matched to an air of just suitably restrained intellect. Thirtyish like Mr. Hughes, the same height, unmarried as well, but there the resemblance ended. For Marin Montserrat had wavy black hair, lively dark eyes, elegant features and languid gestures. He taught math, French and history. When Perpetua announced that Harriet would be working with him on an extracurricular bridge building competition, his nod in her direction was as graceful as his name.

A DAY LATER, Harriet received a summons to Perpetua's office. She was aware of butterflies as she tapped at the door.

"I wanted," said Perpetua, "to welcome you, of course." She gestured Harriet to a chair. "This is a big year for you, Sister, spiritually and vocationally."

You would never have mistaken Perpetua for anything other than senior management. She seemed not unkind, but her quiet authority gave it away. Harriet had already seen her in action at the staff meeting. She felt a jab of fear mingled with respect: no doubt exactly what Perpetua wanted her to feel.

"You will have all our help and support. And don't hesitate to speak with the senior sisters"—she named three in a deliberate way—"or myself for any reason. Your academic qualifications are, of course, stellar."

Perpetua's eyes scanned Harriet thoughtfully. "I wanted to mention the school bridge competition for a moment. Mr. Montserrat will give you the necessary details. We set up the project last year. The goal is to demonstrate student talent naturally, and we also want to mark for Saint Reginald's this exciting upcoming year in the history of Bothonville."

Harriet must have looked blank, because Perpetua added, "The Bothonville Bridge. You would have seen it coming in? It will be inaugurated in June and will mark a new chapter for the city."

Harriet's mind skittered back to her dream-like first impressions from the train. She felt curious. She'd supposed the school competition would be the usual busy work masquerading as science. This was a fancy way to talk about coffee stir sticks and glue.

"The older girls are being paired with younger ones in teams, where both can learn in different ways. There is more to this competition than enforcing rules and deadlines and judging, although you'll do that too, of course. Mr. Montserrat and you will have a very particular responsibility."

Harriet's mind roved willingly over possible problems. Mr. Montserrat couldn't handle the girls? The seniors and juniors weren't working well together? That probably went without saying. Maybe the girls couldn't handle Mr. Montserrat. But why involve Sister Harriet, the greenhorn, in all this? It was always the way though, wasn't it?

Perpetua's gaze wandered to the view of trees from her window. "Now Sister, there's another role you will be taking up this year. You're expected at the Bishop's Palace next week. He is in need of an assistant—it's a sort of secretarial and representative role—on the work of a municipal committee. It's called the Bridge Design Committee, although I assure you you won't be expected to lend technical support.

The bridge is anticipated to usher in a new era for Bothonville, and the wisdom of the Church is always needed during such times. Your role will be to liaise as the Bishop's representative. His Excellency will himself want to explain its intricacies to you. The role is sensitive, but not time-consuming. There are meetings in the municipal council chambers. You'll have the use of the station wagon."

Harriet perked up at once. Patricia had travelled from Bothonville with another nun who would be staying at the motherhouse, her second duty being to accompany Harriet back to Saint Reginald's. Nuns rarely went anywhere alone. Except, seemingly, when behind the wheel of the convent's Rambler Custom Cross-Country wagon. Vistas of opportunity opened before Harriet. She'd begun to wonder if she'd have a chance to revisit the scenes of her youth. With a car you could accomplish a lot.

"Do you have questions, Sister?"

"Oh no, Reverend Mother." Harriet looked eager and agreeable, yet meek, also not too distracted.

For there was a plethora of distractions here, from handsome Mr. Montserrat, the known distraction, to unknown competition politics, to stick shifts she hoped she remembered how to work. And she had a vivid picture of herself driving to see Rhonda's old clapboard house. She and her family had moved away to distant parts years ago, and Harriet had lost track of them. But she still remembered the house: its faded aqua clapboards, the overgrown lilac by the door, and the cracks in the buckling sidewalk out front, which if you stepped on could break your mother's back. Although time might have erased the clapboards and the lilac, and even traded the cracks for new cracks, offering play drama to new children.

That she was to meet the bishop and that she, the new nun, should be thrown into this odd-sounding committee to funnel—somehow—ecclesiastical soundness, didn't strike her as it might have, had she been less distracted, or wiser.

PERPETUA REPRESSED a sigh.

Bishop Aloysius and Perpetua were friends of long standing, but Perpetua knew there was still a limit to what she as convent superior could say to her bishop, whatever her private thoughts. He'd been quite specific about wanting the academy's new teacher for the unusual committee role. He'd apparently talked it over with Mother Alexandra, during some diocesan event, and whatever had been discussed—Perpetua remained unclear—he seemed to think Harriet was just what he needed.

There was therefore nothing to say, which didn't stop Perpetua from wondering. She knew about Harriet's qualifications through the hiring process; it was the personal angle she sought. Of the young woman before her, she knew the general type. Suitably guided, she would make an excellent teacher and an adequate nun. The gleam of idealism in her eye worried Perpetua a little, but in 1962 this was to be expected. Harriet was attractive, an inherent risk where Mr. Montserrat was concerned, but she had run out of options for someone to place with him on that irksome project, the idea of which had long ceased to appeal. She'd asked Miss Edison as a last resort, and Miss Edison had flat out refused. "Nothing I teach is going to be an iota of use with the girls' bridges," she'd maintained. "Also, I am allergic to glue."

As for the bishop's work, Perpetua had no choice but to let things unfold. From what she understood of the committee it was composed of the sort of men she had little use for, who thought they ran everything in Bothonville, which they did, although not quite everything. There Perpetua had fewer worries, for Harriet, whose face could look as severe as a saint's, seemed eminently capable of taking care of herself in that department.

No, on the whole, Perpetua wasn't too worried. *Que sera, sera,* anyway, as the song went, and she frowned faintly that a billboard hit should have popped into her head, and this one in particular, in relation to a new nun she must now foster and guide.

ON SUNDAY A SPECIAL high mass was celebrated at Bothonville's ornate basilica, with Bishop Aloysius officiating. Harriet, in a pack of nuns near the front, was glad of the opportunity, ahead of their meeting next week, to scrutinize him freely. He seemed your usual sort of bishop. Tall and old, craggy-faced, with bushy eyebrows that might take getting used to. He could, she suspected, be fierce. His sermon went on and on, the doctrinal pitch taking its time to wend towards its obscure conclusion. He preached with a kind of private zeal, while one by one his flock drifted into the realms of sleep and heat stroke.

The basilica was packed, with Saint Reginald's girls en masse, who made a fine showing and kept several designated nuns on their toes, and a cross-section of Bothonville dressed generally to the highest Bothonville standard. It was one of those early September days, that might have been high summer but for a wine-like mellowness in the air. The church was stifling, yet Harriet caught glimpses of ladies in mink stoles. The nun beside Harriet pointed out the mayor and his wife in a whisper. While Saint Reginald's and its *rentrée* featured prominently in the celebration, clearly it also attracted Bothonville's leading citizens.

Sartorially deprived as a child, Harriet still engaged in the shallow pastime of envying the well-dressed during mass. Her eyes took in the elegant frocks and pert veiled hats. A tame and mainly prosperous congregation, she concluded, as the Communion queue advanced with a lethal sluggishness towards salvation and the afterlife. Then her eye picked out a discordant movement at the back.

She'd passed the usual swaggering posse of young men at the church doors, who nipped in for the Eucharist on a technicality. A few of these had just surged in, bringing with them an electric air of the wrong side of the tracks. She supposed they were young mill workers. One had an especially undomesticated look, whether because he was wolfishly handsome or because he moved like a professional fighter, she couldn't decide. As she stared unwillingly, her mind suddenly supplied his proper setting: not this airless basilica but the cindery railway track that led out of town, along which, in her inward eye, he dissolved from view over the misty horizon line.

HARRIET WORKED LATE into the evening in Saint Reginald's quiet library, and then had scant sleep. It hardly mattered. An assembly took up the morning and was followed by homeroom business, and an extra good lunch in which the day girls joined the boarders in the paneled dining hall. A little work followed, mainly talk about work. A night of rain had auspiciously poured freshness over the land, seemingly concentrating on Saint Reginald's, which gleamed in the rinsed air. Harriet knew there would be drudgery ahead. The day despite this was dazzling, light bouncing like shards of glass around Harriet's high-windowed homeroom, everything to her tired mind somewhat fragmented; pictures and scenes forming and reforming while cries of "Sister" flew across the room like birds.

She looked forward to an unbroken sleep, but woke much too early after a nasty dream. It had been so vivid she'd been obliged to get up. First, she'd heard faraway sirens, then urgent voices whispering just outside her door. She'd gone to the window and seen a pallid glow beyond the trees. All at once she was outside and running towards it, aware of galloping spectral figures around her in the blackness. The old barn loomed, a swollen flower of orange flame. As in the way of dreams, rescue took forever to come and dreaming Harriet mentally forced firetrucks onto the scene. The putting out of the fire by the firemen thus seemed contrived, not assured; but everyone including Harriet melted obediently away into the darkness. No one spoke a word: better not to ask questions about the fragile safety that had returned.

## 3: Exegesis

"FOR THE COMPETITION we've snagged the best space in the school," Marin Montserrat said, with what in him passed for enthusiasm, as he ushered Harriet into a multi-purpose room, practically a small auditorium, with two walls of windows. "It was designed as a space for a theatre programme, but Saint Reginald's doesn't have one."

There were tables set up everywhere and a few dozen girls worked in pairs, with some flow from table to table, too. The chat quietened at sight of the teachers. All the work took place here in this room. Most of the learning about bridges, the art and the science of them, their social and economic impact, had happened during the previous school year. The construction itself, said Montserrat, was about to begin.

Harriet felt surprise. "The teams get to spy on each other?"

"Spy? They can see the actual construction. They won't have much chance to copy, there won't be time. These will be very big bridges. Strength, weight, materials, craftsmanship—all subject, Sister, to time." Montserrat was sounding almost metaphysical. "At home would have been difficult—teams of two, transportation. And at least half a dozen of these girls' fathers could be engineers. In Bothonville for the bridge."

"Oh. Do we already know the winners?"

"Sister, you have a suspicious mind."

You don't need to worry about Ella Burnhouse-Raquette, Sister."

"She's not a senior?"

"Grade eleven. There are one or two of them in the competition."

Harriet let the silence stretch, as if this had been all in a day's work for a teacher. Which in a way was true. Montserrat's head swivelled to the clock. "Five more minutes." He was returning to his mellow self. Had he been afraid? He wouldn't show something like that. He stood a good six feet tall, but he looked small, or perhaps just alone, among all those girls. Harriet hadn't had time for fear.

"Good job, Sister," he added, with his inevitable irony.

Harriet had gained a new appreciation for Mr. Montserrat. Not every man would have taken on without hesitation those changeling spectators in their destructive joy. She also wondered whether perhaps Mr. Montserrat had a new appreciation for her.

The whole thing had been curiously disturbing. Harriet knew perfectly well it would not be the contestants smashing their own bridges, as the judges had calibrated weights and special pulleys to bring them down, rewarding strength while penalizing weight. Yet, after this scene, she knew her imagination would inevitably associate ravishing girls and feral impulses with bridges tumbling to their destruction.

"NOW, REVEREND MOTHER likes us to refill the tank after a trip. Go to the Esso at the corner of Birch and Fairmount, the convent has an account there, you won't need cash." Patricia handed the keys to Harriet. They were in a secluded work area, with a kitchen entrance from which an aproned sister—Sister Mildred, if she remembered correctly—watched with lukewarm interest. The station wagon was parked in front of the convent garage.

Thunder peeled in the distance.

"Have a good meeting with the bishop. You'd best be on your way, we're in for it." Arms akimbo, Patricia considered the clouds.

Soon Harriet was driving north along secluded country roads.

Behind the wheel, she began to feel nervous. That sky really didn't look good. The thunder continued, a strange thunder, low, growling, leisurely, nowhere and everywhere as the atmosphere thickened. Barely four in the afternoon, but darkness was already engulfing the land. Still, you didn't stand up a bishop.

She had other reasons besides the weather for being nervous. It was bad enough to lead a double life at Saint Reginald's. She had acquired a certain facility in dissimulation through practice at the motherhouse. A bishop was another order of magnitude.

There was never much point in reviewing her spiritual journey for the precise moment when doubt had surfaced. The bright scaffold of her faith had continued day to day from her girlhood, seemingly impervious to the outer world. And then one morning, as if the soil under the scaffold had shifted, she woke to the great question of what if. She tried not to dwell on it too much, but she soon discovered that doubt played out like the worst disillusion, and it altered everything.

Harriet didn't have the time for the haunted melancholy you read about in trashy novels or the little Catholic pamphlets. She tumbled into an undignified panic about practicalities right away. They were huge and, to her, horrible. She'd joined the Order of Saint Thomas Aquinas as a postulant at age seventeen, inspired by pictures of Thomas with his nose stuck in a book. And she had managed to wangle, in addition to her teaching certificate, a significant education, first a degree in science and then a Bachelor of Arts with a double specialization in history and English. Without these credentials, acquired admittedly from a small regional university, teaching at Saint Reginald's would have been impossible. It had been her dream to teach at a place like Iona, to be among girls like the ones she'd known, but in the flowing robes of the scholar. Was she to risk this coveted future?

She needed a job, to use the secular phrase. Judging from her workload, Saint Reginald's needed her. It didn't seem too wrong if she thought of herself now as facing the future in a spirit of making do. She would turn sisterhood into a kind of career with heavy lifestyle implications, while she worked out the year.

One result of this decision was chronic guilt. Guilt at the weakness of her doubts, guilt at the depths of her deceit, even guilt at the self-congratulation with which she proposed to prosecute this fraud. But good and bad Catholics alike were used to guilt.

Harriet studied the threatening sky. The countryside was lonely. She wondered in passing why diocesan cathedrals and palaces were often in the sticks. A noisy wind had risen and was flinging broken branches across the road. The sign announced she was near Saint Angus, population 4097. She estimated she had a reasonable chance of beating the deluge.

After the loudest thunderclap yet, the clouds opened and rain battered the landscape. Even with her windshield wipers on high, Harriet could barely see. At least there was no traffic. The Rambler took a long steep hill, the view opening suddenly at the summit. On a rise, far yet close in that way she was becoming used to, the Bishop's Palace loomed. Its towers and battlements were illuminated by a dancing circle of pink lightning, while another cannonade rent the air.

A turnoff across from a graveyard led her into a tunnel-like laneway that went on and on. At last she pulled in before the entrance of what, up close, was just a big well-lit stone mansion. She sprinted through a wall of water. A youthful nun in a gray apron met her at the entrance and led her down polished corridors to a waiting room. A mirror told Harriet she looked a rumpled fright, and the empty fireplace beneath it made her feel cold.

"Welcome, my child," said Bishop Aloysius, erupting into the room just as Harriet was trying to stuff tufts of hair into her wet veil. "Come into my study, there's a fire. I told Sister Grace to bring us tea. A bad storm. I would have cancelled, but it was too late. What an intrepid servant of God you are, allied to your fabled discretion."

He extended his hand and Harriet kissed the ring. She felt glad that in the bustle she didn't have to reply; his words didn't entirely make sense. He guided her into a room with a crackling fire and took the armchair facing hers. Sister Grace appeared on cue with a laden tea tray and scurried away.

"Let it steep and I'll play mother. Have a sandwich."

Harriet was still trying to come to terms with the agreeable room and the tea tray, not to mention the whole tone of the greeting, when the bishop spoke once more.

"Evil is everywhere," he said, leaning forward.

Harriet froze. Was it so quickly to come to this?

"I'm in the middle of writing my sermon, you see," he went on, sounding slightly less lunatic. "I know it's partly pride not to want to use my old sermons. Most do. But I feel I've come to understand more about the world, God, the nature of evil, over time. The finer points should come out."

Remembering the basilica high mass, Harriet wondered how the rustics of Saint Angus were absorbing these finer points.

Aloysius poured. "I'm so glad you're here. As Mother Perpetua would have told you, the perspective of Holy Mother Church is important in a project like this one, that will bring such change to Bothonville. We have had our bridges in the past"—Harriet now remembered a dull causeway-style bridge from when she was twelve, and wondered what had happened to it—"but this bridge is like nothing before. As I'm sure you are fully aware."

What *was* the bishop talking about? She nodded cautiously.

Pressing a sandwich on her from time to time, he spoke of the committee. Amanuensis, liaison, the perspective of Holy Mother Church. He brushed aside her question about the mandate of the committee. As for her contribution, she would learn as she went. If she had expected a better explanation than Perpetua's, the meeting proved a spectacular dud. She found herself wondering why she'd driven through the storm for this.

"As specific issues arise, Your Excellency, I won't always be sure I'm identifying the diocesan interest. I've done my share of committee work, of course"—no need to mention on a novices' committee to develop a rota for cleaning the common room, after Mother Alexandra had complained—"but the scale here is so different." She resorted to blather. "I'll do my very best, of course. The role of religious sisters in the modern world is changing, and I for one embrace..." She tried again. "I presume I should take notes?"

"Notes? Why, I suppose so," Aloysius said, as if pleased by this original idea.

He continued to scrutinize her, a faraway expression in his eye. Harriet felt a prickle of sweat on her neck and tried to look enthusiastic. What in the name of everything holy did the man want?

ALOYSIUS TOOK IN the nun before him with satisfaction. Bright and full of energy, these young ones were, and of course educated to a high standard nowadays. She looked so fervent. Call it an old man's foible, but he was sick of the way the Romanesque, with its sickly odour of Enlightenment, had crept in everywhere nowadays. Like evil, if he could be accidentally witty for a moment, but this was the very point. Yes, she would do. Surely she would do? He hoped so. Naturally he couldn't ask her directly for her personal views. Still, Alexandra had spoken highly of her devotion to duty, her obedience, her yielding and discreet nature. Wouldn't the superior be in the best position to know?

He contemplated the pale flame of Sister Harriet's face with sudden uncertainty. What exactly had Alexandra told him? They'd been at that crowded event in La Tombe, balancing tidbits on napkins. She had mentioned that one or two just qualified nuns would be heading to Saint Reginald's, where their order hoped for great things. He'd perked up. In his anxiety he'd decided he needed an arm's length instrument—pawn was too strong a word--for the bridge committee, and that certainly didn't describe any of the existing Saint Reginald's nuns.

Alexandra had been praising a particular paragon among her newly-minted sisters. A certain Arrietta. It had been hard to follow in the bustle and noise, but he had grasped the essential and decided this was the sort of cat's paw he needed. When Perpetua told him they were bringing in a Sister Harriet from the motherhouse, he saw at once that he must have misheard the name. And that her arrival was a sign.

The older he got, the less he liked corporate types, who often didn't agree that evil was everywhere. Therefore it doubly satisfied him, as Sister Harriet made steady inroads into the chocolate biscuits, to find this particular one surprisingly engaging.

"Evil isn't something you can first isolate, and then defeat," he said confidentially, delighted to see her eyes grow round and bright. Yes, she would work out very well.

He looked forward to meeting with her again soon, during which he could perhaps expand a little on his notions of evil over more tea. Harriet would never say, like that pup of a curate who'd showed up for confession last week, "but is this not approaching heresy?" And Aloysius shook the young woman's hand with extra warmth at the thought of future doctrinal exegesis.

## 4: Patterns

HARRIET SENSED, on the way back to the convent, she might have overdone the bishop's finger food, but that was all to the good because she'd be missing supper. She'd phoned ahead to tell them she was on her way back, padding her schedule by a good thirty minutes. This would give her a chance to explore Bothonville.

The bishop's enthusiasm had had one practical benefit. She had imagined him with a kind of X-ray vision regarding faith. Thankfully, he had been too busy expanding on his various doctrinal hobby horses to notice much. Whether he was some sort of mystic or a loveable fruitcake remained to be seen. To be fair, he'd been an attentive host. Just not of much use where the Bridge Design Committee was concerned. She would have to take it on a wing and a prayer. An approach she was becoming increasingly used to.

Evening had arrived by the time Harriet found herself cruising the streets of Bothonville. Black clouds still lingered on the horizon but the storm had passed, leaving the city sodden and emptied in the fading light. She couldn't quite believe she was about to set eyes on places she hadn't seen in years. She peered left and right, trying to recognize things. It all felt surreptitiously unreal. As if this wasn't the Bothonville of her childhood at all, but some replica Bothonville with glancing similarities but insidious differences.

For example, the university, in a well-heeled residential district near the city centre, was practically unrecognizable as the old classical college. She could recognize the original quadrangle but it looked slicker, as did the trees. There were new buildings too. An imposing sign out front of one read, "The Bothonville Chemical Company Arthur Brandeis Building". Harriet knew Vivamus College had reinvented itself as a science and technology institution, although you could still study the same happy and useless subjects as in days of yore, probably minus theology. Here at least were signs of life. The students milling around with armloads of books were an engaging sight. Some of her own students would end up here.

It took her a while to find her old neighbourhood and Rhonda's house. Driving by her old home filled her with strangeness. First, the neighbourhood itself, which had informed Harriet's *in absentia* vision of the city, had shrunk to a handful of streets barely a notch up from underprivileged. The house was the same faded pastel, and the lilac shrub by the door was just that, a shrub, and none too big. You couldn't tell who lived there. Dusk bathed it in an eerie neutrality. She drove by twice more, hoping to summon other feelings, until she saw some hard-eyed youths staring at her. It probably wasn't every day a rubbernecking nun in a gleaming station wagon cruised their drab little street.

In heading to the west end, she got on a new bypass by mistake. When she figured out how to get off, she took an anonymous street at random. This turned into a gravel track that petered out before a tributary canal, across which a smoking morass of factory shapes rose up.

She certainly did not remember any of this. She found her way out by heading towards the river, and came to the old canal, suitably mournful and derelict in the dusk. It was when she was driving alongside the canal that she had a clear view of the unfinished bridge, and admitted to herself this had been another goal of her junket.

The bridge loomed as big as before, astonishing big. Surely bigger than such bridges usually are, even when they must reach a far shore you couldn't see. Against an angry sunset, the footings, girders and towers stood out blackly. Its unfinished, upward thrusting spars gave the sense they were aiming for outer space. Harriet couldn't recreate the feeling she'd had on the train, of something threatening. Alien, transgressively bold, but not truly threatening. And she now saw raw beauty.

Her eyes travelled down into the worksite on the river's edge. The immense construction zone looked unreal in the half light, and she didn't know what to make of a sea of small structures strewn higgledy piggledy along the riverbank. She peered, feeling her eyes were playing tricks on her. Lights pulsed and flickered. She blinked and looked up to the crown of the bridge. She imagined seeing movement out of the corner of her eye. Harriet felt a sudden desire for home.

By the time she pulled in near the garage, she was experiencing hunger pangs. There were still lights on in the kitchen and she decided to pop in to wangle a bite. A movement in the darkness drew her eye and, under the glow of the entrance light, Harriet saw a student passing by. She recognized Loretta Mazurek's glossy auburn head. The idea of an assignation came and went. Loretta was eating a chocolate bar. Well, the girl had bitten into it and Harriet was taken aback to see her toss the rest into a garbage can before disappearing. A perfectly good chocolate bar. She felt even hungrier. Old Sister Edwina was still fussing around and greeted Harriet kindly. A tender soul, Edwina did well by Harriet. They had a convivial chat, Edwina calling her *chérie* a lot, a soothing way to end a demanding day.

The bridge she dreamed about that night was wreathed in mist and oddly bouncy under her feet. The mood was shadowy as before, in that sense of much withheld. The downward arc and other shore were just as invisible.

HARRIET'S DAYS fell into a pattern. She became absorbed in her classes. She was always hurrying somewhere, as if default Harriet was this long-legged young woman striding through the halls, her beads clacking, her arms full of books. "Good morning, Sister!" or

"Hi Sister Harriet!" became familiar greetings. Erupting into a classroom, restoring order swiftly and getting down to business required less and less conscious nerve. The larger questions of Harriet's life hadn't gone away, but she put them aside.

Her students, the twelfth graders and the younger ones, began to emerge as individuals. There were mediocre students of course, but her heart warmed to the penetrating intelligence and passion of the few. Florene proved the live wire of grade nine history. Her senior science class was going remarkably well, under the circumstances. She had a strong group, who aced the technicalities and shared her interest in the philosophical questions. Loretta Mazurek in particular displayed brilliance. Her sense of the big picture delighted the teacher in Harriet, and her mathematical insights supplied some of Harriet's better contributions to the bridge project, when Loretta was out of hearing and Mr. Montserrat wasn't.

The project was going as well as could be expected. The room always had a charge, you got used to it. It didn't seem a direct result of the competition, although you sensed competitiveness. Perhaps, Harriet told herself, it spurred on the girls to more work.

One day, when Montserrat was off work with a cold and energy seemed to flag, Mother Perpetua arrived unannounced with a contingent of town ladies to "show" them the project. Harriet was horrified to see the group, some sort of superior Catholic ladies' club, troop in one after the other. She herself was developing a cold. An inspection without warning was the height of unfairness, and for them to walk in when she was blowing her nose into an oversized blue handkerchief was cruelly unlucky.

At least the work pairs were each at their own table, if only from lethargy. She found unexpected allies, however, in the three Ls, Laura Rome in particular, who salvaged the visit as far as she was concerned. Laura stepped forward after the introductions, as if this had been sorted ahead of time, and took the group from table to table, with Harriet floating along in their wake. But Laura managed things so as to suggest that Harriet was the wise sponsor of everything she said. The role of adjusting her face to this fiction was a simple one. Loretta said just enough in response to a question to suggest that Saint Reginald's hatched geniuses, and Laurentine turned out to be the niece of the lady with the biggest mink stole, thus cementing the success of the visit as a family affair.

"I know Laura's nineteen, but she could be thirty the way she behaved," Harriet said afterwards to Sister Patricia. She had developed the habit of visiting the kitchen at random hours, dear Edwina always being good for a snack, and there from time to time ran into Patricia. Harriet had begun to treat her as a sort of kitchen stoop confidante. Her listening skills were undeniable. Whatever you said—and Harriet wasn't always sure she should be sharing so much—Sister Pat's poker face always comforted.

"I just can't figure out why Mother Superior didn't give me warning."

"She might have had no warning herself. She has a lot to do handling the town bigwigs. Saint Reginald depends on them, and we won't mention money because, as you know, Sister, it's the root of all evil."

"They're a little…perfect, those three girls together, but you have to admire them." In this Harriet overstressed the positive, for Loretta, Laurentine and Laura often got on her nerves.

Patricia's eyebrow suggested understanding of this petty reaction.

"They're some kind of club," Harriet said.

"Bothonville, Sister, is just rotten with clubs."

Harriet made a face. She had disagreeable memories of a Rotary Club lady patronizing her mother while dropping off a Christmas basket one year.

Patricia now whipped her brown apron around her shoulders in a swashbuckling gesture against the chilliness of the day. Pat's summer outfit had been replaced with a long-sleeved brown habit similar to Harriet's. We're a bit of a club too, she thought. But with Sister Pat, it didn't seem a bad thing.

THE GIRLS NOW chattered daily about the fall bonfire, a big annual event. Harriet herself began to feel youthfully excited. Kicking through piles of leaves as she hurried along a school path was like time travel straight back to childhood. There was that familiar fall tang in the air, and the golden light brought back other golden days. The nights closing in, which adults clucked about, made any evening business more thrilling. You and your friends being out after supper, cruising cold and empty streets that smelled of oil furnaces in need of a tune up, conjured for Harriet the beating heart of the dying year. The conditions favoured mischief, not that Harriet remembered too much of that. Being out unsupervised under the pale moon felt like mischief enough.

She had begun to wonder when she could borrow the station wagon again.

## 5: Puny Tumbleweed

JUST BEFORE EIGHT, Harriet ascended the steps to City Hall, in one hand a brand new briefcase containing a yellow pad, two ballpoints and a handkerchief. On this damp evening, a mist gave halos to streetlamps and a sense of floating to Harriet. This was compounded by the excitement of officially representing the bishop.

After a fire in the 1940s, Bothonville's city hall had been rebuilt on the same site. The lobby was discreetly grand in the passport renewal architectural style. A commissionaire promptly directed Harriet to the municipal council chamber. She had imagined a big fluorescent-lit room, but modernity had been left at the door. She saw dark wood and muted lighting, with walls of books behind glass. A pack of humanity yattered with civic bonhommie. She hung up her coat and found the diocesan seat at a long table. She sensed she had attracted interest. Now she was a nervous wreck playing it cool. She plunged into facsimile examination of the paperwork in front of her. To her relief, the meeting began without delay.

But she quickly began to enjoy herself. The atmosphere was upbeat, and there were representatives from every sphere you could think of. In a sea of men, she spied a couple of other women: none other than Madame Brunet, Laurentine's aunt from the ladies' club, and, down at the end, one other woman among the technical participants. Harriet's place occupied the top quarter of the table, as befitted the status of the bishop.

She was introduced with due ceremony, and replied to the nods and good words with a judiciously unreadable look. In the first difficult year of her novitiate, she'd fine-tuned the expression with the help of a medieval illustration in which the faces, from the *bourreau* to the individual with the cleaver in his skull, all exhibited the same bland reserve. It had seemed an expression for all seasons.

She furtively surveyed the room. Mayor Larry Martel chaired. A handful of municipal councillors clustered around, and she assumed they would speak with one voice. The voice of Progress. Indeed, there seemed no other voice in the room. The business community was amply represented, from the Retail Council and banks to a private railway developer. There was a four-man bridge consortium. The young editor-in-chief of the Bothonville *Herald,* Dean Carter slouched affectedly in his chair. Harriet could almost see a newsman pencil behind his ear. Police Chief Michael Flynn, a big hearty man who looked well in a uniform, had a place at the table on the left of the mayor. The right side was reserved for a small crabbed individual, a Mr. Byron Slade, who represented something called Salamander Holdings and gave off an interesting aura Harriet couldn't parse.

Madame Brunet seemed to represent the feminine touch, which Harriet assumed included the finer feelings, tempered by common sense and, following a realistic distance behind, common decency. The technical perspective was embodied in that ragtag bunch at the foot of the table, who were often consulted as an afterthought and didn't sometimes seem to hear what was being said. Even the white-haired chancellor of the university, to Harriet's surprise, was in attendance.

As Harriet scribbled dutifully, the impact of the bridge began to dawn on her. The group held a unified belief it would confer untold benefits on Bothonville. An elderly banker brought tears to the committee's eyes when he reminisced about the dark years that had followed the destruction of the previous bridge. A bridge didn't just take you to another place, didn't just move goods around. Wealth and prosperity flowed from a bridge like a spreading Midas touch. The world their bridge would create was practically a new dispensation. Harriet's imagination ignited, as the banker invoked the superb benefit of being linked to the other side of the river. Reaching the Other Side would mean the fulfillment of the committee's civic dreams.

Now Harriet had a flashback. She'd been on the older bridge, when she was twelve it must have been, with two friends. She, Jane and Babs had all made up excuses at home and set out early one Saturday to cross the bridge. It had been an adventure: being battered by monster winds at the bridge's apex; standing with a foot in each country; meeting a sinister gang of boys. When they told the border agent they were going to Sparta, a place they pictured as huddled at the southern footings of the bridge as Bothonville occupied the north end, but in every way more glorious, he told them it was ten miles down the highway and to forget it. Footsore and subdued, they came at last to the far shore, a place of cornfields, empty blacktop and, in the distance, a lone water tower. More than a little disappointing, and Harriet now supposed the committee must be referring to everything that lay just beyond that water tower, with its peeling inscription of Town of Sparta. She and Jane and Babs must have covered fifteen miles that day, and wouldn't have made it home had they not accepted a ride from a stranger in a white van, who drove them back to Bothonville without incident.

While Harriet daydreamed, the meeting wended its way through agenda items with names like Permissions & Next Steps, Secondary Infrastructure (Interim Report), Personnel Planning, Finances Update, and Technical Issues. Here and there something stuck in her brain like a burr. For instance, while private enterprise had been heavily marshalled for this project, Bothonville was to a surprising extent funding this bridge by issuing bonds. It seemed that they would pay for these by issuing more bonds, and so on. The sterling reputation of Bothonville—thirty heads nodded—would do the rest. And if they didn't talk much about Sparta, there were references to Carson

Falls down the river, in tones that struck her as competitive. These remarks were accompanied by an inexplicable side glance or two at Harriet. Then there was the mention of serpentine chrysotile, words that meant nothing to her although they seemed to invigorate the room. Harriet had been idly looking at Mr. Slade just then, and had the peculiar feeling that he changed before her eyes, becoming even more shrivelled and hunched, but also giving off a flood of black energy that set her to nervous scribbling on her pad.

The discussion under Personnel made more sense. Those assembling the bridge were dissatisfied, despite things like wage increases and the "really very much improved" safety record. Someone made a quick reference to tomorrow's expected one-day strike. Everything was under control, Flynn assured them, including that alleged problem with lax security at the bridge site.

The technical issues were quickly despatched. The microphones connected to the engineers at the end of the table just then malfunctioning, as mouths moved down there, the councillor responsible for minutes neatly summed it up as "issues noted."

When Martel asked for a seconder to adjourn the meeting, Harriet timidly called out "I second." Everyone beamed, so that was all right. A pleasant committee all round, and the way they all agreed with each other offered a refreshing contrast to that novices' committee she'd sat on. Once she figured out her role more clearly, she'd feel more at ease. No one had said a thing about design.

And thus, at an astonishing quarter to eleven, the meeting of the Bridge Design Committee concluded. In stuffing her items into her satchel, Harriet was taken aback to see that she'd written at one point in the evening—around the time she'd had that funny impression of Byron Slade—the words, Committee of Dark Designs. She knew immediately the name would stick.

Harriet slid into her coat, left her gloves on the windowsill for later, and headed home.

THE NEXT DAY was filled with lurid accounts of wildcat walkouts on a scale apparently not anticipated, that turned into clashes with the police and rioting. Saint Reginald's stood outside the city centre and therefore in little danger, but Perpetua summoned the entire school to discuss safety. The boarders were to stay on school grounds, and the day girls would have to exercise caution going home. The girls were to remain calm.

It was more a case of them not looking too entertained, although a few students who'd seen grainy pictures on television—black smoke, people running, sirens howling in the background—seemed genuinely frightened. The staff received the news phlegmatically, all but very young Sister Clothilde, who cared tenderly for the academy cat and who began to sob.

All this was something of a contretemps to Harriet, but she went to see Perpetua anyway before lunch. Perpetua seemed only moderately interested in her account of the meeting.

"You role will be evident in time, Sister. You will be visiting Bishop Aloysius soon, in any case."

Harriet nodded deferentially. "I took very thorough notes." She added contriteness to her look of virtue. "I did a foolish thing. I left my gloves behind in the council chamber. I called, I can pick them up whenever I like. It's just gloves, but they were given to me by Reverend Mother Alexandra when I took my vows. They came from that very exclusive clerical garb shop in Rome, the one near the Pantheon—Barbiconi..."

In these allusions, Harriet demonstrated intelligence. Alexandra would have given her the traditional gift in lieu of the family she pitifully lacked. As for the reference to Barbiconi, who didn't know Barbiconi?

"You want to get them today, Sister?" Perpetua sounded uncertain. "The situation in the city is very unstable."

"I was thinking the same thing, Reverend Mother. However, City Hall is away from the unrest. I'll be worried until I retrieve them. I was very careless. The gloves mean a lot to me."

They were top grade kidskin with a frivolous button trim and an unusual Bemberg cupro lining in the fingers, and they did mean a lot to Harriet.

"Very well, Sister, but go before dark. Do you have the bridge project this afternoon? I'm sure Mr. Montserrat can manage by himself. Go right after your last class."

Such an unexpected bonus, although it suggested chance favoured her, left Harriet feeling guilty as she drove into the city later. She'd listened to the news before leaving. Violence was now sporadic, and had moved west to the factory sector. Things might be winding down.

A fog had begun to creep in from the river. She turned on her headlamps and drove carefully, as the day darkened and outlines blurred. Picking up her gloves from the security desk, including a chummy exchange with last night's security guard, took a minute. Then, taking a deep if ragged breath, she headed towards the bridge. She told herself that she wanted to see the bridge up close, closer than she'd seen it before.

She parked at the same spot along the canal. By now the fog was a real peasouper, and the bridge was amorphous and indeterminate. The walkout must have been responsible for the eerie silence. She took a rough incline down to the main gates. These were wide open and unguarded. She saw no one. She entered the vast construction zone.

As she neared it, the bridge took shape, a compelling black presence in the grey. There was a cluttered space to get through—lanes, equipment, huddled structures, you couldn't tell in the murk—and that took some time. The giant curves of the bridge appeared to pulse invitingly as the fog thinned and thickened.

This bridge didn't mess around. You didn't have to cross hundreds of feet of traffic circles, on ramps and what have you. The ground was flat, bridgeless, and then it wasn't, you were between massive trusses, and an aggressive slope rose under your feet. It would have been difficult for Harriet to climb this way: a wall of heavy equipment confronted her, conjuring the tanks of a hostile army.

The other day she'd seen a spiral staircase in a protective cage, climbing the bridge's outward structure at the water's edge. It soared bizarrely high but seemed sturdy, at least from a distance in the dusk. It would bring her by the fastest route to the top of the bridge. To get to the stairs, she descended over broken ground, glad she was wearing flat-soled shoes and not those little cuban-heeled jobs the shorter sisters favoured. The smell of the river became strong, then the dull sheen of gliding water appeared. She came at length to the stairs.

Reflecting that worksite security could have been better, Harriet hiked her skirts and began to climb.

The climb seemed very long. She couldn't assess her progress in the fog. She sensed she was getting very high. The air changed, became fresher and colder, and the fog changed to a brighter solid. Often she thought this must be the last rung. Until finally it was, and she stepped onto a roughly paved surface, into a fitful wind. It took her a few minutes to catch her breath. She looked around.

She stood in a world of delicate pink-tinted mist, that moved continually. When it thinned, graciously soaring trusses became visible, leading her forward, and, when it thickened, she felt like one of those fresco cherubs bobbing in the candy floss of paradise. Was gravity somehow weaker up here? Or was the bridge in its gravity-defying purpose lifting her upward, as it disappeared into the roseate ether?

Along with the bodily lightness, Harriet's mind was curiously transformed. Her burdens lifted. The dilemmas of her life seemed at this moment unimportant. A wordless prayer formed in her soul, and blew away like a puny tumbleweed in the wind. The beautiful iridescent swirls glowed brighter, charged with urgency. She had the impression of a dazzling causeway opening before her, leading her to the point where the bridge ended, to infinite lightness, infinity itself. She was like a deer in the headlights, but not concerned.

She advanced for a while. Then she stopped. Whatever existed beyond the pink wall, this was far enough for today. She sat down on a hard concrete bollard in a mood of waning satisfaction, thinking the wind blew a trifle chilly. Her breath turned into a sigh. She liked it here, but the euphoria was gone. That vertical hamster run had to be tackled in reverse. It would be best to get out of the construction zone before anyone requiring explanations came back. Perpetua would be getting worried.

Later that evening, she thought about what she had done. It had been a heady experience, undoubtedly. Like heroin, maybe? She knew nothing about heroin, but she'd been reading about it, the scourge of modernity that promised bliss. Perhaps heroin would be just as disappointing as her first taste of wine. Climbing the bridge, on the other hand, had been wonderful in its way. She had come to her senses, though. And she had broken half a dozen rules and offended twice that number of niceties today. She felt the irony of her situation: even if she didn't believe anymore, she could still feel the familiar pinch of sin.

## 6: Nuns with Gasoline

THERE WAS NOW a bite in the air, in the procession of these deep blue days. All minds at Saint Reginald's turned to the annual bonfire and the day of fun that would precede it. At staff meetings they discussed how to make the girls work even harder after wasting a day. Harriet's classes were fully underway and most of her girls seemed to be working hard already. She herself felt she had to race to keep up, but even that had its exhilarating aspect.

Perpetua had been genuinely relieved to see Harriet finally return with her gloves. There had been several roadblocks throughout the city that day, only underscoring Harriet's run of luck. Normalcy resumed, both in Bothonville and Sister Harriet.

After her escapade, she redoubled her efforts in all the obvious ways. No lesson prep was too dutiful, no essay commentary too long-winded, no religious devotion too arduous. She forbade herself to think about more gallivanting with the Rambler. She practiced patience with the slow girls and was more generous in giving the smart girls their due. Loretta, who seemed in a way that Harriet couldn't understand, to become a more concentrated flame as the school year progressed, had the mind of a future NASA scientist. Laurentine's intelligence soared also; Harriet didn't see how an eighteen year old could produce such a sophisticated analysis of history, if sophisticated was the word. Her work conveyed a world-weariness, as if willowy, semi-transparent Laurentine had lived for a few centuries and seen it all.

Harriet would have been hard-pressed to offer much of an explanation for why she had scaled the bridge. It had called to her, and she had wanted to. Since everyone in Bothonville was hepped on bridges, perhaps it was a case of contagion. Her first sight of it from the train, a fearful thing possessed, had surely planted a seed, or a spore. Some things were too big for simple or ready explanations. She'd not been afraid, in the pink mist. In that, the experience had been like those recurrent bridge dreams: no fear, but portent on the edge of revelation. Just no revelation.

As for her sense that the bridge had intentionality, a life of its own—absurd. But the things that her faith had led her to believe were potentially absurd too. For a freakish moment she pictured herself discussing these points with Aloysius, realizing sadly they were just too far beyond the thinking of his favourite Gnostic crackpots. Like the rest of Saint Reginald's, Harriet needed a good bonfire.

Bonfire day began with prayers in the auditorium, and letters read out from old girls. They weren't so very old, but it still affected everyone to hear from Carol, married with a baby in Carson Falls, and Suzanne, studying to be a pharmacist in Quebec City. They gushed that their days at Saint Reginald's had been the best of their lives, with bonfire day a favourite. Classes were cancelled, replaced by a controlled bedlam of choral singing and musical performances, a volleyball tournament between the seniors and the nuns, a sort of mass picnic and, in the afternoon, a movie. *Gigi,* a strange choice perhaps as the youthful heroine was being groomed as a courtesan, but it ended on a moral note and Leslie Caron was lovely.

Study hall was cancelled afterwards and everyone was left to their own devices until darkness fell. Then the day girls returned to the school in tight stretch slacks and raffish car coats, some with siblings in tow, and even the lay staff showed up. Mr. Montserrat, in a slouchy black turtleneck and carrying an acoustical guitar, caused general perturbation. He and Harriet were pals by now, having had each others' backs for some time on the bridge project, and they stood companionably together as final preparations were made. In the darkness and excitement, with girls in their hundreds milling around and the reek of gasoline in the cold air, Harriet felt that life was good.

Everyone was assembled in a wide gravelly field well out beyond the kitchen area and mostly encircled by woods. At the centre erupted a pyre, whose size left Harriet speechless even though the older girls had repeatedly rhapsodised on the hugeness you should expect. Eight nuns now came out of the crowd, which greeted them with sharp cries and then silence. They were the beefier sporty nuns, and Harriet recognized Patricia and Rachel, as well as Sister Angela, whose volleyball serve had won the nuns the tournament that afternoon. Half the nuns carried cans of gasoline and stepladders. The others were pushing strange-wheeled contraptions ahead of them that had long metal arms attached. A secondary group of sisters now deployed, to move the crowd away from the pyre. Hundreds backed away slowly, to the tune of a feral murmuring.

The wheeled machines were mystifying. "What are those?" Harriet asked Montserrat.

He laughed. "Just watch. It's all highly orchestrated. We should back away further, Sister, it's not safe." His sweatered arm on her shoulder hardly touched at all.

Harriet could never have anticipated what came next.

Perpetua, wearing her usual long cape but looking different in the context, now materialized and there was a simmering hush. She asked everyone if they were ready. The reply was atavistic and loud. She nodded to the nuns with gasoline. The nuns with gasoline advanced to the pyre—they were dwarfed by it—and set up their stepladders, from which they sprinkled the gasoline over the hay bales and stacked wood. This took some time as they didn't just slosh it on. They were artisans with the gasoline, spreading it evenly, making sure that plenty got in to the centre. They then packed up their stepladders with dignity and left.

The nuns responsible for the armed contraptions had stopped well away from this scene. Now they came forward and lit torches cunningly affixed to the ends of the metal poles. The crowd had to move back yet again, and Mr. Montserrat, sounding genuinely concerned, said, "Let's go over there, they do this year after year and for the life of me I don't understand why it has to be so..." He was at a loss of for the word. "Anyway, you'll see." His guiding arm was even more evident to Harriet, who protested for form's sake.

The nuns on the machines—which now looked to Harriet like some species of medieval war machine—moved forward in careful unison. She could see the torch flames in the darkness but not much else. The long poles had somehow gotten twice as long and in the tricky darkness you would almost think the nuns wielding them wore armour, but evidently that had to be a hallucination. How thrilling it all was. Harriet craned to see.

The word Mr. Montserrat had been searching for must almost certainly have been "explosive." For the next moment, a great ball of white flame edged in electric blue mushroomed into the night sky, sending out a banging whooshing sound and, a split-second later, a sizeable shockwave. Screams rent the air, and Harriet for a reason-dissolving moment thought that one of the nuns had been incinerated. But no, they were all beating an orderly retreat with their machines. It took mere seconds for flames to climb to the top of the pyre, from which black smoke began to spew.

"That, Sister, is the Saint Reginald's bonfire," Montserrat said, turning to Harriet just in time to catch her as she fainted.

SISTER HARRIET'S RELEASE from the tyranny of time and space was brief. The swish-swish of Sister Imelda's white nylon habit was the first thing she heard, and then she opened her eyes and saw she reclined among a handful of patients in a nursing tent set up near the kitchen area. Sweet tea was being passed out by seniors.

"A few people faint every year," Laura Rome kindly explained.

Imelda bustled over. "You're looking very pale, Sister." Whipping out a fifth from her robes, she poured a dollop of brandy into Harriet's teacup.

Mr. Montserrat was still loitering in the vicinity. "I'm better now but I'm so very sorry, Mr. Montserrat," was all Harriet could think to say. She felt embarrassed. Montserrat, himself looking slightly self-conscious, took the opportunity to beat a retreat. After several swallows of fortified tea, Harriet felt much better. Her mind lingered briefly on how she'd been got over to the nursing station—had Mr. Montserrat carried her, had others been involved, had she perchance been trundled on one of those ignition machines?—but there was no point in thinking about that. She decided there was also no point in being embarrassed. The pyre burned away in the distance, and fun was being had around her. She finished her tea and headed back.

As the fire burned, the evening changed in character. Girls gathered in circles on canvas chairs or common room cushions. Small fires had been lit, marshmallow bags appeared. The youngest girls ran around like children at a wedding. Over by the woods a group danced to tinny transistor music. Several nuns sat contentedly at a fire of their own, overseeing whatever they could in the darkness, which wasn't much. Were those "siblings" really brothers? Threading her way through the groups, Harriet had her doubts. Everyone had thrown off overcoats, because the bonfire was still giving off substantial heat. There floated everywhere a crazy feel, of a warm summer night under the stars, and Harriet felt very relaxed.

She felt unsure of what was expected of her. Should she stay with the sisters? Before she could make up her mind, someone seized her hand. It was Florene Pellerin from ninth grade, looking, out of uniform, even more like a Dickensian urchin.

"Sister Harriet!" she said excitedly, "I'd like you to meet my brother, Roger." Roger advanced, dropping and crushing his cigarette with practiced ease, and they shook hands. Harriet started. Roger was a grown man. But there was something else. He looked familiar, she felt sure she had seen him before.

"I think I saw you at the special high mass at the basilica," she said. She immediately regretted the remark. What was she doing looking at men during high mass? She felt sure now it had been him in the communion queue: the hair falling over the feral eyes, the mood of a banked fire.

Florene continued to babble. "Yes, Roger was there. I've so been wanting to introduce you. I've told him, Sister, how much I love history because of you. And I can hardly wait to take your English class next year!"

Harriet tried to look modest and teacherish. "I take a great interest in Florene," she said to Roger. She thought she saw a scowl in the darkness. What was wrong with taking an interest in Florene? He was a grown man, but young, with an aspect of adolescent revolt about him.

He finally said to his sister, "How about we get you home? It's late."

"Oh, I know!" Florene said, grabbing his arm. "But let's look at the bonfire one more time." And she whisked him away, barely allowing time for goodbyes.

There was, in these interactions, food for thought. Roger was a very young man, in his early twenties if that. But there was a tolerance in his voice while addressing his sister that hinted at a protective tenderness. Florene's woefully shabby civvies had confirmed for Harriet what she'd already suspected. The child was poor, one of those scholarship students no doubt. Harriet guessed Roger worked in one of the factories. Florene had taken his hand as they whirled away. His hand, Harriet remembered, had been strong and warm.

She now heard guitar music nearby. Another campfire crackled invitingly, around which many attentive girls clustered in studied poses. At their centre, the firelight glinting off his dark hair, Marin Montserrat strummed his guitar. Several smiles greeted Harriet as she joined the circle, including from Mr. Hughes. The three Ls were there, arranged in an inner circle beside Mr. Montserrat, Loretta closest of all, next to her Laurentine and, last but certainly not least, shadow-eyed Laura Rome. Ella Burnhouse-Raquette stoked the fire.

Montserrat leaned over his guitar, far away in his music like any turtlenecked troubadour trying to get the harmonies right, but when he looked up eventually and saw Harriet he smiled warmly. He said something about Harriet's fainting fit, and everyone laughed including Harriet. Mr. Hughes mentioned his own first year reaction to the bonfire, but few paid attention and he soon ambled off.

Montserrat began another song, and Harriet immediately

recognized the strains of "Greenfields" by The Brothers Four. He sang in an unforced baritone and his hands had a feel for the guitar. He got the slow tempo just right. The heart-tugging music and words wafted over his listeners.

*Once there were greenfields/Kissed by the sun/Once there were valleys/Where rivers used to run...*

Everyone was picturing the greenfields, the valleys, the rivers.

*We were the lovers/Who strolled through the greenfields...*

Everyone now pictured the lovers and a faint movement ran through the girls; they were like wheat rippling in a nighttime breeze.

The song entered a minor key. The lines became longer, spoke of lost love and hopelessness, the driving chords conveying a swelling sorrow. Suddenly, and it was clearly unrehearsed, Laura Rome joined in and the two sang, in lifting two-part harmony:

*I only know there's nothing here for me/Nothing in this wide world left for me to see...*

The shock, in the merging of the voices, the bleak message in the lines, the sheer unexpectedness, travelled through them all. The wheat tossed now, as if before an approaching storm.

Harriet experienced a tearful squeezing under the ribs. The girls were to the last one of them in a volatile trance. Something close to panic rose in her. Mr. Montserrat, at the moment, was a force of nature. As the lone responsible adult, she had to do something. When the song ended and Montserrat looked up with an oddly innocent smile, she called out: "Can you play 'If I Had a Hammer,' Mr. Montserrat?"

The brisk tempo and rousing words everyone sang together swept the other mood away. That was the thing about groups of girls, Harriet reminded herself. The collective mood could change in a moment. As for her own mood, it might take longer to rearrange.

# 7: Gothic

DESPITE HER GOOD intentions, Harriet found herself behind the wheel of the Rambler again sooner than expected. A week or so later, a toothache woke her at four am and, by breakfast, it was worse. Pointing out Harriet's swollen face, Imelda declared that the time for self-dosing with aspirin was past. A spot that same day was found at the dental clinic patronized by the sisters, and Harriet drove there after last class. Others had offered to accompany her but everyone was now in peak busy mode and Harriet had resolutely refused.

There was the beginning of an abscess, pronounced Dr. Lapointe, and the molar had to come out. Shakily relieved of a tooth and numb to the cheekbone, Harriet left as dusk began to fall.

The nuns' dentist wasn't in one of those gleaming new clinics in the downtown; Dr. Lapointe worked out of one side of his modest split level ranch, at an intersection where his was the fanciest house. Most of the houses in this area were older, shrunken two-storeys with peaked roofs, the kind of houses unskilled children drew. But here there were no butterflies, rainbows or smiling suns.

She was suddenly very aware of her surroundings. She wasn't far from her half-sister Rhonda's neighbourhood, but it wasn't that. The street signs told her she had come to the intersection of Vine and Marguerite Streets. Then she remembered. Marguerite was the street on which she'd been born, memorable because Marguerite had been her mother's name, although she'd never been called anything but Peggy. Evidently this was a memory from Harriet's second sojourn in

Bothonville, when she had been trying hard to forget a lot, not only her sick mother back in Lafrenière but all that went before including Marguerite Street. Now, with the street lamps coming on around her, Harriet felt the tug of curiosity. The place must be a few blocks away: 214A Marguerite Street, not forgotten either.

The semi-detached still wore its brick asphalt siding, never a great look and now with exposed parts showing the tarpaper behind. 214B cringed behind a spruce, while 214A was half-hidden by unkempt shrubbery. Harriet gazed, trying to summon a response but feeling only a discouraging blankness. This was the place where her mother Peggy and…Tom, that was her father's name, Tom Savary, had resided in the early 1930s, and where Ruth, as they had called her, had first lived.

Her family had made their home in 214A for three years, and for the last chunk of this her father had been gone in search of work. Harriet let her mind drift over what she understood had happened. There had been no work in Bothonville, that she remembered from her mother's accounts. People everywhere were hurting. The Savarys had been lucky to have a duplex to themselves. Many neighbourhood families were crowded into one bedroom with other rooms let out to unemployed lodgers, who were even willing to rent the wretched little leans-tos that sprang up to meet demand out back. Then inflation hit, and everyone including the Savarys had to pay more rent than before too. Tom had had a good mill job, then a bad mill job—Harriet uneasily pictured the factories she'd seen, the day she'd taken the bypass—then no job at all. Peggy took in sewing, but most women still sewed back then so business wasn't brisk.

When Tom left town—had he really jumped a train?— other men were leaving with him. Did they all leave families behind? And where had he ended up, this Tom Savary? Harriet's mother had said something about the West, so she must have heard from him. Much later Rhonda and her family went to the same West, a big place evidently where it was easy, perhaps inevitable, to become permanently lost. Peggy and Ruth/Harriet left Bothonville hardly a year after Tom's departure, back to Peggy's hometown of Lafrenière, where they had the connections Harriet now had such trouble recollecting.

As for Tom Savary, he'd been a handsome man, judging from the one photo of him she'd seen. A catch by Marguerite Street standards, not a bad husband, reading between the lines. Perhaps he even had plans to return to Bothonville, or bring his wife and daughter out to live with him, somewhere amid the plains, mountains and sunsets of this mythic West.

He'd most likely met another woman, said her mother. Obvious, when you thought about it. Little Ruth for her part wondered if he'd met other children.

Behind the wheel of the Rambler once more, Harriet felt an inexplicable reluctance to leave the poky street now shrouded in darkness. She fiddled with things on the gleaming dashboard, pulled out the ashtray and was intrigued to see a cigarette butt. Just one more of the world's mysteries.

It hadn't been that meaningful to gaze upon the home of her birth, of her mother long dead and her father long disappeared. Or so she told herself. But loneliness had crept into the picture somewhere along the way. Harriet felt a shiver up her spine, then an ache in her jaw. She had penicillin to buy and codeine to take. She headed for Saint Reginald's which, on these long November nights, abounded with light and noise, and where a big piece of science prep awaited her.

PERPETUA BUTTONHOLED her a few days later.

'Sister Harriet," she said, "you should make yourself available today, as Bishop Aloysius will be in the city for meetings and he would like to speak with you."

Harriet hadn't yet given him the meeting report, so she hunted down her typed notes. At the appointed hour she met the bishop in the sitting room set aside for convent visitors.

"Sister, it is a pleasure to see you." He sounded like he meant it.

He looked as vague as ever, but slightly tense.

"I thought to save you a trip to Saint Angus." He peered at his watch. "I have more meetings and that ceremonial dinner with the Jesuit delegation from Italy, which I couldn't duck. I was able to avoid hosting them at the palace, there's that. Jesuits can't all be accused of being jesuitical. I am suspicious of their position on charism, which they intend to take to the Second Vatican Council. You know how broad the mandate of the Council is." He looked truculent.

"I sense danger. I will admit to you, my child, that I've wondered why the Holy Father didn't bring the Oblates into his inner circle. Perhaps, however, I'm just an envious old man." Harriet knew about Vatican II, as everyone did, but all this inter-order byzantine politicking sailed right over her head. And while she was ready to adhere fervently to the Oblate vision of charism, she would first have to know what charism was.

"The Bothonville Bridge, as you know, isn't just any bridge."

The change of tone was abrupt and now his eyes bored into her. Harriet's mind flew to her bridge adventure, that had taken on the aspect of a dream. She felt the colour flood her cheeks.

"Would you like me to give you a summary of the Bridge Design Committee meeting?" she asked quickly.

Bishop Aloysius listened and received her written report with grateful thanks, as if a wad of paper was an unexpected and delightful surprise.

"I marked some key areas that could be of interest to you, Your Excellency. I didn't contribute to the meeting. I—ah—feel they have a specific role for me, which they haven't yet mentioned. Perhaps you can tell me about this? I remain dutifully open to your guidance." She'd rehearsed this verbal gambit.

Aloysius gave her a veiled smile.

"What an astute sister you are," he said. "Let me make things plain. Although construction is well underway, you will know by now that design is ongoing. The Church, and I personally, have an interest in some aspects of this. The gothic, Sister Harriet, is much more than a symbol. You will know that."

For a change, she did. "Yes, Your Excellency, gothic architecture embodies the energy, it *is* the energy of our Catholic faith. In a manner of speaking."

"More than a manner of speaking!" The bishop now looked slightly possessed. "The bridge is many things to many people, but it must channel and be a symbol of our faith and the goodness that flows from it. For the simple populace, the bridge must daily remind them that their life's journey is not a trip to those American outlet malls—all very well in their way and I have no issue with outlet malls—but a journey towards heaven. I greatly fear, Sister, that this message could be forgotten. The material world is so much with us. We confuse the satisfaction of desire with love. A bridge is a beautiful and useful thing, but what is God's purpose for a bridge, Sister Harriet?"

"Does God have a purpose for bridges, Your Excellency?"

"How can He not, since He has a purpose for everything?"

Harriet's mind ran over the illustrated catechism manuals of her early school years: the simple Qs and As, the plentiful dos and don'ts, not to mention the line drawings of white milk bottles to represent virtuous souls, the patchy and black ones indicating the stages of venial and mortal sin. She didn't remember anything about bridges.

The bishop carried on triumphantly. "Which is why, Sister, we can't have a bridge with a Romanesque superstructure. Evil, we are both agreed, is everywhere. That, we can take as a given. As people cross this bridge, they must look upward and see, between them and the limitless firmament, the pure lines of the gothic pointing unambiguously towards heaven. Not sliding down towards outlet malls."

Harriet unwillingly pictured some sort of highway to hell, luring unwitting souls with attractive markdowns.

"That is my message, Sister, for you to deliver to the committee!"

Harriet's mind returned to the pink mist, to the fitful wind that blew it aside to show possible glimpses—she wasn't sure—of some sort of superstructure far ahead of her. Had she seen the beginnings of rounded arches or pointed ones? Had she been anywhere near the middle of the bridge, to see anything at all? Now, though, her imagination filled with a spectacle of soaring gothic arches, so dramatic, so decisive in the filmy air, so like a stairway to heaven, that she couldn't think how anyone could want anything else.

"I quite see your point, Your Excellency."

"I knew you would, Sister."

"But many beautiful Catholic churches rely on Romanesque architecture, Your Excellency," she murmured. She only said this because she wanted to hear the irrefutable reason why Romanesque would not do.

The bishop sat back complacently. "That, my child, is the doing of the Jesuits."

Perpetua put in an appearance just then, to say the car waited in front. Goodbyes were rushed, so Harriet may have imagined a certain look in the bishop's eyes. Her questions would have to wait for another time.

Throughout the day, these grew. There were, to begin with, perhaps engineering issues, but neither she nor the bishop could really be concerned with these. Superstructures sounded decorative. What parts of a bridge were decorative, if it came to that? Fewer than you might at first think, Harriet suspected, and her mind slid uneasily to the notion that engineers could well share the bishop's views of everything being connected to everything. Well, she would find out soon enough when they tested those stir stick bridges at school.

She knew the bishop had attended some of the planning committee meetings early on. Why hadn't he brought this up when he had the opportunity? Such as when they were all looking at blueprints together. A difficult question to ask a bishop. Bishops, she supposed, had their reasons for distancing themselves from decisions at times. This thought offered no comfort. Best not to think about things too much. How to pitch this to the committee was presumably up to her. As soon as possible from the sound of it. Some tips would have been welcome.

When she was grading papers after supper, other questions came to her. She'd asked Aloysius if he knew what the committee wanted from her. He hadn't answered. Harriet felt now more certain than ever that the committee had a plan. They probably knew all about the bishop's fixation, she couldn't imagine him holding back on so cherished a topic. Perhaps they were waiting for her to bring it up. *Quid pro quo* was at the heart of deals. The wheeling and dealing of the novices' committee had taught her this. Perhaps everyone, even Perpetua, knew what the committee wanted.

Amid all the unsettling practicalities it was tempting to forget the more metaphysical question posed by the bishop's fixation with the gothic. Aloysius's zany enthusiasm was always convincing in the moment, but now she wondered. In grade eight, she'd written a heavily cribbed essay on gothic versus Romanesque architecture, and still remembered the symbolic import attributed to the soaring gothic in a time of faith. It had seemed farfetched, quaintly medieval. How important could a symbol be? Extremely important, if Aloysius was to be trusted.

The most metaphysical question of all, God's purpose for bridges, would have to wait.

## 8: Stairway to Heaven

SISTER HARRIET HAD A few anxious days after her meeting with the bishop. Then the air cleared. She wasn't sure why this happened. One afternoon she passed two girls in the hall singing along to Doris Day's "Que Sera, Sera" on a transistor. The words seemed strangely soothing to her, almost as if they came straight from Perpetua herself, not that she had shown any interest in advising Harriet about her committee role, quite the opposite. After that, Harriet was able to relax.

When she walked into the municipal council chambers a week later, she found herself able to chitchat with the best of them before the mayor called the meeting to order.

Harriet had decided to meet the challenge directly. Feeling bold, she'd telephoned to ask that Church Contribution to Bridge Design be added to the agenda. This, she was interested to see, had become the first discussion item, rebaptized as Ecclesiastical Perspective, Ongoing Clarification: Mayor, Sister Harriet of Bingham, et al. Never had Harriet seen friendlier faces as they dove right in.

After assorted mayoral verbiage, Larry Martel turned the floor over to Harriet. She had memorized a paragraph, and now she delivered it. Wanting to downplay the bishop's loopy fervour, she was still obliged to come right out with gothic and Romanesque, and the symbolically propulsive force of the pointy. She stressed values, as people rarely questioned such a soft and gentle term. She also relied on hackneyed messaging. The day after the labour riots, she's read a *Herald* editorial on sending a signal, not merely to the malcontented elements but to the whole town, if the bridge was to realize the benefits expected. A signal about the importance of pulling together and setting aside differences, stepping up and being counted, backing off, pulling up socks and buckling down. No shillyshallying, as Dean Carter, whom she hoped would recognize the language she was borrowing from him, had said.

She's spent time on her little spiel, although the delivery was quick. Everyone seemed agreeably interested. Someone filled up her water glass. Madame Brunet brought her a cup of tea with a digestive in the saucer.

Martel thanked her, adding compliments about the richness of such ideas and "how you keep us all on our toes, Sister Harriet." He then turned the floor over to Henry Gillespie, one of the bridge consortium principals.

It was all about Salamander Island.

Salamander Island occupied the middle of the vast stream, miles from either shore. It was also a fair distance downstream, as close to Carson Falls as to Bothonville. Few had ever visited it, for it was privately owned. As well as being very large—your islands like Anticosti weren't in the running—it had an extraordinary asset, one of the world's largest deposits of serpentine chrysotile. Complex shoals and peculiar currents surrounded the island. The geomorphology was especially challenging. If the world was to benefit from all that serpentine chrysotile, a bridge link was necessary. The Bridge Design Committee wanted Bothonville's bridge to be that link.

Harriet, Gillespie said, would recall that Mr. Slade of Salamander Holdings had attended the previous meeting. Salamander Holdings owned the island, and Mr. Slade was *very* interested in what Bothonville could do for him.

Expropriation was impossible, due to the uniquely absolute nature of Mr. Slade's possessorship rights, and also certain political factors. Slade to an unprecedented extent held the cards. Bothonville had been in discussions with him for some time. Nods all around the table. Salamander Holdings had been engaged in similar discussions, however, with the city of Carson Falls. They too were in the middle of a big bridge construction project. Why, you could drive down the highway any day and take a gander at the ungainly thing.

The issue at stake was whether Salamander Holdings would partner with Bothonville or Carson Falls. Bothonville was ready to play the game, to go the extra mile, but the recent riots would perhaps give Harriet an idea of the challenges. Their offer needed to succeed, but the committee members agreed the sky could not be the limit.

They needed a better understanding of the nature of the discussions between Carson Falls and Salamander Holdings. They had to find out how advanced the Carson Falls bridge really was, because time, for Slade, would always be money. And they needed to know the specific nature of Carson Falls's offer, so they could top it.

Gillespie waved a bulging cerloxed document before Harriet.

"This is our Plan," he said, "the critical information related to the Bothonville bridge, from the engineering and budget information to constraints and their mitigation. It's updated regularly, so you would see, for example, detailed information regarding the state of our discussions with Salamander Holdings. It would of course be fatal to us all if it fell into the wrong hands." Polite laughter. "What we need, Sister, if we are, ah, to be inspired to consider your points about design to the extent they so richly deserve, is our rival's Plan. And we feel sure you can help us to acquire it."

He stopped abruptly here. No one else said anything either. Mr. Gillespie's mellow voice had lulled Harriet into something like a hypnotic state, in which picture after picture scrolled agreeably through her imagination. She therefore let the silence stretch, the way you did after a particularly good movie, before it occurred to her everyone expected a reply.

"Thank you, Mr. Mayor and Mr. Gillespie," she said. "For your kind words about what I've put forward on behalf of Bishop Aloysius"—was it spiteful to want the old man's name minuted here?—"and for the explanation. I'll have to take this back to him, of course." She'd worked this out ahead too. "Meanwhile, as you've mentioned a role for me, I'd like to hear more."

She could have said something like "about this proposed industrial espionage heist or pilferage scheme." But let others name it.

Martel now took over. In the folksy manner so popular with voters, he said that Carson Falls had a similar confidential steering committee to theirs—although Carson Falls called theirs Carsonites for a Better Tomorrow—and the committee believed that Harriet was well placed to make contact. Carson Falls also had diocesan representation, very naturally. To Sister Harriet's puzzled look he explained, "Not the Saint Angus Diocese but the adjacent Diocese of Sainte Claire. Bishop Labrecque is just as interested in his own spiritual criteria, as is very proper." Solemn nods. "The diocesan representative is aware of the need for—em—an integrated archdiocesan approach."

"Brother Cyprian has been on Carsonites for a Better Tomorrow for some time, and is aware of their discussions with Salamander Holdings. There is no one better suited to provide"—the word "leak" now hovered in the air—"the information than him. Nor will he be surprised when you approach him, you need have no worry." Martel beamed. "As it happens he teaches at the Carson Falls college for boys, Saint Mark's. Like you, Sister Harriet, he's a teacher. Of science, I think." He looked over at the chancellor of Vivamus College, who endorsed the accuracy, or fitness, of this with a gracious nod.

Harriet said that she would take up all this with Aloysius at the earliest opportunity, remarks that well satisfied the committee members.

"But there's something... Perhaps this is a question for Mr. Gillespie. If our bridge will cross Salamander Island, won't the trajectory have to be altered? Won't it have to be much longer, but also wouldn't it have to curve downstream, several miles? I'm just asking out of curiosity, but it would help with my general understanding."

Gillespie's consortium colleague, a Mr. Len Silverman, took up the relay, launching into an enthusiastic description of what it would involve, but leaving her with the general impression that, first, horizontal curves in bridge mega-projects were structurally sound and, second, working a huge curve into a bridge already under construction was all in day's work for the engineering brains. Harriet knew better than to look towards the end of the table where the technical staff were having the usual problems with their microphones.

The discussion moved on to other agenda items. There was plenty of talk about the recent riots, but Flynn had an answer for everything, and soon the minute-taking councillor was writing, "Adjourned in good order at 9:58 pm."

Harriet had kept her face composed in a suitable neutrality during the meeting. And she felt quite calm, even detached. The words of "que sera, sera" continued to circulate in her mind to tranquilizing effect.

Back in her room, she wondered what the Diocese of Sainte Claire would be getting from this, but who better to ask than this Cyprian, who would be divulging so much anyway? As for her committee role, now she knew. She didn't fully understand why it was that she, Sister Harriet of Bingham, had been elected, but was pleasantly distracted in contemplation of her new identity. As many girls would scribble imaginary married names for themselves, Harriet musingly wrote on a scratch pad, things like "Harriet of Bingham, industrial spy," and "Bingham, special agent." There seemed no end to her disguises. Surely this made her more interesting than the average religious sister.

Anyway, there was no refusing this job. Everyone she needed to worry about, which meant Perpetua and Aloysius, judged this work worthy and necessary, and she was the suitable candidate to undertake it. Presumably there was nothing illegal in what she was about to do—the police chief had been right there at the table. Besides, the worse role, mole if not traitor, was surely this Cyprian's. She pictured him as an old grump with a tendency towards bitterness.

Stillness wrapped the convent wing that evening and Harriet stayed up late, enjoying the unusual calm. For once she was caught up in her prep. The school bridge project was fully underway too. Or rather, rude forms had begun to take shape on the girls' tables that represented, as Mr. Montserrat had observed last week, the laws of physics in one way or another. Despite the Committee of Dark Designs, could she now relax just a little?

In the night she dreamed about another bridge—the dream made it clear that this consisted of a second bridge, and not just the regular dream bridge in another form—and she once again walked the deck alone. This time, although she still felt no fear, she was aware of yawning space and the surging currents of the fast-flowing river far below.

## 9: Loretta

WHAT HAPPENS WHEN a student goes missing at a reputable girls' boarding school is generally not known, because the school goes to such great lengths to hide it when it occurs.

Harriet met anxious faces at early prayers, but it wasn't until breakfast, a special one of pancakes because the kitchen had to use up eggs, that she found out. Loretta Mazurek hadn't slept in her bed the night before. A bolster and cushions were all the supervising nun found when she investigated why there was no sign of life that morning. The senior girls slept in rooms of three to four beds, randomly assigned. Neither of Loretta's roommates, heavy sleepers, could clarify when Loretta might have crept away. She was in her bed at lights out and immediately after. They were sure about this because it was Loretta's turn with the dorm's smuggled copy of *Forever Amber,* and they had seen the flashlight glow through her covers.

Everyone worried, and you could only imagine the difficult conversations Perpetua must be having with the Mazureks in their exclusive Bothonville suburb. The vivacious redhead boarded because her family wanted her away from undesirable neighbourhood friends—this from Patricia who was nothing loath to share some context. It was especially unfortunate that Saint Reginald's should have somehow gone and lost her. The bolster and cushions screamed escapade, which capped the worry, but only by a little.

Perpetua herself came to fetch Laurentine Artois out of Harriet's history class. Everyone knew why. Someone had taken the opportunity, while bringing a box of chalk to Harriet, to glance adroitly out the window and the whole room knew that a police car was parked outside. Harriet did her best to keep the girls focused, but it was a lost cause. They swapped sidelong glances, interspersed with yearning gazes in the direction of the windows, beyond which more might be happening.

Sister Pat, later in the day, told Harriet that Laura Rome had also been summoned to Perpetua's office and, yes, the police—that chief himself and another officer—had been in there with them. Her duties having taken her to that part of the building, she could add that the interview had been an interesting one, if you happened to be standing near the door.

"Did you hear?"

"Oh, yes," Patricia said. "Well, bits. They were grilling those girls. Not the cops. The cops were listening. Mother Perpetua was laying it on hard and heavy. Smart, because that way they didn't need parental permission. The cops just happened to be in the room, see? Laura and Laurentine sounded upset, but they kept insisting they had no idea where Mazurek was."

The nuns were outside the kitchen door. Now Patricia gestured towards a row of sheds off to their right. "Let's go over there, we'll be away from the wind." As they huddled out of view of the school buildings, to Harriet's surprise Patricia pulled a pack of cigarettes from her pocket. She lit one in a no-nonsense way and inhaled deeply.

"Everyone's got to go sometime," she said.

Harriet recognized this for what it was, Patricia opening up on an unprecedented scale, and she took advantage. "What did you hear?"

The nicotine was doing Patricia a world of good. "Neither of them knew when Loretta left the school or where she was going. They didn't 'aid and abet' her. ventually Laura breaks down and says Loretta has a secret boyfriend, who she meets off school grounds." Sister Pat waved her cigarette. "But she swears they know nothing about him. Loretta wanted it that way. Laurentine is agreeing with all this. Police Chief Flynn asks how a boarder could carry on a secret romance off the school grounds. You could picture everyone looking at him pityingly, and Reverend Mother gave that small cough of hers."

"Hmm." Harriet frowned. "Something about Loretta seemed to be off lately." She couldn't put into Pat-friendly words the sense she'd had of Loretta burning more and more intensely like a Bunsen burner on high. "Mr. Montserrat told me the three of them are a secret club. Do you think they were lying to cover for her?"

"Our Mr. Montserrat," Patricia said drily. She gave Harriet a considering stare, which made her wish she hadn't brought him up. "They could be lying. All kinds of things go on between seniors and boys. Some are Saint Mark's boys with cars, some are even young men from the mills. Or the shanty towns, that's considered extra wild. You've heard about those wild dares, like scaling the bridge after dark. Myself, I'm doubtful. But you never know—what do you think, Sister?"

"Far-fetched."

But that first evening, hadn't Harriet seen movement high up on the deck of the bridge? Patricia was giving her a hard look, but she couldn't resist asking, "Have students been caught in the act up there?"

"In the act? Not that I'm aware of, but I don't know everything."

Harriet watched with admiration as Sister Pat carefully stowed her butt in a metal box that disappeared into her robes.

MONTSERRAT COULD ADD little, from their window spot as they watched the girls work on their bridges later in the week. Loretta was still missing, and the police had returned to the school. They'd had to rejig the work teams—"temporarily," Montserrat said it was important to stress. Loretta would be found. She would come back. Of course she would come back, Harriet thought, with something like fear.

The mood in the multipurpose room was tense, but not very

different from other days. Laura and Laurentine were there, stoically bossing the young girls around. They looked stressed and no wonder, after more than one session in Perpetua's office from what Harriet had heard. There was a disturbing translucence about Laurentine, and Laura had mauve shadows under her eyes. But there was something steely in the way they carried themselves. The idea of nighttime escapades by students on the bridge had continued to occupy Harriet's mind. She could somehow imagine the three Ls doing something like that, with or without boys, while maintaining their grades in the 90s.

Montserrat himself seemed tense. Today he wore a charcoal corduroy jacket with a black turtleneck, which reminded Harriet of bonfire night. The sombre colours brought out all the shadowy charm of his face. Not that all that attractiveness wasn't irritating on some level too. Men really did cause a lot of problems in the world, she mused. But the ugly ones too, and she continued to take in the elegant planes of his face.

"Did you hear about the secret boyfriend?" she asked, to re-establish herself a little.

Mr. Montserrat didn't look surprised. "Sister, at least half the senior girls have secret boyfriends. It's mostly quite innocent. Why, last year that novice who was helping in the sports program, Sister Eleanor, had a special friend. A gymnastics teacher from the public high school." He suppressed a laugh. "It blew over. You look shocked, Sister." He seemed to enjoy Harriet's blushes.

Since she had fainted into his arms, she felt at a continued disadvantage with him, with a corresponding need to bolster her persona.

"I may be a religious sister but I'm very much of this world, Mr. Montserrat," she said, adjusting her face to a medieval saintliness, and her eyes to a distant galaxy.

Marin Montserrat, who had accidentally seen Harriet out on the frozen pond the night before—there'd been a period of hard frost, although no snow yet—had a sudden moment of Deja vu.

He hadn't been sure if it was the whimsical blue figure skates she must have cadged from a student, or the meticulous way she executed figures in the moonlight, oblivious to everything else. As he watched her move, to the eerie rasp of the blades, her self-containment had to him seemed total—and she herself otherworldly. A romantic way to describe a flesh and blood woman, even with the expected sisterly reserve: but the effect, under the cold moon, of her unattainability persisted. He experienced this sensation again in the dusty multi-purpose room.

Covertly scanning his handsome face, Harriet for her part was having momentary trouble with the picture of Montserrat as a secret boyfriend. A thought to skate over and banish. Not that she didn't suspect him of leading a double life hardly less involved and perhaps even quirkier than her own. Nevertheless, when you stopped being reduced to jelly by it, it was a confusing face. Mingled with its sensuous lines was a deeply antithetical look. A familiar look: and then the bishop's face was before her. Not his crackers look, the other one, when you sensed you were in the presence of something both haunted and endlessly tender. Troubling, unnerving in its way, but making you feel like a defenseless child, who had strayed by happy accident into a garden filled with every scent of spring and hoped against hope you would never have to leave.

## 10: Masters in This Hall

LORETTA MAZUREK'S disappearance dragged on. Rumours persisted, but came to nothing. Harriet had heard that the Mazurek family was on the attack, and she could imagine how difficult this must be for Perpetua, especially now that the *Herald* had gotten hold of the story. Evidently, it was far more devastating for the Mazureks. Harriet was all too familiar with losing family members. Days turned into a week, then two. Life at Saint Reginald's went on. There was a sinister aspect to this, a hint of cosmic callousness at odds with a loving God.

Everyone at the next meeting of the Bridge Design Committee was extra cordial to her, either out of respect for Saint Reginald's difficulties, or because the bishop had sealed the deal. The gothic design features, Mr. Gillespie confirmed, were being integrated even as they spoke. It would be up to Harriet how she approached Brother Cyprian, but she might like to know he worked in the parish soup kitchen and had been given a head's up she'd be there on a Saturday afternoon at two pm, when he was usually just finishing up.

On a brutally cold afternoon that made her think it was already winter, just without snow, Harriet set out to Carson Falls in the Rambler. Her drive took her along the river, through a world of grays and browns scored everywhere by the tracery of naked branches. The river came and went in her view, a sheety vastness visible through the trees.

Harriet was in a good mood. She had always loved the bleak natural harmonies of this time of year. The small riverside villages had a tightly wrapped up look and made her think of small hibernating animals. The Rambler handled beautifully at higher speeds. She wasn't sure what to expect from this Brother Cyprian, but she'd take things as they came.

Carson Falls, when she arrived, seemed both similar to and different from Bothonville. It had an equivalent bustling downtown, newer, if she was to judge the architecture, busy tree-lined streets, a painterly haze of factories on the edge of town, no canal, but an even better view of the river because the city was built on an escarpment.

She had no trouble seeing the Carson Falls bridge, visible from most vantage points. Regardless of the disparagements of the Bothonville committee, construction seemed to be going well and it stretched out into the river. The river seemed just as wide here as it was at Bothonville, and she couldn't see to the other side. She tried to judge whether this bridge was curving or about to curve back in the direction of invisible Salamander Island. She didn't think so, but perhaps you needed an engineer's eye.

Her job was to get the plans from the contact, and get out. She pictured a cerloxed document as fat as Bothonville's with "The Plan" neatly handwritten on a cover label. Just like their own, maybe a different colour. Manila buff, instead of red rope rust.

Saint Felix's Church was an aged brown brick building in an established neighbourhood near the downtown. The soup kitchen was in the basement and forlorn types milled about. She'd delayed her arrival to half past one, to let the queue subside. "All welcome," said a sign by the side entrance, and Harriet grabbed a tray, to eat while casing the joint, as she liked to think of it.

You entered a soup kitchen with lowered expectations, evidently, and yet the smells rising up the stairs were not unappetizing. Inside were rows of tables filled mostly with men although she was glad to see small clusters of religious, male and female, among the diners. It was cafeteria-style, figures moving around behind an open counter display. There were bouquets of paper flowers on each table and it was warm.

She took a bowl of mystery stew and a bun to a table from where she had an unimpeded view of the counter. She counted one aged nun and three male religious, one of these middle-aged and middle management looking, the Saint Felix pastor at a guess, a young one with sandy hair and the bald old duffer she had been expecting. And yet he greeted his regulars with a smile and a joke. The men were all working hard dishing out food. The elderly nun seemed in charge.

Harriet planned to approach the bald one at a propitious moment. She was therefore surprised when a low voice behind her said, "Sister Harriet?" and she turned to see the young sandy-haired cleric right there at her elbow.

"I'm Cyprian," he said, filling her water glass from a jug. "I've got more to do here but we could meet by the presbytery door around the other side? Father Brennan said we can use his sitting room."

He gave her a pale smile, and went off to fill other glasses.

Dutifully sipping her tap water, Harriet owned to a certain surprise. He proved a willowy young fellow, the real Cyprian, so much for her hunches. Neither friendly nor unfriendly. And certainly with the look of a high school science teacher. He also reminded her of someone, and a mental picture formed. Bertrand had been a brainiac fellow student at university. Similar schedules had brought them together. Bert had the same sandy colour scheme and the same smooth-featured face.

He had been a physics major, and it was his pastime before class to broach with the young novice uninvited debates on religious faith versus science. While obsessively sharpening his pencil, he'd bring up, the way others chatted about homework, Copernicus or Bruno or Einstein and their various cheap shots against religion. She especially remembered his busy flat eyes.

Father Brennan's sitting room was one of those drab spaces reserved for the importuning faithful. Harriet felt awkward but Cyprian started a breezy line of chat about highs and lows of teaching and the varieties of student—the good, the bad and the ridiculous, as he put it. He also inquired about job opportunities at Saint Reginald's. This puzzled Harriet, for she knew the Saint Mark's brothers were Marists whereas they were the unrelated Sisters of Saint Thomas Aquinas, and you didn't just apply for jobs outside your order. Still, it was a relief to see this unBert-like side to the brother and she cautiously relaxed.

"I'll take you on a tour of Carson Falls afterwards, and we can swing by Saint Mark's if you haven't yet seen it," Cyprian said. "Is there anything in particular you want to see?"

"The Falls? There must be some." Harriet felt guilty at this touristic impulse, but she reasoned that diplomacy was a necessary part of her role, not to be confused with fraternizing. Cyprian's laugh told her a change of subject was overdue.

"I'm not sure what you've been told about—about the agreement between our two dioceses," Harriet began.

"Everything," he interrupted.

This could save some time. "How specific do I need to be about what we want?"

"Try me," Cyprian said, settling back in his armchair.

"Anything to do with Salamander Holdings. Records of meetings between members of Carsonites for a Better Tomorrow and that Mr. Slade, any agreements. Alterations in blueprints as a result of those meetings, up to date information on the construction timeline..." She paused. "Money. Offers. Money changing hands. But it's the plans they want, Brother, where the bridge is going and by when."

Cyprian nodded matter of factly and Harriet suddenly thought, what a turncoat. But if she had no business criticizing Aloysius, then surely she had no business criticizing Bishop Labrecque, nor this brother who was, after all, under orders too.

Cyprian was now all business, scribbling in a notebook. "This will take time, but it's all there. I've seen some documentation. I presume you want copies of cheques, which I don't usually handle." He underlined a word or two.

"Brother Cyprian," she asked, unable to repress her curiosity, "what do you know personally about meetings between your committee and Salamander? Is Carson Falls really thinking of building its bridge to Salamander Island or is Bothonville wrong?"

"We've had plenty of confidential chats with Slade, well, not me but an inner circle of the committee. It's been considered, I'm ninety-eight percent sure. Slade has come to a few meetings, everybody kowtows to him." Cyprian pursed his lips. "There's a spirit of competition on the committee. We enjoy a little light slanging about Bothonville and the Bothonville Bridge. Gossip about its progress. If there's more under the table, no one's told me."

"What do they say about Bothonville? This slanging..." She was slightly miffed.

A conspiratorial smile. "Bothonville is too big for its britches. We're not the only ones who think that. Apparently, Sister, the history of Bothonville's city fathers dreaming too big goes way back. To the notorious Sieur de Bothon, my history colleague told me. Did you know he burnt down the whole city—I mean, it was a handful of squalid shacks—because he wanted a blank slate? For urban renewal. He was never a patient man. Carson Falls, on the other hand, has always patted itself on the back for knowing its limitations. They've used that as an excuse for everything for two hundred years. Our bicentenary year slogan was *Secundo ibi nobilitate*," he added airily.

"I think you're making up part of that, Brother." She tried to sound severe.

"I might be, but what part. Well, I can give you nothing today, but in a week or two. Now would you like to see the city?"

To Harriet's slight dismay, he slid into the Rambler passenger seat, saying, "I walked from Saint Mark's so we'll need your ride."

They were far too visible driving around town together, two youthful religious side by side. She hoped they would escape notice from the wrong quarters. This affected her pleasure in seeing Carson Falls. And it turned out the waterfall was in a secluded woody area, something Cyprian didn't tell her until they were well on their way, so that its magnificence was lost to her as she fretted. She felt relief when she dropped him at Saint Mark's, refusing to "meet us brothers."

But as they said goodbyes, she had to know. "I have another question to ask you, Brother, but if you can't reply I'll understand. My bishop has his own reasons"—she wasn't going to get into the stairway to heaven here, not that Cyprian seemed interested anyway—"but can you tell me why Sainte Claire agreed to share confidential information with us? I mean, what do they get out of it?"

"It is kind of Benedict Arnold of us, isn't it? I'm tempted to say, guess."

Harriet was shocked. And also intrigued. A spy should understand basic motivations, or she wasn't much of a spy. "Well..."

"I have all the time in the world, Sister."

Harriet knew she always overthought things, so she spoke at random. "Love or money. It's got to be money."

"You are correct, Sister." Cyprian affected awe. "The Bothonville committee cut a very substantial cheque to the diocese of Sainte Claire. That was one cheque I cast my beady eyes over. *Very* substantial." He shook out his fingers to indicate hypothetical heat. It reminded Harriet of Elvis Presley doing the same. "Really, Sister, I'm impressed. You are one for surprises."

The compliment didn't mean much to Harriet. Cyprian's unfeeling answer had put her off. Still she would not be diverted. "What is the money supposed to be for?"

Cyprian opened the school gate. "Oh, good works, Sister, good works." And now, in looking into his unusual eyes, dark blue with golden flecks, Harriet felt she was accidentally inspecting the chill reaches of outer space.

WORK CONTINUED on the Bothonville bridge. If Carson Falls thought Bothonville was getting above itself, no one in Bothonville seemed to think so. The *Herald* featured a series of articles boosting the bridge, and paid a visit to Saint Reginald's for a fluffy piece for the Women's Section on the bridge competition. Madame Brunet from the Catholic ladies club appeared and her niece Laurentine was among those photographed with the half-built bridges in the multi-purpose room. Also Florene, Ella, Perpetua, Harriet and Mr. Montserrat. Florene and Ella were thrilled at being in the paper, in contrast to Laurentine who, as well as looking a million miles away, didn't seem well.

Harriet saw her in class but here, where all must smile for the camera, it jumped out that something was wrong. The continued disappearance of her friend Loretta must be weighing on her. The girl was naturally pale at the best of times, but today she looked almost ghostly.

The overhead pendant lights were all on. These, plus the camera flashes, dazzled Harriet's eyes, so that she had the impression sometimes of looking right through Laurentine to the window frames and shelves. And it didn't help that, when the *Herald* published the pictures, Laurentine wasn't in any of the shots. Florene displayed her toothy smile, Ella looked sardonic. And the adults were all there too, Madame Brunet appearing to be under attack from the minks comprising her stole, Perpetua not fully concealing impatience, Mr. Montserrat exuding a sort of movie star aura, and Harriet herself, repressing, so she thought, a look of guilt. But where Harriet thought the Artois girl had stood, there was only blankness. People would be cropped out of pictures if they blinked or moved suddenly. Harriet supposed this must have happened.


SOMETHING CALLED THE mid-semester trough arrived, and you could really see it at staff meetings. Everyone was jaded and everyone did their best to keep up appearances. That the Mazurek girl had apparently vanished without a trace didn't help, but, since Perpetua had banned gossip and rumour-mongering, Harriet was left to her own uneasy thoughts.

Twice she saw a police car at the school, and caught a glimpse of Flynn and a plainclothes policeman exiting the principal's office. If there was ever a reason to pray, it was surely now for the missing girl, and Harriet prayed with a troubled ardour. It was hard to think that your prayers might be going nowhere, maybe just floating into outer space to rub shoulders with the radio signals of aliens. But futility wasn't the worst of it. For Harriet, despite having no control over her religious doubts, experienced these as a religious lapse, and therefore feared her prayers were somehow tainted, like Cain's offering, and that sin lurked at her tent flap.

She wanted to get behind the wheel of the Rambler and drive, increasing her students' homework twofold to discipline herself. This didn't help with the loneliness that hadn't left her since the night on Marguerite Street, through an oppressively cold November. The sisters were her community, and in that regard she felt close to all of them, but they weren't her friends. Sisters were discouraged from having personal friendships in the secular sense. You were fellow brides of Christ, not pals in a divine harem, although of course you couldn't help clicking sometimes, the way she had clicked with Patricia.

As for the lay teachers, Miss Edison had proved willing to help her junior colleague with any curriculum bumps, and had an entertaining wit besides. Mr. Hughes was invariably warm and courteous, perhaps a little too warm, for there was nothing more unrewarding than being the target of an unrequited shine.

It had been hard, after the bonfire, the guitar, the fainting into his arms, to think of Montserrat without emotion. They'd be in the multi-purpose room together, and she would find herself too aware of his proximity. She feared occasionally she had turned a key in a lock that night, letting them both into a zone of femininity which sisters were permitted to occupy with a great naturalness, as long as there were no men in there with them. Even a zone of shared humanity was a risk. Evidently not with a Mr. Hughes, whose budget haircuts and drip dry shirts showed a sadly misplaced inclination, for a young unmarried man, to save money, but Marin Montserrat was different. If only, she thought from time to time, he wasn't likeable.

It undermined efforts to mock him.

Cyprian called fairly soon to tell her the package was ready, coded words that thrilled Harriet in spite of herself. She also spoke via telephone with Aloysius to tell him that all was proceeding according to plan. She was disappointed that she wouldn't be squeezing in another visit to Saint Angus. She had decided after their last meeting that the bishop was a visionary and therefore the usual rules and categories, sanity for example, didn't apply. That there was kindness and humility mixed with his various eccentricities, she had come to see.

Perpetua approached her after breakfast that Friday to tell her that, if she had to get to Carson Falls, she'd better take the car today, because the convent had need of it all weekend. It was a professional development day, but Perpetua was happy to excuse Harriet, as was Harriet to be excused. She still didn't manage to get away until after lunch, which meant that she might be driving home in darkness.

She'd agreed to meet Brother Cyprian at Saint Mark's today. It seemed preferable to a perambulation about town or a pick-up style coffee date. Cyprian waited for her at the side entrance where the friary joined the school, with the same unreliable smile on his face. This time, however, Harriet, in need of company, found it pleasing. He was an original, she'd decided.

"Sister Harriet!" he said, as if they were old friends. "Come in, we lit a fire." He dropped his voice although there was no one around. "I've got the binder for you in my room. But come and warm up first and meet some people. We're making tea."

He led her through corridors that were museum-like in their age, however with the signs everywhere of men and boys in residence. Of the men and boys, there were none.

"We're like the Mary Celeste today," Cyprian said as he led her into what was clearly the brothers' common room, where a fire burned in the fireplace and half a dozen smiling men in clerical garb rose to greet her. "That's because all the boys left this morning, on a weekend religious retreat. Several of the brothers have gone with them, the old and reliable ones being best, it was decided, after that regrettable incident a couple of years ago when the young brothers drank more than the boys they were supposed to supervise. Which is why us low-budget junior brothers are left guarding the fort." He indicated his brethren.

"Brother James is making the tea, is he? Sister, sit down, we have reserved the best armchair for you. Isn't the fire nice? It's the first one we've lit this season. So here you are—welcome to our humble abode." Enthusiastic agreement, as the other brothers dragged chairs into a semi-circle, commenting on the unseasonal cold and arguing about whether the fire needed another log.

She was well and truly trapped, Harriet realized, not without admiration for the way it had been contrived. The tea took a long while in coming, and a Brother Andrew produced a bottle of sherry in the meantime. Harriet could, of course, have refused the miniature glass—but why, after all? They were a lively bunch. The conversation was equally lively, as the *mores* of Catholic boarding schools were endlessly fascinating to compare and contrast, and everyone found much to say also about the future of education, Vatican II, whose city was better, and plans for Christmas. They were on their best behaviour with Harriet, as the sherry circulated. The tea when it finally emerged was worth the wait, accompanied by two sorts of cake. Harriet could not deny she was having a good time.

Then Cyprian whipped out an acoustical guitar from somewhere—dear God, not another guitar—and he led the way in an assortment of modern folk and traditional songs. Although he was no Mr. Montserrat, he had a good singing voice.

So did the other brothers. When they launched into "Masters in This Hall," which they would be singing for the holiday concert and to which Harriet should really come, she suddenly felt wafted away from her ordinary life, whether by the ancient song or by the richly joined young voices on that early winter afternoon.

She could see the light disappearing through the windows overlooking the garden, and she knew she had to leave. The brothers told her to come back soon and she said she would try to, although she would probably try not to. Cyprian then took her to another wing and effected the handover of the materials.

"All there as you asked, Sister, in an easy to carry and fashionable Marimekko tote, courtesy of my forgetful visiting aunt." He now sounded slightly bored. "And after looking over everything I'm still not sure that Carson Falls is even in this race, or dog fight."

"Was it difficult to lay your hands on this?" Harriet hefted the heavy binder.

"Oh no. I'm secretary of Carsonites for a Better Tomorrow, so I had extra copies of most things. But you can make what you want of it, he's fishing, we're fishing, but remember what I told you about Carson Falls being a slacker city." He practically winked.

"Well thanks, also sincere thanks on behalf of the diocese and the bishop." Harriet knew she was making the whole thing sound nobler than it was. "Bishop Aloysius, he, well, he has spiritual aspirations connected to our bridge."

Now Cyprian looked positively mocking. "As long as he doesn't have spiritual aspirations connected to serpentine chrysotile."

Harriet, who'd been meaning to look up serpentine chrysotile but hadn't gotten around to it, said nothing.

"The brothers were glad to meet you," he said abruptly. "One or two of them might have seemed even almost sad to you? Not everyone who joins a religious order at eighteen feels as sure of their vocation ten years later. It gets to be a drag, no women around, all us men. Plus, I mean, teaching at a Catholic school. Plus Carson Falls. I'm from Montreal, one of those old Catholic Westmount families, more Catholic than the pope," he added morosely.

"Was I a canary in a coal mine, to test their vocational soundness?"

He laughed. "You are one." His mood abruptly altered, and his dark blue eyes, their star-like flecks suddenly more pronounced, were now fixed on her. "I sometimes go to Bothonville. Next time I go could we maybe meet—for a coffee?" Seeing her speechless, he added, "Oh, all above board, I'd just like to talk to you, about things. Nobody around here, in this crumbling bastion of faith, wants to chit chat with me about post-relativity physics, can you imagine how difficult that is?"

"I'm not sure, Brother. We'll have to see."

They were in the doorway, and Harriet was buttoning her coat. "I'll take that as a big maybe." He seized her hand and squeezed it without warning. "Don't mind me. Until we meet again, Sister."

As Harriet drove back to Bothonville, one anxious eye on the lengthening shadows, she thought about Cyprian's crumbling bastion of faith remark. His tone had been semi-joking, but even that was a tip off. Once again, in his odd remote eyes—beautiful eyes, she could not deny—she'd imagined she could see the emptiness of space. She suspected that he was even more advanced than she in his doubts. For all she knew he was a flaming atheist. Shoehorned by his family into the religious life, finding nothing there anymore. If they met up in Bothonville, Harriet felt pretty sure, it would be to have Bert conversations, with Cyprian doing all the talking. He hadn't made a pass at her today, not really, but that could change.

Whether his current circumstances truly bothered him she couldn't say. He'd looked genuinely carefree during the singalong, like a modern young brother who'd found his calling in hard work and slightly childish pastimes. Had he been going through the motions? She realized she should pay more attention to details. Perhaps the hair just covering the tops of his ears offered a clue. And what about the guitar?

This made her think of Mr. Montserrat, and she wondered, with feelings that took her attention off the road, about his social life. It was oblivious of her never to have thought about this before, what a single man with his looks did, when he was far away from Saint Reginald's and Perpetua, say on a Friday night like this one, to supply himself with romantic distraction.

## 11: River Flats

AT DUSK HARRIET arrived on the outskirts of Bothonville. Here the route became tricky: one turn would take her on a ring road back to Saint Reginald's, another across the highway and into some fields. In the dying light, Harriet took this one by mistake. Only when she was crossing a desolate little overpass did she realize this.

I'm on the wrong road, she thought, and kept driving as people did. She peered left and right. Nothing looked promising. She saw fallow fields. She had a recollection of someone telling her about such neglected and disorderly pockets, where half-acre hillbilly farms rubbed shoulders with disreputable neighbourhoods, hidden where you wouldn't expect them. They were hard to get into, and harder to get out of. At the moment she couldn't see any turnoffs. She might have to drive back the way she came.

She gave the pedal a little gas, then more. Something didn't feel right. Why was the Rambler slowing down? The fuel gauge registered plenty of gas. She pressed down hard and the engine surged, changed its mind and died. She had just enough momentum to bring the car to the verge.

Her hands were jumpy as she tried repeatedly to restart it. Dismay hovered. She looked around. Empty fields rose everywhere to the treeline, no sign of human habitation, no traffic. She would stay calm. The thought surfaced anyway: this couldn't be happening to her.

There was no point in sitting here. She hid the binder under the floor mat in the trunk, wishing it didn't bulge, and locked doors.

Should she go back the way she'd come, a long way on that rutted road, or take her chances and go forward? The overpass was a good mile away, and from there she would still have a hike.

To the right in the other direction was a dim glow and scattered lights beyond the trees. She should probably go forward. But the road before her melted unnervingly into the dark. As she peered uncertainly, she thought she sensed motion, and faint sound, as if something or someone was coming in her direction. Maybe people walking in a group? She squinted. She definitely saw movement—a car advancing towards her? A car without lights. Something didn't feel right. The disturbance seemed to churn and swell.

In seconds she'd retrieved the binder from the trunk, cleared the wire fence, and was leaping from frozen ridge to ridge, the tote bag hitting her leg as she ran. Half way up the slope to the treeline, she turned to look over her shoulder. Was she imagining movement around the abandoned car? Sounds—waves of something sinister similar to sounds—made their way to her. Thank goodness, she'd be completely invisible by now. Except for those touches of luminous white on her habit. She felt calamitously exposed. She ran into the trees, pushing her way with rasping breath through undergrowth to higher ground. Finally, the view opened.

Beneath her lay the city at last. Block after block of bungalows and tumbledown apartments crouched in rows under dingy street lamps. Not much of a neighbourhood, and shuttered on this cold night. But she could hear sounds ahead. The kind ordinary people in groups make. Several streets away and half-hidden by the crowding houses, an illuminated Shell sign flickered. Let it be open, she prayed. She looked at her watch, only to find that she'd lost it, probably back among the trees. She went down among the puny houses.

The Shell station was closed. There were several open establishments on this busy street, mainly bars, and milling people everywhere, mainly drinkers. So this was where everyone was. A rough crowd, their faces like masks: there was an edge to the mood. People were already beginning to stare, for she drew attention in her nun's habit. She'd better move.

She settled her veil and set off at a brisk place. Too fast. She slowed down. Not too much though—she had to convey she knew where she was going. It seemed to work. She was occasionally cat-called but she was allowed to proceed, just another little nun lost in the drunken masquerade. She kept looking for a phone booth, she didn't want to go into any of the places she passed. And then she was in a kind of no man's land, and it was too late. Eventually the street came to an end at a row of cement barriers. A footpath headed off to her right through tangled brush. A painted arrow pointed the way.

Feeling she was in a worsening dream, Harriet took the path, which plunged downward into a ravine. In the darkness she couldn't see her feet. If she fell, it would be because the dream ordained it. She felt the gripping cold through her coat. If she died of hypothermia, so be it, the dream would decide. She'd begun to resent the heavy tote filled with Carson Falls secrets. Why had the bishop made her do this? If only she had a match, she could use the paper for tinder to keep herself warm. But only until the fire died out. The dream would determine all.

Harriet's mind being distracted, she wasn't looking ahead. The dense undergrowth suddenly cleared and she stepped out into the open. Now she had absolutely no doubt where she was. She stood on the edge of sloping waste ground leading to a massive construction zone, all of which looked very familiar by now. Directly in front of her, the Bothonville bridge, a glare of construction lights, soared into the night sky.

She was no longer lost: there was that. But how far she had come boggled the mind. And the sudden sight of the bridge was a shock. She had avoided it since she'd perambulated its deck in an altered state of consciousness. She hadn't wanted to see it again. And now, here she was. She almost felt she'd been drawn to this place by the bridge itself. But where did such thoughts end? Had the bridge arranged for the fuel pump, unless it was the alternator, to fail, summoned a hillybilly black hole to trigger flight across the fields, painted that sign saying "this way" to lure her into the ravine? One thing consoled her: there would be people here and a telephone to use, to call Saint Reginald's, a cab, a tow truck.

As before, she walked unmolested through the open gates and past the unguarded gate house. Further in, there were plenty of men around. Yet when she tried to approach someone, he had the habit of disappearing behind an outbuilding or driving off faster than you would suppose possible in a forklift. She kept going. Eventually, she left the tall stacks and heavy equipment behind, coming to an area of crowded small buildings.

There were quite a few of these minute sagging structures, resembling huts or cabins, with crooked footpaths running between. Here and there a dim glow escaped through cracks. Beside low doors, jerry-rigged lamps fizzled and flickered. The light did little to push away the shadows, and woodsmoke moved sinuously through the lanes. She blinked when she saw it: someone had tied a bunch of holly in a red bow and nailed it to a door. Where was she? Did people live here? It seemed so. She kept walking, discovering lane after twisting lane, realizing this shanty town was bigger than it looked.

Despite the improvised electrical supply, phone lines might be too much to hope for. Although she thought she saw fleet-footed shadows disappearing between houses, and the lights and woodsmoke must mean something, she met nobody. She came eventually to an open area like a miniature town square, and was about to knock at a door, when a low voice whickered in her ear: "Welcome to River Flats, Sister."

Four boys surrounded her. But were they boys? They had the reed-like quality of underfed boys, but their smiling faces on these withered stems were like the faces of men. One held a bottle, another a length of pipe. Harriet had never been more afraid in her life.

They started a line of talk, ostensibly to her, but really to each other, about what the sister could be doing here, whether she had come to pay them a visit, what she had in her bag, what she was hiding, what was under her veil, what was under everything, would she be fine to kiss, could Reg pick her up?

Reg, the biggest one, pinned her arms in a bear hug that swung her high off her feet, to whoops of laughter. The others came nearer, a tight circle enclosed her. One of them tried to grab her bag, someone else held the hem of her habit, a third grabbed her crucifix.

Harriet began to struggle, and they laughed louder, pushing up against her. But she wouldn't go down, she decided, without a fight. She swung her foot, landing a solid shoe on someone's leg bone. A yell, more whoops, a growl. Someone grabbed her ankles, but she worked a foot free and her second kick produced a scream.

The mood plunged into ugly. Reg said, "See what's under her veil, Mal!" Mal, the one with the bottle, pulled her veil off, tearing it almost in two. As loud as she could, Harriet yelled "Help!"

Almost immediately she heard a shrill echoing "Help!" and a child ran out from between the cabins. "Help, help," the girl cried.

The next minute, two of her attackers had crumpled to the ground in quick succession. A third flew backwards from a fist to the jaw. There was the sound of breaking glass as the bottle smashed on the ground. Reg dropped her unceremoniously and stepped forward, a threat. A punch levelled him. The first two had gotten up by now, the girl yelling, "Watch the other two!"

But the man the girl was with had picked up the pipe and the broken bottle and stood there, swinging each in a hand as he looked them over calmly. Whatever their plans, in a moment they changed their minds and retreated, Reg and Mal half-dragged by the others.

Her body electric with adrenalin, Harriet stood where she had been dropped by Reg. One hand gripped the tote, the other, her veil. She stared at the two in front of her, the girl and the man.

"Oh—Sister Harriet," said a familiar voice.

Harriet felt the shock of recognition. It was Florene Pellerin. And beside her lounged Roger, looking like a relaxed killer machine with his improvised weapons, although he had always looked like a killer machine, now that she thought about it.

"Florene. And Roger."

Florene stared. Harriet needed to say something. "Four against one isn't fair."

"You got in one or two good ones," Roger conceded. The man knew his way around compliments. Florene still looked horrified.

"I'm fine, Florene, don't worry." Harriet made the mistake of waving her torn veil for emphasis. Florene stared mesmerized at it, and from the veil her eyes travelled to Harriet's head, to take in the hair she now saw for the first time.

A snowflake pirouetted over the scene.

"You have nice hair, Sister." And Harriet, who had light brown hair which she cut herself, but which didn't look uneven because of an attractive wave, found something to smile about at last.

Roger cut in. "Let's get out of here." To Harriet he said, "Your ear is bleeding, did you know?"

Harriet put up her hand and felt wetness. It must have happened when they yanked her veil, attached with metal clips.

"We've got a place down this lane," Florene said. "We can give you a bandage, Sister, we can"—her eyes flickered to the veil—"fix that." She passed Harriet's bag to Roger, taking Harriet's hand in hers. "It's this way."

The three entered the crooked lane together, as snow began to fall.

THE REST OF THE evening was out of focus for Sister Harriet. They walked through more lanes and came to a cabin like the others. Roger ushered her inside. It was small and dark, but Florene stirred up the fire and Harriet could see a table, chairs, camp beds, and a bicycle propped by the door. A twenty watt bulb sizzled in a corner, where a doorway led off somewhere.

Florene tended to her ear—"just a scratch"—and took away the veil. Roger gave her tea and they talked. She began to calm down.

He told her there had been an "incident" on the bridge earlier, a walk off, some rioting among factions. Things were still tense. She remembered the edge to the mood back among the bars. She told him about her misadventures, the car breaking down, her own incident on the overpass road, the walk through that neighbourhood, coming to the shanty town.

"I was afraid all evening, but back there I was angry more than scared." She shook her head. "I just kept finding myself in rough areas." She blushed. Hard though it was too believe, it seemed the Pellerins lived here.

Roger must have read her mind. "We don't live here all the time. We have another place." He added, "In the woods."

Florene reappeared with a woefully stitched together veil. "I don't think Sister Rachel would approve," she apologized. She'd made big stitches with emerald green yarn and the veil looked like something Frankenstein's bride might have worn after a religious awakening.

"It's safer in the woods," Florene added. "Although those boys will leave us alone, now." She surveyed Roger with pride.

"Who were they?" They had seemed to Harriet like something from an alternate reality. As did this whole shanty town. It was as if modern go-ahead Bothonville, with its bustling streets and civic aspirations, had been a mirage, or else Harriet herself had been sucked through a portal.

"Oh, they live here, they work on the bridge," Roger said. "They weren't always like that," he added broodingly.

Florene added brightly that Roger also "sometimes" worked on the bridge too.

Nothing made sense.

"Would there be a telephone?" Harriet knew the answer was no, but she had to ask. It was getting late, exactly how late she had no idea since there were no clocks in the cabin. And even though the fire was delightful, she couldn't stay here all night like a rescued character in a fairy tale. She was Harriet of Bingham, teacher of advanced academic subjects at Saint Reginald's. Although she wasn't really Harriet, was she, but come to that she didn't feel she was Henrietta of Baumgarten either and, as for that child Ruth, well she was the least real of all, belonging as she did to the irrecoverable past. She started to feel sleepy.

Roger stood up. "I'll see if I can start your car. I'll take the bicycle."

Florene cracked the door. "The snow is covering the ground, Roger."

But he pocketed Harriet's keys, slung a bag over his shoulder and just said, "I'll be back."

An hour passed, then another. Florene asked Harriet if this would be a good time to talk about her history project, and Harriet said probably not. It was warm in the cabin, and Harriet drowsed. When Roger appeared suddenly in the doorway, she opened her eyes with a start.

"Just the ignition switch. I parked it by the canal. I'll go there with you."

Florene insisted she would come too and the three set off through gently falling snow, which was already up to the tops of Harriet's shoes. They met no one, and soon they were saying goodbyes as Harriet revved the engine with immense relief.

"Come back and see us another time," Florene said. Harriet's eyes swivelled briefly to Roger, and she murmured something vague.

As she drove through the snow-hushed city, she rehearsed what she would say back at Saint Reginald's. They must all be badly worried by now. And how would Perpetua react to Harriet's frightful veil?

But nothing had been her fault. How was she to have refused the brothers? The breakdown had been unforeseen and getting lost just one of those things. Someone should really put a map in the glove compartment. It was a pity about the Timex, purchased out of the small stipend provided to her for such necessities. She'd have to tell Perpetua about that. Perhaps she shouldn't have walked into that shanty town after dark, but she hadn't even known it was a shanty town when she entered it. The entire day had consisted of things beyond her control. And despite her misadventures, it was a case of mission accomplished. She eyed the Marimekko bag on the passenger seat, thinking she'd be happy never to see its garish pattern again.

Still, she felt guilty. There were things she would minimize for Perpetua, such as the real danger she'd been in with the louts. But how to minimize the fact that she had spent most of the day in the company of young men—one of whom had made some sort of pass at her, if she was being honest.

And worst of all, somehow, was the veil. However clever she could be with her explanations, the veil shrieked of things that must not be. Harriet felt sure that Perpetua would forbid her from ever leaving the convent alone again. She felt a surge of anger. And it was all their fault, Perpetua's and the bishop's, for without that committee they'd foisted on her none of this would have happened!

Her ire didn't last. If she were in Perpetua's shoes, she'd be sick with worry. She might even have called the police by now. Harriet had just come upon a clear view of Saint Reginald's among the trees. She felt confused. Everything was too bright. There were pulsing lights everywhere, bouncing off the snow. And she realized with mounting horror, as she pulled into the grounds, that she was looking at the flashing lights of multiple police cars. Perpetua must have called the authorities, and she was in for it now.

## 12: Laurentine

HARRIET DROVE THE car around the back, and entered by a side door she hadn't expected to find unlocked. She would go straight to Perpetua's office, where she'd most likely find her despite the hour. The Marimekko bag smacking her as she went, she half ran through the hallways, not slowing down to make sense of the mood. The girls' dormitories, which she cut through, were filled with the buzz of a disturbed hive, and there were sisters still dressed and hurrying places. Harriet couldn't understand why everyone ignored her. You would have almost thought they barely saw her. Had she become invisible? Had her tousled hair become invisible?

The lights were on in Perpetua's office and Harriet could hear the voices of men within. Right outside the door was a row of hooks from which hung Perpetua's long cloak, and beside it, the bonnet-scarf combo sisters wore in winter. Harriet whipped this off its hook and pulled it on before presenting herself. Perpetua stood behind her desk, and four large policemen, including Flynn, sucked up the remaining space.

"Reverend Mother, my apologies...here I am." She bowed her head, while still keeping an eye on the mood.

"Yes, what is it, Sister?" Perpetua's voice was crisp. The men took in her presence, with no great interest.

"I'm very late, I'm afraid."

"What? Yes, you are indeed late, Sister." Perpetua looked at her watch, frowned in a distracted way. Harriet now noticed her superior's pallor. "We'll have to discuss that another time." She looked quickly at the Marimekko bag, over to Flynn, then back to Harriet. "I trust all went well?"

Harriet was bewildered. But this wasn't the first time tonight she'd had to think about survival and she played along.

"Yes, Reverend Mother." She hesitated, calculating. "Now that I'm back…is there anything I can assist with?"

Perpetua's headshake betrayed impatience. "No, at least not immediately. Just try to stay out of the way, Sister. The police may need to speak to you, along with others, so you will be in your room, of course."

Harriet retreated dutifully, hardly able to believe her luck. What could possibly have happened? She raced back to her room, threw the tote bag into a corner with unnecessary violence, and switched to the one other veil she possessed. She hurried to Patricia's door. Harriet tapped lightly, but the door opened immediately.

Patricia too was fully dressed. Harriet had long ago decided that Sister Pat's mobile eyebrow was the only really expressive part of her face, so she was disturbed to see her grave look.

"I need to come in." Harriet brushed past her without ceremony. "I had a just terrible day, but never mind that. I need your help. But first, tell me, what happened? I saw the police. Did they find Loretta?"

"No, Sister, they did not."

Sisters weren't supposed to use each other's rooms for socializing, but Patricia offered Harriet the armchair. Out of the corner of her eye Harriet took in the decor. The walls were adorned with prints in the holy picture style of religious art, of saintly saints, proficient guardian angels and cherubic shoeless children, against backgrounds murky with threat. Despite a fixation with lambs, they gave a certain pizzazz to the bare white walls.

"What, then?"

"Another girl has gone missing. Laurentine Artois."

"That's terrible. What happened?"

"She pulled a stunt like Loretta's, pillows under the covers. One of her roommates woke up and, I'm not sure why, went over to Laurentine's bed to check, found the pillows. The girl sounds the alarm, the police show up in force, we're all awake—waiting."

"Another boyfriend?"

"Well, maybe. It looks like it. Deliberate, anyway."

Harriet thought of the reserved girl, whose cynicism mingled with a studied innocence would have a fatal effect in the right quarters. It had to be a boyfriend. Hadn't she seen Laurentine dancing with a boy on bonfire night? She remembered the girl silhouetted against the fire, doing a casually cool Watusi in the general vicinity of a gyrating partner. This image thinned in Harriet's imagination, and Laurentine became insubstantial and translucent, her shape dissolving into the fire.

"Get a hold of yourself, Sister," Patricia said quickly. She pushed a glass of water on Harriet. "Did you eat? I can tell you didn't."

She pulled from her closet a box, labelled "Missals—two dozen, leatherette cover," but overflowing with unauthorized foodstuffs.

"Let the police do their job, is what I say. We need to think of the girls, we need to think of ourselves too." She offered Harriet a chocolate bar. "Eat up. But you came here for something else."

"I'm in a jam. Setting aside details, this happened tonight." Harriet pulled from her robes the stitched veil. "I've got to repair it better than this. Because it's the last one I can wear. Because of this." She held up the end of the veil she was wearing, displaying a highly visible cigarette burn.

"Oh that. Yes, well, I said I was sorry about my cigarette. That wind out back is tricky. I'm down to one, too." Patricia examined the green stitches. "A grisly sight. No, you can't wear this." She scrutinized Harriet. "You're all right, though?"

"Yes, fine. And I'm down to none, not one. I need to make a better repair than this, and I need to make it now, before tomorrow."

"It's after midnight, Sister." She could tell Patricia's wheels were turning. "Hang on." She slipped out of the room, came back in a minute. "Get your coat, don't forget your boots. Let's break into the

Home Ec house."

But they didn't have to break in. Shortly after they arrived, Sister Rachel appeared with keys and ushered them in. Upstairs under the eaves, with only the light of sewing machines to work by, as they didn't want to attract attention, Rachel had a close look at the badly repaired veil.

"And what," she asked Harriet, "do you think I can do with this?"

Harriet had managed to escape almost all Home Ec while at school, which had seemed a great idea at the time. "I read something about invisible repairs?"

Patricia guffawed behind her. "Well, I'll leave Sister in your capable hands, Sister." She stumped down the stairs, the door slamming after her.

"I'd need a miracle."

Harriet wanted to cry. "Even with black thread? Is there nothing you can do? I've had a very trying day and evening..."

"There now, Sister. I didn't say there was nothing I could do. Get me that bolt of black cloth over there. It's not veil material, it's that new Dacron so it's a bit shiny, but it will have to do. It's left over from the boarders' Halloween project. They shouldn't really have—witch costumes—but I didn't have the heart. Sister says it can't wait? Sit down out of the way and I'll make you a new veil."

A lot of measuring, marking and cutting followed, considering it was a big black semi-circle. Harriet watched in a sleepy trance, as Rachel explained that this veil would be without snaps or buttons but she'd sew on twill tapes, which Harriet could tuck inside and no one would be the wiser.

"You can tie a bow, I hope, Sister?"

At this point Harriet was impervious to sarcasm. It was immensely soothing, really, at 2 am, to watch Rachel sew and to listen to the hum of the machine, the only sound in the quiet dark pavilion. How useful, had she but known, were the womanly arts, she rambled on to herself, and how restful a school could be without girls. Due to her exhaustion, she didn't remember just then that Saint Reginald's had one less tonight.

THE SNOW STAYED. Saint Reginald's had never looked lovelier, in its setting of pristine slopes and shrubbery, at the top of its tree-lined drive. There was just that one area in front where police cars coming and going had made a mess, and continued to make a mess, for they came daily to the school now.

Harriet submitted to an interview. She was summoned to an alcove off a blind corridor behind Perpetua's office. A plainclothes officer entered, doffing a fedora whose impeccable angle she had had time to notice. He introduced himself as Inspector Alain Moreau, of the Bothonville Criminal Investigation Bureau. She recognized the man she had seen before with Flynn. He seemed in charge of the investigation. An accompanying uniform with a notepad melted into the background in the approved fashion.

Moreau was also in the approved fashion, early forties, suspicious gaze. Harriet has worked herself up anticipating this interview. She knew nothing about the disappearance of Loretta and Laurentine, but she taught them and supervised them on the bridge project, so perhaps she should have known. Her case of nerves was really less specific, to do with her inner conflicts. She was also uncomfortably reminded of her no-doubt illegal escapade onto the bridge.

"Where were you"—he looked at his notebook—"Sister Harriet, on the day and evening when Laurentine Artois disappeared?"

"Diocesan business. I'm on the Bothonville Bridge Design Committee. Mother Perpetua, or Police Chief Flynn, may have told you?" Moreau gave nothing away. "After lunch, I drove to Carson Falls, to Saint Mark's College. I was there for two hours, no, three. On the return, I took a wrong turn off the highway that took me onto an overpass. The station wagon broke down between some fields. walked, found myself in East Town"—she had since learned the name of the neighbourhood with the sad streets and many bars—"but wasn't able to find a service station. I ended up in central Bothonville. I ran into a student and her brother, and he went back and got the car started. That took another two hours, probably. When I got to Saint Reginald's it must have been midnight, and the police were here. So I was nowhere near the school for most of that day, I'm afraid."

Moreau looked taken aback. "East Town," was all he said.

"Yes." Harriet arranged her face into womanly ruefulness. "I would have called from there, but there was no place where I wanted to stop in."

This was almost the same account she'd given Perpetua. She'd decided not to mention River Flats.

"No, I could imagine." His gaze lingering thoughtfully over her. "How well did you know Laurentine Artois?"

"I taught her and I supervised her along with another teacher in a science project. But this is my first year teaching and I believe other teachers, other sisters, would know her better." She hesitated. "A very good student. I keep hearing she had a secret boyfriend, but I don't think she's the type."

She suspected Laurentine was more a collector of worshippers. If she ever had condescended to a secret boyfriend, he would be anything but your run of the mill teenager with a car. She could see Loretta Mazurek picking off a Saint Mark's boy with the cachet of Montreal on him. But Laurentine moved through the world with a robed hem for the male to kiss. She was a *noli me tangere* type.

"Unlike Loretta Mazurek, maybe?"

"That's right. But again, Inspector Moreau, I hardly knew that girl. She and Laurentine are friends with a girl called Laura Rome. She's the head of the student council. Laura might know. They're all top students though, from good families, it's hard to associate elopements with that kind of girl. It's very worrying. But as a new sister, I know nothing."

For emphasis, she adjusted her veil, which happened to be the Halloween fabric one. Moreau looked resigned, which had been Harriet's objective in repeating trite generalizations and gossip. Harriet didn't mention that in her recent glimpses of Laura Rome she'd seen there a tautness that made her think of the underlying bones, and an implacability, wholly unreadable. A part of Harriet wanted to corner Laura, to give her the third degree. Presumably the police had the same ideas. Meanwhile, where in the wide world were the girls?

DAILY LIFE AT Saint Reginald's carried on, except that a few parents took boarders out of school "early for Christmas," according to the transparent phrase. Harriet redoubled her teaching efforts. It had been the dictate of Perpetua to keep the students focused on work. The young girls were more distractible. The outward decorum to the seniors didn't fool Harriet. The Saint Reginald's way was well inculcated in them, but Loretta and Laurentine were their classmates, and Harriet recognized a watching and waiting. From staff room gossip, Harriet gleaned that the girls knew nothing—or they weren't speaking up.

Florene was discreetness itself about the events of Friday night. But then the child had as much to lose as she did, were the River Flats story to get out, since what Saint Reginald's girl would want to admit to such a home? Harriet kept turning over in her mind how the Pellerins lived. Florene was so neat in her uniform, which she wore better than many of the girls. It boggled the mind that every morning she came from a cabin without running water. Unless of course she came, at least sometimes, from the other place in the woods, a cabin too no doubt. How much better was a cabin in the woods, and what woods?

Harriet continued to feel gratitude. Roger, especially, had displayed know-how bordering on magical. His particular skills were part of the reason she had decided not to bring up his name with Moreau. Who knew what interactions he'd had with the police? If Reg and Mal and the other two were River Flats delinquents of one sort, Roger might be more dangerous still. As for the four boys, she tried not to think about them too much. The ugliness of the encounter had left its mark and her craving for those car trips subsided. Her own experiences mingled in her mind with the continued disappearance of Loretta and Laurentine, and sometimes she felt quite sick at the dangerous world these young girls faced.

More snow fell and she and the other teachers busied themselves making a ski trail and a toboggan run, Mr. Hughes and Mr. Montserrat being invoked according to custom to do the heaviest work, as if they were collective school husbands. They also layered the ice on the pond to a perfect surface. Harriet had finally managed to save up enough from her stipend for a pair of sober black figure skates, so that she could now return the other skates Laura Rome had so kindly loaned her. She often took a spin, with a gaggle of girls and teachers or by herself in the evening. These activities helped take everyone's mind off the trouble that had come to Saint Reginald's.

The school bridge project had become difficult, without two of the senior participants. Ella Burnhouse-Raquette, who previously had a floating role, replaced Loretta and, after the grade nine partner of Laurentine burst into tears at the prospect of being the third wheel in another team, Laura Rome offered to team up with her directly, effectively doubling her work. The bridges themselves continued to grow, visually stunning in their fantastic lines, although time would tell whether they were any use at all when the judges tested their strength. Mr. Montserrat and Harriet had their work cut out for them now, as the construction rules were complex—some braces were not allowed, there needed to be a certain clearance for the load apparatus, even too much glue could result in a disqualification—and they were expected to head off the more obvious errors.

They were still able to find time to occupy their two customary chairs by the window and engage in desultory chat. With effort, Harriet had rebuilt her outward self with Montserrat so that she wouldn't always be so conscious. It had worked, to a certain extent. But now Mr. Montserrat seemed the withdrawn one. His gracefully chatty way, that elevated talk to a pleasure, had retreated somewhere. He seemed distracted, even anxious. Everyone was worried, but Marin Montserrat looked like he carried within himself a heavy burden, and his face fell from time to time into a passing bleakness. She sometimes had to repeat herself. He would come back to reality with a fleeting smile, which made the lapse all the more apparent.

"I can't believe the police are making so little headway," she said to him one day, as a wind rattled the window frame and chill seeped into the room. "Two girls like that, disappearing without a trace. And nobody knows anything?" He nodded dispiritedly.

"I believe someone knows something, and just isn't saying. Look at Ella, she's now very pally with Laura. Look at her face, she's different than before." Although the girl's face was no less closed, Harriet detected a suppressed excitement in its set. "And Laura. Well, maybe the police are getting something out of her and we just don't know it yet. Do you ever think, Mr. Montserrat, that one of us should be talking to her?"

Mr. Montserrat had practically no reaction at all to this. Drat the man, was he even listening?

"I think Laura Rome will come forward with anything she knows when it suits Laura Rome," he finally said.

"Do you credit the elopement with secret boyfriends?"

"It's the most likely explanation, Sister. These are young women."

"I don't credit it." Harriet felt mulish. "They aren't just any high school seniors, they all want to go to Vivamus College at least, they're high flyers. They want everything." Thinking of Laurentine, she added, "I can't see the boyfriend they would risk their future for."

A spat broke out and they had to intervene. Then one of the girls had a coughing fit and needed water. A box of tissues was found for two other girls afflicted with the latest cold. A general coughing and blowing of noses erupted, including Mr. Montserrat into a fine linen handkerchief. Harriet ordered a spotty child with a feverish glow to go to the infirmary directly after they finished. She hoped she wasn't coming down herself with another bug. As she watched Montserrat put his handkerchief away—the man could turn pocketing a used handkerchief into an elegant gesture—she thought he really wasn't looking good.

"Sister Imelda recommends wine for colds, did you know, Mr.

Montserrat?" she said, for something to say, as the girls began to put things away. "You should have a dose tonight."

"An excellent suggestion, Sister, and since I heard you sniffling will you join me at a distance?" This was the old Mr. Montserrat, but for the tone. His heart, it was wretchedly obvious, wasn't in the sally.

Was this yet another person Harriet had to worry about? Because in discussing the runaways she hadn't just been passing the time with Montserrat. In her kind of world, people could slip between your fingers. She hadn't expected her life at Saint Reginald's to remind her of this so soon.

SAINT REGINALD'S traditionally celebrated the first Sunday of Advent by attending mass in a group at the basilica, and Harriet there had a brief discussion with Bishop Aloysius about her work for the civic committee. He had preached a long sermon on doctrinal disputes involving Advent, about which Harriet for one had not previously heard, and seemed inclined to carry on in this vein when they met in the vestry. The Carson Falls papers had been picked up and handed to the minute-taking councillor. He'd been unctuously thankful and Harriet rejoiced to get the files off her hands.

The bishop was equally enthusiastic in his gratitude. But these accolades only went so far with her. Her success in this task had been hard won, more so than she could really divulge to anyone. Except maybe to Brother Cyprian. Therein lay the problem, one aspect of it anyway. Also, the more she had had time to reflect on gothic superstructures and what they would do for humanity, the more she'd wondered.

And yet now, as altar boys scurried around them in the vestry and he began once more to carry on about his vision of the—ahem—issue (since little pitchers had big ears), she felt once more the pull of his vision. It was partly the way he called her "my child" a lot, and how he repeated his wish that she visit him soon again, before Christmas if possible so she could see the lights they had strung in the trees. She'd met bishops before, and they'd mostly seemed to her like tired businessmen with a smooth streak and too much on their plates. Their eyes did not light up when you mentioned Saint John of The Cross as your favourite Advent saint, speaking as he did about dark nights of the soul in this season of darkness.

Thanks to Aloysius, Harriet enjoyed the rest of that Sunday. The nuns and boarders put up the big outdoor crèche in front of the grotto. Then modest amounts of holly and fir were strewn about indoors and out, Perpetua having drawn the line at a foyer full of five hundred pulsing bubble lights proposed by the Christmas decoration committee. A stack of grading sat waiting on Harriet's desk, but she was still able to take time to go tobogganing. She had school dinner duty, never a recipe for digestion, but musical performances in the decorated dining hall enlivened the evening.

The icy delicate moon sent diamonds running through the snow as Harriet took the shortcut across the quadrangle back to her room. This was a blessed time, Perpetua had said at dinner, a time when we were schooled to hope again. Perhaps this was so, Harriet thought, perhaps this was so.

Bodies are not so easily found in night and falling snow. And yet some snowmobilers, taking a nighttime ride along the river, had no trouble finding the bodies of Loretta Mazurek and Laurentine Artois, in a bay halfway between Bothonville and Carson Falls where the detritus of the river had a tendency to wash up.

## 13: Henry

INSPECTOR ALAIN MOREAU sighed. A few days had passed since the discovery of the bodies, and the shrill moanings of the school womenfolk he'd had to deal with daily had abated to some extent. Not that that mother superior was the moaning sort, but her problem was she asked too many questions. The families could be the hardest to deal with normally, but in this case he'd found the girls to be worse, at least in sheer volume of grief. There were just too many tears for a man to think straight.

He looked out his office window in the fading light, to the back of city hall, the emptying parking lot and the odd sad tree under its weight of snow. A case like this, if he played it right, would get him out of Bothonville, and he didn't mean only as far as Carson Falls. And yet, with so little to go on he was as likely to fall flat on his face.

Had any crime been committed? Flynn was on him for a pronouncement. The problem was a lack of evidence. Rumours and gossip were flying around the town. What more suitable crime victims could you hope for than two pretty young women from good families at a Catholic girls' school? There must have been a crime. White slave trader sightings on the river you could dismiss, but when people began to harp publicly on the need to deal with the various shanty towns—and by people he meant the *Herald*—Flynn developed his whingy baby look and upped the pressure on him with a malice that would have surprised others but not Moreau. To complicate matters, it was all tied up with the blasted bridge, and the need to avoid more civic unrest during this final winter of construction. And how in hell would some showy raids on River Flats and Turpentine Flats, maybe East Town and the Factory Alley warrens, help with that? The message was clear: solve the case so that people stopped talking about it.

He cut off a recurring fantasy about arresting, to the acclaim of the city, the holiest little nun in the pack, maybe that one with the big hazel eyes whose veil glimmered unnervingly like a halo, and opened his paper file once more.

The photographs weren't pretty. Although the faces were the worst, everything had been heavily altered by time in the water. The autopsies would tell him more, but if there'd been superficial signs of violence they were all mixed up now with the effects of hungry aquatic life and decay. That was the biggest problem of all, along with the absence of the mythical boyfriends.

Yes, many interviewees had opinions, but in neither case were there any actual leads. Pinning down the specifics had been a nightmare. The girls and even some of the nuns experienced an unholy joy in repeating rumours. But when he tried to pinpoint, for instance, secret nighttime escapades, a chaotic picture emerged of constant excursions of this kind by the senior class. It seemed to be a cultural necessity, a rite of passage. Earnest and not so earnest descriptions gave him a picture of a transplanted Berlin Wall with a nightly traffic of Saint Reginald's girls scaling it in brisk succession.

The families for their part pushed back with a grief-stricken violence against the idea of secret boyfriends and, although the Artois's were out of towners, he had to tread carefully around the Mazureks, prominent Bothonvillers who could make his life difficult.

The final insult had been running into that damn Montserrat during interviews. He'd never wanted to see the man again, and there he was suddenly, lounging across the table with his superior good looks, professing to know nothing whatsoever about anything, something Moreau didn't believe for a minute on principle. Little Maureen Phayre, with her big brown eyes, her laughter, her curves, may have been young for Moreau, quite young for him, and he couldn't honestly say he'd thought he had a future with a lunch counter waitress. She hadn't been the first of his casual girlfriends and she probably wouldn't be the last. It had been humiliating just the same to have her snatched so easily by that Lothario in tweed, on only his second visit to the diner where she worked. And then, to make matters worse, Moreau had heard that they must have gone steady—what a joke—for no more than a couple of weeks before either he ditched her or she ditched him. He'd also heard, in a final stab of fate, that Maureen was now seeing someone else. This kind of thing made a man weaken when some of those grade thirteen girls, practically the same age as Maureen, flirted with their eyes. Not that shadowy Rome girl, but some of them. The Rome girl, likely to know the most, gave absolutely nothing away. There was something almost terrifying about that one; and a part of him knew he would never be able to shake a thing out of her.

He slammed the file folder shut. He would go after the men, he decided. There were several: Montserrat and the other male teacher, the brothers of some girls who showed up regularly at school events, certain Saint Mark's boys who were known to visit. Maybe the males would give up their secrets. This was, in one way or another, a case of boy trouble. Besides which, it would be a pleasure to grill Montserrat.

AS PARENTS TOOK more girls out of the school "early," and the students became virtually unteachable, it became the task of the teachers to hold them all together. Perpetua harangued them daily on this. Looking at the faces at staff meetings, Harriet knew she wasn't the only one suffering. Everyone looked heavy as lead. At the same time, as the police came and went daily, hysteria hovered in the wings. It didn't help that a flu prowled the school for more victims, and that two girls were hospitalized with pneumonia. Miss Edison's and Mr. Montserrat's colds wouldn't go away, Mr. Montserrat looking especially grey. The school rang with bronchial coughing. Imelda was looking swamped, the only reason Harriet didn't approach her about her own sleeplessness.

Harriet slept all right, just never more than an hour or two at a time. Her nightmares didn't directly involve Loretta and Laurentine. She sometimes found herself back in the hands of the River Flats louts. Other times, she was making her way at night through tangled woods, like on the night the car broke down. Only, in the latter dreams, she was looking for a childhood cat named Henry that had gone missing. The lout dreams were nothing in comparison to the missing cat dreams, for their clutching anxiety, their bleak heartbreak, their general hopelessness. She was always staggering over uneven terrain, calling out in the darkness. Henry, in her dream imagination would sometimes be aureoled in gold, almost like a whiskered saint. He had aspects of a beloved baby gone missing as well. And it was always her fault.

She hadn't thought of Henry in years. By choice, the same way she avoided the convent cat Lester. When Harriet had gone to stay with Rhonda, she'd left not only her sick mother behind, but Henry too. During those two years in Bothonville, while doing her best to put her mother's illness out of her mind, she'd given scant thought to Henry. Then had come the end: the too-late summons to her mother's deathbed, the empty funeral, the emptier return to Bothonville, her exile to Iona Prep. And the gradual disappearance, in thought and actual fact, of the remaining shreds of whatever family she had left.

During this entire time, not once had Harriet inquired about Henry. She'd wanted to, but she hadn't been able to summon the nerve. Her mother's and her pitiful goods had just been thrown out—she'd overheard contemptuous conversations at the funeral to this effect. She feared hearing that Henry, old and one-eyed, had been thrown out too. If she just didn't ask, she could hope. Over the years her silence became wedded in her mind with her fatal carelessness in letting everything slip between her fingers. Her family, her mother, Henry.

These feelings she outgrew eventually, along with a taste for cats. Harriet just wasn't a cat person. But if so, why dream of Henry now?

As for Loretta and Laurentine, she puzzled over the how's and whys: how the girls had ended up in the water; and from where, a question that always made her think of the ill-intentioned bridge.

Childhood had also left Harriet with a distaste for funerals. Everyone from Saint Reginald's would be attending the Bothonville funeral for Loretta, and a large delegation would be sent the next day to Laurentine's funeral out of town. Harriet was glad she wasn't part of that delegation, but wished Perpetua hadn't chosen her to put in an appearance at the Mazurek wake with a group of sisters. They said funerals made the living feel better. Harriet didn't remember her mother's that way, but perhaps she might feel differently as an adult.

She had taken to spending the time after dinner in her room, needing to be alone. Late one evening, when she was looking out the window at yet more falling snow and wondering whether she would have the courage to go to bed, she heard a knock at her slightly open door. She turned around, surprised to see Laura Rome framed in the entrance.

"Could I see you for a moment, Sister?" Laura asked.

Letting students into your room was even more frowned upon than letting other sisters in. But the *passe partout* aspect of Laura had its effect and in any case these were strange times, so Harriet gestured Laura to the armchair.

"What is it, Laura?" Harriet tried to sound kind. The girl had purple smudges under her eyes and her face was almost gaunt. Being Laura Rome, she still looked eerily beautiful. Harriet for a brief moment wondered if a revelation was at hand and emotion flared in her. But that wasn't what Laura had come to say.

"I haven't had a chance to take any of your classes, Sister," the girl said in a low voice, "not like Loretta and Laurentine. I won't be able to now, as I'm in my last year." She'd replaced her uniform, as the grade thirteens were allowed to do outside class, with a pullover and a pleated skirt, whose pleats she now fingered rhythmically. "I wanted to tell you, though—I mean, nothing will make us feel better for a long time, but I wanted to tell you how much Loretta and Laurentine thought of you and your classes. Because they can't now." Her gaze drifted past Harriet. "They never stopped talking about how much they learned from you. You inspired them, Sister. I thought you should know."

"That—that is really very kind." This was the last thing Harriet had expected to hear. "I'm touched. I'm touched also, Laura, that you thought to come and tell me this." She felt a lump in her throat and wondered what Laura could read on her face.

"Sister, I've seen you in bridge project, I could see the sadness in your face. I mean, we're all sad. But it was the least I could do." The rush of feeling from poised Laura Rome was disconcerting. "I had to make that part right."

Harriet had started to speak herself, and didn't quite take on board the last sentence. She felt a strong need to lift the mood or the two of them would be weeping on each other's necks in a minute.

"I have a face that's easy to read, like a bad novel. But Laura, I know you're struggling too, and this is the time when we must all look out for each other." Now she was sounding like Perpetua. "And work, as Reverend Mother says. Your work on the bridge project is magnificent and you've no idea how much I rely on you." More Perpetua. She forced a smile. "We must look a sight in the multi-purpose room, me with my long face and Mr. Montserrat with his hundred-day cold."

Laura smiled back, her face taking on the public Laura look she would wear so well at the funerals. The pleats dropped from her slim fingers. "I just wanted to say this, anyway," she murmured. "My apologies for intruding, Sister, but you're not often in the library, so I looked you up."

Her exit was as composed as her entrance. No, Harriet didn't mind in the least. From a very unsimple girl, such an act of kindness was all the more striking. That Laura had been sincere, she was sure. Truthful in relaying what the others had thought and truthful in her impulse to share it. What Harriet didn't think about until later was what, if any, special meaning there was behind Laura's words about making things right. When they came back to her, she worried over them, although not to any productive effect. Which may have been why she didn't think about the abruptness with which the conversation had come to a close, right after she'd tried to change the tone by mentioning the bridge project.

IT WAS CLOSE to christmas. With all the snow Saint Reginald's had never looked readier to celebrate. Harriet's bad Christmases had faded in memory, but the feeling of being on the far side of a gulf from something joyful now came back to her. Not as strongly as before, for she knew things now she hadn't known then: the benefits of self-discipline, of refocusing on others. This time, however, she faced a new and pressing question: for whom exactly was Christmas supposed to be? The people on that Bridge Design Committee, with their dreams of avarice, would be untroubled by the question. What about the Artois and Mazurek families, who might never recover from their loss? What about those lines of down and outs at the Saint Felix soup kitchen? What about the people of East Town, where she hadn't seen a single wreath?

It seemed to her important to answer this question. Yet she faced a blank wall. Perhaps Bishop Aloysius would know, but he wasn't around to ask. Was this how Saint John of The Cross felt, during one of those dark nights of the soul he wrote about? Probably not, almost certainly not. He was a major saint of the faith, a Mystical Doctor of the Church. Catholic royalty. While she was Harriet of Bingham, composed of muddled impulses and misrepresentation, from her name to her veil. A venal wayfarer on a pilgrimage she didn't understand. Let there be no further trouble, she prayed daily—to herself mainly. Just let things not get worse.

# 14: Laura

INSPECTOR MOREAU eyed Harriet suspiciously across the table. This was a new one for him at Saint Reginald's, a nun seeking him out rather than the other way around. She looked nervous—as far as he could tell, because she was one of those tightly-strung ones at the best of times.

"I wasn't completely honest—no, I told you the truth but I didn't include some details I want to tell you now," Harriet said. She looked unhappy.

He leaned forward expressionlessly. "Go on."

"About the night Laurentine Artois disappeared. You remember, the convent car broke down, and I ended up having to walk forever after I took a wrong turn. Well, after East Town I walked in the woods for a while and that led me somehow to the construction zone in front of the bridge, and then to River Flats."

"You said you ended up downtown."

Harriet looked injured. "I believe that area is technically part of the downtown."

"And I believe your lot aren't supposed to rely on technicalities when it comes to the truth." Moreau hadn't meant this to slip out, not so soon. But River Flats? This flibbertigibbet had been in River Flats that night and not told him? Really, these women were too much.

A humanizing smile on Sister Harriet's face surprised him. "You're right, Inspector Moreau, we're not supposed to. It was remiss of me, although I meant it for the best."

"Go on," he said, mollified. She was a good-looking little thing in her way. Why in the name of God, if he could put it that way, did women become nuns anyway, when the alternative was a happy life undeprived of men? This question nudged up against why Maureen had dumped him, and he brushed it away.

"I did meet a student from the school and her brother did get the car running for me. But when I was in River Flats some youths accosted me." She went on to tell Moreau about the four boys and how they'd roughed her up, mentioning the names Reg and Mal, and recounting how the Pellerins had appeared.

"I didn't want to mention the Pellerins before, but now I don't know how not to." She briefly dropped her gaze. "I'd met Roger Pellerin before, at bonfire night, other school events. He seems like a respectable young man. He might have saved my life." She didn't need to add "or my virtue."

Moreau sat up straighter. Was this the beginning of a break at last? The autopsies had revealed signs of violence. The deaths were now officially suspicious deaths. The bodies had sustained significant internal damage, damage consistent with impact blows, or being hurled from a height. Water in the girls' lungs, which meant they'd been alive on impact. It didn't bear thinking about. Whatever that gasbag boss of his said, security was a joke some nights at the bridge. It depended on the level of rioting by day. Who knows what might have gone on there? And here came new information at last.

He questioned Harriet about the thugs, and then slipped in some questions about Pellerin: where they went afterwards, how she spent the evening, how long he was gone. He knew all about Pellerin, an agitator at one of the big mills, and the last remaining male—a virile specimen so probably not for long—of that multi-generational small-time crime family, whose curated focus on things lying around on construction sites and in open trucks made the Pellerins unique among the tribe. You wouldn't associate violence with the Pellerins, not normally, although he'd had a question about the beating of that security guard at the mill during the union drive.

"While you were there that night, Sister, did you see anything else that seemed strange to you, any activity, for example, close to the bridge? Or even on it, unbelievable as it might seem that anybody would go climbing up there?"

This question provoked a squirm. The woman clearly had no imagination, or no head for heights.

"Nothing, Inspector." She sounded sincere. "But then there was fog and I wasn't exactly looking at the bridge a lot of the time, River Flats, once you're in it, is a kind of warren. And then I was indoors until Roger came back." She frowned. "But..."

He didn't say anything.

"I do remember driving by the bridge...after my dentist's appointment, no, I'd been to Saint Angus in the car...and seeing what I thought was movement on the deck. Very far up, it might have been a trick of the eye." She hesitated. "There are rumours that young people climb the bridge at night for kicks. One of the kitchen sisters"—a low blow to Sister Pat—"told me this. Girls and boys together sometimes. Evidently it's not the night in question, but I saw movement—I believe."

She cleared her throat, blushed again. Moreau bundled her out of the room in a hurry, because he had some thinking to do.

LORETTA'S FUNERAL was the next morning. The basilica was packed, and more people, including reporters, hung around the doors. Harriet could hardly bring herself to look at the white coffin piled with flowers, or at the Mazurek family, the women heavily veiled, in the front row. She focused instead on the ocean of Saint Reginald's girls, the Advent decorations, the slanting light through stained glass. Afterwards, Perpetua, Rachel and Harriet, accompanied by Miss Edison, drove over to the Mazureks.

They lived in a sprawling split-level ranch in one of Bothonville's prosperous suburbs. The house was packed with visitors when they arrived. Perpetua knew what to do and carried her delegation along with her. The parents of Loretta looked frozen, possibly beyond thawing. Mrs. Mazurek was a plump woman with a shockingly gaunt face, as if she'd lost weight so quickly in recent weeks her body hadn't caught up. The house itself seemed to have the latest in everything, new-fangled items and finger foods unrecognizable to Harriet, whose existence for years had been passed communally in an aura of institutional floor polish and stew of the week. She welcomed the distraction of all this, and did her best to loiter in the shadow of Perpetua. A strange smell stole through the house, not unpleasant, and Harriet at length found the source when she attempted to hide a half-eaten appetizer: a sort of electric vaporizer discreetly tucked behind the nubby orange drapes. The smell reminded her of the flytox her mother used for spraying closets, but tangier.

THAT WEEKEND, SHE plunged into prep for the ninth grades' history project, one of those ambitious headache projects that set Saint Reginald's apart. On Monday Florene was predictably prompt with a topic requiring approval.

"It fits the criteria, Sister. It must have been a *terrible* time for Bothonville. There are so many questions."

The students were to pick a local historical event, and write it up using a specified number of records, from county archives to newspapers to library resources. Thereby did Saint Reginald's hope to nip in the bud the habit of summarizing heavily from one source, before omitting it from the citations.

Harriet took cookies out of her desk drawer—they were in the empty homeroom—and offered one to Florene.

"There have always been shanty towns in Bothonville," the girl said, causing Harriet to start.

She went on to talk about an early twentieth century murder, of the daughter of a prominent citizen. A local man who lived in a place called Bourbon Flats, since cleared, had been arrested. The trial had been "sensational," according to the *Herald*. Florene was well into the project already.

"He was convicted and hanged, Sister. In the courtyard of the town jail—it's where they hanged people. I found a library book on famous Bothonville court cases. I only need a third source."

Harriet felt vague doubts. Florene must have picked the topic a while ago, but it was now a little close to home for turmoil-ridden Saint Reginald's. The type of project that parents would complain about afterwards. Not that she could picture Roger asking what the bloody hell the teacher had been thinking. Perhaps it would benefit Florene to work on this. Although it was hardly a "shanty town child makes good" story.

Distracted by indigestion, the result of too much refectory coffee, Harriet weakly said, "This sounds acceptable, but give me a one page write-up."

"Thank you, Sister. The trial pivots on a getaway car. But there were things—flaws in the investigation, feuds. The jail had snitches, guards turned a blind eye. You could buy anyone's testimony for favours. Sister, you don't look well."

Harriet wasn't going to get into the lurid aspects of Florene's topic for now. "I'm all right, Florene, I'm going to take something. You'll be late for class. Here, have Edwina's cookies."

After Florene left, Harriet thought it should have been she asking the child how she was. You almost got used to the subdued faces all over the school, but Florene had looked pitiful. The deaths had to be the reason. She continued to excel in her schoolwork, so it wasn't that. Her life with Roger would never be easy, but what could Harriet do? Approve her project and give her cookies. She went looking for the Bromo Seltzer.

THAT EVENING, PATRICIA asked Harriet to take a spin on the rink with her. Harriet's upset stomach had passed, but she was in a restless mood and she decided it would be a good way to distract herself.

It was a bitterly cold night and the students were all in pre-exam mode. They expected the pond to be deserted but found Mr. Hughes and Mr. Montserrat there, wearing skates, shoveling the rink and serpentine. This recent addition, an effort of the senior girls and some nuns, and a condoned distraction, curved gracefully away towards the trees and looped back behind the grotto.

The sisters decided not to be put off by the presence of the male teachers. They were all Saint Reginald's staff; and it was really too good of the men to take care of the rink in their off hours. Harriet for one felt obliged to show proper appreciation. Besides which, the newly-surfaced ice, brilliant under a lone lamppost, was bewitching.

Soon the shovels were ditched and they were skating in a brisk foursome, Harriet and Patricia arm in arm ahead, Mr. Montserrat and Mr. Hughes behind them, not arm in arm. Harriet's spirits lifted in spite of everything. The cold air now merely braced, and she felt she belonged to this winter scene and these congenial people, her peers. The scrape of their blades reverberated through the night.

Then Elsie Edison appeared, in a species of loden winter getup that gave her a disconcertingly different look, and joined them on the ice. Harriet was an adequate skater, and the others knew their way around a rink, but Miss Edison put them all to shame with her speed and agility. Harriet and Patricia lost their balance trying to keep up with her and went flying. They were helped up solicitously by the men, who then took a tumble themselves. The skate turned into a kind of race, then a crack the whip during which Harriet could not refrain from shrieking, and finally a tag game. The result was an explosion of spirits and skaters scattering in all directions, Elsie Edison's disappearance at lightning speed along the serpentine somehow drawing Harriet along behind her.

But Miss Edison became quickly lost to view and Harriet found herself alone in the darkness, the laughter receding behind her as she skimmed the ice faster and faster, reckless with a sudden euphoria. Then a dark figure on skates loomed before her. They both swerved in the same direction and the collision was rapid and impressive, flinging them in a tangled knot into a snowbank.

"Oh, Mr. Hughes!" Harriet cried, and threw a small handful of snow in his face, only to discover that it wasn't Mr. Hughes at all but Mr. Montserrat; Mr. Montserrat whom she should have recognized due to the halo of his beauty, which shone even in the darkest of settings. And he was trying to help her up, despite a face full of snow.

Harriet was horrified and mortified, much more so than had it been Mr. Hughes. Then a sudden spite swept away this mixture of emotions, as if the collision and her feelings were all Montserrat's fault. Before she could stop herself she threw another handful of snow in his face. This was terrible! What had possessed her? She began pitifully with a gloveless hand to wipe the snow from his features, revealing thereby an expression she had never seen before. He moved quickly now, seizing her fingers tightly and planting a kiss on her cold lips—his were warm—which, if it wasn't passionate, was at least juicily deliberate. She pulled away, just in time, for Ron Hughes and Patricia were skating up to them in raucous argument. The foursome carried on together back to the grotto, where Elsie Edison rested on one of the benches.

In shock, Harriet acted as if nothing had happened. Marin Montserrat was his unreadable self. The argument between Sister Pat and Mr. Hughes had escalated and now went tetchy. Miss Edison complained of a stiff knee. Very quickly the mood dissipated, and they were looking at one another apprehensively. For what would Perpetua have said had she seen them carrying on, just after the funerals of those poor girls? It didn't bear thinking about. Harriet felt ashamed, for this reason at least, if not for any other.

"This did us good, everything has been so terrible these last days," Miss Edison pronounced. "But now it's over and that's as it should be too."

She was the oldest, and they nodded gratefully to her; even though they knew that her presence as a meaningless chaperone and Perpetua-substitute had in fact unleashed the mischief.

The men were gathering the shovels. Everyone quickly scattered with low-key goodnights. On the way back to the convent wing, Sister Pat cast a sideways look or two at Harriet, who was still hopeful no one had seen anything.

In her room, she wondered if she would feel remorse later. They were reading *Little Women* in sophomore English, and that stolen kiss, which to be truthful she had provoked, seemed just like something Jo might have done if she'd paired off with the right wrong man instead of the wrong right one. Anyway, nothing to overreact to, and few would judge it improper if they understood Harriet's current relation to her religious vocation. This didn't stop her from thinking about those lips for a while longer, until such thoughts—always with their accompaniment of resentment—receded, and the old questing mood replaced it.

It had been an enjoyable evening. This was sometimes the case with these fleeting moments so difficult to predict or recreate. And it had released the tight hurtful knot inside Harriet. That night, she slept without dreams.

THE LAST DAY OF classes came, filled with an anticipatory joy hardly matched later by Christmas itself. Joy triggered by seasonal songs in the halls as the girls swapped cards, the unfamiliar feel of the smart dresses and double-knit suits they were permitted to wear, the fragrance of balsam in the air, the glitter of tinsel. The sense that, despite everything, happiness was still within grasp.

The farewell gathering in the auditorium was solemn, for it was partly a memorial to their late classmates, and tears were shed, causing forbidden makeup to smear. Laura Rome, a pre-Raphaelite figure in a gold mesh dress, her face pale under piled-up hair, spoke about Loretta Mazurek and Laurentine Artois. In a composed voice, she enumerated their virtues, and spoke of the aspirations they had cherished which it was now up to the other girls to pursue. Her audience was rapt. Harriet had her blue handkerchief out, which didn't prevent her from thinking that Laura Rome could lead anyone anywhere she chose.

The last couple of hours of class were spent killing time in homeroom. Girls produced candy and visited at each other's desks to show off attire and discuss holiday plans. The class presented Harriet with a box of Black Magic. When the bell rang, the girls who were heading home were gone like bullets from a gun. The teachers spent a little longer on farewells and season's greetings, and Harriet could look Mr. Montserrat in the eye when he wished her a cordial goodbye in the teachers' lounge, where everyone enjoyed sampling Miss Edison's fruitcake.

Since the evening on the rink, Harriet had hardly run into him, giving her time to decide just how cool she would play things. The key had been remembering that Marin Montserrat was of French extraction scant generations back, and these people were always kissing each other on the slightest pretext. It was therefore relatively easy to fix him with her neutral saintly look and reply in good order. And she made sure to be equally cordial to Ron Hughes, while Mr. Montserrat still lurked in the vicinity. Indeed, she'd found Mr. Hughes quite agreeable on that social evening, less awkward on than off the ice, nimble on skates, thorough with a shovel. Some day soon, she realized, he'd be scooped up, for girls and women were as capable of being as practical in some circumstances as they were of losing their heads in others.

As dusk fell, the school, so unusually quiet, felt strange to Harriet, although the ghost of all that elation lingered still. A dozen girls, for reasons sorrowful and mundane, weren't going home for Christmas. The nuns took these in hand, and there were many things planned, outings, special meals, treats, midnight mass unabridged and with extra incense, and an allowance of laxness balanced by beautiful choral singing in the chapel, the whole a little religious for the girls, a little secular for the sisters. You never knew, anyway, what sort of Christmas these girls would have gone home to. Harriet had managed to intercept Florene before she left to give her "for you and your brother" more of Edwina's cookies, and for Florene herself a set of mittens and a scarf that had gone unsold at a basilica charity tombola.

Harriet took a stroll around the dark grounds. The winter evening contrived to fill her with a promise of kindness and peace. She made a lengthy tour along the wall, pretending not to see the usual furtive figures here and there. At peace in the moonlight, she said aloud to herself, "What if" and then "If only…"

That same evening, later, it was Laura Rome's turn to drop from the sky. But this time River Flats carousers saw the figure falling, in a sort of floating fall, from the deck far above, before coming to rest at last on the ice that had already formed beneath.

## 15: Torn Tapestry

THE CITY DECKED in holiday finery, Saint Reginald's in its lovely setting, even the Advent ceremonies, became, to Harriet, like scenes from those finely lithographed Christmas cards decorated with silver and gold. Something to take pleasure in, just not real. The school might rally and struggle on—Perpetua would permit nothing less—but all Harriet could do was focus on dull immediate routine.

It was a practical miracle that school had already been dismissed for the holidays. The police were back at Saint Reginald's, sometimes by the car load, but operations mercifully centered down at River Flats. Perpetua met regularly with Flynn and Moreau and kept the sisters updated. This was no time to keep anything from them.

Laura Rome, still wearing her gold mesh dress under her coat, had died on impact. The investigation was in its early stage, but some had said they'd seen a second figure up there on the bridge. But how could they be sure? The place from which Laura had dropped was so far above the shanty town, it could all be fancy supplemented by hootch. One witness had said "it looked like a fight;" although how in blazes, Flynn said feelingly to Perpetua, could they determine that after the fact? And yet you could picture it: the tension of tiny figures near the rail, a struggle, a fall, a flight. Once you imagined it, you couldn't unimagine it.

The other possibility didn't bear thinking about. Apart from which, Laura Rome, perhaps more than any girl at Saint Reginald's, had

had everything to live for. She had been the most respected girl in the school, and also recognized as brilliant. She'd just received early acceptance and an offer of full scholarship, contingent on her final grades, from the University of Toronto. She wanted to study, she'd told more than one person, under Northrop Frye and Marshall McLuhan. All that, combined with her indefinable wildness and her looks, had made of Laura Rome a captivating example and a living dream.

The prominent Rome family ran a business in Bothonville, but lived outside town in a big house overlooking the river. The funeral, after a speedy release of the body, therefore took place in their rural parish church. This too was a relief to Saint Reginald's, for another grand basilica funeral would have been unbearable. Many of the sisters nevertheless attended. Harriet saw several people she recognized in the congregation, including her three lay teacher colleagues, huddled together in a pew. Mr. Hughes looked blank with shock and Miss Edison was as if beset with sudden age. Harriet couldn't see Mr. Montserrat's face, for he was hunched over the back of the pew in front of him. Some from the convent, including Patricia, went on to the Rome house afterwards. She told Harriet the next day it had been an ordeal. There was a police presence even at the house, and the mood had been tense.

"I heard two people gossiping. One said the parents were going to sue. The other one asked who, and the woman says, 'the school, of course.' 'That's nuts,' the man says. 'It didn't even happen at the school, it happened like the other deaths down at the river.' They go back and forth and the man is sure police are going to arrest suspects at River Flats—the sooner the better. These rich girls are offered the world on a plate, he says, but they like to take risks and this is what happens."

"They weren't rich, not really." Harriet spoke dully. The sisters were by the kitchen entrance as usual, doing their best to escape the wind.

"No, Sister, you're right, but people are envious and like to blame."

"I read an editorial in the *Herald* that called for dealing with the shanty towns 'for once and for all.' It feels like people have already made up their minds. They link the three deaths."

Sister Pat blew a smoke ring. "Well sure, they're linked. But how—that's the question."

She looked at Harriet kindly. "This is turning into a hard year for you. I do feel for you, Sister." She offered a puff of her cigarette. Feeling she might as well, Harriet inhaled. It made her cough, but it was something.

She cleared her throat with difficulty. "Men," she gargled. The single word rang like an incantation in her mind, carrying with it realms of floating charm and gutterish danger. In reality she was too shocked to think: she had no theories.

"Men—yes, probably." Sister Pat spoke the word as if it were the punchline to a secret joke. "The things you read about in the newspapers these days, though…" Even she sounded subdued.

The next evening Harriet had to attend, of all things, a meeting of the Bridge Design Committee. She had begged Perpetua to be allowed to skip it, but the mother superior, in the middle of fielding calls from parents intending to take their girls out of school, had sounded almost hard in telling Harriet it was her duty to attend.

It was the usual long and bureaucratic meeting, with just enough of an update on the incorporation of gothic design elements into ongoing work to make Harriet's presence necessary. It seemed negotiations with Salamander Holdings were progressing and the news, wrapped in gauzy layers of hush-hush, was encouraging for edging out Carson Falls in the great race, via Salamander Island, to the other side. Everyone spoke confidently of June as the completion date for the Bothonville International Bridge, for such was now its name.

Harriet had been told by Perpetua to say nothing about the dead girls. This advice was relevant when, in the middle of the inevitable commiserations, someone with blithe disregard for the agenda floated the idea that Bothonville had a mass murderer in its midsts. Others picked this up, as if it only took one mention to breach a dam of reticence. Harriet's medieval mystic face came in handy when a banker cited the New York Nylon Stocking Strangler terrorizing that city, and went on to say that such occurrences were—tsk tsk—perhaps part of the price you paid for progress.

Martel had had to step out for a moment, but, catching the last of these comments, he brought the meeting rapidly back to order with a raised voice Harriet had never yet heard from His Blandness. The idea that progress somehow entailed killing women lingered, however. The only mercy, Harriet thought, was the absence of Madame Brunet, Laurentine's aunt. Harriet had to get out of these meetings. There were limits.

IT WAS NOW FOUR days to Christmas. No matter external circumstance, the birth of Christ demanded celebration. Harriet, being the new sister, was pulled into various activities. One evening she attended, with a handful of the girls staying over at the school, a performance of *The Pied Piper of Hamelin* at the old Imperial Theatre downtown. Two were grade thirteens and particularly responsible, and it had been the plan for the students to go off on their own. Now, of course, a ticket had to be scrounged for a nun to accompany them and they had to be driven.

Whether the presence of Harriet would have made a material difference was irrelevant. The whole city guarded its teenage girls. Girls weren't permitted to go anywhere alone, end of year dances had been cancelled, and Vivamus College had doubled its security, among various measures. All perhaps useless, since who really understood the nature of the threat.

Harriet might have enjoyed the performance in different circumstances. The show blended the jolly and macabre, with some musical numbers that mixed the rousing with a heart-tugging nostalgia for unblemished childhood, or perhaps just happy human ignorance. With its ornate embellishments and red velvet, the Imperial thrilled the girls. But the play's theme of disappearing children couldn't have been more topical. Few if any in the packed audience seemed to be making the association, however, between the stolen children of the story and the city's own lost girls.

Close to midnight, the Saint Reginald's contingent stepped out into the winter city. It was a bone chilling night and Harriet wearily marshalled her charges to where she'd parked the car on a side street. As they piled in, police sirens howled in various parts of the city. There had been news reports all day of unrest, whether of riots or labour protests Harriet hardly took in, but police operations in the shanty towns, possibly linked to the deaths, seemed to be part of it. Perpetua had almost cancelled the outing, relenting at the last minute.

The next day Harriet and four other sisters went to a shanty town, Turpentine Flats, which you reached by driving down Factory Alley. Factory Alley was more a boulevard than an alley, and a disturbing wasteland to Harriet who'd never been along it before. On the other side of the satanic mills, they came to a semi-rural area of hilly terrain and silent lurking crossroads. A short drive through rutted backroads brought them quickly to an impenetrable forest wall, or so it seemed. But the screen thinned and they were suddenly in a semi-lit world of small crowded cabins under giant conifers. Every year the convent sponsored a deserving family for Christmas, and this year's family, a parish referral, lived in Turpentine Flats.

They spent a strange couple of hours there, strange to Harriet at least, in a squalid cabin with the large Sherwood family. There was a mother and an invisible father—a back door slammed to the tune of a curse, as they entered by the front. There were five children between the ages of two and thirteen. The bleak-eyed woman and the staring children seemed frightened at first. When the nuns unpacked their hampers the family thawed, the fear in their eyes replaced by cupidity that in no way lessened Harriet's sense of being disliked. Nevertheless, the few refurbished toys made a difference, and the youngest children especially, when presented with mended dolls and puzzles with only a few pieces missing, under their influence became children again. The mother's stone-like face, as she watched them play, now took on a look of mere wistfulness that was hard to witness.

There were winter clothes to distribute as well, and the food when it emerged was much the best: a giant turkey, a ten-pound sack of potatoes, various cans and sweets, all donated by Bothonville merchants. There seemed to be a form to these things. Everyone formed a circle near the woodstove—not near enough for Harriet who sat in a terrible draft—and made stilted conversation. The father was again out of work. The youngest was still "ailing" in some non-specific way, and the eldest, a weasel-faced boy, seemed to have problems best not referred to with him right there, as he radiated a sort of muffled rage. Two small ones got into a peculiar game with the dolls, only to be reprimanded by a raucous-voiced girl, who had no qualms about administering irate slaps, and seemed in charge of the whole crew of children despite her youth.

Rachel quickly distributed tangerines to restore order, while Imelda began furtively to look into the ears of the frog-throated youngest. At one point the mother offered the nuns tea. This appeared to require herculean effort, while unlikely to produce tea. Elderly Edwina, who had seemed merely along for the ride, now came into her own. Soon little ones surrounded her as she pulled lollipops and candy canes from her robes in virtually limitless supply. Their snotty noses and none too clean smell were nothing to her, nor were her age-spotted hands and wavering voice anything to them, as they clung to her in a way that raised a lump in Harriet's throat.

"There was another boy, but he died last winter, pneumonia," Rachel whispered in her ear, and sadness flooded Harriet's heart.

Then the children had to sing songs for the nuns. There were discordant versions of "While Shepherds Watched" and "We Three Kings," followed by an off-colour ditty about a Frankie and Johnny pair, complete with local allusions to Bothonville that made Harriet wonder whether she was listening to an original composition of the Flats. Following the lead of her fellow sisters, Harriet smiled blandly through references to red hot guns and snapping garters, crooked cops and copulation, for what else in the context could canoodle mean.

Despite the absorbing entertainment, it was time to leave at last. Imelda murmured something to the woman about a return visit with her medical kit, while two children were sent for the coats. They then had to be sent back for the gloves, which had somehow in the interval fallen out of the pockets.

It was even darker under the canopy now. As the sisters passed along the path in single file, faint lights flickered in some of the windows. Harriet sensed a teeming community and felt they were being watched.

Her sudden thought as they arrived at the place where they had left the station wagon—"hubcaps still intact," Imelda said matter-of-factly—was that this was where the Pellerins must live. Unless there was another shanty town in some other woods. She should have thought of this sooner, even tried to visit Florene. She was glad it was now too late.

The wind, picking up just then, made a rushing sound in the pines. Queued impatiently for the cold back seat, Harriet looked over her shoulder into the trees. Another time, she said to herself, not realizing how soon this would arrive.

ON CHRISTMAS EVE everyone stayed at Saint Reginald's, and the school chaplain, Father Joseph Lynch, a fretful individual from their local parish who spent as little time as possible at the school owing to a fear of girls, was prevailed upon to celebrate midnight mass in the chapel. A candlelit procession and music charmed the sleepy students, and for the nuns it offered an opportunity to pray for the torn tapestry of their world.

A minute into the mass, to the general astonishment, Aloysius made an appearance with a small retinue. He came as a participant not a celebrant and sat near the back, refusing Perpetua's gestured offer to clear the first pew for him. Afterwards, he spoke with everyone in the narthex and wished every goggle-eyed girl and solemn sister a happy Christmas. Not once did he mention Loretta or Laurentine or Laura, but all knew that he had come because of them. To Harriet he whispered an extra blessing which she felt she didn't deserve, as she intended to abandon the Committee of Dark Designs at the earliest opportunity.

Harriet expected a rather dour twenty-fifth of December given over to prayer and contemplation: it had been ostentatiously the way at the motherhouse. Morning prayer got the nuns up before dawn, and then there was mission work for several, visits to various retirement lodges and a home for disabled children, from which the younger sisters came back grey-faced. The girls were left to themselves after breakfast to open parcels from home and practice their *tenue* for later on. Harriet and a few other teachers were added to the kitchen roster under the ironic guidance of Patricia, for the once a year splurge dinner. Harriet was surprised by the family atmosphere at Saint Reginald's, a little tired and grouchy, very informal, subdued under the circumstances, of course, but with open chocolate boxes encouraging you from every surface. Dinner was worth the wait in the candlelit student dining hall, as snowflakes brushed obligingly against the glass.

The evening also surprised Harriet. After clean-up, the nuns reconvened in their common room in pyjamas, and at last got to open their Christmas cards and the gifts of goodies sent to them by the community. The girls came in briefly with small offerings of their own, craning to see the details of their teachers' *déshabille*—a frustrating vista of pastel robes, and veils, which the sisters only removed once the door shut for good.

The evening was slightly marred by Perpetua being called away to an urgent phone call—from the police, according to whispers—from which she returned with a forbidding look on her face. The entrance of Miss Edison, Lester the academy cat on her heels, was a fortunate distraction.

The veils came off and more tea and punch made the rounds. Elsie was told of the sudden appearance at midnight mass of the bishop, and all extolled his kindness in being with Saint Reginald's in its hour of need. The silly child who ate a piece of tinsel on a dare, quickly taken care of by Imelda with ipecac, raised a laugh, as did the pudding flame at dinner which set fire to someone's napkin.

Miss Edison gave news of Mr. Hughes and Mr. Montserrat. At

the funeral Montserrat had been especially cut up, she said, quite devastated. She had run into Mr. Hughes while shopping on Christmas Eve and he'd told her that poor Marin had apparently taken to his bed with bronchitis.

The hour was late by the time the festivities concluded, and Harriet was getting in a last yawn when someone tapped at the door. Patricia and a few other young nuns stagily crept in with the leftover rye from the plum pudding, with instructions to "get out your tooth mug." They didn't stay long and, since morning prayer was leniently rescheduled to a later hour on the Feast of Stephen, Harriet got her night's sleep anyway. It turned out to be much needed for the day ahead.

## 16: Masquerade

AFTER THE GIRLS had been excused from breakfast, Perpetua stood up in a meaningful way and asked everyone to remain. She had an announcement to make. The kitchen staff were summoned back to the refectory.

"I wanted, Sisters, to tell you about a development in the police investigation into the deaths of our students. It will be all over town by this afternoon, according to Inspector Moreau." Never had her face looked so austere. "There is a delicacy in the matter... Another trial for Saint Reginald's, something closer to home than I could wish."

Harriet sensed the sisters tensing.

"The police have made an arrest. I received an update yesterday. This morning the police chief told me that the dawn raid on the Flats had been successful, and a man is in custody."

A murmur swept the room. But why did Perpetua look so stern?

"The complicating factor for us is that the man arrested is Roger Pellerin. Some of you know he's the brother of a scholarship girl by the name of Florene. He's been at the school quite often, for bonfire night, for instance, the family skating party, the open house."

The murmurs had swelled to a low roar. Perpetua raised a hand. "I will ask you, Sisters, to be silent. I am telling you all I know. It seems the police have important evidence, which naturally they can't share. It will be announced at a press conference at 11. The first radio bulletins are expected shortly after. This will be front page news beyond Bothonville."

"I knew it!" shrieked Sister Angela, whose athletic prowess never would be matched by her understanding.

Perpetua's look withered. "It is *extremely* important that we remain calm. Outbursts"—the look became incinerating—"and gossip will not be tolerated. Sister Angela, you will come to my office directly after this meeting."

"The press will be telephoning, perhaps trying to get onto school grounds. There will be photographers at the entrance. Thanks be to God the school is in recess. A police cruiser will be stationed here. I do *not* want to hear of anyone talking to journalists. For the immediate future, we stay indoors. You will not leave the property without permission."

Perpetua let the silence stretch.

"I'm sure you are full of questions. We will know more this afternoon, but we may not know very much at all until the trial, and even then we may continue to have unanswered questions. This doesn't matter. The satisfaction of curiosity we must leave to the secular world. The Sisters of the Blessed Order of Saint Thomas Aquinas trust in God."

Harriet made her face as blank as her fellow sisters' faces. Clothilde beside her now burst into snivels that were at some point to be expected from that quarter. Harriet offered her the blue handkerchief, glad to be doing something until Perpetua's gaze had moved on to rake the other side of the table.

"He was such a nice young man," Clothilde whispered. "That time when my skate lace broke and he fixed it—do you know, Sister, he undid my skates, saying I hadn't done them properly, and he laced them up again after pulling up my knee socks—"

"Dear God, Sister, that's not a story to tell anyone!"

"Why not, Sister?" Clothilde's soft pink lips formed a surprised O and her eyes were as guileless as they were heavily-lashed and green.

"Shh!"

Harriet looked up to see that all were staring at her. She sensed that Perpetua had just spoken to her.

"Did you catch that, Sister Harriet?" Perpetua's tone was clipped.

"No, Reverend Mother, I'm sorry, I was comforting Clothilde."

"Inspector Moreau will be here today and he wants to speak with you, to clarify some matters."

Harriet's breakfast curdled in her stomach.

"I will now ask you to return to your rooms. You may work, you may pray. But you will not treat these events as a subject of speculation and gossip."

And so they were dismissed. Perpetua hadn't sent them back to their rooms to think. But that was what Harriet did, once the first shock wore off. Roger Pellerin! How could that possibly be? But if it had to be someone, why not Roger, who exuded danger like a musk calculated to provoke teenage hysteria. Could he have been the secret boyfriend of one of them? Of more than one of them? That she could credit. Undoubtedly. Just not that he had killed them, one or all of them, after wooing them. Perpetua hadn't said anything about the specific charges.

She remembered how Roger had helped her beyond the call of duty on that frightening night. But then, she was a mere nun, almost elderly compared to him, and perhaps she simply offered no provocation compared to the glamorous and precocious threesome. She knew nothing. Knew almost nothing about him, if she were being honest, and nothing about the dark world that had opened up before them, the world of mass killers and nylon stocking stranglers and what the common room newspapers were calling sex crimes. For what else could the deaths of the three Ls be? And yet, Roger.

And poor Florene. She now remembered how she'd told Moreau about the boys and also her encounter with the Pellerins in River Flats. The night Laurentine Artois had gone missing. Roger had been with her and Florene. Except for at least two hours, when he had gone to retrieve her car. Had he been somewhere else during that time? She'd felt an obligation to tell the police about River Flats. Had she put the detective on the scent of Roger Pellerin instead?

She'd been pacing. She sat down, made efforts to calm herself.

But she felt no better by the time she was summoned to the meeting with Moreau.

At least, Harriet thought, looking wanly across at him, I can guess what he wants to talk about.

"You're looking unwell, Sister," Moreau said gruffly. He had two uniformed officers with him this time and they were both brandishing notebooks and pencils. He filled her glass.

"We continue to receive terrible news."

"Terrible," Moreau said tolerantly, "but we're making progress."

He began with the night at River Flats. He asked her to go all the way back to when she'd left Saint Reginald's, so she was obliged to tell him about her afternoon trip to Carson Falls, the period she'd spent there with the brothers being now difficult to account for. Since she had lost her watch somewhere along the way, she wasn't much use with time. Moreau came close to badgering her: what did she mean by "perhaps two hours, or more," and at what exact time had she arrived back at Saint Reginald's? The school had been in an uproar and she could only remember looking at the clock in the Home Ec pavilion. All this was near useless. In the retelling, her whole story sounded shifty to her own ears.

He also wanted to know about the evenings when Loretta and Laura had gone missing, but here she protested she had nothing to say.

"Laura Rome would have been alone in her dorm. She had student council duties to wrap up and she didn't leave for her parents' right away. No one remembers seeing her after three pm on the day she died. Can you tell me anything about that interval, Sister?"

"I don't see how... Oh! That evening..."

"Yes?"

Harriet frowned "The last day of class. I went for a walk in the grounds after dark. Inspector, you have to understand that with girls going to and from the rink, the Home Ec pavilion, the barn, it would be normal to see people. That night, when I was on the other side of the serpentine, near that corner where the ground drops, I did see two figures..." The favourite corner to scale the wall, according to Patricia, because cars could wait in seclusion along quiet Convent Road.

"Did you *recognize* the figures, Sister?"

"You get used to seeing people and—not looking too closely." What an admission to make. She tried to recollect now. "I would say at a guess that one was male and one was female. The female figure might have had a hood up, but half the school have duffle coats with hoods. The male figure, I think male—he just looked bigger. A longish coat, longer than the girl's? I only saw outlines. We—we show more leniency after term ends. After all, the girls aren't prisoners here." She avoided his gaze.

"Anything else?"

"They might have scaled the wall. They kind of disappeared. Where else could they have gone?" Something else now came back to Harriet. "This could be my imagination, but I thought I saw a flash of something."

"Like a cigarette being lit?"

"Like light bouncing off something."

"In the dark?"

"It was dark, but sometimes you can see things anyway? The girl's coat might have been open. The flash might have been something under the coat."

"Like a dress?"

"Perhaps. Is it important?"

"Laura Rome was found in the dress she'd worn earlier that day, a sort of *lamé* number—as I understand it's called."

Moreau looked as keen as a hound on the scent. He let the silence stretch, then turned to the night, weeks before, when she had perhaps seen movement on the bridge. He sent her to the principal's office because she couldn't remember the date of her trip to Saint Angus. Clothilde, looking fascinated, pulled this up in a moment. Perpetua was keen on recording the comings and goings of her congregation.

"Why do you care about that night, Inspector?" Harriet asked.

"Gathering evidence." Moreau's tone was superior. "Three young women are gone and many nights are important for the police case."

Harriet felt a spike of raw curiosity. She nodded like an impressed simpleton, to spur him on.

"There are features common to the three deaths which will come out at trial."

She waited.

"The case is complex." His tone was dismissive and breezy. "We may be making more arrests."

Harriet somehow didn't think so. She had a hunch that Roger would be charged with everything.

"You aren't alone, Sister, in seeing suspicious movements on the grounds on the day the Rome girl died."

"It's impressive police work." She thought she might be laying it on too thick, but she hadn't.

He sat back in his chair with a satisfied smile. "The sighting of the male in the long coat is pivotal for the investigation. Others saw him too, saw the coat, a kind of Donegal ulster."

For the first time Moreau seemed conscious that he had become chatty. He made some brusque movements involving papers, and told her she would be asked to read and sign a prepared statement later.

On the way to her room, Harriet reflected that she had found out quite a lot. Laura Rome must herself have had a secret boyfriend, the one in the Donegal ulster whatever that was. And she had taken advantage of end of term to make an assignation with him. Following a passionate prelude, they'd gone up together onto the bridge, the place of necking and more, where something else had happened, a quarrel, resulting in rage, a shove. Or had it all been planned, a night of passion leading up deliberately to murder? Is that how sex maniacs did things?

Harriet wondered how the police had decided on Pellerin. They would, of course, have other information which even indiscreet Moreau wouldn't dare blab. She pictured Roger on a hot date in some kind of long coat. She could imagine his appeal to Laura's unknowable side. She supposed Roger would be equally appealing to Loretta and Laurentine, but how could he have pulled off being everyone's secret boyfriend? The three Ls would have shared confidences. And as for Roger killing them all, she couldn't fathom it. Besides which, her instinct told her that Roger wasn't a killer, at least not a sex maniac killer. Not that she knew anything about sex, let alone its dark side, which set her at odds with a good number of the grade twelves and thirteens.

In passing through the nuns' common room, she saw an early edition of the *Herald*. The headline shouted: "Bothonville Murderer of Three Teens Arrested!" She learned that Roger Thomas Pellerin, aged 21, resident of River Flats and a machine operator at the paper mill, had been charged with three counts of first-degree murder. And he languished in the city jail awaiting trial on these capital charges.

DURING THE DAYS between Christmas and New Year's, Bothonville was thrillingly alive with the story of the arrest. It was the top news item and a subject on everyone's lips. Journalists hovered at the gates to Saint Reginald's, but all they could photograph were police cars coming and going. One enterprising fellow with a telephoto lens jumped the wall behind the barn but the police soon dealt with him. In warning the sisters, Perpetua had been wise.

As per the advice of Perpetua to the hardworking teachers, Harriet had deliberately set aside her books. Time dragged. Saint Reginald's was too quiet. The shock of the arrest lessened, just as the shock of the deaths had. The library had a stash of newspaper accounts of the New York nylon killer, which left her with a bad feeling about what men got up to.

Imelda had given Harriet pills—a blister pack with "sample" written all over it—and while a little pink capsule made her sleep, it also gave her technicolor dreams. One night she dreamed she was on the bridge again. She stood on its high deck, from where she looked down on Salamander Island, a cloud-shrouded mass in an ocean of water.

Cloud also tantalizingly cloaked the bridge's crown. Her yearning dream self searched for the place where the stairway to heaven began. Another time she dreamed she was back in the multipurpose room, surrounded by bridge projects and students. The bridges had become huge and bizarre, their coiling shapes suggestive, but they were nothing compared to the girls, who'd all somehow turned feral, or like something glued together in a laboratory that hadn't turned out right. The three Ls weren't there, nor was Mr. Monserrat.

The rowdy New Year's Eve celebrations in the city mingled with a wave of social unrest, to create a busy night for the police. Harriet woke to the sound of sirens. The next day they found out mischief makers had burned down the ruined button factory outside town. The *Herald* had spectacular photos of the mill going up in flames, its hundreds of windows like raging eyes, its crown of flames towering into the night sky. The fire supplied a permitted topic of meal-time conversation for the nuns.

The first day of 1963 still saw them confined. Harriet decided she might as well get back to work. The first folder in the pile included Florene Pellerin's project proposal, and Harriet now asked herself what was happening to the poor girl. It seemed wrong to wonder about this only now, but she been so preoccupied. School reopened next week. Was she even returning?

A few girls who lived out of town had spent the break with relatives in Bothonville. Ella Burnhouse-Raquette, for instance, had told her she would be with her favourite cousins. Had Harriet assumed Florene would be taken care of by relatives? What relatives? The girl had lived precariously with a brother barely of majority age. How likely was it that she had any relatives willing to step up under the circumstances? Harriet wasn't the only person in the world with no family. For all she knew, Florene was utterly friendless. That the Pellerin name would now be pure evil to the community only made things worse. But what could or should Harriet do?

Sister Clothilde told her Perpetua had gone to the chapel.

"Well, I don't want to interrupt her prayers, but I'll go there and wait. It's quite important."

Clothilde looked sympathetic, and Harriet added, "It's just that I've been wondering about Florene Pellerin. I should have thought about this sooner but, with her brother under arrest, what's happening to her? She *is* our student."

Clothilde nodded eagerly. She placed on the desk the cat she'd been hiding on her lap.

"Reverend Mother doesn't think Lester should be in the office but he keeps following me." She leaned forward. "I know she's been concerned about Florene. I heard her talking to Chief Flynn. I didn't overhear everything, but I guess they were still looking for her."

"Looking for her? Do we know where she is?"

"Not at River Flats, anyway. Probably not." Clothilde shrugged. "I heard something about a cousin."

"I wonder whether she'll be coming back to the school."

Clothilde fondled Lester's ear. "She has to go to school somewhere. It might be better for her and for Saint Reginald's, though, if she went to another school, under another name. She could take the name of the cousin, for instance. Let's say the cousin is called Hickinbottom, she would go the public high school under the name of Florene Hickinbottom. No one would know her true identity. She'd seem a sad sort of a girl to the others, when they noticed her at all. She would do her best to be invisible, living a double life, with this dark secret that she could never shake off, that would blight her life."

"Roger Pellerin hasn't been convicted," Harriet felt obliged to remind Clothilde, although impressed by so much imagination. "Anyway, Sister, didn't you say you thought he was a nice young man, because of the way he laced up your skates?"

Irony was lost on Clothilde. "A very nice young man." She had the grace to drop her gaze. "But, Sister, we never really know."

The chapel doors were ajar. Perpetua knelt in an attitude of prayer, and Harriet resolved to wait. She sat down in the hallway, at first thinking she'd say a decade of her rosary for old time's sake and then deciding against it as Perpetua would hear the click of the beads.

A minute passed. Harriet became aware of a sound from the chapel, repetitive, awful even before she recognized it. Tears. She peeked in again. The chapel was in shadow, but she could make out Perpetua's head sunk down on the communion rail, shoulders shaking.

Harriet was horrified. Mother Perpetua weeping. Who had ever seen this—or wanted to? Perpetua, their rock and foundation, would have wanted it least of all. Harriet felt a painful urge to comfort the other woman, but it just wasn't possible. Nor was this a time to place one more burden on her superior's shoulders. She must leave Perpetua to her tears.

The day wore on and she went by the principal's office, only to be told that the mother superior wasn't well and was lying down. Perpetua didn't attend supper. Harriet would have to sort this out on her own.

HARRIET HAD DOUBTS about what she was about to undertake, but the arrival of the fire department early the next day for a timely inspection—they were going to have a couple of overdue fire drills once the girls were back—seemed to her a propitious sign. Perpetua assembled a band of nuns to do a walkabout with the inspectors, but some of the nuns were in the middle of things and so others were substituted. The resulting mild bedlam, making her absence easier to miss, smiled on her endeavour.

The keys to the senior girls' dorms were simple to extract from the office, with only Lester to witness the act. The fire team had moved on to another part of the school by the time Harriet let herself into Laura Rome's old room. Each boarder had an alcove of her own, with a bed, a closet and a desk. It wasn't hard to find Laura's cubicle, the attractive clothes set it apart.

Harriet felt odd, going through the dead girl's effects, but how else could she leave the school grounds without being noticed by the reporters still camped out front? Things were being boxed up for the Rome family to pick up, and someone was coming tomorrow. Harriet could have borrowed some other girl's clothes. But with the first students coming back at the end of the week, that could lead to complications. A little voice told her she would hang onto what she borrowed today.

Trying on Laura's clothes felt even odder. She ignored the dress up clothes and uniform, the latter somehow hardest to look at. She wanted casual and warm. She settled on a woolen turtleneck and corduroy pants that she only had to roll up a little at the ankles. She grabbed a shoulder bag as an afterthought. She burrowed through the boxes before she found an oversized pompom beret she could pull down over her face, and an insulated pea jacket. The whole thing worked. The hat hid her no-style choppy hair, and with a scarf to cover her lower face, she was unrecognizable. A boyish young woman in a modish getup stared back at her in the mirror. She swung by her room to pick up the Marimekko bag—better than Laura's purse—and slipped out the back exit.

She scaled the wall behind the barn where the trespassing journalist had entered. When she emerged in full view of the news teams out front her heart was thumping. She got a glance or two, but there was nothing to interest them in this young woman with a tote, probably a Vivamus coed, crossing the intersection.

Harriet was practically giddy with success when she got the same reaction on the half-filled bus: casual glances, but so different from the furtive no-look looks that greeted her as a nun. She'd never ridden a Bothonville bus before and she enjoyed the passing scene in the sunshine. She knew where to transfer for the bus to Turpentine Flats.

It had occurred to her that Florene must be there, if she was anywhere. The shanty towns had an on-again off-again, but mostly off-again, relationship to civilization and officialdom, for everything from taxes to electricity supply. The police had known to go to the River Flats address. Roger had been described as a resident of River Flats. Did anyone even know about the existence of a second cabin at Turpentine Flats? If Florene was missing, and not in the hands of welfare authorities or the supposed cousin, it was possible she was there.

The second bus let her off at the mouth of Factory Alley. The walk through towering grey walls and belching stacks was eerie, and she almost lost her way when she was once again crossing the frozen fields. *I'm always here, always doing this.* A peculiar thought, perhaps not even true, and yet it felt true. Her booted feet balancing on the snow-crusted ridges, the fence of trees rising up on the horizon. Surely she'd done this before.

She plunged into the twilit world under the canopy. She remembered the footpaths leading to the Sherwoods' place. She knocked on the sagging door. The weasel-faced boy gave her a shock when he suddenly wrenched open the door. She didn't introduce herself. What could she say? "You won't recognize me but I am one of the sisters who visited?" Confidence was the key.

"I'm looking for Florene Pellerin." No reaction. She gestured to her bag. "I've brought her some things." The boy's eyes dropped to the bulging bag, back up to Harriet's face. He frowned, as if something nagged at him but he couldn't think what.

"Things she needs." Harriet hefted the Marimekko. "I know she's being helped by neighbours, but you can't do it all by yourselves."

The hostility lessened. He looked behind him into the house, made up his mind. He grabbed a coat and stepped outside.

"I'll take you." He gave her a shove along the path.

He was bigger than he'd seemed before, and she didn't much care for walking ahead of him through the semi-darkness. The back of her neck and the space between her shoulder blades tingled. He occasionally called out "left" or "right." The place was big, it went on and on. Cabins and huts crouched amid the roots of great trees in a way that made River Flats look positively suburban. She became disoriented. It grew darker, as if evening could decide to come whenever it felt like it in this alternate world.

When he told her to stop, she didn't see the dwelling at first, for the rudimentary door was half-concealed down a tunnel of vines. She could just see the shape of a structure behind it, camouflaged by trunks and shrubbery. She wouldn't have thought anyone lived there.

"Is this where she lives?" But Harriet spoke to herself.

She knocked. Presently she heard slight noises. There were cracks in the wood and she tried to look benign. The door opened, and Florene appeared.

"I'd know you anywhere, Sister."

## 17: 1963

"ROGER IS INNOCENT," said Florene, once they were seated in what Harriet supposed was the living room. She had expected these words, and had other things to say first.

"Are you living here alone, Florene?"

"For now. When I'm back at Saint Reginald's I will tell everyone I'm staying with a cousin. I do have a distant cousin, but I won't really stay with him. He's a creep. I have other plans."

Florene's composure was unexpected. She seemed to have done some growing up in a hurry.

The living room was basic, but a step up from River Flats. It was reasonably well furnished and had a glowing woodstove. There seemed to be other rooms in the back. Harriet saw an oil lamp on a table, with Florene's homework beside it. All of sudden the idea that Florene would not return to Saint Reginald's seemed absurd. The school existed for the likes of Florene.

Harriet emptied the totebag of its contents. "Sister Edwina is always giving me food so here are cookies, other stuff. Some things from your desk. I had the idea you'd like to get ahead with your schoolwork." An eager nod. "I didn't know what you needed, so here's something else." She handed Florene four five-dollar bills. During term Harriet had written to a teacher, an old friend, for some curriculum materials. Eleanor, who'd been a postulant with Harriet but had returned to secular life, had sent the twenty dollars in an envelope tucked into the worksheets. Eleanor knew Harriet wasn't supposed to have money other than approved by Perpetua, but had ideas of her own about the rule.

"Oh, Sister, that's kind! I don't need a lot of cash but there's bus fare…"

Harriet felt she should be directing this conversation better. "Can you tell me, Florene, about those plans of yours? No one lets a thirteen-year-old live alone. I heard at the office they were looking for you."

"I know. Don't worry, Sister. I won't be staying with the cousin, but Ella says I can stay with her uncle and aunt in the city. The aunt already called the school."

"Ella Burnhouse-Raquette?" Harriet didn't realize the girls knew each other. This sounded like quite a good plan. Had she been worrying for nothing?

"Ella's aunt just said she was my cousin, so it was simple."

Florene smiled. "Please don't worry. Also, I won't actually be staying with them, the Raquettes, hardly. It's easier for me here, the buses are better. I like the people, they're our friends. We have that place in River Flats because Roger works extra hours on the bridge. Turpentine Flats has always been our home."

Harriet looked around. She saw dishes on an old painted sideboard, paperbacks on a shelf, a basket of apples, a rag rug by the door. The place looked like home. A home the police didn't know about.

"I can't argue with that, but, Florene, if this arrangement stops working, if you need something, I want you to tell me, or someone. Will you promise me? I can come here. Now that I've disguised myself once, I guess I can do it again." She cleared her throat. "Everyone at Saint Reginald's wishes you well." She wasn't really sure it was true. There would be those for whom Roger's arrest was all they needed to know. If not ready to blame the girl, they would still hold it against her that she had brought him into contact with Saint Reginald's precious student body.

"Lots of people will hate me." Florene looked at her hands, no longer confident. "But nobody knows Roger better than me. You think I'm just a kid, you think the police have a good reason for arresting him. I don't know what you think. Why is there so much miscarriage of justice in the world?"

"I'm sorry, Florene."

The girl crossed to the desk and brought back her Hilroy notebook and a library book.

"These are my history notes. Do you know how many similarities there are between that case and my brother's? Ethel Gleason was the daughter of the mayor, who was also rich. Yves Martin was white trash. She was beautiful. Kind of wild. He was even wilder. She went to bush parties. People connected their names. But she knew other men too. The men used to fight over the women at the parties, there was a knifing. Rich kids mixing with poor kids, anything could happen. Someone said they saw Yves driving away from the place where they found Ethel's body. I'm reading an account of the trial now. Just one witness."

She leafed through the book. "There was another man, I guess he looked like Yves, tall, blond. It could have been *him* behind the wheel of the car, his car was black too. Ethel had given him the shove. Everyone in town who counted hated the Martins, they had a history with the police. Everyone *wanted* Yves to be the killer."

"That's interesting, Florene, but—"

"History repeats itself."

Harriet needed to stop this. She herself was now noticing the similarities between the two cases, but this soap opera Florene was spinning seemed unhealthy. She didn't want to say the police sometimes knew what they were doing.

"Does your brother have a lawyer? You can't go investigating on your own. It would be dangerous."

Florene looked mutinous but said, "Yes, he has a lawyer. Ella's uncle found someone. He's supposed to be good."

Once again Harriet felt surprise at the support coming from that quarter, although obviously glad.

"I should go," she said, but didn't move.

"Sister Harriet...I wanted to say how sorry I am about Laura Rome and the others, Loretta and Laurentine. Not just sad. Terrible. What could have happened? Who could have hated them so much?" Now Florene was looking like a child again, her eyes bright with alarm. "Those are Laura Rome's clothes, aren't they?" She spoke without emotion.

Harriet had to explain. "I hope—it may seem irreverent to you, Florene, but this was the only way to leave the school undetected." She looked at the pea coat she still had on because the cabin was chilly. "The jacket is new, it's hard to think Laura will never wear it. Her school blouses were still hanging in the closet. One looked new. It's hard to think Laura won't wear that new blouse, and will never remember when she wore the old ones. It's hard to think there's just—no one there anymore." She couldn't go on.

"Oh, Sister," Florene cried, "I'm sure Laura wants you to wear her clothes, she will love thinking of you jumping the wall like a senior!" And she sat beside Harriet, anxious to console. "I saw your face though the crack, I recognized you. But your disguise is marvellous; you look like another person entirely. It must have been fun to ride on the bus like anyone."

Harriet wiped her eyes. "It was nerve-racking."

They heard a muffled thump at the door. Harriet stood up in alarm.

"It might be Ella," Florene said.

"Ella? I have to get out of here." Harriet affixed her eye to the crack. There, startlingly close, hovered the face of Ella Burnhouse-Raquette in all its fine and sardonic lines, sly, dogged and impassive; and now, with no awareness of being watched, careworn.

"Out the back," whispered Florene, shepherding her through the passage. Another low door appeared.

"The bag!"

Florene retrieved the Marimekko bag and shoved it into Harriet's hand. "This path is simpler, take every left. Peter just led you in a roundabout way. Sister, thank you for coming!"

Harriet didn't calm down until she was half way back to Saint Reginald's. Seeing Florene had to some extent lifted a weight. It had felt good to give her the money too. She wished she had caught herself when she spoke of Laura Rome—not as the newest of heavenly princesses on a fleecy throne but as an absence, an immaterial memory dissipating into an empty universe. Florene hadn't seemed to pick up on it though. Harriet found it worrying to hear the stories she was spinning to herself about Roger. The stories meant everything to Florene, they were the scaffold of her life now.

DURING THE REST of that week Perpetua held meetings to discuss the new term. Her fighting spirit was a thing to marvel at. The school community would mourn but they still had their responsibility to the other girls. There were new security measures at Saint Reginald's, and leaving the school grounds after dark was now a grave offense. A dozen girls had been taken out of school, but time and the school's excellent reputation would replace these numbers. Saint Reginald's mission was being tested but they would emerge stronger. As for Florene, she continued to be a respected member of the school. Perpetua provided exact instructions regarding what the teachers were to say in their homerooms.

Harriet was not so lost in admiration that she couldn't hear the occasional undertone of baloney, as when Perpetua volunteered the moral benefits of the refiner's fire to put a better construction on their current ordeal. hat else could the woman do? She had a school to run. She wisely relied on fear. Harriet felt a frisson each time Perpetua said "there will be consequences."

After the staff meeting Harriet met with Mr. Montserrat to discuss the way they would run the rest of the bridge project, now well advanced. They were in agreement. Another of Harriet's science seniors would replace Laura Rome. She and Montserrat would pitch in. The goal was to hurry things along, hold the contest, proclaim a winner and then walk away from the project for good. Hardly another school project bore so clearly the imprint of the three Ls, and the sooner it came to a conclusion the better.

Montserrat looked changed, to Harriet. Well, everyone looked changed. In Montserrat's case, however, it wasn't like before Christmas, when strain had been visible. He seemed a different person. Older. And without the sparkle, uninclined to flirt.

Harriet sometimes imagined she was interacting with a shadowy duplicate of Mr. Montserrat. If there had been a deceptiveness before, it had been smart and playful and not too hard to parse. This new Mr. Montserrat went through the motions, but he seemed to have hidden himself away. Then again, the truth might be simpler. Charming Mr. Montserrat wasn't deploying his charm in her direction anymore, and it was like looking at a house in darkness with all the lights on, but which you knew had been abandoned. And this was the man who had kissed her on the rink. There was no accounting for men.

He was fed up with the bridge project, that much was clear: just as fed up as she was. They were of one mind there. She felt herself almost nostalgic for the old Mr. Montserrat, as if she had lost a friend, although perhaps only an imaginary one. But the day to day, she had to admit, was fine with the new facsimile.

Monday arrived, and the school came back to life once more with the chaos of girls, with further distraction provided by a major snowfall. The rest of the week was a race, and by Friday everyone had found their rhythm again. The police attended a special assembly. This seemed to invigorate the girls, reassuring those in need and entertaining all. There would be a memorial service in the spring for the three Ls, when everything felt less raw. Positively brutal amounts of homework would keep everyone occupied in the interim.

Harriet kept an eye on Florene. She was glad to see that the other grade nines were kinder than she'd expected, after a frozen day or two. The girl carried herself with an impressive dignity. Ella spoke with her, sometimes sat with her, in front of the others. Ella had a quirky status of her own, and Harriet could see the students taking this in, adjusting their attitude. Things that to Harriet had seemed impossible a week before seemed possible again.

THE BOTHONVILLE International Bridge had now become a thing to see.

At first, it was just the people from up and down the river who came to gape at its soaring skyward mass and its enormous swerve downriver to where, well beyond view from the shore, it would join Salamander Island. Among the gawkers there were presumably envious Carson Falls residents, for Carson Falls's bridge remained an uninspiring thing. As the Bothonville Bridge's fame spread, pilgrims from further afield came to goggle, standing in groups and even small crowds on promontories where the perspective was unimpeded. On some days, from favoured places on the shore, the gothic superstructure became visible. It was a thing of beauty when it appeared, conveying that sense of looming close and yet being far away that was a unique effect of Bothonville's distance-bending atmosphere. To Harriet, it resembled one of those vertigo-inducing cloud pictures that became many things the longer you stared.

The bridge would put Bothonville on the map. Surely the biggest bridge ever built, everyone said, a wonder of the world. The city proclaimed triumphantly that they were right on target, despite ongoing civic unrest, for a June completion.

JUST AS WELL, perhaps, that Bothonville had this to be proud of, for the city woke up one morning to the news blaring from every source that Roger Pellerin had escaped from jail in the night. A giant manhunt was already underway, involving numerous police forces, and the citizens were assured that he would be captured without delay. And yet, as the days slipped by and one of the harshest winters in memory set in, the hunt produced nothing. Roger Pellerin, presumed mass murderer, remained on the lam. After forty-eight hours of panic, Bothonville calmed down with almost unseemly promptness. If he was smart enough to make a jail break, the reasoning went, he'd be smart enough not to stick around. He might be Carson Falls's problem by now, or Montreal's. He might even have crossed the river in a boat, possibly the best outcome of all.

Saint Reginald's students stared at Florene for a few days, but then got tired of this in the preparations for the Saint Valentine's pageant. Florene's newly-adopted stoical demeanour continued to serve her well. The police came once more to the school and brusquely questioned Florene. What the girl thought of her brother's escape she shared with no one, but Harriet could imagine relief. She herself felt relief, mixed with other things.

Florene had her share of struggles, apart from this. The bitter cold made the Turpentine Flats cabin practically unliveable on some nights. And yet, according to Ella, she resisted packing up and going to the Raquettes. A scholarship girl like Florene, Ella had been a boarder before Christmas but now lived with her relatives in town—a concession to the troubled circumstances. Her presence there should have been an inducement to Florene. For three days the thermometer dropped to thirty-two below, and Florene spent those nights with Ella's people, but moved out again promptly despite pleadings and advice.

"Everyone is happy to have her at the house," Ella told Sister Harriet, "but we couldn't get her to stay."

Harriet and Ella regularly had such semi-conspiratorial chats nowadays and, although Harriet never sensed she got to know the real Ella, they had developed a kind of companionship. Ella had thawed to her, partly thawed.

Harriet hadn't resorted to her disguise a second time. She found it easiest, with all the new security and rules, to employ Ella as go-between. Saint Reginald's participated in a diocesan emergency clothing drive, for it was a winter of unprecedented want in some quarters. Harriet, heavily involved in the drive, had been able to set aside blankets that she bundled up, along with the few dollars she could spare from her monthly allowance, to hand over when the uncle came to pick up Ella in his car.

The Turpentine Flats cabin was still a grim place for a thirteen-year-old to spend winter evenings alone. Florene herself admitted she and Roger had spent the worst of other winters at the River Flats place, smaller but closer to town. Harriet had tried to ferret out a snug and secret spot somewhere in the school where Florene could spend the hours after classes, at least to do her homework, before taking a later bus home to the Flats. Although the school was large, with many wings, nooks and crannies, this proved to be impossible. She'd even wondered whether Florene could hole up in the home ec pavilion, but the boarders were always over there working on various projects.

Finally, on a day when Florene showed her her chilblains, something Harriet thought she would never see on an actual person, she thought of the barn. The barn offered more than the cabin in the forest. After the school had stopped using it as a covered rink in winter, the nuns had winterized the building. Then, while repairing it following August's fire, they had replaced doors and put in double-glazing. It was now a dual-purpose space, offering indoor amenities. Although without electricity—next year's project—a big new wood stove in the corner provided heat. Harriet found it easy to set up a workspace for Florene. Best of all, she was able to check on Florene during the long evenings. There arrangement was highly irregular, and she felt chronically in over her head. Perhaps next year Florene's scholarship could be modified and she would be a twelve-month boarder, the way Harriet had been at Iona Prep.

Patricia found out about Harriet's nightly sorties before long, often with a steaming mug of something, in the direction of the barn.

"Smoke above the trees, but of course I was looking and most wouldn't. I put two and two together. I can see why you're doing this, Sister, indeed I can. No, don't feel you owe me explanations.

isten, the girl must be eating rubbish. Pure rubbish. We've got our kitchenette."

After that, Florene began to eat good suppers. Entering into the spirit of the thing, Patricia filched excellent leftovers from the kitchen, which they reheated in the kitchenette and brought to the barn when the coast was clear. Some evenings, the two nuns would stay to chat with Florene, trim the lamp and see that all was well.

"The whole plan is mad, if you want to look at it that way, but what else can we do? It's a mad world, Sister."

As always, Patricia summed things up well.

## 18: Outer Space

THE RITUALIZED WORLD of Saint Reginald's was a very complete one, and by now Harriet had become used to the way it could push away the bigger world. The Saint Valentine's pageant was no less the highlight of this February than any other, along with a one-day winter Carnival on the Saturday after the 14th. The seniors had their own quasi-Masonic rites of passage, in which Harriet was minimally involved except for the preparatory masses and a forthcoming weekend religious retreat to Carson Falls; but the excitement in her senior classes was palpable.

Loretta, Laurentine and Laura were not forgotten. There would be a special mass and remembrance ceremony for them at the grotto, scheduled for lilac time. The whole school seemed to be involved in the planning of this and Bishop Aloysius himself would celebrate the outdoor mass. The girls would wear simple white dresses they would make themselves in Home Ec. It would be unfair to say that the sewing of these dresses, and deliberations related to accessories, preoccupied the girls more than the spiritual aspects. But, undoubtedly, discussions of the respective merits of *peau de soie,* layered muslin and linen-slub synthetics had a soothing effect. The school's collective grief had entered a new phase. The dead girls were often spoken of, but increasingly in nostalgic terms. Any flaws were forgotten. Only the ideal remained.

The atmosphere in the bridge project sessions had improved. The absence of the three Ls allowed Harriet to notice other girls for the first time, girls less perfect than the three Ls but still worthy of support. Everyone had been so sure that the dead girls would lead brilliant lives, their future educational achievements, their careers and marriages, their exquisite children, all bound to occupy a higher plane. But no one really knew the future. And dumpy Hilda here and persevering Sandra there might as easily seize the torch of life and run victorious with it.

It was soothing to think of the three Ls and their imaginary perfect lives, of course. It was far more comfortable than suspecting their own mistakes had killed them.

On the weekend when the seniors and accompanying nuns were in Carson Falls, Harriet received dispensation to meet with Brother Cyprian. The meetings of the Bridge Design Committee continued, and Harriet had not gotten around to pitching her resignation to anyone yet. She had come to realize her opportunities to leave school grounds would shrink to nothing without them, given the new climate of heightened security.

When Cyprian had contacted her at the school to say he had more materials to hand over, she realized she was curious to meet up with him again. She presented herself as before at the brothers' wing of Saint Mark's. Determined this time not to find herself a semi-willing guest at a brothers' jamboree, she'd invited him to lunch at a previously-scouted corner restaurant so mundane and out of the way it would surely be proof against gossip.

Cyprian's appearance astonished Harriet. His sandy hair had grown out—he had acquired an accompanying hand gesture to toss it off his forehead—and there was no sign of his *soutane*. He wore a casual suit over a striped T-shirt. His manner was just as la-dee-da as before. He handed her a slim envelope.

"Notes from a meeting between Carsonites for a Better Tomorrow and some Salamander underlings." He shrugged, smiled his characteristic off-beat smile. "Nothing much probably. But passing notes is what I signed on for." His gaze emptied. "My condolences for what you're going through at Saint Reginald's. We've had our share of tragedies. In 1899, a bobsled carrying Saint Mark's boys fell through the ice on the river. Six dead. The bodies were only recovered in the spring." Despite the solemn expression, Harriet had the usual trouble deciphering the tone.

"It's good to see you again, Sister." He took a look at her across the small and none too clean table at Joe's Corner Lunch. Joe or a delegate had just deposited their hamburgers in front of them, with a Seven-Up for Harriet, a beer for Cyprian. "I wanted to see you again, this way I didn't even need an excuse. I see you're frowning at my garb."

Remembering her recent disguise, Harriet said apologetically, "Oh well, I just wondered if there was a reason. I mean, are you engaged in work off site?"

"We do a lot of work in the town. Did you know the diocese is opening a big homeless shelter? We'll be renovating that closed down orphanage where I think you lot are having your retreat, a wing for women and children, a new kitchen and cafeteria. Deluxe, all mod cons." He took a thirsty swallow of beer. "Did you think we were just lining our pockets?"

"I still don't know why you're dressed like a beatnik."

"It's not against the rules—technically. The world is changing and we have to change with it, Sister. One day, who knows, you yourself might give up that little black dress of yours. Although it's more flattering than the old habit, I'll say that, and gives me a peek of your neck and stockings."

Harriet couldn't be bothered to take offense. "You're out of date. Stockings are square. We're now allowed to wear tights. But the Sisters of Saint Jolene in San Francisco got rid of their habits last week. Skirts and cardigans, any blouse they feel like. No veil. They had a picture in the paper. Strangely boring."

"I could see you in cords and a turtleneck." Harriet couldn't prevent a blush. "I'm right, I see."

Cyprian ordered another beer and emptied half of it into Harriet's glass despite her protests. "No one can tell what you're drinking in that green glass and they're not expecting you back any time soon, give yourself a break," he urged.

There were three hours of small group discussions planned for the afternoon, on topics such as "Tuned In to the Holy Spirit," "Sacrificial Love," "Jesus and the Pure Heart" and, eagerly awaited by the seniors in a spirit of derision, "Going All the Way with God." No, Harriet didn't want to return to Saint Hilda's a minute sooner than necessary.

Joe's Corner Lunch proved an odd place, grafted onto old row housing in an odd part of town. The lunch rush, such as it had been, was over and a new clientele drifted in, many of them dressed like Cyprian. "Joe" pulled down the green shades, creating an evocative penumbra, and yelled that the kitchen would close in ten. Brown bottles appeared on the tables.

"This place turns into a midafternoon speakeasy," Harriet said.

"I thought this was why you picked it."

"I saw an ad in the *Herald*. It said 'Try our all-Canadian lunch.'" She looked at the other tables. Not only did she see no one whose opinion she needed to worry about, she sensed they might as well be invisible to the other patrons. "That has to be the last." Cyprian had just finished pouring her another half beer.

He nodded noncommittally. "What difference does it make, Sister?"

His gold-flecked eyes, staring into hers, were a very dark blue. Harriet, who, like all sisters, had been invited to think about lust during her novitiate, the better to repress it, now realized with slight surprise it could take you different ways. For example, her attraction to Mr. Montserrat, as unambiguous as Montserrat's unambiguous charm, could wane surprisingly when he dialed down the flirtation; whereas Cyprian, certainly not the kind of man Harriet would have gone after in secular life, now seemed to her, in the half-light, to be aureoled in attractiveness. His eyes could be so remote, so interstellar, but now they were promising magic carpet rides to those same corners of the universe.

"What are you thinking of?" she said.

"That's for me to know and you to find out."

They might have been sixteen.

"I wonder if we'll get out of this alive," Cyprian now mused, without apparent distress. "I visited Bothonville last weekend. I would have contacted you, but what good would it have done? I knew you were coming, anyway. I saw your bridge. Very impressive. You win. I surrender."

She surrendered too. She told him the most uncensored version of the Committee of Dark Designs she had ever shared with a soul. She even imitated some of the participants. "I thought at first it was a good committee. And I even thought that Bishop Aloysius's quest was a good one. I guess you either believe everything or you believe nothing. It unravels, that way. The bishop seems a very holy man. He has a way of making you agree with his enthusiasm, but it just doesn't last."

She wondered as she spoke whether she might be grossly overstating all this. Cities all over the world were built by people like those on the committee. Gothic architecture had always been more than a way to hold up a roof. And if everything had fully unraveled, how had her prayers at Sunday mass been so agonizingly fervent when the souls of the departed girls had been mentioned?

"It unravels," he repeated. He took her hand, not especially libidinously. Something very like sympathy, only not quite, appeared in his eyes. "When did it start to unravel for you, Sister?"

"I can only tell you that this year at Saint Reginald's has been very bad, that way. Seeing the youngest girls, their faith is so simple... realizing you haven't felt that way in a long time? Coming back here, where I used to live when I was like that myself, hasn't helped. But I think the deaths of those girls was the worst. To think there are people, supposedly made in the image of God, who would push three girls off a bridge. There's no way to *explain* that..."

"They arrested someone."

"I don't mean that, Brother. No explanation will ever be good enough to explain that. It's been so—"

"Hellish. But what's death, after all? Just extinction." Portentous words, yet he looked as flippant as ever.

The beer was having a hypnotic effect on Harriet. More brown bottles had found their way to their table.

Softly, a drum began to beat. She looked around. On a small dais, a bearded man had begun to play hand drums.

"Bongos," Cyprian said appreciatively. The drummer kept the beat low and slow, and then began to intone. She could only catch fragments—"by this teaching the earth came to an end" and something about "human bones" and "vain lines" and the "whole universe" being a "mold of stars."

To Harriet, who had no head for booze and had now arrived at the everything is magical phase, the words and rhythm spread like lava through her being. The chanting seemed to affect Cyprian too. He took her hand once more, squeezed it to the point of pain, and said cajolingly, "I'd like to crush your illusions."

His eyes had become impossibly beautiful, a dark swallowing blue, and the flecks made Harriet think of swirling galaxies, although it was in fact her head that was going in circles. A small part of her brain hectored her that Cyprian lacked proper feelings. But she settled back in her chair, now as comfortable as a mattress, and looked up at the ceiling, only it wasn't the ceiling, it was the deep vault of the sky, and no, she wasn't looking, she was travelling into it, into the airless interstellar void. Stars and whole galaxies flew by and the chair became like pillows, that were hardly needed since she seemed weightless, without worry, entertained and novocained from head to toe, perhaps except for her finger bones, which Cyprian still gripped. Light years passed and still Harriet flew and rhythmically floated through the universe, aware that a revelation was at hand. And when it came—it was that Cyprian could be a jerk—it came with a sense, out there on the remote edge of the universe, of roiling unease, unease that came closer, until she realized it was her stomach.

She just made it to the bathroom in time. More light years passed and her nausea was so thorough she eventually returned without swaying to their table. Cyprian had the grace to look contrite. He'd ordered coffee and mineral water and pressed these on her.

"We should wait, before you go back to Saint Hilda's." He sounded rueful. "You look better, but just in case. Your pal Joe said you should eat some of these." He handed her a two-pack of saltines. She nibbled suspiciously, but Joe knew a thing or two and she reached for more.

"I'm not a drinker," she confessed.

"No kidding." Cyprian patted her hand. His face bore a worried expression and he was looking much more human now. "When you get back to the retreat, you should just plead a headache and go to bed. You won't really be over this until tomorrow. Trust me, I know. A night's sleep will make all the difference."

A few coffees and much bongo lament later, they were able to leave the restaurant.

"Thank God I don't have to listen to those bongos anymore," Harriet said.

Cyprian flagged down a cab at a busy corner and escorted her back to the retreat house. "You still smell a trifle—ah—beery, Sister, if I were you I'd go straight to my room. Here, take my Dentyne, chew assiduously. Wait, you're forgetting your spy papers, the whole purpose of your afternoon out. I do apologize, Harriet—may I call you that?—my mother would be disgusted with me for leading you astray, but I've tried to make it up to you."

"Good bye, Brother."

The vivid picture she formed of him as she said goodbye, slouchy in his beatnik getup, the eyes knowing and almost bleak, stayed with her afterwards, even when she saw him again, much later, under dramatically changed circumstances.

She went to her room without meeting anyone. She was lying down when there was a knock at the door.

"You're unusually fortunate, I'll say that." Patricia didn't seem to need an explanation. "I'll tell them below at supper that you have a migraine. I'll find you some ginger ale." She sat on the window ledge.

"How did the group sessions go?" Harriet asked weakly.

"Oh, they went swimmingly. It was purely the luck of the draw that it was that young bashful Father Rivard, I don't know if you know him, leading the "Going All the Way with God" session. The seniors got their money's worth. The only fly in the ointment was that half a dozen girls played hookie. That many, Perpetua couldn't overlook."

"What happened?"

Patricia smiled appreciatively. "She sent Sister Sophia, and now you know why Sophia is along for this ride, after them. They were discovered in the downtown Woolworths buying make-up. It wasn't even that they went. They made it so obvious. Six of them, in uniform. They are in there now, with Sophia and Perpetua and they even brought in the security guard, Trevor, or is he a custodian, anyway he has a uniform and they should have signed out with him. That's what I mean about you being lucky, Sister. Perpetua has no time for you tonight. There'll be an emergency meeting in ten minutes with a stiff lecture on Catholic responsibility, and if we hadn't already paid for the rice pudding she'd be docking dessert."

Harriet smiled wanly. "We have a Woolworths in Bothonville."

"Oh yes, Sister, but I don't have to tell you what girls are like. They were hoping for some new shade of eye shadow maybe, Carson Falls blue. Well, I'd better go, don't want to miss Reverend Mother at her best. You'll be all right for an hour or two? I'll leave the door off the latch in case you're sleeping."

When Harriet woke up it was dawn, and two bottles of ginger ale stood on her bedside table. Despite a headache, she threw herself penitently into retreat activities all day, with such zeal that Perpetua and several sisters complimented her. This only increased her remorse. There seemed no end to her double life.

## 19: Fire

LATE WINTER CRAWLED. Harriet was summoned to Saint Angus. This time, Perpetua had some business with the bishop as well, and Harriet had the novel experience of a road trip with her mother superior. Perpetua veered to the topic of Vatican II, which took them safely to their destination while Harriet drove, minding her manners. At the palace they separated, and Sister Grace took Harriet once again to the room with the fireplace.

There wasn't anything to tell Aloysius that couldn't be said over the phone. She realized when she was there that she had mythologized her previous visit on that stormy night. Now he seemed tired and distracted, although eager for news of the gothic crown. Since she hadn't had but the one glimpse, when it had looked suspiciously like a cloud formation, her account relied on imagination.

She had been summoned to receive thanks, she decided eventually. He made one or two conversational side trips down doctrinal byways. He got her to agree tiredly to the controversial existence of an intermediate state between life and death, only to unsettle her by crying out, "But what about Eusebius?"

She would have liked to talk to him about the dead girls, and the crisis of faith she could now conveniently say had been thereby triggered. But she sensed the bishop would offer her little, and bringing up the killings might only cause him needless sorrow. He did seem frail today. His gaze was withdrawn and dim. Harriet saw this with fear. He was, she realized, dear to her.

"His Excellency seemed under the weather," she cautiously said on the way back. Perpetua didn't immediately reply. She had been discussing money, and was not in the best of moods.

"Bishop Aloysius is only eight-one," she said. "Mind the lane change, Sister. Signal. *Signal.*"

Only eight-one? A good way to look at the world, unless it exemplified everything that was wrong with the Church in 1963. Harriet suppressed a sigh, perhaps not well.

"Let's stop here. You are driving so decorously, Sister"—a note of irony?—"we'll have missed lunch."

Harriet was surprised to see that Perpetua pointing to the Dominion Family Restaurant, an old stalwart on the station road. It had provided predictable food to three generations of Bothonville.

Taking Perpetua's lead, Harriet ordered a sandwich but Perpetua was having none of it. "You need building up, Sister," she said. She half-bullied Harriet into getting the meatloaf platter, that looked like it would feed a pair of lumberjacks. And when she ordered them coffees, Perpetua insisted Harriet get pie. They had to box it.

"Thank you, Reverend Mother," Harriet said in the parking lot.

"I don't think I've eaten so well since Christmas. I'm grading all afternoon, the pie will give me energy."

Perpetua's smile was short and business-like, although warm for her. "Just don't fall asleep over your copy books." That was as warm as Perpetua got.

Harriet did fall asleep over her exercises, which backed up her schedule for the week. A girl burned herself in science class, requiring a trip to Hotel Dieu. She herself fell on the rink and managed to cut her lip. Montserrat, who had seemed to her to be rallying, took a day off for a "personal emergency" and she had to deal alone with a squabble among the bridge builders, a squabble so bitter and byzantine it reminded her of the days when the three Ls had spread their iffy magic about the room. Florene had played a role, and Harriet wished everyone would apply the brakes to their enthusiasm and just get on with things. Florene still did her homework in the barn on weeknights and, while it wasn't onerous to help the poor child, it was one more burden.

The Saint Valentine's pageant arrived, a student-produced event ostensibly about Christian *caritas,* which the girls had infused with increasingly shady humour in a licensed outbreak of spring fever. As she watched them carry on in red and pink crepe paper outfits, celebrating chocolate and boyfriends past, present and imaginary, Harriet felt like a crow, and not only a crow but an old unloved crow. Had the finger-squeezing Cyprian been there that evening, when the nuns on her floor got together with their own chocolate for records and reminiscences of former boyfriends, to which Harriet had nothing to contribute, who knew what might have happened? Nothing would have happened. As for warm-lipped Mr. Montserrat, just come back from a restorative weekend in Montreal, where he'd bought himself impressive new duds which had been that week a wonder to behold, nothing would have happened there either.

The get-together in Patricia's room soon broke up, and Harriet still had to pay a visit to the barn. Patricia was tidying, and Harriet told her not to worry about Florene. Still feeling a bit put out by celibacy, she didn't rush to make the cup of cocoa she usually brought.

Harriet opened a copy book on her desk. In no time she fell asleep. In the middle of a dream in which she was looking for her childhood cat Henry, something wakened her. It had seemed like a bang, or a knock on the door. But the corridor was empty. Had it been part of the dream? She thought it might have come from Patricia's room, but she could hear nothing through the door. Yet she had heard something. Without knowing why, she was afraid.

She hadn't gone to see Florene. Surely the girl would have caught her bus by now. Still, she would go. She grabbed her cape and slipped out the side door. It was a calm winter night, under a mist-shrouded moon. Harriet began to run towards the barn.

The peaceful scene beckoned, the Home Ec pavilion to her left shrouded in darkness, the door of the barn beyond slightly ajar and emitting a flickering light. Flickering? In the doorway, Harriet froze.

The scene before her eyes made no sense. Tentacles of flame danced in several directions—one towards a stack of hay bales, another towards the woodstove with its pile of logs. And framed in the fiery ring, the table, the knocked over oil lamp, Florene's papers beginning to ignite, and Florene herself, asleep or unconcious.

"Florene!" The girl lifted her head sleepily, her expression dissolving when she saw the flames.

Harriet leapt into the circle, grabbed the girl by the arm and dragged her away. "Get outside!" She gave Florene a hard push. Too late to summon help. She wrenched off her cape and began to beat out the flames. Florene had disobeyed, and stomped on the line of flame moving towards the hay.

At first, the only sensation was horror: the nightmare feeling they were having no effect at all. But quite quickly the fire subsided. A final sizzle. Harriet and Florene stood together, breathing heavily, still in shock. Harriet had grabbed hold of Florene's arm once more and couldn't seem to let go.

"It's out, Sister," Florene said. All that remained was the stink of kerosene and a charred mess.

"Are you all right, Florene?"

"Yes. Do I still have eyebrows? You do. But my boots... And my project!"

"I'll give you an extension."

Harriet wouldn't relax until they had filled the bucket several times with snow and dumped it everywhere. They shared a few more minutes of blank staring. Then, by silent accord, they began to hide what had happened.

The table was a write-off. Florene's notes were ashes. The mess on the cement floor could be cleaned. They took the blackened remains of the table outside and hid it in a pine hollow. They returned the scorched metal chair to the back of the stack of folding chairs in the corner. The scorching, seen at some future date, would be a minor mystery. It was very late when they were done. Harriet would return in the morning, but it didn't look too bad.

"We can't have you working here anymore. If you can't stay at your cabin you'll have to go to Ella's." Florene said nothing before Harriet's expression. "You can't go anywhere tonight."

"I'm *very* sorry. I suppose I knocked over the lamp when I fell asleep."

Harriet set up the rollaway cot from a closet in her room. Florene, in a borrowed nightgown, fell asleep midway through another apology. Harriet had no such luck. In a remarkably few hours, she had to dress for Morning Prayer. When she returned after breakfast, Florene was gone. Her note said, *I am so sorry again. Thank you for sheltering me. Sister Patricia gave me breakfast. I will see you in class. How long is my project extension?* And then, ridiculously, *I was finding out some interesting FACTS. Do you think I have ennemies?*

Patricia helped Harriet expunge the rest of the evidence. They carried the table parts to the kitchen dumpster. Patricia found the cement floor paint they had used before and did a touch up. Everything looked as good as new. It had to be, for some carnival events would take place here on Saturday.

"You are a true friend, Sister."

Harriet and Patricia were eating pretzels in the kitchenette. Patricia brushed this aside.

"Least said, soonest mended. Where will the girl work now?"

"With Ella Burnhouse-Raquette's family, I hope. Perpetua thinks they're related, cousins or something." Harriet shrugged. "Florene will decide. She likes that cabin in the woods. She says the neighbours look after her. That's either very true or very untrue."

The only other damage was a week's worth of bad dreams for Harriet. However, Imelda only too willingly resupplied her, no questions asked, with more of the sample bubble packs, so it was indeed a case of least said, soonest mended.

## 20: Two Wrongs

"I'LL NEED YOU TO check up on something for me, Sister." Mr. Montserrat had regained a determined seventy percent of his original suavity, which Harriet now remembered always contained a grain of bossiness.

They were in the multi-purpose room to plan the bridge judging event. They were surrounded by the smell of glue and the room's persistent drafts, along with twenty-four finished bridges in all their outlandish glory. If appearance had been the sole criterion, it would have been a tough job to pick a winner, for the bridges, on a much larger scale than typical for these events, were all magical to behold.

Mr. Montserrat had a sheaf of papers in his hands, all the rules and rituals for bridge building competitions as prescribed by some minor Welsh university with time on its hands. He rifled through the paperwork.

"Let me just go over this. We're going to shrink the process down, naturally. We'll have the walkabout on Friday, just the girls and staff. If they want to show their parents their bridges, they can bring their Brownies. The newspaper will take some pictures too, in and out fast. I think you asked Sister Clothilde to make those arrangements?"

"The photographer will come at 11."

"Now, Saturday. We've got the judging panel, you, me, the school superintendent from the public board—around him we'll need to keep our wits—and the engineer. Handy finding an engineer who'd judged these things before." A Mr. Urban Shorto, a stalwart of the parish. He had assured them he had everything, the weights and pulleys, the rating forms he had himself devised, and he knew exactly how to proceed.

"We'll let Mr. Shorto take care of the actual smashing."

"Why do we even need a panel of judges?"

"Because, Sister Harriet, there are points assigned for aesthetic considerations, and we'll be like those corrupt figure skating judges, assigning points to our favourites." He pointed to one of the bridges that had a sort of fantastic Chinese pagoda look. "Like that. What price orientalism? You decide. Then we do the math." He was in a strange mood today.

"You said, Mr. Montserrat, that you wanted me to check something?"

"Mr. Shorto reminded me we should find out if any of the girls have engineer fathers. There'll be a few. It makes a big difference to the outcome. Another school had a juicy scandal. The three first prizes went to the kids with dads who were civil engineers. It all came out amid recrimination and hysteria."

"Our students signed papers attesting they're getting no outside help."

"So did those other students."

"But what can we do now? Surely it's too late?"

Mr. Montserrat sighed. "Not at all, Sister, we can have this information when we give the bridges discretionary marks. Well, not the superintendent, of course, we'll leave him out of it. Mr. Shorto says one engineer's kid can win, but better not make it a first prize." A breezy smile. "Sometimes two wrongs must make a right. Therefore, I would like you to find out what the girls' fathers do for a living if you wouldn't mind. All that should be in their files. And don't worry about Perpetua, I dropped a word."

"Very well." Harriet hadn't expected a rigged event, but she wasn't going to get worked up about it either.

"We fill out forms, perform basic arithmetic, adjust basic arithmetic, pick three winners. The awards ceremony for these events can sometimes be elaborate, but Perpetua and I discussed devoting a part of a future Friday assembly to the announcement, short and snappy with three of those rented trophies to hand out. A kind of swimsuit girl on a pedestal for the first prize, a cup for the second, and a little cup, about the size of a coffee mug, for the third. Everyone applauds, the end. We're buying some pictures from the *Herald* photographer, we'll have blow-ups of the winning bridges in the main hall."

Some of this, Harriet felt she should have been consulted about. Yet she couldn't fault Montserrat's executive vigour.

She considered him across the table. He wore another of his tweedy get ups, with a cashmere turtleneck in a deep wine, a Montreal purchase according to the general consensus. His wavy black hair was either in need of a cut or else he was trying out a rakish new style. Whichever the case, it made him look predictably irresistible. Just as well he wasn't being flirtatious. Thank God for that.

"I know you're dead tired of this, Sister, so I thought I'd take some of it off your shoulders," he said to her in the hallway. "We three lay teachers got a lecture from Perpetua about showing support for the sisters etcetera. This is all I could think of. Well, other than my endless toboggan run maintenance and rink clearing duties. One day, the five of us, or even the four of us, should skate again. Mother P. didn't come right out and say you need more recreation, but she implied it." He flashed her the facsimile of one of his old smiles, so that Harriet forgot all about being thankful.


CYPRIAN HAD LEFT a message for Harriet. When she called back, under the scrutiny of Sister Clothilde, he said he had more information to share.

"This time, Brother, could you perhaps put it in the mail? I am very busy just now, and this Saturday in particular we'll be judging a school science project."

Was this tone of independence for Clothilde's benefit? It was true about the bridge judging, although she had little idea how long the event would take.

"Oh dear, no," Cyprian said. "Your committee and mine made a pact and they all expect me to hand things over person to person. Bad as they are here with prying into our letters, I know it's worse for you lot. Nuns have no privacy whatsoever, as befits what they consider your lowly femininity. What if an unauthorized person were to see what I'm sending you?"

Harriet felt annoyance. "You're exaggerating. How important is the information anyway?" Clothilde was putting a file away in the cabinet. Had her hands suddenly stilled?

"That's not the point. I would like to see you."

In as bland a tone as possible, Harriet agreed to the visit.

"I'm not sure whether the Rambler will be in use, Saturday after next," said Clothilde, proving she'd been following the conversation. This irritated Harriet even more.

"Well would you book it now, Sister? If it has to be changed later, so be it. This is priority work, for Mother Perpetua and the diocese."

Lester came out from behind the filing cabinet just then, and two pairs of green eyes studied Harriet as she left the room.

ON SATURDAY SHE and Mr. Montserrat met in the staff room for a quick confab before going together to the multi-purpose room. He had his guitar with him and wore all black. Harriet didn't ask about his plans for the remainder of the day. Urban Shorto and a Monsieur Gareau, the school superintendent, had just arrived.

Things went smoothly. Everyone wanted their weekend to begin. Mr. Shorto knew everything there was to know about judging bridge competitions. Soon swan-like structures were tumbling into ruin, as everyone busily jotted down comments and assigned marks. Sure enough, the first and second prizes, on unadjusted numbers, would have gone to teams with daughters of engineers. The third-prize bridge ended up in first place. It had been built by a twelfth grader whose father was a family doctor and a ninth grader who had no father at all, being parented by an anxious widow. It verged on humdrum and its use of materials exceeded the norm, but it was the strongest bridge in the room. The eyes of Harriet, Mr. Montserrat and Mr. Shorto agreed—there was no safer choice. They then deliberated the second and third prizes. Loretta Mazurek's bridge looked likely for a prize, but that could not be, and numbers underwent adjustment once more. The whole event was too short for Harriet to be bored, and she realized she could have gone to Carson Falls after all.

"Are you the one who has to clean this up, Sister?" Mr. Shorto asked jocosely as they said goodbye.

"Why no, Mr. Shorto." Harriet's tone was prim. "We have a debrief with the girls about what the judges said, minus the scores. And then it's the girls who do the cleaning up."

Montserrat raised an ironic eyebrow behind Mr. Shorto, but the latter took Harriet's statement as wit. Monsieur Gareau was already half way to his car.

Later that afternoon, Harriet came across the expected glossy spread about the competition in the *Herald*, complete with photographs of clustered smiling girls and the bridges themselves from flattering angles. She hadn't managed to avoid being in one picture, along with Perpetua and Mr. Montserrat. The tone of the short article was light, gushy and congratulatory, with all due references made to Saint Reginald's, youthful femininity and the Bothonville International Bridge, the sponsor of it all. Harriet sighed. The *Herald* made everything look glamorous and exciting whereas, from her perspective, the project had been a long slog, needlessly stressful in the beginning, and increasingly tricky towards the end. From the Herald's article you would never have known that three students had recently been murdered.

Perpetua came in to the common room while Harriet held the newspaper.

"Yes, I saw that. It's to be hoped it will attract enough new students to the school next year to make up for our losses. Some of the pictures will do very well for the brochure." She sounded weary, yet businesslike. Harriet knew Perpetua wasn't referring to the dead girls, but to the ones taken from school in the aftermath. Still, there was such a thing as being too matter-of-fact.

"It was a good project, Reverend Mother," she said meekly. Just not for Loretta, Laurentine and Laura.

## 21: Watusi

DURING THE FOLLOWING week, Clothilde apologetically told Harriet that she couldn't have the car on Saturday, as it had been claimed for some senior class event. She could have it on Sunday or even Monday, a day slated for professional development. Harriet didn't want to examine too closely why she had been looking forward to the Saturday trip, but she felt disappointed. Monday would be no good, and Sunday was Saint Mark's turn to have a retreat.

Cyprian could have nipped out from the retreat to deliver the papers to Harriet, but that wouldn't have suited her at all. Not that she described to herself in exact detail what she imagined them doing on Saturday. But their visit last time to Joe's, nausea aside, had evolved. in retrospect, into a memorable interlude. What a frivolous person she must be, she thought as she handed back tests to the tune of rebellious murmurs and squeaks of dismay. She would be thirty this summer, and she was no better than these girls, who had clearly not studied, so what did they expect? That the car was needed to take several of them to a social event seemed especially unfair. Unlike them, she had something to be rebellious about.

On a fine Saturday, a leggy young woman in a pulled down beret and pea jacket slipped out the Saint Reginald's side entrance and made her way to the back wall.

They really should be policing this part of the grounds more, Harriet mused. The girls had always used the corner diagonally opposite to meet their waiting swains; and the security guard who now wandered around seemed oblivious to this other perfectly good escape route, cut off as it was by the barn, a stand of pines and some snowdrifts.

She'd had the revelation that the Rambler wasn't her only option. A milk run train travelled between Bothonville and Carson Falls, and the Carson Falls railway station was a convenient two blocks from Saint Mark's. It would require her travelling incognito, of course, but in Harriet's mind this was no longer a drawback.

It was the usual busy Saturday at Saint Reginald's, and she'd been encouraged to sign up for whatever weekend chores were going. She'd been able to tell Edwina she'd be assisting with the clothing drive all day, while informing Sister Angela she'd be involved in the annual kitchen cupboard turnout. In either case, she would be exempt from lunch in the refectory. Why would the sisters even discuss her? What could go wrong?

From the railway platform Harriet watched the locomotive rounding the curve. It shimmered in the sunshine and shook the ground like a juggernaut. She felt a sudden happiness. Amid the Saturday travellers she hardly attracted attention, and soon she got off at the picturesque old Carson Falls station. She'd realized she couldn't appear at Saint Mark's in plain clothes. In the Marimekko bag—how many were its ongoing adventures, and how faithfully it performed them—she had her habit and veil. She nipped into the washroom and changed. With little time to spare, she made her way to the friary side of the school and rang the bell.

Brother Andrew, the one who'd passed the sherry, opened the door.

"I'm here to see Brother Cyprian."

"Cyprian! Oh dear, Sister..." He looked over his shoulder in a furtive way. They were in a vestibule and the hall beyond was deserted.

"We were to meet at one o'clock." Harriet began to feel confused.

"Were you now, Sister? There must be some mistake." He looked over his shoulder again, cleared his throat. "There is no one here by the name of Brother Cyprian."

"What are you talking about?"

Brother Andrew was a boyish redhead and she remembered him as the life of the party. Now he looked apprehensive as well as furtive.

"Oh, very well, but that is what they are telling us to say. Or that he became overtired and is on a rest cure at monastic HQ in Schenectady. Sister, can you come back? I can't talk now, but I can meet you around the other side in an hour. The door beside the Michael Archangel statue will be unlocked. You come up the lane, it's off limits to the boys."

Harriet just stared. "I don't understand."

"I'll explain everything. *But we can't talk now.*" Echoing footsteps drew nearer. Brother Andrew bundled her out of the vestibule with a muttered apology. He practically slammed the door.

Harriet felt disoriented. Bizarre explanations aside, it seemed Cyprian wasn't there. Had she made the trip for nothing? It looked that way. But what could have happened to Brother Cyprian?

Her uncertainty gave way to annoyance. She decided to go back to the railway waiting room. By the time she arrived, even more annoyed, she had changed her mind. She would go for a walk instead, and she might as well do it out of her habit. She popped back into the washroom and changed once more. When she adjusted the beret in the mirror, this time beside a plump teenager who was assiduously plastering her face with Miami Tan, it struck her that she looked washed out under the beret. With her light hair and winter skin, off-white just wasn't her colour.

"You'd look great in a deep rose lipstick," the girl piped up.

Harriet felt out of sorts already, and didn't need fashion advice from a teenager. But she bit her tongue.

"The light isn't especially flattering at this time of year." She hoped she sounded blandly secular.

The girl now applied lipstick in a deep coral. She'd already rimmed her eyes Cleopatra-style. Harriet couldn't help but gaze. The girl worked the tube like a Picasso. The colour scheme wouldn't have been Harriet's first choice, but it was effective.

The girl laughed. "You're right if you're thinking my mother would kill me if she knew I wore all this makeup. She'd skin me alive.

You're so lucky." It was her turn to gaze at Harriet. "No one tells you what to do. I can hardly wait to be old."

"Thanks. But be careful what you wish for."

"I'd love your cheekbones. And your eyes. I'd do things with your eyes."

"Oh—would you? Er—what exactly?"

"Well, I'm sure you buy your makeup at the Helena Rubinstein counter at Ingham and Marsh and those places, but me I go to Woolworths. They're having a makeup sale this weekend. If I had your face, I'd go with gray eyeshadow and a classic dark rose lipstick. Your mascara and eyebrow pencil should be brown-black. You hardly need foundation, but cream tone powder would work. That's what I'd do if I had your face."

Two girls barged into the washroom, shrieking "Hurry up, Diaaaane!"

Diane said, "nice chatting with you, Miss," and the three departed in a flurry of noise, leaving pale Harriet to scrutinize herself in the glass.

Was it her fault that the Woolworths, a big one with a gleaming red and gold sign, beckoned practically across the street? Diane had been right. Harriet could see markdowns and two for one offers everywhere. She knew nothing about makeup, and stared uncomprehending at the wall of face paint. There were boxes, cases, tubes and bottles, and the stuff came in every colour. What did some of these words mean, they surely weren't English. She tried to remember what Diane had said. It took her a while. The cost, even with slashed prices, was a shock. For a handful of containers and wands? Thank goodness her teacher friend had sent her another twenty dollars, this time tucked into the jacket of a dull book on Catholic curriculum.

Back in the station washroom, she cautiously dabbed her face. The cream gray—called Waterfall Gray—went on her eyelids. You drew a sort of feathered line with an eyebrow pencil, the box said. You could poke your eye out with mascara if you weren't careful, but she was careful. She patted her nose with the powder puff. Her pores disappeared. She applied the lipstick, wiped it off with a paper towel, applied it again, wiped it off again, and finally left it on. How in God's name did you get used to your lips looking like this? Harriet supposed you just did. Her eyes in the mirror looked big and sparkly, and she guessed provocative clown lips were necessary for balance. She tried a toothy smile. Eek. How could she even think about appearing in public?

And yet, when she emerged onto the busy midday street, a couple of men gave her glancing looks, otherwise she saw no reaction.

Harriet enjoyed her walk in the sunshine. She bought a little bag of fudge in a candy store. She nibbled it daintily, not wanting to smear her lipstick. She kept catching glimpses of herself in shop windows—a graduate student, perhaps, with a loose-boned step, swinging her Marimekko bag as she walked, her face eerily magazine-like in a way she'd never seen before, full-lipped and bold-eyed.

This was how she presented herself at the back entrance to Saint Mark's. It hadn't been worth the trouble to change again. Andrew had to be talked down from his amazement before they could discuss business.

"Brother, you will promise not to speak of how I'm dressed, won't you?" She made an effort to sound stern. He nodded, bug-eyed. "Well, where is Brother Cyprian?"

"First, Sister—should I call you that, yes, yes—he left this for you. Paperwork from that committee work, I think?"

Harriet was mollified. Her journey hadn't been totally useless then.

"You might think, Sister, because he trusted me to pass this on to you that he trusted me with an explanation. But I'm as much in the dark as anyone. Cyprian just disappeared. He's been missing for five days now. We called the police, all that, but they haven't been much use. Since he left a note that said *Adieu, my brothers, don't look for me, I am in the wind that blows,* the police aren't treating his disappearance as a criminal matter."

"But that's extraordinary. He said he'd meet me here this

afternoon."

"He did say I was to tell you, what was it exactly, he knew you would understand."

""Well, I don't!" Or did she? He had been turning into a real flake right before her eyes. "Do you have any idea where he is?"

"Maybe back in Montreal? Or Schenectady? He has friends there, from the time of his discernment. They're making inquiries, but they're striking out. He really is in the wind."

They discussed the mystery a little longer, Andrew's eyes roving over Harriet as they talked. Whether Cyprian was in the wind or full of wind, he had decamped.

Back on Carson Falls's sunny streets, Harriet found herself wandering without aim. She'd just missed the midafternoon train. The next one wasn't until well after six. She could just afford a cheap lunch. She had come to a residential neighbourhood now, of sagging row houses picturesquely frosted with snow. She remembered Joe's Corner Lunch was five minutes away.

The place was bustling and it looked like they were still serving food. Someone led her to the last vacant table, a tiny one jammed up against the stage. She ordered a hotdog and a fountain drink. Some people were still eating, but the green blinds were already lowered and brown bottles were multiplying. She sensed a mood of anticipation among the turtlenecked patrons. As she began to eat, the lights dimmed, while a spotlight illuminated the dais. A guitarist came out and sat down before a microphone. With a sense of the earth falling away under her feet, Harriet recognized him.

Marin Montserrat, attractive as always in espresso brown this time, began to tune his guitar. He spoke to someone rearranging the electrical cords and looked out over the audience with a self-possessed smile. His eyes landed on Harriet, who sat after all less than five feet away. His face didn't change at once. He looked, did a double-take. The look became a puzzled stare. Then came the jolt of recognition.

He got up and did some things with the chair and microphone

that brought him to her table.

"Harriet—how unexpected to see you," he murmured. His face showed awe, amusement, calculation.

"It's not what you think." Harriet's words were thick and slow.

"I'm sure it isn't." He scrutinized her face. If only she hadn't reapplied Passionate Rose just before entering the restaurant. She imagined her lips glowing like a beacon in the penumbra. She pushed her plate away.

She must look horrified, because now he grew concerned. "I'm doing two numbers, I'll come and join you afterwards. Don't worry. I'm not looking for explanations although I'm sure you'd have a good one. Also, I'm not a rat." He looked sympathetic, but his eyes roved as had Brother Andrew's.

"I have to catch a train."

"I think the next train isn't until just before seven? I'll see you in fifteen. We can have a beer."

Harriet's mind must have wandered after this because, when she next became aware, Montserrat was singing the Brothers Four song, "Greenfields," the one that had mesmerized everyone at the bonfire. Here, with a microphone, the effect proved even stronger. The room was still, listening. Montserrat held the beatniks in his hand and Harriet noticed pretty swoony girls now, as if they had been spotlighted by their own yearning. She could feel the wave of emotion when he came to the words, *I only know there's nothing here for me/ Nothing in this wide world, left for me to see...*

And she remembered the sparks flying upward, and Laura Rome joining in with her young voice. And now Laura had died, and here was she, Sister Harriet but the plainclothes version wearing Laura's clothes, listening to this song again. The audience clapped enthusiastically, as Montserrat's gaze swivelled her way with a smile meant just for her, although that was always what you thought.

He fiddled with the guitar, while carrying on light patter with the room. His second number, he said, would be familiar to anyone who knew last year's Bob Dylan album—Harriet didn't—although the song was older. More fiddling, the lighting changed, Montserrat's face became closed and remote, and the song began on an urgent rhythm in the E chord.

If the other number had hit home, this had the impact of a gale blowing through the room. The song seemed to be called "In My Time of Dying," an old spiritual, Harriet guessed. It was dirge-like, but catchy like a fishhook to the heart, and Montserrat's voice sounded different, rich, plaintive and urgent, as he sang about dying easy and the hope that Jesus would take his body home.

When he came to the words, *Well, meet me Jesus, meet me/Meet me in the middle of the air/If these wings should fail me/Lord, won't you meet me with another pair,* Harriet felt transported back to the deck of the unfinished bridge, with the moving mist all around her. A sense of her destiny overwhelmed her, the common destiny, the same as everyone's. But simultaneously the cradling melody carried her back from the brink, to this random room on this random afternoon, to the strangers around her, to the man on the stage. A man she knew, at least, although his face was unrecognizable now, its planes and moving parts subsumed into—what? You would have thought grief, but that must just be the song.

*Lord, in my time of dying don't want nobody to cry/All I want my friends to do is come close my dying eyes.*

The last notes summoned a wave of sighs and a storm of hoots and hollers. Montserrat came back as if from a distance and didn't seem too fussed one way or the other about the acclaim. He talked to the electrical guy, pushed the chair to its original position, and looked around. Then he lifted a hand briefly in Harriet's direction and exited via the back, leaving the whole room and not just the pretty girls dejected with the sudden chill of his departure.

When Montserrat surprised her five minutes later by sitting down beside her, Harriet had herself in hand and had worked out how she'd explain herself to her fellow teacher.

"Two beers, I think?" he said. Two brown bottles appeared. Wherever his music had taken him, he was back and studying

Harriet's face as if he was trying to memorize it.

"You're a wonderful musician—guitarist and singer. You could be professional."

"You are kind. If Mother P. fires me, I'll have something to fall back on. I just do it out of enjoyment. It passes the time."

Harriet shook her head. Whatever Montserrat was doing, he wasn't just passing the time.

The beer started to work on Harriet, and she told him, over the sound of two girls with tambourines, about her reason for being in Carson Falls, which led inevitably to the mystery of Brother Cyprian. Montserrat seemed unsurprised by her diocesan project—Harriet suspected everyone at school knew some version by now—and was intrigued by Cyprian's abscondment.

He didn't ask her about her change of clothes, although the question hung in the air. She offered a limping excuse about civvies being easier when you took the train alone. He pretended to accept this explanation, although his eyes appraised, and Harriet supposed he thought of her as another young religious gone rogue. Perhaps she and Cyprian even romantically involved.

This annoyed her. "We weren't seeing each other, in case that's what you were thinking. Cyprian is a square peg, and maybe that's what I am too." She picked at the beer label. "You have to talk to someone. It's not easy, being a sister in 1963. And it's been a terrible year at Saint Reginald's."

He made a manly *moue*. "You have a right to friends, whatever the papal encyclical says."

"There's a papal encyclical?"

"No. Or I don't believe so. But I told you, your secret is safe with me, Sister."

The conversation roved, after that. Montserrat, she was surprised to discover, had been born in New York City, although his family had moved to Montreal when he was young. A picture emerged of wealthy enigmatic people who didn't like each other, a sister now dead, the getting of teaching qualifications almost an uninteresting accident along the way. But what *was* Marin Montserrat's way? The story offered no keys to the man himself. Harriet, on the other hand, felt she was filleting herself for his inspection when she talked about her connection to Bothonville, Lafrenière, Rhonda, the death of her mother, Iona Prep and her vocation. She even revealed her birth name, Ruth Savary. Although not the Henrietta of Baumgarten moniker; she had, after all, some remaining survival instinct.

Told to him in the free flow of a second beer, the story of her life in her own ears sounded pitiful. Marginal existence, childhood suffering, retreat from reality, religious crutch—throw in a *sainte nitouche* role at school and a generous helping of repression, and voilà: Harriet of Bingham. However, he didn't seem to take what she said that way.

"I can imagine how important an education was." He spoke seriously. "That would have been a waste of a brain— you not going to university."

Now a threesome of young Black singers in spiffy loungewear were doing a version of the Orlons' "Wah Watusi." Not a beatnik hit, but the cool cats in attendance must have watched their share of Canadian Bandstand because several began to writhe in the open space before the stage.

"Will you dance, Harriet?"

"That would be a firm no."

Just then a girl with a pony tail—perhaps the top pretty girl in the room, wearing form-fitting turquoise stretch pants—came over and asked him to dance. He looked at Harriet once more, but he was already getting up.

Thus did Harriet get to watch Marin Montserrat dance, perhaps three or four feet away from her; and if his partner did a mean Watusi it was really nothing to his, so understated, so well-timed to the music, so neat in its moving syncopated parts. The girl held a cigarette while she danced, a mere affectation. But when he picked up his bottle and had a sip, while executing a casual little twist accent at the twist reference, Harriet thought she had never seen a man dance so well.

He disengaged himself from his partner after the dance but, when he returned to their table, Harriet discerned a glow, along with a whiff of some fresh aftershave. The world, she thought, was unfair. The top pretty girl, back at her table, may have agreed. Montserrat took Harriet's hand as he said, "Why don't we cool off with another beer, and then I'll drive you home. It's getting late, Sister Ruth." The space between the green blind nearest her and the window frame had turned indigo.

They drank—their chairs had somehow become squeezed together after the dance—and finally he paid, including for her meagre lunch. She waited for him out on the sidewalk while he retrieved his guitar. The wind had picked up and, after Joe's cozy fug, the night air pinched. He took his time and she began to walk up and down, attracting looks from passers by. When he did reappear, he came up behind her and managed to give her waist a quick squeeze before propelling her along the pavement.

"I parked my car a few blocks over."

Harriet wasn't sure how Montserrat felt, and she didn't even ask herself whether he was fit to undertake the drive back to Bothonville. She herself had come to the carefully drunk stage, in which no one would notice as long as she was careful. Inside, however, her thoughts churned. The mention of the car reminded her that Montserrat drove a 1955 Chrysler Imperial, the kind with the roomiest back seat going, a back seat hilariously discussed by the girls for its potential. The thought that she was about to embark with Montserrat in his make-outmobile filled Harriet with panic. She wasn't afraid of him, rather of the connection between dark cars and alcohol-fueled kisses. He came very near her as they hurried along, his long coat swinging open, still radiating warmth and that manly smell. She had to do something.

"*Wait*, Mr. Montserrat."

"Oh, it's Mister again, is it?" She didn't recall addressing him as Marin at Joe's, but she must have.

"I can't go back to Saint Reginald's like this. I'd better change into my habit." She gestured to the tote. "I need a place to change."

Montserrat looked at the Marimekko bag as if he had a question or two, but all he said was, "Do you want to go back to Joe's?"

"No, it's too full. Could you take me to the train station?"

So they drove to the railway station, or rather to within a few hundred feet of it, for it was near seven and Harriet didn't want to be seen by any Bothonvillers. Montserrat stopped the car on a ramp to the freight yard, saying like an impatient husband, "Don't make me wait."

"You made me wait while you said goodbye to your pony tail partner."

Harriet nipped in and out of the train station washroom in a jiffy. After all, she was getting used to these changes.

As she hurried up the ramp, a sustained gust of wind blew snow like smoke around the Chrysler. Montserrat leaned against the car, lit up by the sodium light overhead. The wind blew the hem of his coat around him. She sensed, as she came up to him, that the picture was telling her something. Mystified, she said at random, "That's an attractive coat. Tweed, is it?"

"Yes, Sister, tweed." He did up a button, as he opened the passenger door for her. "Donegal. I got it when I visited Ireland last year. You can't find Donegal ulsters in Canada, at least not in Bothonville."

In the time Montserrat took to walk around to the driver's side, Harriet had rallied. She was apparently absorbed in perusing Cyprian's papers when he got in beside her. Anything to avoid looking at him, looking at the Donegal ulster Moreau said had been seen on the grounds the night Laura Rome disappeared. And anything so Montserrat wouldn't see—she brusquely refused his offer to turn on the interior light—the emotions on her face had she been forced to meet his stranger's eyes.


INSPECTOR MOREAU couldn't believe his eyes.

Also his luck. The chances that he might have passed that Montserrat on a dark back street in Carson Falls weren't so very slim, after all. It was a Saturday night and Carson Falls, Bothonvillers in the know were aware, had the best music scene. And if the Saint Reginald's nun liked to dress in plain clothes and nip over to Carson Falls for some obscure reason known only to herself—well, these things sometimes happened in 1963.

But what luck to see her in the company of her fellow teacher. He'd never have recognized her otherwise. He'd scrutinized her—the better to torment himself with Montserrat's latest conquest—and the light bulb had come on.

He was at a table at Joe's, cogitating while his meal arrived. The woman had been walking up and down. And then Montserrat had emerged, guitar case in tow, and they'd waltzed off together. A date? Unless she'd been his backup singer. A meeting between friends, anyway. He was so excited, he wasn't sure he would be able to eat his blue plate special.

Moreau had been to hell and back with the Saint Reginald's investigation. The escape of Pellerin had been a bitter setback but, thank goodness, that could be blamed on the jail, and the manhunt was a federal responsibility. His biggest problem had been the actual case against Pellerin. In discussing it with the new prosecutor, holes had begun to appear. "This is ninety-nine percent circumstantial evidence," that jumped-up bastard had pointed out. "What do you think I can do with this?" And so on. Flynn had yelled and told him, "God damn it, *find* the evidence." And everyone knew what that meant.

Worst of all, in a way, were his own doubts. He would have been more than happy to see the right man swinging from the end of a rope. Justice served and Alain Moreau promoted. Yet the case against Pellerin had begun to seem thinner even to him. The ticklish question had arisen, what if Pellerin was innocent? He had no other serious suspect. Of course, he wasn't sure. Say they found Pellerin, gave him the third degree, he might well up and confess. A confession would be a good thing. Doubt, on the other hand, was a terrible thing. He was a man acquainted with suffering all right.

And then that blasted Montserrat had sashayed by, arm in arm, practically, with a Saint Reginald's sister, for pete's sake. Could this open new doors? The possibilities were endless, and he didn't want endless possibilities. A secret romance, while interesting, might mean nothing. But Montserrat, along with the other male teacher, Hughes, and half a dozen or so miscellaneous brothers and boyfriends, had been on a shortish list of suspects. The killer had to be associated, directly or indirectly, with the school. They'd looked closely at a few of these, Montserrat included. It had been impossible to pin anything on him, that was the trouble.

If a man can play the field in one way, he can play the field in other ways. If he can have one dirty secret, he can have others. Besides which, the involvement of another person, a woman in a situation as delicate as this one, gave Moreau opportunities. He'd always thought that nun, with her holier than thou look, had been holding back on him. Now he had leverage to make her talk. That, roughly speaking, was the opportunity. Of course he'd have to think it through—a lot more.

For example, the full implications of a secret romance between Montserrat and the sister, who looked a whole lot better out of her habit. How possible was that, after all? Quite possible, for the world seemed to be as lucky in love as he was unlucky.

His bouncing thoughts were violently interrupted by the appearance of Maureen in the doorway with her date. The real reason he was here was to spy on her and that loathsome specimen Bill. Yes, his Saturday nights had sunk to that. The pair of them settled at a table across the room, happy as larry and laughing over some joke. It must have been a funny one, for their laughter went on and on. The sight of Bill's white teeth made him grind his.

Despite the ambient noise, scraps of their conversation wended his way. To Bill's leering compliment, of which he heard only the words "more dancing later," Maureen giggled with pleasure and riposted, "Oh Bill, I'm not that kind of a girl!"

Moreau scoffed inwardly, for who more than Maureen was that kind of a girl? Yet she was a sweet kid. The sweetest, he dimly sensed; and another part of him could scarcely hold himself back from rushing over and knocking the vile scoundrel's teeth down his throat.

But the *coup de grace* came a moment later. When Maureen

eventually shrugged off her ratty fur, Moreau recognized her expensive green angora sweater. He'd given it to her. She filled it beautifully, too, as Bill's bulging eyes attested; all of which only increased his pain. Indeed yes, he was a man acquainted with sorrow.

## 22: The Ava Arundell

NUNS CAME IN ALL SORTS, Alain Moreau thought. What a contrast Sister Patricia presented to that other one. Could this be true of women generally, that they came in all sorts? Saint Reginald's was the only large community of women he'd dealt with professionally. He'd questioned just about everyone at the school. Tears and lies. He shuddered. It had been more than enough. But he had a good memory for trivia, and he'd recalled something he wanted to follow up on.

"Sister," he said, "could you just recapitulate your whereabouts on the night Laura Rome went missing?" His tone was casual.

The sister considered. "The last day of school, Inspector? It's been a while. After dinner, we did breakfast prep. Then...I went for a skate."

He beamed. "I'd like you to go over that evening. Times, whether you saw anyone."

Raising an eyebrow, Patricia complied. The serpentine had been deserted; she fancied a long spin by herself. She estimated times.

"And could you remind me, Sister, what you saw?"

"What you call 'sightings' are common as mud, well, they were before the new rules." Moreau nodded patiently. "I saw Sister Harriet. I don't know where she disappeared to, but on my next lap I saw two figures in that corner where Convent Road meets Fourteenth. I didn't see the woman, or girl, clearly. The male wore that tweed coat."

"And you know it was tweed because..."

"Inspector, I used to teach Home Ec, until the Department of Ed wanted us all to have teaching degrees. I know my fabrics. A heavyweight Donegal, midtone with flecks. There's a streetlamp at the corner there."

She was apparently Moreau's only witness for the Donegal ulster. It was now important to get the details confirmed. The sister's smugness irritated him but this level of detail was potentially critical. Her calm confidence would make her a good witness. He picked at her answer, but she stood firm: winter weight fabric, fashionable this season, the beige/brown all the rage.

"That's good, Sister." He made a note, then asked as if in afterthought: "There was an evening earlier when you and Sister Harriet went for an evening skate, you mentioned it last time. Can you tell me about that evening?"

Patricia looked surprised. "The five of us? We didn't see anyone else. At least, I didn't. You should ask the others. We weren't always together."

Was that the smallest twitch?

"Naturally I'll speak to the others. Miss Edison, Mr. Hughes, Mr. Montserrat, you and Sister Harriet. If you were all spread out…it's a big skating surface." He waited.

Patricia shrugged. "Miss Edison used to be a competitive figure skater. When she showed up, everyone got competitive." How was he to read that Mona Lisa smirk that came and went on her face? "We got separated trying to keep up with her. We had mishaps on those curves, ended up in snowbanks." Another twitch. She was holding back.

"Modern times, Sister, modern times. I'm sure Reverend Mother Perpetua wouldn't have minded."

Patricia looked alert. "I don't think anyone told her."

"Why would you? Good clean fun. I love a good skate. Who fell into snowbanks, by the way?"

"I think we probably all did." But he could see her calculating. She had no way of knowing what the others would own up to. "Well, Sister Harriet for one. Mr. Hughes too, I think." Moreau felt sure he was the red herring. "Mr. Montserrat had snow on him too." Patricia looked wary.

Moreau nodded, asked her a few more questions for form's sake, and dismissed her.

He ruminated while staring out the window. The trees lining Saint Reginald's drive were thrashing in a rising wind. The weather report promised a gale, but he wasn't worried about the weather.

That Patricia was a sly one but he fancied he'd outsmarted her. He'd asked everyone about all evenings out on the grounds. Harriet hadn't mentioned the teachers' skating party. The omission had seemed unimportant at the time. Now he had a thread to pull with her, linked to what he'd seen in Carson Falls. A little thread to trigger little lies, before he pulled the big thread to unravel the big lie. He hoped.

He pictured the two of them on the rink together, Montserrat and Harriet. Probably not hand in hand, there were others about. Then, a fortuitous and fortunate tumble into the snowbank. A struggle to disentangle themselves and get up, brush themselves down, some interesting etcetera etcetera, and then, *Oh, here is Sister Patricia coming, do stop, Marin!* The whole thing was all too vivid. A bit like those paperbacks his sisters used to read, that he looked through in case there was any sex, although there never was. But there was a lot of truth in them. Well, he'd mull over how he would approach Harriet for maximum impact. No matter how hardened she proved, he now had other strings in his bow.

As the wind began to howl, Moreau looked with disfavour at his trench coat with the button-through lining, which had seemed at the time so right, and wondered when he could next get to Montreal to look at ulsters.

CYPRIAN LISTENED TO the wild wind all day, from the relative safety of his friend's cabin near the river. This was a better place to lie low than Schenectady, where he kept almost running into people he knew. Richard being one of them; but they had been the kind of pals who covered for one another back in the day. Cyprian had spent one night in Richard's room at the monastery. Then he'd slept in a little-used outbuilding.

This would suffice until he could get his hands on some money, which he felt confident his family would cough up. But between the discomfort and the risk of discovery, they needed a better plan. Richard suggested his family's unused cabin upstate. No one had gone there this winter, so he'd maybe have to share it with mice. It had been shut up properly in September, and it offered a generator, canned food and a non-nosy neighbour who ploughed.

Cyprian wasn't on the lam. Legally, he had every right to leave the order. But he wanted to live in peace for a while with the aftermath of his draconian decision. He wanted time to reflect, without interference or static. For that, Richard told him, the cabin was perfect. And it wasn't far from Sparta, where there were banks, phones, shops.

Cyprian used the last of his cash to buy an old jalopy, and made the journey north without mishap. The place was all Richard promised, plus it had a library of only slightly mildewed books and a transistor radio that pulled in stations far and near. He'd made contact with a bank in Sparta, and now all he had to do was wait for money, from the branch of his family that had disapproved of his becoming a brother, that is, disapproved of *him* becoming a brother. He had time to read Theillard de Chardin and other Catholic luminaries, for Richard had dumped his old classical course textbooks here.

It was a little late for Theillard de Chardin, he realized soon enough. The radio cheered, but commercials for local Sparta restaurants with all you could eat buffets and winter sales on men's suits left him yearning for money he didn't have. Plus, he felt lonely. He'd be lying if he denied that the appealing young nun from Saint Reginald's was sometimes on his mind. She was across the river from him now. Did she sometimes think about him? Whether she did or not, she was a universe away. He consoled himself with long walks through the bush and the pleasure of his guitar.

He had been making inroads into the battery supply, but it was worth it to listen to the radio reports of the storm. All day, the news had been dire. Power outages spreading across the countryside, compounded by freezing rain. Several freak deaths in Sparta, as people were swept into traffic and big objects flew from their moorings to crash down on the unsuspecting. The order came to shelter in place.

And the nearby river was supposedly raging, although Cyprian wondered if he's misheard, for surely the river was still mostly frozen over. Perhaps the icebreakers had gotten to work early. In the darkened cabin (the day was bizarrely overcast), Cyprian could imagine he heard a watery roar over the wind. Through a surge of static, the newsreader spoke of worse out on open water: hurricane force gusts and thirty-foot waves. Now Cyprian felt confusion. And a part of him was deeply stimulated.

He picked up his book again, a volume of Victorian poetry. He had come to the middle of a poem called 'The Scholar Gipsy,' about an impoverished student who dropped out of Oxford and became, to summarize, an addle-brained flower-picking wanderer and, then, an inspirational ghost. That, plus a lot of Doubt and topography. He fancied himself a kind of elusive scholar gipsy, at least until his money came in. He thought about composing a song, using the poem as a general model. When he came to the part about a sighting on some bridge during a snowstorm, *Have I not pass'd thee on the wooden bridge/Wrapt in thy cloak and battling with the snow*—hot stuff that, a definite yes for the song—he suddenly thought he should be outside right now. It was too good a storm to waste.

The day was darker and the wind even stronger, but the sleet had stopped. He calculated. He was hardly a quarter mile from the river. The pines would give him shelter; unless one squashed him, but why be negative. The trail would lead him to the top of a steep escarpment, from which the view was spectacular. There were oilskins in a cupboard. In two minutes, he was out the door.

He struggled to the point, through thrashing trees that seemed to be calling to him to get the hell back to the cabin. There was everywhere a dull roaring sound. The undergrowth began to thin out. He felt a glow of anticipation, which became tinged with anxiety as the noise of the storm increased. To turn back seemed the coward's way, running counter to the purpose of his escape from safe Saint Mark's. The river was almost in view. Wasn't the sheer sickening thunder of the storm a command he couldn't refuse? There would be ten years' worth of inspiration here: inspiration for the songs his soul craved to write and, of course, perform to large audiences. Cyprian muttered a brief prayer, because it always came back to that, and crested the rise.

Miles of wind-contorted icescape extended before him, under a violently shifting firmament in which the Bothonville Bridge appeared and disappeared like a monster in the clouds. To add to the monster movie effect, lightning flickered everywhere through the turbulent mass of the sky. Perhaps the announcer had been right: far out he could see what he thought must be an open channel. In addition, even a ship! It was too distant to be sure, but it seemed a big one, a mid-sized Seaway freighter or an icebreaker. Its lights appeared and disappeared eerily in the murk, as the vessel rose above the waves and disappeared into their trough. Over this forsaken scene, the storm unleashed its fury.

Here were giant poplars, their huge rubbery arms flying this way and that and offering meagre shelter. Brother Cyprian crouched down and began to tune his guitar. He made a few false starts. The first words that he half-liked were *You never can know/Where the love of God goes,* but he dismissed these as ponderous and tried again. It should begin like a fable. In the key of C major, he started over: *It was the winter of sixty-three/The coldest that the world did see...* This was true somewhere anyway. *Dark days were on the river and land/Something something God's heavy hand...* Maybe. He needed a hook. And the music too, it had to be rhythmic and tense, but grave, building up to tragedy. As darkness fell, he carried on.

Cyprian thought he had something in an hour. Although it might have been two; he'd lost track of time. He'd have to get back to the cabin to listen properly, for he could now barely hear himself above the storm. He stood up, casting another look over the river. It was almost completely dark, and the bridge had retired to its nighttime lair.

Strangely, he could see the ship still out there, in roughly the same position. Its lights continued to do their appearing and disappearing act. There was something subtly sickening, as he continued to watch, about the intervals of darkness, which seemed to be getting longer. His unease grew. Why was the ship still there? Was there something different about what he saw now? He suddenly wondered, had the pattern of lights changed? Were they at an angle? Could the ship be listing, in distress, taking on water? Just as the question formed itself in his mind, the ship dipped from view once more. He waited for the lights to rise again. The minutes passed. The lights didn't reappear.

He must have taken a step towards the edge without realizing, because suddenly his foot began to slide, the rest of him, guitar included, following in a useless scramble towards the brink. They said your life flashed before your eyes, in such moments. All Cyprian remembered afterwards was his determination not to drop his guitar, which made him one-armed. But that one arm seemed to know its purpose, for he reached up to a poplar branch swinging wildly above him and grabbed on. His feet flew out, but the rest of him hung on. And as the greatest gust yet clawed at him, he and the branch swung together, like an acrobat and his trapeze over the void.

Somehow, he got back to solid land. The wind subsided, his hand didn't slip; his feet found ground and he launched himself backwards. And then he was in the shelter of some rocks, his guitar case dinged from landing on it. Deprived of its prey, the wind renewed its fury. It took him several minutes to compose himself.

But no matter how long he stayed there watching, the lights of the ship were gone.

## 23: Waiting Game

ONCE AGAIN, HARRIET rode the bus, on a gray Saturday hinting at winter's end without promising spring. After her last trip to Carson Falls, she'd told herself it was past time to set aside her secular disguise. And yet, here she was again in cords, turtleneck and pea jacket, although she'd acquired another hat from the clothing drive bin, a face-hiding mohair hood and scarf affair, blue and more flattering. Now, in the reflecting surface of the bus window, her appearance didn't cause her a second look. With the Marimekko bag slung over her shoulder, she imagined herself off to the Vivamus library to work on her thesis.

She had maintained her *sang froid* during the drive back to Bothonville with Montserrat. If he wondered at her change of mood, he could attribute it to an attack of conscience. She was good at sisterly reserve. She had experience in misrepresentation.

She had told no one about the Donegal ulster. Fear and suspicion, with surprising ease, had given way to simple confusion. During a busy work week she managed to avoid Montserrat, while watching him on the sly. He seemed the same Montserrat, or rather the same Montserrat who had emerged following the deaths of the three Ls, for that sense she had, that she looked upon something reconstructed remained. He'd always been an enigma. And after all, what was a coat? She just couldn't latch onto the idea of him as a murderer of young women.

Nevertheless, she continually pictured herself telling Moreau.

She rehearsed versions of a Donegal ulster discovery, such as seeing Montserrat up close one day in the parking lot and "suddenly realizing." They sounded hollow, and Harriet sensed that every admission she now made would threaten the secrecy of her double life. She felt pressure, but put off action.

She had other things to think about. Florene had agreed to move in with Ella and her relatives. She was better out of the barn, which seemed to attract more than its fair share of fires. The world seemed always poised to go up in smoke; but at least Florene was safe. Then Harriet overheard Florene by the lockers, talking to another girl about "where I live," mentioning paths and trees. Belatedly, she realized Florene must be back in Turpentine Flats. She couldn't ignore this. The situation had its complications, it would require yet more subterfuge. Even when she thought of others, it seemed, her actions never fully synchronized with the world's.

The fields on the other side of Factory Alley were just as deserted as before and the barrier of the forest, when she arrived at it, just as secretive and mournful. She hoped she remembered the way. She passed a few staring children among the trees. They didn't seem to be playing and she didn't feel like asking them for directions. Eventually she recognized the tunnel of vines and the entrance.

The door stood open a sliver and Harriet stepped into the room. The woodstove was going, and Florene, wrapped in shawls and scarves, bent over her books. When the girl looked up, her eyes changed from anticipation to surprise and a shy gladness.

"I hope you don't mind me interrupting."

"It's time for a break. So you knew I was here, Sister. Come in."

"Your door was unlocked, did you know?"

"Oh, was it?" Florene's tone was disingenuous.

Harriet unloaded the contents of the Marimekko bag onto a shelf. "Here, I'll put these away. Sister Edwina is always giving me things."

They sat by the stove.

"Are you ever at the Burnhouse-Raquette house?"

Florene looked ingratiating. "Yes. But I come here on weekends." She added, with an air of pleased improvisation, "Ella's house is noisy and I like to do my homework here."

"I thought they were actually your relatives too."

"They might be." Florene switched topic. "I like your hood, Sister. It brings out your eyes." Harriet accepted defeat.

They chatted about this and that. The wreck of the freighter Ava Arundell during that terrible storm came up. It had been Bothonville's favourite topic recently. A horror, they agreed. Forty hands and the captain had gone down with the ship, all lost to the waves. The wind outside the cabin whispered agreement.

Harriet felt a draft on her neck. "Did I shut the door?"

As she turned, it swung open. Roger Pellerin stepped into the cabin.

Harriet was not even particularly shocked. Florene looked self-conscious and Roger, advancing into the room, cool as a cucumber. Harriet sensed he'd taken her in from a crack in the wood, and knew all he needed to know. He wore a sort of hobo getup which, as he peeled off the layers, looked eminently weatherproof. Underneath he seemed much the same, only darker, whether from dirt or the effects of exposure who could say. Also thinner. He put a small roll of bills on the table.

Florene broke the silence. "Roger comes on weekends, when he can. That's part of why I'm here, Sister. No one seems to know we have this house. You know what it's like, the authorities don't come here."

Harriet sensed his calm audacity as he gripped her hand. She said nothing. What could she say?

"Sister Harriet just came by to see how I'm doing. She brought cookies. I'll make us coffee. You miss my coffee, don't you, Roger?"

The coffee, when Florene poured it from a battered percolator, made her heart race. They settled before the woodstove. Harriet's efforts to leave were rejected, by Florene, but also by Roger. Florene brought out bread and butter from the larder, an end of ham and another of cheese, and made sandwiches. Roger poured something from a flask into his cup and offered it to Harriet.

"I won't tell you where I stay, Sister. I like to come and see how things are with Florene. Other people here help us. I reckon to leave for good, in the summer." He paused. "I didn't murder those girls."

"I know you didn't," she said. Although she wondered how his not guilty plea would sound in the dock. His expression was calculating, rapacious, jokey. The cards were well and truly stacked against him.

That only made her feel worse. She was so confused. What should she do now? Her silence, faced with this outcast pair, seemed so wrong. This tergiversation had to end.

"I guess it's easier to get around, without your habit," Roger said. "Less staring and people wouldn't recognize you." Harriet didn't like the implication they were partners in dissimulation. At a disadvantage, she accepted the reoffered flask.

"Whisky," he volunteered, pouring generously. "Near as near, anyway."

It tasted like nothing much in her cup, but moments later a numbness flooded her limbs. She sat back in her chair. The fire smiled tenderly upon them through the woodstove door.

"I'm glad you can stay for a visit," Florene said, although Harriet hadn't mentioned staying. The girl contemplated her brother. "I wish you wouldn't drink that stuff, Roger."

"You know I can't sleep, Florene."

A little domestic bickering ensued. The conversation moved on, touched again on the Ava Arundell, and from there ranged to other shipwrecks and olden times in Bothonville. Once again, Harriet found herself telling her life story. Because it was so complicated or, at least, fraught, she soon wallowed in detail. Unless it was the "whisky." She told them about her recent visits to the semi-detached on Marguerite and the house where she'd lived with Rhonda. She spoke of Lafrenière, the place of her intervening years, their home so close to the river you could smell it from the backyard on a summer night.

It was Roger, after all, who left first. As he put on his coat, Harriet fished several of Imelda's sample packs out of the tote—where she now kept all questionable items such as her makeup—and offered them to Roger.

"These pills might help you sleep? I have trouble sleeping too, our nursing sister gives me these. They're pretty strong."

Roger accepted them with a cagey nod and slipped away. Harriet felt disposed to take this as her signal, but Florene prevailed upon her to stay, saying she was all caught up with schoolwork anyway. It seemed the girl would be returning to the Burnhouse-Raquettes only on Sunday night.

Florene beamed. "I had notes on my notes here for the history project, so doing it over wasn't such a big job after all."

Harriet wished Florene had the lighter distractions of other girls. "I'd be telling you this on Monday, your project is impressive. Impressive is a word I don't often use for student assignments."

Florene bloomed like a flower. "Oh, Sister, thank you, and thank you for *everything*. Roger comes when he can. He's not without friends." In her enthusiasm, she added confidentially, "When summer comes, he's thinking of joining the circus."

"The circus."

Harriet knew she sounded startled, and Florene became defensive. "You can be another person in the circus. No one can find you. The biggest circus in North America is coming up the river this year. It stops in Bothonville and he would leave with it." She fiddled with her wraps. "He wants me to come with him."

"Leave Saint Reginald's?" The circus idea sounded fantastic. Harriet had been entertaining the notion of Florene as a boarder next year. "You're only in grade nine, Florene. You're my best student. Well, now that those poor girls..." Could she have been less adroit?

Florene didn't seem to mind being bested by the dead. "Laura and Laurentine and Loretta, they were wonderful students, weren't they, Sister? They were so...perfect." Her voice became dreamy. "Perfect. But you can go to school in the circus, you know. They have a teacher."

"But—where?"

"The classroom carriage, on the train. The train we would live on. Although when they put up the big top somewhere, they set up a classroom in the corner. I guess it makes a change?"

Harriet didn't know what to say. The classroom carriage? Florene, for all she knew, was making up most of this. And yet, circus people had children. However, the idea shocked her.

"If anybody will make use of a Saint Reginald's education it will be you, Florene. Other girls were turned away so you could attend. I always saw you at Vivamus College. Making something of yourself." This was not coming out right.

"Thank you, Sister," Florene said demurely. She thought for a moment. "The thing about these top schools is they give a girl like me something precious but, then afterwards, you might not know what to do with it. You might carry it around for the rest of your life. Like a fancy box that gets heavier with each year. And you still don't know what to do with it. But it would always remind you of the things you were supposed to have done."

"Education is never wasted."

Harriet was thinking how, in her own case, teaching at Saint Reginald's seemed a very random sort of result after all those years of aspiration and swotting. But you had to do something. There would always be randomness. Much less, of course, if you joined a religious teaching order, for then religion and teaching were an entwined destiny. As she mused, she saw herself briefly from the outside: her stolen clothes, her Woolworths makeup, the Marimekko bag—not to mention her repeated adventures and her relentless rule-breaking. She sensed a blush coming on.

"You are my favourite teacher."

Harriet couldn't ignore the tone. She left soon afterwards. Her mind, in a caffeine-induced commotion, continued to review her misdemeanours on the bus home. She'd sometimes thought the young nuns at Saint Reginald's broke nearly as many rules as the girls, but this was faint consolation, for the scale of her own rebellion surely set her apart. Climbing onto the deck of the unfinished bridge was of course the most outlandish of them. In Harriet's mind, however, the bridge was a separate category, that she would defend without knowing why. And eclipsed surely by kissing a killer. A potential killer, but still. What should she do? Roger Pellerin as fugitive was one thing. Faced with Florene also on the lam, she felt more pressure to act.

A picture of the girl disappearing across the horizon chilled her. Her anxiety spiked. Would these disappearances that happened around her never cease? The three Ls, in their combined perfection and tiresomeness, were before her like summoned ghosts. And the pattern persisted. Where, for instance, was Cyprian? She saw Montserrat's handsome features swallowed by the hangman's hood. She violently pushed this image away.

Her thoughts were becoming wild. She resolved to have two of Imelda's pills when she got home to calm herself down. And she vowed to stay off caffeine for a week.

AS THE WORK TO COMPLETE the Bothonville International Bridge ratcheted up to meet the June deadline, a fresh wave of civic unrest and labour disturbances dominated the headlines. The girls were warned as before about going into the city, but this hardly made a difference to them, the new rules being so strict. It became a pastime at Saint Reginald's to look at television images of burning vehicles and police charges. It was surprising what you got used to. And what you could forget. Preparations for the memorial for Loretta, Laurentine and Laura were in exciting full swing, but the deaths, burnished by time and therefore less atrocious, began to seem as if they were a very touching story you had once read.

As for Mr. Montserrat, although Harriet's sense he had checked out on some fundamental level continued, she saw nothing in his demeanour to trigger action. Exchanging a sly witticism with Miss Edison, or dropping his car keys in the snow and mouthing a curse while two girls giggled nearby, Marin Montserrat did not convey killer.

One morning, she had the rug of procrastination pulled out from under her via a summons by Moreau to the anteroom. The interview took only ten minutes. Moreau hadn't minced words. He manoeuvered a bit, cornered her, and came out in no time with everything he had seen on that fateful Saturday night in Carson Falls.

Harriet wasn't the first person to face unexpected calamity in a meeting. She was surprised to realize that you didn't stop thinking, even calculating. Quite the opposite. She moved with glib speed to mitigate damage. She fumbled a pitiful excuse for her disguise, which he took the time to savour before breezily brushing aside. She dramatized a little, expressed remorse, while fine-tuning her strategy. She found the moment to introduce, naturally enough, an ersatz sudden memory about the infamous coat Montserrat wore.

"It just came to me now, Inspector Moreau—about Mr. Montserrat's tweed ulster. I don't know why I didn't make the association sooner." She added craftily, "I forgot, I suppose, that you'd mentioned that piece of evidence to me."

She had the uncomfortable feeling of throwing her colleague under the bus, simultaneous with the thought that it was quite easy to throw a colleague under the bus if the circumstances were right. You said something, and there they were, under the bus. Moreau didn't seem worried about her treachery, in any case. He dismissed her with a gleam in his eye.

As she hurried to her next class, Harriet had trouble grasping what had just happened. So much for her cautious dithering. Even as her weasel brain optimistically weighed the chances Moreau wouldn't rat her out to Perpetua, she succumbed to a lurking panic. She carried on like an automaton on high speed for the rest of the school day.

It wasn't until late afternoon, when she drove another sister to the dentist, that Harriet had a chance to take a breath and think. Instead of sitting in the waiting room while Sister Frederica had her ordeal, Harriet decided to take a spin. Freddie would be in there for a good hour, poor thing, having sadly neglected her teeth, and Harriet for one didn't want to hear anything disturbing, such as Freddie's pitiful cries, through the door.

When she pulled onto deserted Canal Road in view of the bridge, she felt a slight surprise.

Although melting snow lay drearily everywhere, the sky above shone a tender blue. The bridge, from the Bothonville side, looked completely finished to her eye. Its gigantic curves, disappearing at an extreme angle downstream, shone silver in the blessed light. The bridge's promises, today, seemed as without malice as the fleecy pink clouds above it. She made a mental note yet again to look up serpentine chrysotile.

If only she wasn't Harriet, if only she was in someone else's skin, she would feel elevated by the scene before her eyes, nature and human ingenuity harmoniously joined for the betterment of all. All she could think about was whether she was safe with her secret. Now she clutched at hope. There could be many reasons for the detective to share his knowledge with Perpetua. But then, he might not. Perhaps he would take pity on her, even see the humour in her Carson Falls escapade. Although, there were things that maybe a policeman couldn't ignore in a convent school teacher: in particular going to Joe's, where alcohol was served and the Watusi danced, although at least in this case she'd share the blame with Montserrat.

Montserrat would be in the soup too. It was proof of how unclear her thinking was that she was glad of this. Evidently the consequences, she reflected with rancour, would be graver for her. She was a nun, subject to convent discipline. She'd put aside the part of this disaster where Marin Montserrat would be charged with multiple murders.

She wound down the window to change the air. Cold filled the car but, with it, the freshness of the day. She took a deep slow breath, the first she'd taken since the interview. Unless she went rushing to Perpetua to confess proactively, and she'd rather chew glass, it was now a waiting game. If things got too bad, she could always bolt like Cyprian.

It was strange that her hand reached just then for the radio dial. Naturally, the nuns didn't drive around the city listening to the top thirty. The radio, perhaps due to the seniors, was nevertheless tuned to the only happening station around, a Sparta station with a strong signal. And Harriet caught the announcer just as he introduced a new folksinger, from the Sparta area, whose song, "The Wreck of the Ava Arundell," had become a local sensation.

The singer was a new light on the horizon, the announcer

enthused. Going by the stage name Cyrian, not much known about him, a mystery man. Some claimed to have seen him at local coffee shops, late at night when the cigarette smoke was so thick you wouldn't recognize your best friend. The single had popped out of nowhere, and now everyone talked about "The Wreck of the Ava Arundell," although apparently not the B-side ditty, "*Viriliter Age.*"

Harriet listened, with a mixture of shock and bemusement, to the song. She recognized Brother Cyprian's voice. A good song, more than good. It was catchy, the music well suited to the words. It seemed to be about many things: the tragedy of the Ava Arundell, the absence of God and the wintry harshness of life, and it even managed to weave in a voguish harangue against shallow and duplicitous women. You got a sense of the singer himself, someone half in one world and half in another, whom you might meet in the middle of the air, or think you had passed on a bridge, at nightfall, during a snowstorm.

A car backfiring brought Harriet back to herself and she noticed it grew time to get back to the dentist. Frederica, puffed up like a chipmunk, needed her ministrations and it wasn't until she was in her room after supper that she thought again about Cyprian and his song. She still worried about her interview with the detective; but the song had subtly operated on her in the interval like a balm.

Was it the sense of inescapable fate it contrived to present so aesthetically, or was it the sheer cheek of the singer, who had gone AWOL in the middle of a school year and found the resources to produce a catchy local hit in another country, that left her calmer? She remembered his charm, the space travel effect of his golden-flecked eyes. Better to think about that than dwell on Mr. Montserrat and what might be coming for him.

## 24: Truth Sets You Free

IN THE DAYS THAT followed, Harriet resorted to fantasy. Evidence would emerge to exonerate Roger, and he could come back from whatever limbo he was hiding in. Montserrat for his part would never know he'd been in the authorities' crosshairs. They would have to arrest someone else for her fantasy to succeed; but her imagination supplied a killer utterly remote from Saint Reginald's. As for Harriet herself, her various offenses would slip away into the past, and she could get on with her crisis of faith unmolested by lurid circumstance.

She knew now that next year she wouldn't be at Saint Reginald's. How could she be? It was a decision but also a realization. Her doubts, her multitudinous infractions, her chaotic inner life: these weren't the stuff of a religious sister. She lacked practicality, the specific virtue needed for the long haul. She lacked many other things as well, but the contrast between her nervy approach to the world and the other sisters' matter-of-factness particularly leapt to mind. She might become like them in time. The problem of her faith would always be before her like a widening pool.

The other half of her identity wasn't safe from such musings either. She didn't mind teaching; some days she enjoyed it. As a nun in a teaching order, it was also the only game in town. Thought of otherwise, it seemed a good deal less inevitable. Perhaps this was the effect of Cyprian's sudden career change. Montserrat's attitude had left its mark too. He was an excellent teacher. But he conveyed the sense that, just as easily as Cyprian, he could leave it all behind for—what?—life as an independently-wealthy folk singing boulevardier? The terrible poverty of her upbringing smote her. If *she'd* had money, she would have made something of herself. She wouldn't be back in Bothonville, teaching at Saint Reginald's. Some days, however, all occupations felt the same to her, from teaching to potato mashing. Except that, in her current disaffected mood, potato mashing seemed almost more appealing.

But she held no illusions about how much she would miss her fellow sisters. Especially her own little community in the overflow wing, which included stalwarts like Patricia and Rachel, and where being slightly cut off had proved to be nothing but an advantage. If she ever regretted her decision, it was on those evenings when a few of them were assembled in the kitchenette for a freewheeling conversation.

Tonight they were trying out a comfy old sofa dragged over from a redecoration of the common room. Food appeared as usual, Patricia saw to that. It was a little like dorm life, but better than any real dorm life. And if the inner lives of these sisters remained largely a mystery to Harriet, this seemed unimportant to the bond she felt.

Patricia, for example, who was she? Harriet couldn't say she knew her. Had Patricia, eight years her senior, made her peace with convent life? Harriet sensed things Patricia revealed only in small gestures like smoking. Harriet would probably never know more about her.

Sisterly reserve didn't extend to gossip. As the first rain of the year began to fall, they got to swapping tales of sisterly breaches. The conversation was probably triggered by Harriet, who had shared a colourful version of an elopement of a postulant and the janitor's son at the motherhouse. This led to a general trashing of postulants, who would, all agreed, do anything.

But Elizabeth, the group veteran, assured them that older nuns could get up to all sorts of things as well. Without malice she launched into a story, from her former convent, about a nun, a pretty woman, a good thirty years old, who had fallen in love with the widowed father of a student. Harriet felt a premonitory apprehension. Apparently this woman, whom Elizabeth called Sister X, used to sneak out of the convent in disguise to meet her beau.

"They found a whole wardrobe of regular women's clothes, quite becoming clothes, in her cubicle when they searched it. Even some makeup. The thing had gone on for six months, before someone spotted them in a restaurant. Can you imagine being so foolhardy?"

There had been no reason to think the two had engaged in anything really improper—the nuns all blandly considered what this would entail—but it was more than enough. The mother superior there had been a gentle soul, for the most part, but the consequences had been harsh.

"I can't imagine what Reverend Mother Perpetua would do." Rachel's rueful remark caused Harriet to go the counter so no one could see her face.

"We can only imagine, Sister," Elizabeth murmured. "In this case, as well as various smaller penances—no leisure reading, no television nights with the other nuns, no dessert, what else, oh, *endless* extra prayers—they took Sister X off teaching for at least a year. It was the shame of it that I remember. She might as well have worn a scarlet letter. Even if, like I said, I don't think there was actual *activity* to warrant that." Another pause while the nuns pictured scenarios once more.

"People can't help falling in love," Clothilde piped up.

The other nuns surveyed her with favour. With her big eyes and adolescent look, sitting there in her fluffy dressing gown with Lester on her lap, she was an approved recent addition to the wing. Remarks like this were very properly hers. Someone always had to speak up for love, and it wouldn't be Sister Pat, who instead offered, "Now Sisters, before you get ahead of yourselves, the widower was probably potbellied and bald."

"Just as well nothing like this happened here," Rachel observed, "because Perpetua's wrath would be the wrath of the gods."

Harriet rearranged her face as best she could, but slept poorly that night. From being lulled into thinking that her worries might just go away, her fears now sprang back to life, more persistent than before. She had a nightmare in which she scrubbed the main lobby on her hands and knees, in a species of sackcloth and ashes garb badly sewed with lurid green yarn so that bits of her were showing that shouldn't, while people pointed and said loudly, "who's mashing the potatoes now?"

Perpetua, meeting Harriet in the hall, said she must be coming down with something and sent her to Imelda. But no sample pills would help her now. And to think, Harriet said glumly to herself, as she popped a pill anyway, she could be in just the same pickle as Sister X, and she wouldn't even have had the benefit of a romantic interlude.

A FEW DAYS LATER, at the end of a staff meeting, Perpetua turned abruptly to Harriet and Montserrat, who happened to be beside each other.

"Sister—Mr. Montserrat—I would like to see you both in my office, if you please." Her tone was business-like, which in Perpetua could mean anything.

Everyone stared discreetly, while Harriet's stomach cramped. She and Montserrat made their way to the principal's office without looking at each other. Perpetua was on the phone and Clothilde had covered the chairs in the outer office with files. They were therefore obliged to wait on the hall bench, typically reserved for delinquent students.

Harriet wanted to say things like "Admit nothing" and "Let me do the talking." As people went to and fro—the usual traffic, and everyone seemed to be inspecting them—Harriet was very aware of Montserrat beside her, and of her clashing feelings. Despite her susceptibility to the man, she experienced an atavistic impulse to throw him, killer or not, under any passing bus.

Perpetua wasted no time. "There's been a complaint."

They kept their mouths shut.

"A parental complaint about the judging of the bridge competition." Harriet suppressed her relief, but she could have got up and danced, perhaps even the Watusi.

"A Mr. Gorman. Father of Lucy, the senior member of the Gorman and Riley team." Harriet remembered they had adjusted the score on that particular bridge, a well-performing structure but a showy thing, in order to exclude it from the top three. Mr. Gorman was an engineer.

"I really do *not* want us to spend too much time on this. This is, in my opinion, frivolous. But the Gormans are a well-known county family."

"We would need to look at the scores, Reverend Mother." Montserrat was at his most reasonable. "But the choice of winner was unanimous." Harriet nodded. Monsieur Gareau had caught on pretty fast.

"What he is alleging is that the Martineau-Williams team received excessive help from a parent, who is an engineer."

"*He* is an engineer, Reverend Mother," Harriet protested. "Mr. Sholto said it was practically a given that engineers' children win and—" A nudge to the ankle silenced her.

"The Martineau girl's father is a doctor." Perpetua betrayed mild amusement. "But Gail Williams's widowed mother is an engineer."

"How were we to know *that?*" Something more kick-like came from the size eleven City Club loafer.

Perpetua suggested they look over the scores, and then she would offer Mr. Gorman a propitiatory meeting with the two of them. "What, exactly, was wrong with the Gorman-Riley team bridge?"

"It was vainglorious."

An amused Montserrat nodded in agreement. "There were points for aesthetics."

Perpetua raised an eyebrow. "Make sure you have a diplomatic and solid explanation for him. Mr. Gorman has been exercised enough to speak about this publicly. He buttonholed Mrs. Williams at some engineers' social and accused her publicly of having built the bridge herself. He said Mrs. Williams's handiwork was visible in the bridge's pedestrian lines." She frowned. "I feel we are dealing with professional rivalry."

Mr. Montserrat promised Perpetua they would deal with the issue expeditiously. He got Harriet out of the room. Down the hall from the principal's office, he said, half-jokingly, "That could have been worse."

But Harriet, remembering the ankle and more, didn't see things his way. "There is nothing to be amused about, Mr. Montserrat," she said crisply. "Perhaps you can schedule the meeting while I retrieve the file. We'll have to be as honest as we can with Mr. Gorman."

A good general principle. But if the truth set you free, Harriet nevertheless felt relief they had some flexibility to work with.

In Harriet's bridge dream, that night, she walked the deck. It was a spring morning, deliciously mild, but the mood changed as she advanced towards the bridge's mist-shrouded crown. Something lurked there she wanted at all costs to avoid. Then the scene shifted, and she stood in Perpetua's office. Perpetua's eyes bored into her in a horror movie way, as she said, "you may want to consider, Sister X, whether a religious vocation is right for you." Why was Perpetua being cruel—to her, Ruth, only a child? Once again the scene shifted, and she lay in bed in Rhonda's house, overhearing a conversation between Rhonda and her husband. "It was her mother who didn't want her to come back," Rhonda said, "not the other way round. But let her think whatever she likes."

When she woke in the darkness, she was unsure whether this last scene had ever really occurred. She had often overheard adult conversations at Rhonda's house; her bedroom had been a small box room off the kitchen. As the sleepless night dragged on, she became more confused and discouraged. She had hugged her guilt feelings for so long. Imagine if they had been unnecessary.

THE BOTHONVILLE INTERNATIONAL Bridge neared completion.

Warm June was still far away, but Bothonville had already begun to think of the Grand Opening and Inauguration. Like the Seaway, coffer dams had been used during the construction phase. Unlike the Seaway, the destruction of the coffer dams would be spectacular, for the water would run in all at once and not take the whole day and half the night, disappointing the crowd picnicking on the shore in the hope of seeing something good.

The meetings of the Bridge Design Committee had become infrequent. Harriet, who had never gotten around to extricating herself, received the invitation with surprise. She hadn't thought there was anything left to discuss.

On a cold evening with the sounds of run-off everywhere, she climbed the steps of City Hall. There was still light in the sky, the better to see the dog poop revealed by the melting snow and the muddy patches where it was difficult to imagine flowers growing in a month. She was early, and the council chamber was like a cocktail party minus the booze. Mayor Martel bustled over to her to chat. Harriet found herself thinking he wasn't such a bad sort. She saw, for the first time, a kindness in his eye. She realized her feelings for the committee members had undergone a mysterious revolution. There lingered an atmosphere in the room, a kind of melting golden thought among them, that they were only human. Pursuing the Good as they saw it, even as they were lining their own pockets. Even their specious bonhomie seemed to suggest fellowship of a higher order. We're all imperfect, Harriet thought. Also, everyone loves a bridge.

"We'll be discussing the inauguration," Martel said. "That's why everyone's come, tonight."

Harriet looked around. "It's a full house."

"We aren't the inauguration committee, of course, that's another working group, all bells, whistles and fat budget now. But we've done the work, and we do have an interest."

Across the room, Harriet now saw Madame Brunet, Laurentine's aunt.

"Oh, Madame Brunet is here. I wasn't sure she would come back."

I hardly recognize her."

Still swaddled by her minks, Madame Brunet looked like she had lost the battle and been half devoured by them. She was in there somewhere, but she looked a human ruin. Her face was a map of sorrow.

"Tragic, what happened to that family," Martel said. "And the Mazureks too... Maybe you didn't know, Loretta's mother died a few weeks ago."

"How terrible. How did it happen?" Harriet feared the answer would be suicide.

In the months following her daughter's death, apparently, Loretta's mother had just wasted away with sorrow. "Although"—Martel dropped his voice confidentially—"her system was just chock full of chemical insecticide. We store it in our fat, John said to me the other day at the club. The pathologist. A great one for housekeeping, high standards and the newest of everything. But we all use insecticide, it's everywhere. Seems like it doesn't do us harm, but if you lose weight fast like poor Mrs. Mazurek it kinda floods your system. That's according to some, anyway. The Chemistry Department at Vivamus College says that's all bunk and communist propaganda." He added cozily, "Me, I'm just the duly elected mayor, I don't take sides."

Harriet stared. She remembered the fly-tox vaporizer hissing away behind the drapes at Loretta's wake.

The secretary called the meeting to order. Despite the long agenda, the mood was upbeat, if edgy. The old familiar faces were all there. The Retail Council said its members would hold several special sales around the time of the inauguration, on the unstated yet attractive principle that the more you spent the more you should spend. The bridge consortium members waxed lyrical on the cooperation they had experienced. Aloysius and "our astute Church representative, Sister Harriet of Bingham," came in for their share of compliments. Len Silverman added ten minutes of technical effusions about the innovative design features of the bridge, from the horizontal Double Curve to the load-bearing gothic superstructure. Dean Carter ironically thanked the rest of the room for providing the *Herald* with two years' worth of fodder. He looked over at Flynn and it was clearly on the tip of his tongue to make a similar remark about the rioting, but the Vivamus chancellor leapt in to thank the police chief for remaining at the helm during these troubled times. Even Madame Brunet received thanks for the sandwiches.

Harriet became hungry. The refreshment table beckoned, but she would have had to edge by Mr. Byron Slade of Salamander Holdings. A mere human shrimp, and yet, as before, he exercised the effect of a black hole. She must have been staring, and Mr. Slade may have sensed this, for suddenly he looked at her. Harriet once more felt she was witnessing the gates to the underworld beckoning.

During the refreshment break, the atmosphere of a dry cocktail party returned. Harriet was perambulating the room when a timid voice spoke behind her.

"Sister Harriet?"

Before her stood the third woman on the committee. She wasn't noteworthy at the best of times and Harriet had hardly noticed her tonight.

"I thought I'd introduce myself. Since we have another connection out of this room. My name is Mrs. Williams." The name pinged. "My daughter, Gail, is a ninth grader at Saint Reginald's. She was one of the builders of the winning bridge in the competition."

"Gail Williams. Of course. Such a bright girl."

So this was the engineer, the "anxious widow." It had been Mr. Montserrat's expression, he must have had dealings with her. Whatever the reason for the epithet, everything about the woman conveyed tiredness tonight: her bun was tired, her shoulders were tired, every line of her faded face proclaimed tiredness.

"I know Gail's and Karen's prize award is the subject of a complaint," Mrs. Williams said, taking Harriet by surprise. "I felt terrible when I heard. The girls put so much work into their project, and I feel responsible."

Harriet felt alarm. They had just met with Mr. Gorman and had offered what they hoped was the right mix of blandishments and inducements. The last thing she wanted now was a confession from this Mrs. Williams.

"Oh, I think the matter has been resolved."

"That's good, then. Gail was so keen that she made a study of bridge design during the summer. I recommended reading, and she even built a practice model in the basement." Mrs. Williams tucked a wisp of hair behind her ear. "She told me she wanted to win the prize and make me proud, as a member of the engineering team for the Bothonville Bridge. Of course, I sometimes feel I've barely seen Gail since the work began. If my mother hadn't been able to look after the little ones—I also have two boys, three and four—I don't know what we would have done."

Harriet hesitated. "We reviewed the complaint thoroughly, as per the, ah, procedure. The judging was careful and fair. Your daughter's bridge scored the highest."

Harriet wasn't going to disappoint Mrs. Williams, or young Gail, whose face she could only vaguely picture, not to mention Gail's grandmother or the little boys. Although she had spoken as if Gail was well-known to her, this wasn't the case. She had been one of those mouse girls whom it was easy for teachers to overlook. Once the professional engineers' oeuvre had been excluded, as she thought, Harriet had been surprised that the Martineau-Williams bridge had won. Strange, considering even Mr. Sholto had said affably he wasn't sure he had enough weights to pull this one down and they might have to beat it to death with a stick. All this only made Harriet more determined to give Gail her due now.

Even if the woman was telling a tissue of lies about her role in the construction of the winning bridge, Harriet's back had been since yesterday. She would have squared off with Gorman, but Montserrat offered a transparently ridiculous story of certificates of merit long held up at the printer's owing to the strikes, one of which certificates, the one with the most gold leaf, would soon go to Lucy. "You should have just bought him off with a bottle of moonshine, in the other sense," Harriet had said afterwards. Montserrat had been surprised by Harriet's cattiness. But that was the way you sometimes felt, when you didn't know if a man was a mass murderer.

Madame Brunet now approached. She hadn't done much circulating, but Harriet had seen her endure a constant procession of condolences. She seemed eager to attach herself to the women. Mrs. Williams scurried off to get her a plate of grub, for no one had thought to do so. They agreed the meeting was going well, but quickly moved on to general topics. The two others complimented Madame Brunet on her spring hat, which frankly looked like a pot, but a pot with perky flowers on it. It was the only thing about her appearance they could be complimentary about. They urged more food on her, which she admitted with surprise she needed. They even played interference with a couple of Retail Council types who were disposed to butt in. When Madame Brunet said she had made the egg salad sandwiches herself, Harriet sincerely said they were her favourite. Mrs. Williams then declared she had seen the first dandelion today, and weren't they more reliable than any daffodil? They had never longed so for spring. Had they seen a robin? All three had seen their first robin of spring. No word of sympathy was permitted.

They were lightheartedly deploring the length of the meeting when Martel called everyone back.

The last item, Inauguration Participation: General Discussion, could have ruined the mood of good will. But thanks to Harriet, the discussion was short and went well.

The Inauguration Committee had told the Bridge Design Committee that there were six spaces on the crown reserved for them on inauguration day. There would be many locations from which the tens of thousands of people expected could watch. But the spots on the crown of the bridge, so perfect for being able to see everything, the dynamiting of the coffer dams, the great waves of water that would result, the cheering crowds in both countries, not to mention any fly-bys, snowy white doves or balloons the Inauguration Committee had lined up, were the best. Up there in the ether, there would be heads of state and generals, crates of champagne, comfortable bleachers, girls in bathing suits, possibly with bunny tails, and pre-positioned telescopes for the myopic. And the Inauguration Committee was telling the people who had just done all the work, they could have only six spots. The room was irate.

It looked as if they weren't going to get out of there on the right side of midnight when Harriet spoke up.

"Surely, on the biggest bridge in the world"—was it?—"there's room for the entire committee? How many of us are there? Thirty-two? Thirty-three, if we count Bishop Aloysius. That's only one more coach, or three shuttles." Then she had her stroke of genius. She looked humble. "Why—I don't want to speak out of turn—but why couldn't Mr. Slade speak with them? I'm sure he could persuade them to let us all attend?"

A protracted silence. Everyone stared in the direction of Byron Slade. His head was up now, he looked straight into the room. Then his mouth cracked into a wide rictus and he smiled his fearful smile. In a voice Harriet had never heard before, of dead caverns and crumbling bones and endless darkness but, even so, a merry voice, he spoke.

"Consider it done!"

## 25: Novel Flu

THE DAYS AT SAINT REGINALD'S passed as in other springs, with intensifying work pressure even as hearts lifted towards summer. The Easter break cheered the students. For the sisters, it was a time of prayer and fasting, beginning at dusk on Holy Thursday. Harriet participated as keenly as the most devout. Strange how prayer still satisfied when you were an agnostic, an agnostic at the very least. It took on a new intensity, mixed as it was with the painful yearnings of loss and exile. Perhaps her prayers were as good as anyone's, she ruminated during the third hour of the Saturday vigil in the chapel. This thought perked her up, as she considered her rigorous sincerity in comparison to the expedient faith of others. Perhaps God, had he existed, would have preferred her prayers, as being more haunted and sophisticated. She had heard rumours that there were *avant garde* theologians in Europe advancing such perspectives.

She sighed, just as Father Lynch finished up his dreary homily on sin, causing gentle Edwina to squeeze her hand. No, the Edwinas of this world would always be ahead of her in any moral queue. The European theologians were entitled to their beliefs, but there were limits to what would work for Harriet.

If the students hadn't been able to find time to study before, they had no trouble throwing themselves into preparations for the special memorial for Loretta, Laurentine and Laura. The Home Ec pavilion bustled with girls long into the evening sewing their simple white dresses, and unpicking them under the frown of Rachel and her henchwomen. Some of these dresses were not especially simple, for the families who could afford it had invested in costly fabrics and often had a seamstress in the wings should something go wrong. Looking as good as you possibly could became, in the minds of most, a show of caring for the dead girls. Harriet quickly realized Florene might have nothing pretty to wear. She found a cocktail length wedding dress in the clothing drive bin, and Rachel stayed up late transforming it into a dress suitable for a thirteen-year-old. A debate about headgear raged, squelched by Perpetua who ordained simple floral wreaths. They were already spending a fortune on floral arrangements for the grotto, so what were another few hundred circlets?

The Saturday of the memorial dawned promising. The sun brought out the fragrance of the lilacs, blooming right on cue. At three pm, a crowd had assembled in the outer reaches of the grotto area, and nuns and girls all in white made a fine showing closer in. The families of the dead girls sat in the reserved front seats. Around the altar, amid a banked mass of flowers, the three girls in blown-up photos looked out benignly. The bishop said a quick mass, followed by choral singing, speeches with a five-minute limit, on positive themes, and then obscure girlish ceremonies in the approved Saint Reginald's style, one of them being a presentation of bouquets to the families of the three girls. This affecting interlude introduced more choral singing to move the doings along.

Everything was heart-wrenching and yet beautiful. Harriet wondered about the choice of Ella Burnhouse-Raquette as the leading girl. Saint Reginald's could never have a special assembly without a leading girl, and it had been necessary here to choose a friend of the dead girls. It turned out that Loretta, Laurentine and Laura had hardly any friends, beyond each other. The only half-exception to this was Ella, and so Ella had been selected for various showy roles, such as carrying a tall candle at the head of the procession and leading the bouquet giving. She also spoke briefly. Her face, above a rather sack-like white shift, gleamed more secretive than ever, her eyes alight with something fierce and triumphant, or so Harriet thought.

Harriet drifted away from the grotto afterwards with the lay teachers.

"That was very nice indeed," Miss Edison said, working her hankie discreetly.

Ronald Hughes nodded feelingly. "Appropriate and well done." Mr. Montserrat may have frowned. He looked a million miles away, perhaps the result of a Friday night date, Harriet thought snidely.

For reasons she couldn't readily explain, she felt contrary. "It was long. It was uplifting in that Saint Reginald's way. It helps us pretend that everything's been sorted out and we can all move forward."

She hardly meant anything by the words. Yet, astonishingly, for she had never seen Montserrat like this, he turned towards her with all the force of naked judgment.

"I'm sorry if it didn't earn your approval, Sister. Unlike many here, you didn't have time to get to know the girls. To people who knew them, nothing will make a difference. But to those people, a memorial is all they have."

This shut everyone down in a hurry, and all Harriet could think to say was, "You're right, of course, Mr. Montserrat, I didn't think."

She ruminated uncomfortably about his reprimand for the rest of the day. On one level, where did he get the colossal nerve, if he was in fact the killer? On another, how could he possibly be a killer when he said things like this, like a chiding character in a Jane Austen book? In her heart, though, she felt quite furious with him and, unlike an Austen heroine, she contemplated withering repartees and other forms of petty revenge.

THE SPRING DAYS went back and forth between mild weather and harsh gales that sprang up out of nowhere. Perhaps this was why a novel flu virus now began to make the rounds. One by one, the teachers and the students fell before it. Doctors began to visit the school. Some of the infected had to be hospitalized with complications such as pneumonia. Miss Edison, so fit, became one of them, and two Saint Reginald's girls followed. Other girls were sent home to be nursed.

Then, quite suddenly, Mr. Montserrat was hospitalized too. The news came in an odd way. First, without any additional detail, the information that Montserrat had been admitted to hospital. General discussion about how he hadn't looked well. By the end of the morning, people began to say that it might not have been the flu. Around midafternoon, the term "nervous prostration" began to be heard. As the news continued to evolve, curiosity surged. A hint of unease surfaced. What was nervous prostration? It sounded mysterious, on purpose. Perpetua, seen around the school in the course of the day, looked like a ghost. Then an ambulance with siren howling came to the school to bring elderly Sister Edwina to the hospital, and once again the flu was all people talked about.

A disturbed Harriet had gone to look for Patricia but couldn't find her. She decided to take a walk around the grounds. It was a chilly evening, although that horrible wind had at last died down. The grounds were mournful despite the new foliage everywhere. The grass under her feet squelched with recent rain. She had begun to think she would turn back when, in the notorious corner by Convent Road, she came upon Clothilde.

Harriet's first thought was that Clothilde had come for an assignation. In a moment she saw this was unlikely, unless her lover was up a tree. Clothilde leaned against a tree trunk and looking up into its branches. She was weeping.

"Sister Harriet," she cried, "what am I to do?"

Harriet hurried forward. It transpired that Lester had marooned himself up there, unwilling or unable to come down. Harriet couldn't see much and even began to doubt Clothilde, until she heard a sad and frightened mew above her head.

"There he is! Lester! I've been here for hours, I've called and called."

"Maybe he will come down on his own?"

"That's what people say, but cats don't always come down on their own. They can lose their nerve and don't dare try. And they get tired, and they can fall and injure themselves terribly!" Clothilde was beside herself. "That wind is supposed to come back tonight, with rain. What will poor Lester do up there, in the wind and rain and darkness? I can't leave him! First Mr. Montserrat and Edwina and now this!"

Harriet thought. "Maybe we can get a ladder from the shed." Lester mewed again, more faintly, as if he were losing confidence in the humans down below.

"That's higher than any ladder we have." Clothilde's sobbing increased in volume.

Harriet felt rattled and peered up into the dark canopy. "You could climb. With a bag or something."

Clothilde now silently extended her hand to Harriet. In the light of the street lamp, Harriet saw a long ugly scrape, only partly covered by a handkerchief.

"I did try and climb, of course." Clothilde spoke mournfully. "But I fell. I have other cuts, I hope not as bad as this. The trouble is, Lester fights when you want to rescue him. I'm clumsy, too."

This was true. Clothilde could hardly stand on skates and every flight of stairs was for her a perilous encounter. Harriet, on the other hand, had spent a childhood climbing trees.

"Well, he'll scratch me too if I try to bring him down. I need something like a bag."

"My laundry bag? I went back for it."

The bag, big and sound, sealed Harriet's fate. Tossing her coat and belting her skirt higher, she began the ascent. The branches were well spaced and solid. Her feet remembered the way to find footing, and her hands to grasp. It was not too much of an effort, and it had a delicious gravity-defying feel. It didn't take long before she was on eye level with Lester.

He looked pitiful, but ready to fight his saviour. He hissed at Harriet, to set the tone.

"Clothilde," she called down, "he's like a wildcat, I don't know how I'm going to get him into the sack. He'll scratch my eyes out."

"No he won't," Clothilde called back up. "But let me think. I will call out something to distract him, and then you put the bag over his head. He won't see you and the rest of him will fall in."

"Fall in?" Lester's dilated pupils were pools of darkness. "Darling Lester." Lester hissed again and his paws slipped on the branch. This made him madder.

"All right, when I count to three." And Clothilde counted to three, yelling out afterwards in a loud voice, "Fish paste!"

Lester heard the call of his favourite food, and this distracted him for a mere fraction of a second. The fraction was enough for Harriet. Over his head went the sack, and in a berserk reaction he actually did fall in. It was like holding onto a giant demented jumping bean as Harriet made her way down, to Clothilde's cries of encouragement. She fell the last few feet. The sack got away from her and Lester burst out and streaked off unerringly in the direction of the kitchen.

"Oh, Sister Harriet!" Clothilde now shed tears of joy. "You are wonderful!" She hugged her. Harriet felt shaky and sat down on a nearby decorative rock.

Clothilde sat down beside her and linked her arm in Harriet's. "I just couldn't stand the thought of something bad happening to Lester, after such a *terrible* day," she said. "I will be eternally grateful to you, Sister Harriet."

"Poor Sister Edwina, yes. We must pray for her."

"And Mr. Montserrat. We must pray for Mr. Montserrat too."

"The flu is a terrible thing." Harriet nursed her wrist. "Well, we should go and patch ourselves up, you especially."

"Oh, with Mr. Montserrat it wasn't the flu. Not the flu at all." Clothilde's voice, although they were alone, had dropped. She sounded confident and portentous.

"I'm not supposed to tell you this. I'm not supposed to tell anyone." Her eyes were round with what she could hardly wait to share. "But I will tell *you,* Sister. You've been so good to Lester and me—and I know Mr. Montserrat was your special friend."

"Well, I don't know if he was—"

"He tried to kill himself."

Harriet stared speechlessly into Clothilde's face, where the pleasure of gossiping had been replaced by unease.

"I'm not making it up. I've been in the office all day. I heard it all. Mother Perpetua..."

Harriet still said nothing.

"But don't worry, Sister, he's all right. He didn't jump. They stopped him in time. The rioters. They saw him, they stopped him in time. I know it's hard to believe."

It had happened the evening before. There had been an after-class singalong in the barn, mainly for morale, and Mr. Montserrat had been prevailed upon to play his guitar. The songs he sang, Clothilde said, were about longing and dying, meeting Jesus in the middle of the air, that sort of thing. But she certainly didn't associate these themes with his own mood, besides which all those songs, as Harriet must know, were really about sex. That was the last anyone at Saint Reginald's saw of him before the report came through, early the following morning.

There had been another of those nightly riots at River Flats—a spring ritual between police and strikers—and he was seen up on the bridge, about to jump. Some men swarmed the bridge. During his rescue, the police and rioters stopped fighting for a while; strange the way these things happened. Perpetua could hardly credit it, of course, but she was assured Mr. Montserrat had been about to jump. It wasn't a question of Montserrat admitting this, apparently. At least, Clothilde didn't seem to think so. But everyone was sure, just the same. Why else would he be up on the deck in the darkness? He had been in the hospital ever since.

"I suppose he never got over the three Ls," Clothilde said. "What else could it be? Sister Harriet, he is being looked after, remember that. But you must tell no one. Perpetua wants to keep this a secret, from everyone. You can imagine why. Poor Mr. Montserrat deserves his privacy, she says. The reputation of Saint Reginald's has been 'just dragged through the mud,' she said on the phone. I think she was talking to the police? She also had a call with the bishop. She's worried the school won't survive."

"Of course I'll tell no one. But the police...?"

Clothilde studied her injured hand. "She's always talking to the police these days. Maybe because suicide is wrong?"

"Well, still."

"No, who would think like that? I mean, the Church, but what do they know? Lester isn't supposed to have a soul, according to *them*. I can't think of anything more obviously wrong. You only have to look at him."

"The police though…" Harriet's skin prickled.

"That detective, Moreau, even came by later. I didn't hear that part, I was getting office supplies." Clothilde sounded regretful.

Harriet found the rest of the evening difficult. Clothilde was well-placed to get the goods, and perhaps her construction of events was the true one. But Harriet's feelings and thoughts were all over the place. She couldn't imagine Montserrat deciding to end it all in this way. Now that she thought about it, if she had to choose one person who fully embraced life, who seemed to love it in all its provoking, boring, rich, absurd, petty and thrilling aspects, it would be her fellow teacher. He'd been going through something in recent months, there was that. But still Harriet couldn't help associating Montserrat with a comprehensive joy. Perhaps, though, she was dead wrong. Why had he been on the bridge, why was he now in the hospital, and what did the police have to do with any of it? None of it made sense. The man was a puzzle she couldn't solve: strange that this should produce such dread.

The next day little news of Montserrat surfaced, just that he was "resting in hospital." Edwina had passed a worryingly uneven night. Miss Edison was on the mend. There were prayers at assembly for them and for everyone else in hospital and suffering from the flu. A dedicated mass would be held in the chapel after classes. Several students began to look frightened. More parents would be coming to pick up their girls today. Everyone acknowledged Perpetua's heroic resolve.

## 26: Love

THE NUNS HAD FALLEN into the habit of driving day girls home after class, if the news of the rioting warranted it. It was Harriet's turn to chauffeur today. Ella Burnhouse-Raquette, going to her aunt and uncle's house, was her last drop-off.

"How are you finding Florene?" Harriet asked.

Florene spent most of her time with Ella and family these days, with occasional weekends in Turpentine Flats for the now obvious reasons. When Ella didn't reply, Harriet looked at her.

"Sister Harriet, I have to tell you something." Ella sounded tormented.

Harriet knew this was serious. "I'd better park then, Ella."

They ended up on the road running alongside the canal. Even in the spring sunshine the place had a melancholy air. Those eroding black iron mushrooms lining the water made Harriet picture ghost vessels that would never sail this waterway again.

Ella stared at the bridge. "I hate that bridge."

Harriet felt remiss. "We can go elsewhere."

"No. It's as good a place as any." Ella looked at her hands. Harriet waited.

"Those girls—Laurentine and Loretta and Laura—were friendly to me. Especially Laura. I think they thought I was funny. I wasn't part of their club, but I was around them enough. Enough to find out things. They swore me to secrecy. I don't know what to do any more."

Her mouth dry, Harriet said, "Go on."

"It's because of Mr. Montserrat. Mr. Montserrat and Laura were—going steady. It was a secret, I wasn't supposed to tell. Laurentine and Loretta knew too. Even after Laura died and they arrested Florene's brother, I didn't think I should tell. I mean, since Roger had killed them, why would anyone need to know?" Ella fidgeted. "It isn't fun to carry around secrets in you. It gets heavier and heavier. But now Mr. Montserrat is in the hospital—" Ella began methodically to pick pills from her cardigan.

"Ella, hold on." Harriet was stunned, but also confused. "You need to back up."

"Sister, no one believes that about Mr. Montserrat and nervous exhaustion." Her tone was withering.

"It's flu, isn't it?" Harriet said weakly.

"Oh, pulease, Sister." Ella frowned. "Maybe it's just me, though. Maybe I'm the only one who knows. Mr. Montserrat tried to kill himself." She sounded like she were explaining this to a child. "My family has friends at River Flats. They saw."

Harriet felt an instinct to proceed with the utmost caution. "What exactly are you trying to tell me, Ella?"

"Mr. Montserrat tried to kill himself from *remorse* for *seducing* Laura." Ella had alternated between frightened little girl and her usual cynicism, but now she sounded like any sixteen-year-old who watched too many soap operas.

"Are you sure Laura and Mr. Montserrat were actually—dating? Sometimes, girls like to make up things. He *is* good-looking..."

"We helped her hide it. Once she told the school she was going home, and told her family something else and she stayed out all night with him. You can call that dating if you want. Pulease. Laura wasn't like any other girl at Saint Reginald's, she could have anyone. She wanted Mr. Montserrat. And of course he would want her."

Harriet's soul was in revolt against the suicide story, but she couldn't fault Ella's logic. Morality and *mores* aside, Marin Montserrat and Laura Rome were made for each other. Blatantly obvious when you thought about it. A moron could have seen it. Should have seen it.

Ella frowned. "Or did Mr. Montserrat just miss her too much to live? I also thought maybe Laura was expecting and he couldn't face the loss of his unborn child. Especially if it was a son. Anyway, now I feel terrible, because I think I should have told someone sooner. But every time I thought about telling someone, it felt like I should keep my mouth shut. But now with Mr. Montserrat trying to jump off the bridge, I can't stand it."

"You—did well to tell me, Ella. But the police need to know."

"That's why I'm telling you, Sister. You're not like the other sisters. You won't mind pretending to be the one who knows this and telling the police yourself. This way you can keep my name out of it entirely." She encouraged Harriet with a smile.

"What? Ella, you should be the one to go to the police."

"We *never* go to the police."

"But Ella, for me to pretend that I knew this all along... I'd get into terrible trouble. I'm an adult. Anyway, it wouldn't be credible." Imagine keeping such a secret for that snake.

"Oh, you wouldn't need to pretend you knew all along." Ella was reasonable. "You could give them *this*. Laura left it in a book I borrowed, but you could say you had just discovered it in the pocket of that jacket of Laura's you wear. Don't look like that. Florene told me. Well, it came out. Personally *I* have no problem with you dressing up like that, but, well, others might..." The beady-eyed stare belied her airy shrug.

"This" was a folded paper. Harriet opened it. It was a short letter from "MM" to Laura, not much more than the details of an assignation, but he called her *cara mia* and signed off with *It's been eight months, one week and three days*. Tenderly counting the days of their romance? Why did everyone in love sound sappy? But this bordered on lovesickness; it significantly qualified her picture of aloof and dry Marin Montserrat. Of the mysterious MM. What difference did it make that he didn't sign in full? Harriet recognized his bold black Waterman pen strokes. As Ella liked to say, pulease. She folded the letter carefully. This provoking girl had cornered her.

"I put my hands in those pockets, I would have found it before,"

Harriet said.

Ella nodded like this was a normal conversation between student and teacher. "In the lining, then?"

"That's from Perry Mason, the episode with the nurse who poisoned her patients."

Harriet pictured Alain Moreau, who had that way of going cold and focused, especially with people about whom he already knew discreditable things. But then she remembered the shoulder bag of Laura's. She had never used it. It was the sort of thing people did—open a purse one day for no particular reason, go through the zippered compartments, find that bus ticket they'd forgotten about, or that letter from their high school teacher arranging an assignation with them. What an utter bastard. But that wasn't really what she thought. What an innocent she'd been.

"I'll see what I can do. Meanwhile, you talk to no one about this."

Hours of wallowing later, Harriet still had many questions and two thoughts. The first of these was that something as terrible as suicide wasn't motivated by soap opera feelings for unborn heirs. And the Donegal tweed ulster dangled in her imagination again as much more than just a coat. The other thought was that Ella hadn't connected the dots as she could connect them herself—and as the police probably would too. The girl had seemed in a muddled way more worried about Montserrat than anything else. With Roger Pellerin in the frame, few felt the need to look further.

HARRIET AND MOREAU agreed to meet at the basilica. She would be there anyway because of the clothing drive. The basilica was hushed and empty when Moreau sat beside her in a pew. The last time Harriet had seen him, she'd offered up Montserrat's Donegal tweed ulster. But she knew they weren't yet square. Today, she hoped, would settle things.

"Inspector, I have some information for you. With Mr. Montserrat in the hospital I thought it was urgent—but I just found out, as I'll explain. I have an old purse of Laura Rome's"—she'd brought it as a prop—"and when I went through it a couple of days ago, I found this." She handed him the letter.

The detective read it quickly. "Well, damn. Sorry, Sister." He read it again, seemed to tense up. His face changed. "MM—Marin Montserrat. Tell me how and when again."

She admitted she had hung onto the note for a few days. This would give him something minor to chide her about. Did she recognize the distinctive handwriting? She did. "I don't really understand." She spoke in a lowly nun voice. "But it doesn't look good…"

Moreau stared at her for a minute, taking in her little show. He must have thought it was a good little show because he said, in a lofty voice, "What it means is obvious. You did well, Sister, to come to me."

"Inspector, this is the second piece of information I've shared with you. Does this make me a police informant?"

He looked like he wanted to laugh, then wasn't so sure.

Harriet applied the next layer. "First I had to be a sort of industrial spy for the bishop and"—slight emphasis—"all of Bothonville really, and now here I am again sharing information that may be related to a murder case and that I feel quite uncomfortable sharing. A lot of people would think these weren't suitable roles for a Sister of Saint Thomas. Can you assure me my particular role won't come out? Mother Perpetua especially might be upset. Anyone could have noticed the tweed coat, or found the letter in the purse?"

He considered her with a hard look on his face. "You sat on this letter for three days, you say. Some informant." Then he relented. "I see no reason why Perpetua should know." A cynical smile. "This might shock you, Sister, but, when I saw the two of you together outside Joe's, I thought *you* might be having an affair with Montserrat."

"But I told you how we met by accident—"

"Yes, and this letter proves what you say."

Suppressing annoyance, Harriet nodded. "I understand. Your discretion is appreciated."

As she drove home, she reflected yet again on her tangled web of motivations. On the plus side, she'd covered for that poor child Ella, who sat on the letter for months and could have been in a lot of trouble. Also, she'd given the police information that was rightfully theirs. They could withhold the letter's existence from the Rome family, which might be useful for a few reasons. As in confession, obligation had driven her in these matters. Including the obligation to get herself off the hook.

Under the circumstances, how could she feel absolved? Handing over the letter had been driven by Ella's blackmail hints, conveniently supplemented by her need to curry favour with Moreau. And maybe, while she reviewed her grubby reasons, resentment against Montserrat. He owed her nothing, he'd done nothing to her, Harriet. Led a double life and kept it secret from her, which was exactly what she had been trying to do all along with him. But she felt such a fool. And revenge was so tempting, and had a way of slipping in incognito.

His secret romance with Laura Rome maybe only proved how little she'd known him. She was always finding out with a sense of shock how ignorant she was. That crack Clothilde had made, for instance, about gospel and pop songs being all about sex. Was sex just everywhere? She had made an effort to recollect song lyrics, and it made sense. How could she have been so ignorant? She pictured Montserrat singing about his time of dying. It certainly shed a new light on the song's intensity, not to mention Marin Montserrat's delivery.

As for whether Montserrat was a mass murderer, and whether, under the circumstances, Harriet's plain duty was to stop second guessing the police, the thought never crossed her mind.

When she parked the station wagon round back she saw Patricia having a covert smoke and joined her. Patricia was as always a soothing presence, but even with her Harriet couldn't share some things.

"I can hardly wait for the end of term," she said to Patricia, who replied, "Sister, I can hardly wait." They stood there side by side in the late afternoon sunshine, each lost in thoughts that were too difficult, and perhaps dangerous, to share.

PERPETUA HAD GONE to the chapel to pray. If prostration before the altar, like those characters in *El Cid*, would have made a difference, she'd have done it. But she didn't believe in such tricks to make God listen. There must be a divine reason for what was happening at Saint Reginald's. She prayed for an explanation, because she for one, was stumped.

In hiring Montserrat, she'd worried about many things. Principally, of course, was that he would tie one on with another teacher. There were so many pretty young nuns about nowadays, and the spirit of change was everywhere. Even clandestine romance could be framed in an exalted way: joy mingling with pain, the ecstasy of idol smashing.

Blue-robed Mary, crushing snakes under her bare feet, gazed down at her. Across from Mary stood the Sacred Heart. These were her idols. She had always loved them. The reckless courage of Mary, stepping on poisonous snakes. The Dionysian beauty of Christ, augmented somehow by his wounds.

Moreau's call had come through that morning. After so many shocks she should have been inured. But she had literally staggered.

"Mother Perpetua," he said, "there's no way to sugar coat this. Right now, my men are arresting Marin Montserrat at the hospital. He's being charged with the murder of Laura Rome."

She cried out, and he made sympathetic noises. As the investigation progressed, new information had come to light. They had evidence of a secret relationship between Montserrat and Laura Rome. The River Flats witnesses had seen more on the night of Laura's death than they'd admitted. A man answering to Montserrat's description and a dark-haired younger woman in a shiny dress and duffle climbing the circular stairs.

"But how in God's name could they have made their way up there?"

"Mother Perpetua, that's hardly the point. If you want to get up on the bridge, you'll get up on the bridge. A fact of life."

More back and forth ensued, as the catastrophe opened in all its ugly potential before Perpetua.

"Inspector Moreau," she finally said, "we've always wanted to know what happened to our girls, but this is a death blow for Saint Reginald's. First our best girls die. Then a brother of one of the students is arrested. That is bad enough. Now we find out a teacher is responsible. A teacher who's been having a love affair with the president of the student council. Whom I myself hired as the school's first male teacher, just three years ago."

Put that way, it didn't sound good.

"Yes, Mother Superior, it's unlucky for the school, but—"

"So the arrest of Roger Pellerin was all for nothing? It brought gratuitous shame on us?"

"What? Well, we were working with the evidence."

Steel entered Perpetua's voice. "The question, Inspector, is whether you are certain this time you have the right man? Before you destroy this school, it's a question to ask yourself."

He stuttered a bit.

"I understand the pressure the police are under, Inspector Moreau. All I can do now, as the principal of this struggling academy, is throw myself on your mercy. I *must* ask you to keep the information secret. At least until the end of the school year."

It took only moments for him to capitulate. He said the police had kept bigger secrets, and no one in Bothonville needed to know, not yet. Montserrat's few relatives were in New York, and he'd more or less lost touch with them. However, Perpetua had to remember trials were public. But for now he thought Flynn would agree. He sounded reasonably confident, so they had probably discussed it. The chief was a friend to the clergy.

She had the presence of mind to ask, before they hung up, whether Laura Rome had been, ahem, with child. Moreau's voice expressed weariness. "The girl wasn't pregnant."

This, Perpetua told herself now with pardonable pride, was how it was done. She had gotten through the rest of the day somehow. A terrible day, for the realities penetrated in waves and by degrees. She had felt positively ill. That they had nursed this viper in their bosoms.

As light fled the chapel, she shook off this thought. In the soothing shadows, the face of Jesus seemed suffused with pity. The face of Mary was drier. The statue might have been saying something tonic and astringent. Not necessarily about necessary evils, but about pulling yourself together and carrying on. A little salty advice between women.

She had bought time with lies. Like many before her, Perpetua had a fleeting fantasy of being hit by an opportune bus. But there was no use thinking that way. She meditated on the perfidy of men. She told herself, legitimately under the circumstances, that the Saint Reginald's experiment with male teachers—notwithstanding the blameless Mr. Hughes—had come to an end.

She relaxed. Half-light made most things better. The important thing to remember was that she alone at Saint Reginald's possessed this terrible information.

In this she erred, for Clothilde had slipped into the outer office at the beginning of Perpetua's call, and had heard everything. And Clothilde shared it the same evening with a stupefied Harriet, her new special friend since the heroic rescue of Lester on that dark and stormy night.

## 27: The Merry Clown

AT LEAST THINKING about Montserrat as a killer made a change from thinking about him as a shameless Lothario. So said Harriet to herself, a few days after Clothilde had shared her information, when she could think at all. She had envisioned Montserrat as a murderer on and off since Carson Falls. It was almost soothing to know. And yet, not really: she couldn't banish a vivid picture of Laura being shoved off the bridge. Her own personal problems and the ominously lengthening list of her peccadillos only exacerbated her angst. She sometimes felt a visceral urge to run away. On the whole, in leaving Saint Reginald's, Harriet felt she'd be going while the going was good.

She stood at her open window one evening, procrastinating, when it struck her that someone should tell the Pellerins. It was complicated, though. The police could hardly announce charges being withdrawn without a reason. Perhaps an accused Roger, out of sight and out of mind, remained a good distraction. They might not even care. Unfair, but no one cared about the people of the shanty towns. The least she could do, however, was pass on what she knew.

By midday the next day, Harriet waited at the bus stop in a warm weather version of her student getup, supplied by the continuing bounty of the clothing drive. There was something about spring, in Bothonville, that took you by surprise. First came fake spring, the sound of runoff really. Next came doppelgänger spring. Balmy air and a smell of putrefaction; but interspersed with snowstorms, so that once more you crushed down hope. Before you knew it, you were being suffocated by lilac. And then, still in your winter tights, you were in the middle of a heat wave. Her madras capris were light, and the belted cotton shirt, she hoped, gave them a varsity air. She had tied back her hair in a kerchief and wore sunglasses. It was a delightful seventy-four degrees, and the bus was filled with Bothonvillers out and about.

Turpentine Flats was the same world of shadows, but Harriet saw small flowers peeking out among the roots of trees. The walk seemed longer than ever, as if Turpentine Flats repositioned itself from time to time, just to be on the safe side. But the Pellerins' door appeared at last, framed with some kind of thorny blooming vine of the folktale species. Florene, in her white memorial dress which she must have worn to mass, flew to greet her. Roger Pellerin sat at the table.

"I came with news for Florene, but it concerns you," Harriet said. "Good news," she added hastily, for Florene had turned as white as her dress. She told them what she knew—that Montserrat was in jail, charged with the murder of Laura Rome, and that this information was a closely guarded secret. She felt reluctant to bring up the love affair, but found herself mentioning Montserrat's letter and so the rest came out.

Florene was shocked and yet overjoyed. A light flared in Roger's eyes, but he said nothing.

"It seems strange they can keep this under wraps, but another sister overheard exactly this between Mother Perpetua and that police inspector. It seems improper, but I don't understand the law. Are you supposed to be their filler criminal?"

Her words provoked a dark smile in Roger. He seemed thinner than before, by now he really had the look of someone who lived rough. His face bore the lines of want. He asked her many close questions, and she answered as best she could.

Florene was still trying to visualize her teacher being a murderer. "I can't believe it, Sister, I just can't."

"I can't either," Harriet admitted.

"I can picture him and Laura *in love* though." Harriet made a grumpy sound. "In love," the child repeated dreamily. "Like Romeo and Juliet that we read about this year"—when would grade nine stop teaching that play?—" beautiful in a kind of Mediterranean way...an age gap, although of course Laura Rome was a grownup woman...and then, their tragic deaths. Well, Mr. Montserrat isn't dead yet, but—" She looked queasy. She turned to her brother. "I can't believe it, Roger."

Harriet put her offering, a pound cake and some string beans, on the table. "There are things you will never understand and can't do anything about, even if you did." She didn't like her own irritated tone. "Here, courtesy of Sister Patricia; Edwina is semi-retired." The gesture seemed inadequate and she rooted around in her tote. "Some more of those pills, Roger?"

Florene looked at her brother. "Will you be able to come out of hiding now, Roger?"

"When I see it on the front page of the *Herald*."

Harriet stood up to leave.

"Thanks, Sister," Roger said. "For sharing the letter with the police. You didn't have to. You could have worried more about Saint Reginald's."

Embarrassed, Harriet shook her head. It was just too complicated to tell him about Ella's hinted threat, or that she planned to leave Saint Reginald's anyway. She mumbled, "I'm not that corporate."

The Pellerins hadn't been ecstatic. Roger trusted no one, especially the police. Why would he trust the police under the circumstances? She pictured Flynn's rosy-tinted and freshly-shaved face, his pseudo-earnest eyes and ready smile. A mother superior had to do what a mother superior had to do, granted. But these were deep waters, with many sharks about.

SPRING HOVERED ON the brink of glorious summer. The race was on to the end of the school year. The girls threw themselves into preparation for a final pageant. This year's was a depiction of the founding of Bothonville by the Sieur de Bothon, played by Mr. Hughes, and a mob of leering white-frocked *Filles du Roy*. Mr. Hughes looked well in his acetate knit doublet and breeches, but Harriet imagined how much better Montserrat would have looked.

Perpetua got Harriet to drive her to Saint Angus on a fine Saturday. During the ride, she seemed disposed to probe into Harriet's feelings, specifically how she'd found her first year at Saint Reginald's, and then, more intrusively, how her vocation was going. Harriet's vocation was going, yes, that was one way to describe it. She wanted to say to Perpetua, how is your cover up going?

The cover up, as it happened, was going well. A supply teacher had been pulled in to replace Montserrat, and "nervous breakdown" was the new phrase bruited about. If he wasn't at the hospital anymore—Miss Edison also had tried to visit—that only "proved" that he had gone to some institution providing longer-term care. Which in a way was true, as he'd been remanded into custody in the city jail.

Perpetua had a funeral to attend in Saint Angus. She told Harriet that Bishop Aloysius expected her. Harriet waited in an airy apartment with windows on a courtyard garden filled with statuary. She was curious. Why had she been summoned in this way?

Aloysius arrived, a tray of sandwiches and lemonade following. He had aged since Harriet had last seen him, but he was his old kindly self. He asked Sister Grace whether there was still some spumoni ice cream, as if Harriet was ten. He had been writing his weekly sermon, he said chattily, on the fascinating topic of religious doubt. "I don't know why it is not examined more closely."

Harriet squirmed.

"And what is doubt? What is faith, for that matter? Some consider atheism its opposite, but some consider doubt the *true* opposite of faith. There is a third way to look at it, doubt and faith being different sides of the same coin. There is much richness in the question. Some of our greatest saints, Paul of The Cross, the Great Theresa, suffered doubt." The bishop's voice became dreamy. "Faith, darkness, then consolation."

He seemed to expect her to jump in here. "I suppose, Your

Excellency, many Catholics experience brief episodes of doubt."

"Well, in Saint Paul's case, it was forty-five years. For decades, all the poor man saw was the darkness of the universe, and his own inner darkness. Theresa writes that she once thought atheists terrible liars, then decided it was believers who were cheats. Sitting down at the table with these atheists—oh, it was the bitterest meal for poor Theresa." Aloysius now looked less ecstatic than sad. "A necessary meal, perhaps. Bitter herbs. Of course, like a lot of people, she went back and forth."

"Is that the theme of your sermon?" Harriet wondered if the man needed protection from himself.

"No, my child. Much as the half-light of our days can be both a grief and a balm. My theme is abandonment. Doubt's dark twin. To be forsaken. Our greatest trial on earth. "Although —" his eyes probed Harriet's inner soul, "there is great suffering also when we ourselves forsake. Perhaps, even—" he cleared his throat, "greater suffering. Would you not think so, Sister Harriet?"

Harriet felt a confusion at these words. Mr. Montserrat, pining pitiably in jail but still a murderer for heaven's sake, appeared and faded from her mind, to be replaced by Henry the cat, nevermore to be found.

Bishop Aloysius rambled on. "It's the way things disappear. Disappearance. That is the thing I am trying to get across. Are you quite well, my child? You look under the weather. You young ones work so hard. I insist you finish these sandwiches."

They went out into the garden. They stopped before a bronze effigy of Francis feeding a cat. The air was warm in the sunshine and cool in the shade. The perfume of a nearby flowering shrub filled the air.

"What advice will you offer the faithful in your sermon?" Harriet had to wonder.

Aloysius looked at her in an interested way, as if the idea of advice was a thought-provoking and novel one. "Indeed, indeed," he murmured. "I often wonder. Sister, would you like a bouquet of this weigela to bring back to the convent? Two bouquets, one for you and one for your Reverend Mother, who's had such a painful year. There is something else I want to give you. Sister Grace will make up the bouquets, come inside."

With an eager smile he presented her with an elaborate ticket, and a lanyard attached to an identification card, on which she was surprised to see a photo of herself.

"I had these made up for you. I've been invited to the inauguration of the Bothonville International Bridge, in the special seats at the crown. As you sat in for me and did such an exemplary job, you should come too. Don't worry, I've cleared this with Mother Perpetua. They will be in touch and give you specifics. I hope this is a small compensation for your committee work." He had the grace to add, "That you may not always have found easy."

Harriet couldn't pretend this wasn't exciting. To be present among the Bothonville elite but, even more, just to be on the bridge—legitimately—at its very highest point, seeing everything at last, both shores and everything in between, Salamander Island and even Ella's island, like green jewels in a sea of blue.

"They say the crown of the bridge is halfway to heaven," the bishop said. "Which is of course blasphemous. But, as you told me, it is the largest bridge in the world."

"Thank you for thinking of me, Your Excellency. I think, perhaps, it was *you* who told me it was the largest bridge in the world?"

A rumble of thunder stole through the open garden door, and a breath of wind skittered through the room. The old man was too busy boxing up the remaining sandwiches to reply.

THE WIND DIDN'T LET up that Saturday, and blew fitfully through Sunday. On Monday morning it strengthened—1963 was a year of winds—and by nightfall had a driving force. Harriet and Rachel were out in the blustery twilight, sorting arrangements for the final assembly. It had been decided, with the dry weather, to hold it out of doors, in the grotto area. The sisters were out late because every other moment of the day had been crammed with things to do.

"If this wind keeps up, we'll be moving it back into the auditorium," Rachel said.

"It's three days away, we should be all right." The gusting wind unsettled and Harriet felt out of sorts, wary. The big lilacs, denuded of flowers, tossed around them.

Some raindrops flew by in the dark, and then Harriet suddenly thought, *but they're snowflakes.*

"Snow! How can we be getting snow?" Despite the wind it was a mild night.

Rachel looked at her oddly. "Sister—your face." She touched Harriet's cheek, and there was just enough light to see the smear on Rachel's fingers. More flakes whirled by them in the air.

"Soot," Rachel said.

In the distance—in several distances—sirens began their cry.

Perhaps strangely, Rachel and Harriet kept working. Sirens continued to play on their nerves and cinders to float and dance in the air. They finished staking out the space for the various performances—the janitorial crew had wanted a seating plan on paper—before going inside, just as a smell of burning reached them. They hurried to the nuns' common room where two groups had formed, one around the television set, and another leaning into the radio.

"What's happening?" Harriet asked a grave-faced Elizabeth.

"There's a fire in the city, Sister, a very substantial fire. Five alarms. A number of buildings on a downtown block."

Several sisters nodded and Clothilde cried out, "It's terrible! They've just announced a General Alarm! It's the wind."

"The air is full of blowing soot outside," Rachel said.

Perpetua, her presence among them indicating the gravity of the event, looked up quickly. "Do you mean live cinders?"

Rachel exchanged a look with Harriet. "I don't know. Black smuts, lots of them." Now everyone stared at Harriet's smudged face, while she rummaged for her handkerchief.

The news had just come in. It was like the button factory all over again, although more worrying. Bothonville's historic downtown was crowded, four and five storey buildings squeezed together with narrow lanes behind. It seemed the fire had started in a factory that had no business being there, a survival from older zoning rules, and had spread in two directions at once, thanks to the wind. Several adjacent buildings were now alight. The narrowness of the lanes and other barriers were preventing access by the firetrucks. A multi-block evacuation was underway. The General Alarm would bring in a few old fire engines from the surrounding villages—of what use these decrepit trucks?—as well as pumpers and ladder trucks from Carson Falls. But Carson Falls was far away, and the fire seemed to be travelling so fast. There was no news of injuries or casualties.

Perpetua stood up. "We must see about the roof." Her eye fell on Harriet. "Please come with me, Sister." She looked at the excited nuns. "As we wait for news, Sisters, I would counsel you to pray." A few nuns dutifully whipped out their rosaries, while others turned up the volume on the television, still broadcasting the chatter of a journalist over grainy pictures of chaos.

"Do you know, Reverend Mother, where it started?" Harriet said as they climbed the stairs.

Perpetua named an intersection. The old heart of the city, the worst possible place.

On the building's fifth floor they came to an industrial-looking door. The stairs inside were metal. Perpetua led the way to another door, and they stepped out onto a railed platform, suspended vertiginously between gables. It provided a magnificent 360 degree view above the trees. The wind blew strong and blustery as ever and a fine ash floated by.

While Perpetua surveyed the roof with eagle gaze, Harriet stared in the direction of downtown. There on the horizon hovered a substantial brightness, a fluctuating wall of lurid yellow and orange. Considering how far away they were, the fire must be huge. Harriet's eyes tried to penetrate the distance. Streaks of molten red appeared and disappeared, presumably in a vast curtain of smoke. The flames must be hundreds of feet high. She listened. Sirens still threaded the night air, and was she imagining a dull roar that wasn't wind? Also, was there a popping sound, like thousands of paper caps set off at once by a legion of small devils? From anxious and excited, Harriet's feelings swivelled to horror. Beside her she heard Perpetua mutter, "*Defende nos in proelio, contra nequitiam et insidias diaboli...*" Harriet's unsteady hand reached for her beads.

When they returned to the common room, the faces of the nuns told the bad news. Reports now stated that several people were trapped inside the popcorn factory where they thought the fire had begun, with a sizeable explosion. This was the Merry Clown Popcorn Works. No Bothonville child had escaped tasting its rubbery over salted product, with and without caramel coating and pink sugar. Following the explosion, the flames had almost immediately engulfed two other buildings on one side, one a tenement filled with apartments—casualties from this building unknown—and the other a furniture warehouse storing varnished wood items that had apparently all gone up at once in a gigantic flashover. While the firemen were trying to contain this inferno and extract survivors, no one had noticed that the Bothonville Jail, on the other side, had caught.

It was a fine stone building, but the roof was of wooden shingles, which the city had always been meaning to replace, and the exposed frame was of seasoned wood. The flames had invaded the attics at once, where who knew what was stored, and penetrated down via the electrical system, although this information wasn't available until days later. What the fire crews on the ground knew right away was that a choking smoke rapidly filled the building. The few canister oxygen tanks they had were inadequate, but in any case, they could see nothing once inside. When a third floor collapsed onto a second floor, badly injuring two men, the crews withdrew. The narrow lanes and a lovingly preserved historic stone wall prevented the trucks from getting anywhere near the main building. The jail went up like a torch.

No one could estimate at first how many were trapped inside.

But a hysterical jail guard who looked like he'd been dipped in soot, questioned by a television reporter, croaked that he was sure none of the prisoners, sixteen in all, were able to get out. The next day, this number was confirmed, and augmented by five guards.

Most of the nuns stayed in the common room until well past midnight, when they finally announced that the fire had been contained. It would still burn for hours. Two whole city blocks would be ruins. At least it wouldn't spread, like those dreadful historic conflagrations you read about. Relief began to appear on faces.

This wasn't true of Perpetua, stony-faced, Clothilde, convulsively hugging Lester, or Harriet. These were the three who knew that Montserrat had been among the prisoners that night, none of whom was likely to have survived.

INSPECTOR ALAIN MOREAU, man of sorrow, stared out his office window as usual. Since the fire two days ago, he had been bothered by the same thoughts over and over again. The terrible death toll, now estimated at eighty-nine, hovered constantly before him, but it was one death in particular he focused on. There were so many associated tactical and strategic considerations, more or less intriguing; and, suprisingly, he felt the pressure of human considerations as well.

The Saint Reginald's murder case, he decided, must be jinxed. How else to explain losing two perfectly good suspects? First, Roger Pellerin, and now, Marin Montserrat, incinerated via the Merry Clown Works fire. That Pellerin was still the official suspect in the public mind was probably good, since there was now no other suspect. Although it was also perhaps—what was the word?—unfair. This unfamiliar acknowledgement made Moreau wince. Perhaps one day something could be done about that, but not before that little dragon lady in charge at Saint Reginald's got off his case.

Complicating matters, Moreau didn't feel one hundred percent convinced of Montserrat's guilt. He hated these second thoughts. Had he remained sure they had their man, he would have been happier.

They had sweated Montserrat thoroughly—was this something else he had to feel guilty about?—but the man, looking like some saintly heartthrob with his suffering face, had stuck to his story. He had admitted to an affair with Laura Rome. He said they had planned to marry. Well, maybe they had. A picture of Laura wreathed in orange blossom and Montserrat in a suit appeared, Moreau couldn't afford a cluttered mind, and he uncluttered it, but not before Laura's smiling face became Maureen's. Montserrat had refused to say whether he had been on the bridge with Laura Rome. This made it hard to grill him about what had happened up there. And as for the deaths of Mazurek and Brunet, Montserrat insisted he had nothing to do with them. This, Moreau was unfortunately inclined to believe.

It was all less troubling now that the man would never be tried. At some point you could announce he had been charged, and quietly drop the case against Pellerin. The city would have its scapegoat, for one girl or all of them, take your pick. Burned to death, so no one could say he had got off unpunished. Perpetua would still have her PR problem, but she had asked him for time and he had given her time. And Pellerin would be allowed to come back to Bothonville. From a personal perspective, Moreau liked this outcome best. The safest one, since a man couldn't come back from the dead to deny the charges. The arrest of Montserrat would remain a feather in Moreau's cap.

He frowned. This could all spiral out of control. Time would probably run out in connection with the identification of bodies. It would be weeks before they found Montserrat's calcified remains. Even if they never did, entirely possible due to the heat, lists of incarcerees existed. That slice of the truth couldn't remain buried for ever. *Que sera,* as the song went. He realized he didn't mind the *que sera* aspect. He was growing weary of all his career connivance.

He wandered over to the window, on whose ledge two cock sparrows shrilly fought for a plump crumb. Yes, Montserrat as the guilty party was the best outcome. Or so he tried to believe, he really felt very mixed up inside.

And another point of confusion: had Montserrat even been

planning to jump, on the night they'd detained him? The River Flats rioters had sworn to it. The officers had been too busy to get a good look. Montserrat had refused to discuss his reasons for being on the bridge that night. Not that it mattered one way or another now. Not knowing made it difficult to get a handle on the man, to break through the enigma that was Montserrat. Moreau didn't even know why this bothered him as much as it did.

Maureen here infiltrated his thoughts again. He had been doing a lot of thinking about Maureen. He had seen her another time with that grinning ape Bill. She'd looked happy. And why wouldn't she look happy? She deserved to be happy. He'd been good to her in the way a detective inspector with his hand practically on the brass ring is good to a young woman who worked at a lunch counter and was always willing to give him a good time. In other words, maybe not that good at all. He had no idea what Bill had that he didn't have, and no idea what Montserrat had either—well, barring the glaringly obvious. Whatever they had, Maureen had preferred them, and there must be a reason for that. Moreau wrenched his mind back to the various conveniences of Montserrat's death, but an inner voice said to him, very clearly, no wonder she moved on.

He went back to his desk. He had a sandwich crust somewhere. Those hungry birds needed more than a crumb.

## 28: Exposed

SISTER HARRIET WAS IN a bad way. She had gotten over the immediate shock of the death of Mr. Montserrat, but she was still inconsolable. Now that he was dead, she forgot all about the charges that had been hanging over him. At least, they no longer counted for much in her mind. Which was remiss, or perhaps just confused. All she could picture now were Montserrat's virtues—she ascribed them to him one by one in her thoughts—and, like a blade in her heart, their awkward exchange after the school memorial, when he had spoken sharply to her. She had seen him around afterwards in the halls, but those had been their last words together.

Sharp? Had he in fact been sharp? Not really. He had spoken truly. And now she could never talk to him again, never rebuff his flirtations or laugh reluctantly at his witticisms, never tell him he had been right about the memorial. What had that Paul of The Cross said? The world was an abyss. And Harriet, looking into its depths, was hollowed out.

Never had she felt so isolated. Being unable to speak to anyone made everything worse. Not to Perpetua or even Patricia, for there were limits. And she didn't feel like enduring the histrionics of Clothilde, whom she'd heard the other day decrying that no one was mourning the dead jailhouse mice.

The realization that she had no vocation was a daily reminder that her entire experiment as an agnostic, if not atheistical, nun at Saint

Reginald's had been a farcical failure. Just a way to kill time, because it wasn't like she'd been able to set aside a little nest egg. What would she do? The penniless had few choices. She looked at the girls, dizzy with the thrill of ending the school year, and felt like a weary spectator. Everything made her feel exhausted, which may have been why she was careless, and slipped up.

Among Montserrat's sterling virtues she didn't list were his troubadour or Watusi dancing ways, and yet these elements were reasonably prominent in her recollections. This may have been behind her decision to board the train and end up, incognito, at Joe's Corner Lunch on the following Saturday. The place also reminded her of Brother Cyprian. Joe's seemed to be a receptacle of gilded memories. If she had hoped to recapture the glamour of her previous visits, she was disappointed. The beatnik music wasn't up to much and the food portions had gotten smaller.

She had made a mistake in coming here. She'd experimented with a shift dress from the clothing bin, and then she'd had to worry about her arms and legs. Everything about going to Carson Falls had testified to a certain recklessness, her new outfit most of all. The dress was demure enough, but so much arm and leg had hardly been exhibited since childhood. Then there was the makeup, and her hair, which she'd done differently, with Bardot bangs and the rest tucked into a fabric band. She felt depressed inside, but her sprightly exterior and unaccompanied status drew attention. She refused invitations to dance, from lesser men.

One young woman recognized her. Linda Belfast, the daughter of Mrs. Belfast, the basilica's queen of the clothing drive, had on a few occasions met Harriet. Later the same Saturday Linda quarrelled with her mother, who thought she spent too much time at Joe's with that boyfriend of hers, and Linda imprudently defended herself by saying that even a sister from Saint Reginald's went there. The whole story couldn't fail to come out, following which Mrs. Belfast immediately rang up Perpetua. Harriet was summoned to the principal's office to explain herself.

Barely out of her dress and makeup, Harriet knew that this summons was trouble, in fact it probably meant the jig was up. She therefore had precious minutes to compose herself and prepare.

"Sister Harriet," Perpetua began, "it has come to my attention that you've been seen out of your nun's habit in Carson Falls, in a place called"—she paused—"Joe's Corner Lunch, which I understand is some type of musical café. Serving alcohol. Where there is dancing. Is this true?"

Harriet had never seen Perpetua look so cold. And yet her mind was strangely alert. Which visit, she wondered. Likely today's, but she needed to confirm.

"Yes, Reverend Mother, it is true." She meekly dropped her gaze, hoping Perpetua would fill the void.

After a moment, Perpetua did. "I am looking for an explanation, Sister. That a nun of Saint Reginald's would leave the convent without permission and go to a beatnik café dressed in lay clothing…and school not out, with all the girls still around. Anyone could have seen you, and Mrs. Belfast's daughter Linda did. And wearing a sleeveless dress, above your knees! What madness is this?"

This proved enough for Harriet. Soon she'd have to tell Perpetua a whole lot more—she didn't plan to go *vagus* the way Cyprian had—but just now was not the time to talk about her failed vocation. As she'd hurried over, she had examined with lightning speed the various excuses and explanations. The worst, she knew, would be the best.

She composed her face into regret. "Reverend Mother, I'm glad to be found out. This has been a burden to bear. I have found myself, despite ceaseless prayer, in love with Mr. Montserrat." She dropped her eyes. "I've tried to bring my thoughts back to the right path. But I haven't been successful. I was thrown so often into his way, there was the bridge project, for instance"—she meant this as a dig—"and I haven't been able to shake my feelings. I know this is weak, and I beg your pardon with all my heart. Nothing improper ever happened between us. I don't think Mr. Montserrat even knew." She wrung her hands. "At first when he left, due to his nerves, I decided to see it as a blessing in disguise. But his absence didn't make me think about him less. It was torture to be around him, but worse torture not seeing him. I'd heard he played guitar every Saturday in Carson Falls, and I had to see him. And he wasn't even there."

Perpetua's face gave nothing away, but Harriet could imagine her rapid thoughts. With Montserrat gone forever, this could be handled expeditiously.

"I couldn't go to a place like Joe's in my habit," Harriet hurried on, "and then the idea came to disguise myself from the charity clothing bin. All I wanted was not to be recognized, just to sit in the back and be able to look at Mr. Montserrat once more."

Now she looked Perpetua in the eye.

"Because, Reverend Mother, I've started to believe Mr. Montserrat may never come back to Saint Reginald's again. I don't know why I think this, but I feel he might be lost to us."

Perpetua's gaze flickered. Harriet didn't want to give her ideas, so she added in a rush, "I know what I did was wrong, but in a way this trip helped me come to my senses. When I was riding back on the train—"

"Dear God, the train."

"Yes, well, it came over me that I am a wretched sinner. I believe I can overcome this, with continued prayer, and the grace of God. And with your guidance, of course."

Perpetua let the silence develop. Harriet began to think she had overdone it with this fabulous tissue of misdirection. Her being in love with Montserrat had a kind of fluctuating truthiness. All right, she would finally admit this to herself. In reality, her attraction had come and gone and who knew what she really felt. Certainly, she sensed how gross the exaggeration she'd just fed Perpetua was. Perhaps the one simple truth to pass her lips was her conviction that she was a sinner.

It was fitting that a tear should now run down her cheek. Although at first she didn't recognize the sensation, for Harriet hadn't cried since the day her mother died.

A good deal more discussion followed. Perpetua said the things Harriet expected her to say, and a few she didn't. The ordeal wound down at last. Harriet could hardly believe her luck.

"But this transgression can't go unpunished. This has been a grave offense to the school and the order. To begin with, I am rescinding my permission for you to attend tomorrow's inauguration of the new bridge. There will be other penalties. I am very disappointed in you."

And so Harriet was dismissed. She spent the next fifteen minutes boxing her illicit gear and leaving it with Sister Pat, in case Perpetua got it into her head to have her room searched. Patricia asked no questions. Back in her room, Harriet felt awful. Awful that she had let down her reverend mother, awful that she had engaged in such monumental and puerile lying. And, now that she had been forbidden, quite disappointed that she would miss the inauguration. For why else had she had all those eerie dreams about bridges, if not to prepare her for this single moment, when she would stand at the highest point of what was surely the world's most phantasmagorical bridge, and see at last in every direction?

## 29: The Middle of the Air

HARRIET HAD THE LAST of her bridge dreams that night. In this dream she consciously tried to recapture the euphoric feeling of her earlier dreams, but without success. A gale howling continuously in the background stoked unease.

This soundtrack may have been provided by the wind that blew over the rooftops of Saint Reginald's all night long. The day dawned fair, if cool, with ragged clouds racing across the sky. The light had a lemony thinness, which outlined the brittle edges of things. Cast in this unusual light, there was something memorable about the world, but Harriet didn't care. She faced a day of irksome tasks and petty obligations, and she put the much-anticipated inauguration out of her mind.

ALOYSIUS HAD WALKED the parapet of the bishop's palace the night before. He had been out there a long time in the insidious wind, for he felt restless. When the day dawned equally restless, he could barely drag himself from bed. His breakfast nauseated him. He staggered in getting up from the table. His aides got him back to bed, and called the doctor.

The regular doctor came right away, and a second doctor within the hour. This one suggested the hospital. But the bishop refused. Not only did he refuse, he insisted on getting dressed again and called for his car. He had a role to play at the inauguration of the Bothonville International Bridge, and vertigo, fatigue and cold sweats weren't going to stop him. But as the car pulled into the basilica parking lot, where the luxury shuttles were lined up waiting, he lapsed into unconsciousness. The driver raced the car to the hospital and they whisked the old man to the emergency department.

The bishop was seriously ill, so said one nurse to another, in the gossipy Sunday way of Catholics. Aloysius, slipping in and out of consciousness in his hospital bed, knew he was going nowhere but was hardly resigned. He worried that Sister Harriet wouldn't be able to secure a good seat for herself in the bleachers without his ecclesiastical muscle.

MRS. WILLIAMS AND HER family had escaped the novel flu virus. At least until now. And how unfortunate that Mrs. Williams's mother had picked this time to be out of town. Picked might be the wrong word. Her sister in Halifax had broken her hip, and Mrs. Williams had been left unsupported in her domestic responsibilities. The youngest boy, Tim, had been unwell on Saturday morning, and had gotten steadily worse all day. By the next morning his temperature had climbed dangerously high. There was no question of leaving him with Gail or a neighbour. If she was to claim her spot on the crown of the bridge, she would have to leave early and return late. Tim was much too sick. She could go nowhere. Mrs. Williams had no doubt this was the right decision. She attributed her ongoing unease to the strange wind.

She hung up her mint green boucle suit, bought for the event. She put the brand new Instamatic, with its fresh roll of film, back in the drawer. How disappointed Gail would be that there would be no snapshots of the inauguration to show her. Gail, in reality, wanted most of all to see pictures of her mother fraternizing bridgetop with the dignitaries. She'd been fantasizing about showing a photograph of her stylishly suited mother to her schoolmates, especially that bossy Gorman girl.

MADAME BRUNET'S husband was away on business, and so she had the house to herself. It was a big house and, since they had no children, a quiet one. Madame Brunet was still in her robe by midmorning, looking out the window at her garden. In the intervals of acid light, the garden looked strange, the foliage a poisonous green. Plant debris was scattered over the grass. The rose bushes, as usual, had been hardest hit. Really, roses were the greatest nuisance; everything affected them, wind, rain, heat.

Laurentine had loved them best. Especially the old French specimen rose, *Laurentine d'Aragon,* which she had prevailed upon her aunt to plant. Its flowers were the palest of yellows, reminiscent of the girl herself. Fussy beyond belief, its blooms barely lasted twelve hours on the stem. And now there was nothing left of them, delicate petals blasted everywhere and immature hips still clinging to the thorny branches. Madame Brunet decided she was going nowhere.

To hell with the bridge inauguration. She looked over at her bed, where her clothes were laid out. Today, she told herself, she wouldn't squirm into her Maidenform girdle, nor would she squeeze her bunions into her stilletos. And those pearl hatpins she'd bought on the advice of the chair of her club, to anchor her hat against the wind, could stab someone else. She'd stay put, and wouldn't answer the phone in case, for instance, Chairwoman Fraser called to complain she was letting down the sisterhood.

And while she was busy lowering her standards, why bother getting out of her cozy robe? There was surely something to watch on television. She never read the fiction in her magazines, she could start now. She felt an unfamiliar feeling inside her, then realized it was hunger. Perhaps she'd make herself a good breakfast to begin with. When was the last time she'd done that? Something good, something her mother would have made her as a little girl. Blueberry pancakes with syrup. She had the ingredients. She headed for the kitchen with purpose.

EVERYTHING WAS READY.

The crowds stretched for miles on either side of the river. The dignitaries were assembled on the stratospheric crown of the Bothonville International Bridge. It was less dramatic than they had hoped, for television cameras obstructed the view at every turn. But this was necessary, so that all the yokels below could see them and hear their speeches on the giant screens lining the river, not to mention the other yokels watching on their television sets at home. Still, when the jets did their pass in a roar of noise, leaving the skies to the news helicopters, a palpable excitement filled the well-dressed crowd on the bridge. Somewhere else, the technical people had their fingers over the button that would trigger the rapid release of the coffer dams upriver. They'd get a cramp waiting for all the speeches to conclude, but that was the way of these things. Whole chapters of contrivance and delay were required, or how else could a climax be a climax?

At least the sky had cleared. It now blazed forth blue, mirrored with a wine-dark intensity below. Len Silverman became lost in admiration and got a crick in his neck gazing up at the gigantic lines of the bridge. It felt like being in an airplane.

Without a fear of heights, Dean Carter peered over the rampart. The water was far beneath him, its corrugated surface giving the faintest sense of what must be substantial waves, and this even before the dam water rushed down.

The freighters in the shipping lane beyond the velvet hump of Salamander Island looked like their old Tinker toys, men from the Retail Council said to men from the bridge consortium. Far in the distance you could just make out Bothonville on one shore, and even Sparta downstream on the other, their tallest buildings reduced to matchstick stubs.

It was a world between heaven and earth, and they were the chosen ones to occupy it. So said Mayor Martel in a lyrical aside to Police Chief Flynn, although he had to shout, up there in the middle of the air, for the wind was a howling beast.

The speeches took up the next hour. Perhaps the crowds below heard them better than the assembled elite on the bridge. No one heard a thing up there, what with the wind and the various noises made by the innovative combination of flexing cantilevers and quivering suspension cables. Not everyone on the river bank heard very well either. This was the time to get out the picnic, anchor the plastic tablecloth with rocks, and distribute the food, sandwiches, hard boiled eggs, cakes, amid shrill demands and competitive invective. Anyone who'd brought a sweater or jacket was happier than anyone who hadn't. Small children began to snivel and were ordered to shut up or they'd be removed.

"And then you won't see it when it happens," their mothers threatened, while a receding vista of giant mouths moved unheeded on giant screens now less interesting than the Vachon Flakies.

By the time the speeches wound down at last, many on the crown thought they imagined a subliminal bounce in the platform under their feet.

This special feature of the bridge dealt with stress, the Vivamus College chancellor immediately pointed out. A bridge of this size and design required it. For instance take today's wind, which was certainly getting stronger. How else could a bridge like this withstand a wind, except by bending? It was the difference between the oak and the reed. The reed bent, the oak broke. Although, to be sure, the bridge was in many respects like an oak, half a million oaks, and it had to be, for what would the terrible force of the water rushing below do to a mere reed? After a general's wife lost her hat to a broadside gust, a few people moved away from the edge.

The bridge began to hum quietly to itself.

A photogenic girl with a carrying voice was now hauled out from behind the dignitaries to do a countdown for the television. Half a mile upriver, in a plexiglas booth, the real countdown took place. There, the coffer dams crossing the river for miles would be dynamited all at once. Cognizant that the Seaway water release of a few years ago had been a poor show, the adults bored and the children fractious, the engineers had used extra dynamite this time. The idea was for the water to move down to the bridge all at once.

In the booth, a man with binoculars said, "Two, one, zero, Ernie—geez *Ernie*," and Ernie parked his cigarette to press the button, a red one. A rumble like Krakatowa getting ideas rose until sound filled the universe. An instant later the earth shook beneath them and they flinched in their little box as a pressure wave blew through. The coffer dams had vanished in the first split second, replaced by a glittering cloud that grew and grew, and then levitated bizarrely—almost like a spaceship, said Ernie, who now had the binoculars. The spaceship cloud quickly left a clear view below. A clear view of nothing.

"What happened to the dams—sunk, I suppose?" the boss man asked.

"Pulverized," Ernie said.

"Hey, give me the binoculars," said the boss. He focused them. "I just see the river, I guess the river and the sky. Weird sky though—dark."

"It's not the sky." Ernie spoke authoritatively. "It's the water, coming through."

No one needed binoculars now. In the space vacated by the glittering cloud and the pulverized dams, a wall of water, about as tall as Bothonville's tallest highrise, moved downstream at a hundred miles an hour.

"*Geez.*"

Downriver, the bridge began to sing in a higher register.

NEVER ONE TO WASTE his time, Mr. Byron Slade wasn't chitchatting with the other dignitaries. There wasn't much for him to see either, because he was so short. Before the end of the speeches, he'd wandered away in the Sparta direction.

The bridge crown was very large, and he had no trouble finding a place in which to be alone, tucked from view behind immense girders and cables. There was a kind of stairway of ledges here that was just the thing. He first climbed up to the top of the parapet on the downriver side—he had to hold on against the pernicious gale—to survey Salamander Island. It gave him immense pleasure to see that the rail lines were all in place. He had A-plus transportation infrastructure now connecting the island to both shores. He could look down into his huge serpentine chrysotile pits, so far away they were like moon craters viewed from space. His processing works were equally huge. These scorched areas on the great verdant hump of Salamander Island were relatively small still, but he'd soon see about that. He planned to exploit the whole island, which would yield him immense profit.

He tottered down and, leaning into the wind, scuttled across the deck to the upriver side. From this spot he was first among the dignitaries to see the approaching wall of water.

Deep in the bridge's inner structure, something had already begun to change. Byron Slade became aware of a gentle swaying, which developed a cradle-like rhythm whose appeal he couldn't deny. The swaying increased, until it was more like a tossing, and Slade was gobsmacked to see whole soccerfield-sized deck panels begin to lift and billow like bedsheets in the wind. At the same time, the bridge began to emit sounds like a hundred philharmonic orchestras tuning their instruments, changing their minds, and then starting all over again. The wind meanwhile came in great volleys, which added a sort of syncopation to the up and down and now side to side swaying of the bridge.

The cable Slade held onto began to vibrate and shake. The vibrating increased and was joined by an intestinal shuddering that travelled through his body. Slade's teeth rattled in his head. The tuning of instruments was now a kind of frenzy in his ears and he looked up to see the bridge superstructure rising and falling like the masts and yards of a monster galleon in a storm-tossed sea.

It was at this moment that he really looked upriver, and saw between river and sky the dark blue advancing wall.

It took him a moment to take in what he saw. He continued to stare, while hanging on to the writhing cable even as it abraded his hands. He managed to connect the dots pretty quickly. After that, it was somehow easier just to wait.

Far away, as if it had nothing to do with him, he heard faintly the bellows and shrieks of the other dignitaries and the television crews. The blue wall before him rose higher and higher, rolled closer and closer. By the time the water hit the already stressed piers, it was travelling at two hundred miles an hour.

The moment of impact was a strange one for Byron Slade. The bridge roared—he felt sure of it—whether triumphantly or in despair he couldn't say. His bones sensed, before his brain, the disemboweling force of the impact, felt the crumbling of the massive abutments and piles, grasped the splintering everywhere of solid steel. In a staggering movement the bridge tossed him to the ground, where he landed hard, small bag of bones that he was.

With all the strength he could summon, he crawled across the deck to the other side. All around him, against a rushing and roaring sound, the cables, their tension unbearable, had begun to make eerie echoing sounds. And then one by one they ruptured and the air filled with gigantic razor edges flying by him. He pulled himself up onto the other ledge overlooking Salamander Island. The best asset he had ever owned, and he wanted to see it one last time.

The bridge surface suddenly softened, became sponge-like beneath his feet. It was like an unexpected and even agreeable hallucination. But the subsiding was real: the bridge was collapsing. With the sound of a thousand freight trains, the whole structure of the bridge convulsed and began to sag, like a slow-moving elevator at first, then faster. Byron Slade trained his eyes on Salamander Island below. Another convulsion threw him clear of the disintegrating wreckage and thus Mr. Slade began his final journey, down towards the emerald hills beneath him.

Spiralling buoyantly in the wind, surrounded by dust and debris like small shooting stars, he lost his grip on time. The ground beneath him seemed not to be getting closer. Was he flying now, amid the barbed stars? Was he imagining the blackened goblin floating by him in the air? It had a very familiar look. Whom did it remind him of? *I used to have everything, now I have nothing.* Byron Slade was soon borne away on an air current and lost in distance, leaving Byron Slade, tiny human cinder descending, to notice, with failing vision and a sense of surprise, the sunlit beauty of the blue and green world hurrying to meet him.


ON THE SPARTA SIDE, alone at the top of an escarpment far from the horrified yet titillated crowds, two young men watched as the Bothonville International Bridge collapsed. It was a relatively lengthy business, with more water spray and dust than you might suppose, and then there was the fascinating way the travelling water subsided into the great pacifying basin over which the bridge, perhaps unwisely, had been built.

The one with sandy hair said, "Now that's a song subject. 'The Lament of the'—oh, heck, I'm not sure, I'd have to think."

The yellow-haired one said, "They'll love it at the monastery."

"At your seminary too. But you're forgetting, I'm not going back to the monastery—or to Saint Mark's."

"Right." The yellow-haired one nodded. "Your new life as Cyrian the troubadour awaits."

"Well, I'm not so sure about that either. But you seem sure."

"I am."

"Are you headed straight to the seminary, Marin, after I leave?"

"Eventually. Not for while."

## 30: Pact

SAINT REGINALD'S ACADEMY was like a painted picture on this early July day. Not a breath of wind disturbed the leaves on the dreaming trees. Nothing stirred in the heat, or at least nothing was visible on the groomed paths and clipped lawns. Away from the main building, beyond the shady groves, the long grass swayed with secret life under the hot sun. Saint Reginald's, on that afternoon, looked like it was eternal. It gave no sense of its recent tragedies.

The girls were gone for the summer, but for the handful in irregular circumstances who remained. These still slept in the school dorms, but ate their meals with the nuns in the refectory. They were a useful addition to the games of slow pitch and volleyball the younger sisters were keen to organize. On some evenings everyone assembled for a singalong around a campfire. There would be marshmallows to roast, but no guitars. It was a summer like any other. But the mood was subdued compared to other years.

Bothonville had had virtually no time to mourn the dead from the Merry Clown Popcorn Works fire, before it had to mourn all over again, and on a much vaster scale.

That its citizens would mourn, and then rally, there was no doubt; for didn't the Bible say there was a time to weep and a time to laugh, a time to mourn, etcetera and so forth? Thus said the mayor, evidently not Larry Martel since he had perished along with more than three hundred others in the bridge collapse, but the new acting mayor, Roddy Sorenson. And so echoed the lead editorial in the *Herald*, written with stirring adjectives by its editor-in-chief, Clay Bolton, for Dean Carter too had died. Whether the whole city would go along for the rebuilding ride remained to be seen. Sometimes, on a Sunday afternoon, Bothonvillers drove down the highway to Carson Falls for an ice cream cone, and families found their way to the Carson Falls bridge site, where they could view its ordinary sturdy lines shooting straight ahead and think happily about future shopping trips to outlet malls, if not this year then next.

Harriet spent a lot of time helping out in the kitchen. It offered a chance to spend a few hours each day alongside Patricia, who oversaw much of the work now. Patricia was easy on Harriet, whom she privately thought of as all thumbs. She was surprised Harriet threw herself into the more tedious tasks, insisting for example on mashing the potatoes every time. In reality, with most of the girls away kitchen duty wasn't arduous. And Harriet felt a moment of pride when she could claim as her own the peach pie carried out to a singalong.

The reason for all this was to tire herself out. She wanted to be worn out and foot sore, with a backache if possible, after she whipped off her apron for the day. She wanted to sleep without Imelda's bubble packs.

Harriet had still not had her important conversation with Perpetua. She was waiting until after the circus came to town. Why the schedule of the Pickle Brothers Circus, admittedly one of the great travelling circuses of North America, had anything to do with Harriet's spiritual journey was unclear. Perhaps it was because she was going to see it, in a group of nuns and girls, and she wanted to feel she still belonged with them, at least for that night.

Perpetua's threats of punishment, following the discovery of Harriet's escapade, had really not borne fruit. There'd been little things, here and there. A certain tone of severity. But it had been Harriet herself who had taken on the kitchen work, for instance. Perpetua didn't seem to want to punish Harriet much. Nothing had made this plainer than when they had discussed which nuns would accompany the girls and Perpetua herself had fingered Harriet. And how could Harriet refuse?

It was a slow business, weaning herself off the pills. She spent very bad nights, in which she had ample time to review the lurid details of her recent life. The bridge collapse framed everything, naturally. Everyone still thought and talked of the bridge. Private experiences and smaller scale hardships were seen differently. The bridge catastrophe didn't make Harriet feel her troubles were less, but it put them in perspective. She did feel pity for the dead. But the only committee people she'd actually liked, setting aside Larry Martel as a maybe, were Madame Brunet and Mrs. Williams, and they, by some peculiar coincidence, had been spared.

And the bishop, of course. What horror there had been when the sisters thought Bishop Aloysius had been among the dignitaries on the crown. And what rejoicing when they discovered he had been in the hospital all along with a mere heart attack.

The four deaths that had thrown Saint Reginald's into crisis, only three of which were being admitted to, lingered in Harriet's imagination. Loretta, Laurentine and Laura had been seen off to the spirit world, where their youth and imaginary perfect futures could live forever, untouched by harrowing time and sordid reality. Of Marin Montserrat's death this couldn't be said, and Harriet felt it like a wound that wouldn't heal. Other feelings were interwoven. Missing Cyprian—unless this was envy, for his song continued to be popular—was one. Also a sense that her life, after those two glorious trips to Joe's to witness up close the lives of people who danced and drank and could feel the pain of love without a massive accompanying guilt complex, was now quietly subsiding into middle-age. These two brief moments, along with a few others such as the impromptu skating party, had assumed a kind of splendour in the grass brightness to Harriet. The only antidote was moving on with her life. And she would: presently, she would.

If she ducked that, Harriet feared it would be one of those summers during which time slowed, and nothing moved. Caught between past and future, she felt simultaneously young and old. Ignorant and green because she'd hardly yet grappled with life, tired and superannuated because her timid experiences had mocked her heartily before throwing her up on the passing shore. And she was coming up, ominously, to her thirtieth birthday. In moments of restlessness she felt the urge to doll herself up as she had never dolled herself up before, and take the most crowded train possible to Carson Falls without hat or sunglasses. But what would Harriet do once she got there? Someone had told her only the other day that dull Mr. Hughes had gotten himself engaged. So she couldn't even imagine herself, in some floaty summer number miraculously extracted from the cornucopia of the clothing bin, with new coordinating lipstick and a really good haircut—this despite the fact she didn't have a bean—meeting up by accident with him. Not that she wanted to meet up with him by accident. Not at all. Weren't these the fantasies of a much younger woman? It was just that when Harriet had been younger she had been otherwise preoccupied. She also suspected there was something about the threshold of thirty that brought much yearning and folly to a head.

The hot afternoon was easing into mellow evening when Harriet met Patricia outside the kitchen door for a shared smoke.

"I should stop bumming these off you, Sister, and get my own," Harriet said.

"Don't give it a thought, Sister." Patricia took a satisfying lungful of smoke. "It's the least I can do, now that I've made you an addict."

"I could quit any time."

Lester emerged from the shrubbery and entwined himself around their ankles.

"It's shaping up to be a fine summer." Patricia gave Lester a pat.

Harriet pictured the wasteland of weeks ahead of her if she didn't act. She watched Lester slope away into the long grass.

"I'll be leaving the convent," she said impetuously. "I haven't told Mother Perpetua yet. Please don't tell anyone."

Patricia took her time blowing smoke into the golden air. "I can't say I'm surprised, Sister. I wondered about you, last summer. We were on the train together, remember? I said to myself, we'll see what happens with this one."

"Am I that much of a misfit?"

"It's not the word I would use. I'm sure you're a fine teacher—it's what I hear." Patricia pursed her lips. "Anyone who hangs around here for any length of time has got to have a practical streak. I'm not sure you have a practical streak."

"I was trying to be practical. Coming here, after I'd lost my religious vocation, was a supreme effort in practicality."

Patricia nodded comfortably. "Worth a try."

The silence stretched and Harriet felt increasingly let down. She'd wanted more from this conversation. A little emotion, or perhaps she meant drama. She glanced over at Patricia, to see with surprise that the other watched her closely.

"It's all about piloting your boat, Sister. Take me, now. It was a blow to be taken off teaching, but that's long gone. I had a few hard conversations with Reverend Mother, I promise you. Vocation was mentioned. It worked out well for me. I swung a summer in Rome, in the end. A vocation refresher, we called it. There was a discretionary fund. Now, why I wanted two months in a hundred degree temperatures I'm not sure, but the evenings and nights are what I remember. I learned Italian too. I'm from Saint Angus. It was more than I could hope for."

She brushed cat hair off her skirt. "I'm getting a bit of wanderlust again, I'm thinking Lourdes this time. I hear the Pyrénées are beautiful. You need to think strategically, Sister. What does the word opportunity mean to you? Don't get dramatic with Perpetua, decide what you want before you broach the subject with her."

Patricia smiled enigmatically as she ground out her butt, before slipping it into the metal case.

Harriet was mute. Wanderlust? Opportunity? Discretionary fund?

The other tapped her temple. "Practical, Sister. Practical." She added, "For example, I wouldn't think about joining the circus. In some circles, that would go without saying, but with you I'll just mention it anyway."

PATRICIA DROVE, and the Rambler was crammed with nuns and girls. As they headed to the athletic grounds on the edge of town, the nuns had to restrain the girls, who reeked of cologne and were inclined to lower the windows and yell. It was that kind of evening, dimming gold and purple shadow, the air muggy, the anticipation grabbing you by the throat.

The first sight of the illuminated midway, and the various tents and caravans spread out as far as the eye could see, produced actual squeals. The field lights were just snapping and buzzing into life as they parked. Under their harsh glare, the giant red and blue big top dominated the middle of the field like an object in a dream.

Harriet felt her insides unknotting, and surrendered to the evening. They visited many booths, they ate cotton candy, they tried out rides. Rachel won a teddy bear at a coconut shy and gave it to a passing boy. Clothilde disappeared into and had to be extricated from a fortune teller's tent. They visited a hippo in a tank and an overweight alligator in another tank. The crowd was immense and it was a struggle to stay in a group, although this was necessary since the girls attracted their share of attention. As darkness fell, they found their ringside seats in the big top.

It was a circus like any other. Clowns warmed the audience. Then there were the trapeze artists, with more and more daring acts. While their parents performed above, down below in the three rings children on unicycles engaged in intricate manoeuvres with a poise that left every child in the tent in a state of catatonic yearning. Between the acts, hawkers leapt from bleacher to bleacher to sell overpriced bags of peanuts and strange glittering sugar edibles. The evening ended with the much anticipated wild animal acts, introduced by a procession of elephants. The smells were of roasted peanuts and canvas, confined animals and hay, with fragrant puffs of the summer night when boys tried to slip under the tent wall for free.

Yawns and chatter alternated on the car ride home, interspersed with comments by the nuns that it was almost midnight, good gracious.

"You're quiet, Sister Harriet," Rachel said. "I hope you enjoyed yourself?"

"Oh yes, Sister. I'm tired, that's all. It was wonderful, though."

Harriet wasn't tired: she was thinking about Roger Pellerin, whom she'd seen raising the trap doors through which the big cats surged into the round cage to confront the lion tamer. Her eyes had followed him as he darted like a fleet shadow this way and that beyond the glare, loaded gun at the ready. And she also thought about a trapeze artist, whose willowy performance had especially wowed the crowd. The sandy hair was longer, and anyone would look quite different in a cherry red leotard. But Harriet knew she was looking at Cyprian swinging from rope to rope, above the sawdusty abyss. And when he launched himself from a trapeze bar and flew upward, before taking a graceful nose dive down to where another swing miraculously met his finger tips, she didn't scream like the rest of the crowd, because she was sure Cyprian had found his natural element at last.

THE NEXT DAY, Ella showed up unannounced at Harriet's room door. Harriet had been putting her street clothes, as she thought of them, in a suitcase. She didn't bother to hide it. She gestured Ella to the armchair.

"Going somewhere, Sister?"

"Just tidying," Harriet said. The time to speak with Perpetua approached.

Despite her smart aleck tone, Ella looked demoralized and frightened. She clearly had something to impart. Harriet said, half-jokingly, "Are you so eager for September you had to visit us?"

"My parents don't think I should attend Saint Reginald's next year. They want me to go back to the island. It's nicer, now that Salamander Island is a ruin." She added spitefully, "And I don't think

I want to come back, why would I? I haven't decided."

"Ella, I've got things to do."

"When I told you about Laura and Mr. Montserrat, I didn't tell you the whole story."

A coldness clutched Harriet's heart. Ella wriggled her slight body into a better position.

"Sister, I started feeling bad, the longer Mr. Montserrat was gone on his nervous breakdown." She made it sound like a sabbatical.

Harriet chose her words carefully. "You told me he was having an affair with Laura, and he jumped from remorse."

"They *were* having an affair. But there's more to the story. Those three girls, they had a secret. At first I didn't know it and then I started noticing things and then they told me a bit more, and then Laura told me a lot more."

"Yes?"

"They had a pact," the child said flatly. "Well, they had different pacts. You know, the girls at school are always on diets. The three Ls, being so perfect and all, had to be on a *better diet*. They were even in a competition to lose weight."

Harriet frowned. "I don't think they needed to lose weight, quite the opposite." She began to feel uneasy. "But what does that have to do with Mr. Montserrat?"

"They also made a *suicide pact*."

"Ella, of all the untruthful things—"

Ella's shrug was defiant. "I don't care what you think. You know what those girls were like. They always had to be perfect, successful in everything. Everybody expected it."

"That...might be true," Harriet said reluctantly.

"All three girls were in love with Mr. Montserrat. They'd been in love for a long time. They made a suicide pact from *unrequited love*. But last year, Mr. Montserrat and Laura started to see each other. Imagine how the other two felt. Maybe the pact wasn't serious at first. But it became serious. So Loretta jumped."

"But Ella, I just can't—how do you know this?"

"Laura told me. She told me after Loretta and Laurentine were dead. She told me the pact had been her idea. The pacts were always her idea. She tried to stop them from jumping, they pretended to go along. So she was going to have to jump too. Out of remorse. And because it was a pact."

"Ella!"

"Like they couldn't help but copy each other. She said it was too late. Her best friends were dead, and it was her fault. She didn't want to live. She *had* to."

Harriet's thoughts floundered, even as she realized parts of this outlandish explanation could be true. And if Ella had spoken sooner, she might have saved lives.

"He knew too."

"Who knew?"

"Mr. Montserrat knew the girls made a pact to jump. Well, not until after Laurentine died. Laura told him after that, and told him she wanted to die too. She said if he tried to stop her she would *reveal all.*" Ella shook her head. "Mr. Montserrat probably thought he could change her mind. I guess I thought that too, like when Laura was telling me. I mean, if Mr. Montserrat was in love with you, and going all the way with you, wouldn't you change your mind?

"But people saw him on the bridge with Laura."

"Did they? Laura told me he would try to stop her. He was probably doing that on the bridge. So he tried to jump later, from remorse, I guess. It was his fault, really, Laura's death was his fault."

Harriet chose her words carefully. "Mr. Montserrat has been under suspicion. Didn't you think about that?"

"Suspicion?" Ella misunderstood. "He was to blame. All three of those girls were in love with him. If he got tired of Laura, he could have picked out Laurentine, and if he got tired of Laurentine he could have picked out Loretta." She spoke truculently. "Sometimes I think they wanted to punish him."

"Ella, please. Anyway you said it was a suicide pact. Also, you sound like a cheap novel. Everybody in love with Mr. Montserrat..."

She had a rapid intuition. "Were—are you in love with Mr. Montserrat, Ella?"

"No, I am not!" Ella practically shrieked.

Harriet studied the girl. A new idea formed. Ella only ever traipsing along behind the three Ls, receiving their casual attention, never in line for anything that she herself might have wanted, imagined, envied. A pitiful picture, but Harriet's heart was strangely unaffected.

Fitting in the last piece of the puzzle counted for something. But the wind-down of this bizarre conversation left her feeling detached and amoral. She crossed a leg under her habit and stared at Ella.

"Why would Laura tell you these things?" Ella was an original, but Laura was out of her league.

"Laura had nobody else, after Loretta and Laurentine died." Ella spoke soberly. "No one in the world. People like her are what other people want them to be. Someone to be jealous of. She had no one. She had to tell someone."

Laura had no one? What about Marin Montserrat?

Ella seemed to read her thoughts. "Maybe he wasn't the be all and end all for her. He can't have been that important, compared to say Loretta and Laurentine? Maybe she felt guilty." Ella squinted at the wall as if the cheap novel was written there, but with a few surprises.

"I personally think no one could reach those girls." Her expression shifted. "*I* was thinking, maybe Mr. Montserrat has suffered enough? He can't stay away forever, can he? He should be able to come back next year, shouldn't he, Sister?"

"But Ella—what you've told me doesn't let him off the hook. Quite the opposite."

"I thought you could fix things. Fix things like before."

"Mr. Montserrat is gone for good. He was from Montreal, you know, he'd been looking for work there," she lied. "Bothonville was never going to be his permanent home."

"You don't know!" A note of despair rang in Ella's voice.

Had she come here just to issue her royal pardon via proxy, in the hope Mr. Montserrat would then return? Did she really think Harriet could fix things? Or was it a case of Ella too having no one else to tell?

"But I do, Ella. I'm sure he won't be coming back." Harriet again considered. "And now that you've told me, you must never ever tell anyone else. Think of the awful trouble you'd be in."

The girl seemed to agree wholeheartedly with this much.

"We may see you in September, then?" Harriet said. She had walked Ella to the exit.

"No, you *won't*. I'm done with Saint Reginald's."

"What will you do?"

"Sister," the child said witheringly, "we akshully have schools on the island."

BACK IN HER ROOM, Harriet sank into a mood stranger still. She dragged the armchair to the open window. What Ella had told her could be true, or partly true. Or pure fantasy. Thinking about it was like trying to interpret a dream. One Harriet believed the story. Another Harriet thought Ella had a future writing potboilers: Montserrat in over his head after seducing the peerless Laura Rome, unless it was the other way around, which was more than possible; the three girls locked into a destructive end game with each other; Ella finding out more than was good for her, excluded and yet not impervious to a misery of her own.

The longer Harriet sat there, the more detached she became. Her mind began to float. The convent wing was deserted, and summer had cast a spell over the grounds. Yet the summer day was not utterly silent, for the hum of secret insect life stole into the room. Harriet drifted into a place between waking and sleep. The girl's singsong voice now seemed like lines in a play. The rest of the external world seemed more vague too. Far away in the classroom block, a bell rang faintly. But nothing happened, no sound of voices, no rush of feet. A school would never be this silent. Was she really at a girls' school?

She shook herself awake. Girls, men, the universe: anything was possible. The vast secrecy required didn't mean a thing, and who was Harriet to doubt the monumental construct of secrecy and lies? She tried for a tear, for the fate of the girls and Montserrat, and even for the fate of poor Saint Reginald's. But she was as dry as a bone.

She headed for the kitchenette. Que sera, sera. She needed coffee. She filled the French cafetière provided by Patricia, who often spoke of Lourdes these days. Perhaps, Harriet said to herself, she was becoming practical at last.

## 31: Redemption

SISTER CLOTHILDE TOOK the call from Florene in the office, and wandered over to the kitchen to pass the message on to Harriet.

"She wants to talk to you," Clothilde said chattily.

"I'll go and see her then."

"Oh, you shouldn't go and see her, she says. Turpentine Flats is full of mosquitoes."

"I'm used to mosquitoes. Isn't there some citronella?"

"Not these mosquitoes." Clothilde sounded important. "She said the mosquitoes there came back three times as big after Vivamus College had that spraying programme."

"Sister, if you could just step out of my way, this casserole is hot."

"She wants to meet you after supper tomorrow. Clothilde gave a furtive look around. "You're to ring her at Ella's aunt and uncle." A pause. "She said something about leaving?"

HARRIET LOITERED IN the shunting yards at dusk. The place was bigger than she'd expected. She had wandered around in the half-light and had made herself thoroughly lost. Florene had told her to look for the circus train. You would think a circus train would be easy to find. Florene had said it was about to leave town, with her and Roger aboard.

When the girl appeared between boxcars, Harriet didn't recognize her at first. She was dressed like a boy, a boy in a story about circuses, wearing an oversized shirt and jodhpurs held up by suspenders, her hair under a flat cap. Harriet wore a lime green sundress and sandals. They were a pair. They stared at each other for a moment.

"I'm leaving with Roger." Florene sounded apologetic.

"I'm sorry to hear this." Harriet spoke the conventional words, but she didn't know how she felt.

They sat down on a stack of wood, in the blue of the evening.

"I wanted to say goodbye, Sister, but also I have something to tell you."

"I have something to tell you too, Florene." Harriet had thought about this long and hard. "It's connected to Roger's innocence." And she gave the child an expurgated version of the three Ls and their suicide pact, mentioning the sorry fate of Montserrat. Florene listened attentively but it was hard to parse her reaction.

"That's sad about the girls, I guess."

"It is. We adults are all morally responsible, but it's hard to think what we could have done." She pictured the three Ls once more, their sealed off world, their cult of perfection.

"What happens now, Sister?"

"I'm not sure. What will the police do now, with poor Mr. Montserrat dead in the jail fire? Will they officially continue to blame your brother? I can't even see how this will play out."

"We're still going away with the circus."

"I know."

"And then there are the families of the girls," Harriet went on. "Do they want to hear that their girls committed suicide? I don't even know what *should* happen. Take Saint Reginald's, it wouldn't survive if this came out. In the end I thought a lot of this will probably stay secret. You and Roger—when you tell him—and me and Ella know this. We'll be the only ones. Now that Mr. Montserrat is dead."

Darkness and a curling ground mist stole across the yard.

A long-drawn out train whistle sounded, forlorn and impatient.

Oh, about that, Sister." Florene adjusted her suspenders a little consciously. "I think that must be our train. I have to go. But I wanted to tell you about Mr. Montserrat. Roger sprang him from jail, just before the fire."

"Sprang—what do you mean?" Harriet's mind had stopped working.

"We didn't think he killed the girls." Florene spoke patiently. "I mean, how could he? That was just as silly as thinking Roger was a killer. Roger knew a guard, a kind of second cousin of ours. Roger's very good at getting in and out of things. He used those sleeping pills of yours on the other guards and smuggled Mr. Montserrat out. Just before the explosion. They got clean away. Mr. Montserrat escaped in a boat to Schenectady or somewhere like that. But by now who knows. A fugitive from injustice. He would need a new identity, like you read about. But as long as you have the paperwork to back it up, you can call yourself whatever you want—you probably didn't know that, Sister."

Harriet found nothing to say.

"And then we realized, with the coincidence of the fire and all, there couldn't be anybody left alive who even knew Mr. Montserrat escaped. Well, besides us..." Florene hesitated. "So you can be happy about that, I hope, Sister?"

Not trusting herself, Harriet just nodded.

"It's a pity about those poor guards, I mean the ones who were sleeping. But *we* didn't know there would be a fire."

Florene didn't sound especially contrite when she said this: vaguely philosophical as much as anything. In fact, under her oversized cap and behind her glinting glasses, she looked like another person entirely, a hard-edged carny boy. Harriet, whose mind was still reeling, felt she hardly recognized her at all.

The conversation had come to an end. With a subdued goodbye, Florene melted into the darkness behind a boxcar. Left alone, Harriet wondered if the world would ever return to normal. The rail yard now seemed completely empty, but in the distance a radio was playing. For a change she recognized the song: The Weavers' "Lonesome Traveller." Somewhere in the yard, an invisible train began to move and pick up speed. A vivid idea formed in Harriet's mind of imminent departure and the road to freedom.

HARRIET WALKED ALONG the railway tracks towards the blurred western horizon. She planned to pick up the Greyhound bus at Mitchell's Corners; cutting along the tracks was a shortcut. Her open mackintosh flapped like wings on either side of her as she stepped buoyantly along the ties.

She had said her goodbyes at Saint Reginald's. Patricia had given her a canvas backpack, now stuffed with the belongings she wanted for her year off. Perpetua had come through in an astonishing way. She wouldn't let her resign, far from it. This had been a terrible year, and no decision she made now could be entirely reliable. Harriet needed to take some time off, and she, Perpetua, would help. There was even money attached, something to do with Aloysius. This kindly and grateful man, already well recovered from his heart attack and jubilantly on his way to Rome to play special Vatican II envoy for the Oblates, had revealed his gratitude and his deep pockets. She could and should travel, Perpetua prescribed.

Harriet had said she would perhaps go to the United States, where interesting things seemed to be happening with their new president and the civil rights movement.

Perpetua had been enthusiastic. "Above all, you have the whole year to yourself, Sister, to think, to live, to do with as you please. It's *how* we live that matters," she had said to a freely weeping Harriet, offering her handkerchief. "If you come back—and I believe you will come back—we will be waiting to welcome you as your sisters."

Harriet, who had no intention whatsoever of coming back, had never felt more touched in her life.

Now, as she walked into the declining sun on this late summer afternoon, she remembered that she would be thirty next week. This thought took her all the way back to her childhood.

Another evening was now before her, nothing like this one. A cold and blustery evening, in the dying part of the year. She was in the back yard of the house in Lafrenière, along with her mother who hung clothes on the line. The smell of the river nearby competed with the scent of recent rain and dead vegetation. One-eyed Henry lurked somewhere in the shrubbery. Harriet, or rather, Ruth, had tied string between two trees and was using clothes pegs to attach her celluloid dolls, still wet from the shower. With prodigal enthusiasm, she twisted the string back and forth until it resembled a cat's cradle. The dolls bobbed in the wind, and began to pop off one by one, only to be caught in the webbing below.

"It's my suspension bridge," she explained imperiously to her mother.

"It is, isn't it?" her mother said.

And then, in that way she had of telling a story with half her attention on a household task, Peggy Savary began to spin a yarn about a magic suspension bridge made of jute twine that held up an apprehensive child who was on a journey to somewhere. Ruth didn't know where; that was always the way with her mother's stories. What was clear was that the bridge, somehow, held up the anxious and resentful little girl as she stepped out over the abyss, even when she didn't believe it would and, most remarkably of all, when she furiously didn't want it to.

The Greyhound bus, on this summer day in 1963, was full of uprooted people on Pete Seeger's road to freedom. In taking her place among the other lonesome travellers, many of them painfully young, Harriet's thoughts returned inevitably to the three dead girls. They would be forgotten, before they had lived, set out into the world, endured defeat, picked themselves up, carried on. Had they wanted to be forgotten, or just to forget? What had driven them? She saw herself once more on her mysterious bridge of dreams, the pink mist beckoning her forward. She had no answers, but she thought she understood. As the bus pulled onto the highway, she offered them a last goodbye: Laura rhythmically pleating the fabric of her skirt in an anxious code, Loretta taking a bite of chocolate before disappearing into the darkness, Laurentine, under the cold trees, dancing alone.

ON ANOTHER SUMMER afternoon, Father Joseph Lynch adjusted his stole in the sacristy and looked around for his book. This wedding would be over very quickly. Just the bride and groom—he wouldn't be surprised if the bride was pregnant—and two witnesses. Well, that was young women for you, nowadays; and he shuddered slightly at the thought that another school year at Saint Reginald's would commence in a mere eight days and he would be in the thick of things—girls—once more.

He made his way into the garden, a tangled chaos of late summer flowers and triumphant weeds he'd long ago given up on. The bride and groom had wanted the ceremony to be held here. In a fit of indulgence, he'd agreed.

He felt in an unusually mellow mood. He supposed it had to do with the conversation he'd had earlier with that young man who had come to seek his advice about a vocation in the priesthood. Rarely had Father Lynch been so affected by a conversation with a possible new seminarian. The man wasn't so very young; perhaps that was the reason for the passion he exuded. Such thoughtfulness, such depth of feeling, such evangelical fire. Such faith. If this was what the new priests were like, Joseph Lynch felt the future of the Church was assured.

The wedding party waited in a pool of sunlight by the blooming hydrangea, which Lynch had been meaning to prune but now was glad he hadn't. The bride and groom, the priest professionally assessed in a second, weren't an especially well-matched pair. The man, coming up on middle age, was not at ease in an overly fashionable suit, and the bride, perhaps too young, was poured into antique ivory satin several shades off virginal white. Her generous curves, not to mention the oversized bouquet she held, could easily conceal pregnancy. If not May-September, then May-August, he decided. But they had a look of happiness. Things weren't always what they seemed.

Father Lynch leafed through his book as they shuffled forward, remembering once more the man who had come to see him that afternoon. A blond man—quite an unusual yellow thatch, practically like a dye job, but undeniably striking with that olive complexion and those matinee idol dark eyes. He'd looked vaguely familiar, but Lynch knew he'd have remembered the yellow hair. He had joked to himself that the poor fellow, too handsome by half, would need a dye job if he was ever to pass as a priest.

The couple smiled, looking nervous as hell. The priest took a moment to collect himself. This was surely, he realized in a flash of surprise, the most exquisite late summer afternoon he could remember. The burnished light, the woven shade, the still and balmy air, the rioting scents of the garden, all combined in one fragile moment of grace. For the sake of the humble wedding party before him, he gave thanks in his grumpy way.

He began to intone the familiar words that now, to his ears, sounded perennially fresh, "Do you, Alain Joseph Moreau, take Maureen Flora Phayre, as your lawful wife, to have and to hold, from this day forward..."

Anna Dowdall was born in Montreal and, like her protagonist in *The Suspension Bridge,* moved back to the city of her birth twice. Again like the peripatetic Sister Harriet, she's lived all over, currently making the Junction neighbourhood of Toronto her home. Occupationally just as restless, she's been a reporter, a nurse's aide, a graphic artist, a college lecturer, a planner, a union thug, a translator, a baker, a book conservator, a pilot and a horticultural advisor, as well as other things best forgotten. Raised on fairy tales, she began by writing two young adult fantasy novels. These manuscripts made the long lists for the American Katherine Paterson Prize and the Crime Writers of Canada's unpublished novel award. After being told by an agent her words were too "big," she shifted to adult fiction. Her three genre-bending literary mysteries, *April on Paris Street* (Guernica 2021), *The Au Pair* (2018) and *After the Winter* (2017), feature evocative settings and a preoccupation with the lives of women. A lover of prose, she once wrote a poem, which ended up on an electricity pole on Montreal's *rue de la Poésie.*